Praise for Elizabeth Musser

"Elizabeth Musser's engaging novel of the French Resistance is a page-turner! Her knowledge of France plunges readers into the action, and her complex characters—fearful yet courageous—live and breathe. *From the Valley We Rise* is a wonderful story, rich in spiritual depth, that fans of WWII fiction shouldn't miss."

Lynn Austin, bestselling author

"Elizabeth's signature artistry as a storyteller dazzles. . . . Brimming with impressive historical detail, here is a book to remind us that we can honor the past and still bravely embrace the future."

Susan Meissner, bestselling author of
The Nature of Fragile Things,
on *By Way of the Moonlight*

"Musser delivers yet another emotional escape."

Julie Cantrell, *New York Times* and *USA Today* bestselling author of *Perennials*,
on *By Way of the Moonlight*

FROM THE VALLEY WE RISE

Books by Elizabeth Musser

FROM THE VALLEY WE RISE

ELIZABETH MUSSER

BETHANYHOUSE

a division of Baker Publishing Group
Minneapolis, Minnesota

© 2025 by Elizabeth G. Musser

Published by Bethany House Publishers
Minneapolis, Minnesota
BethanyHouse.com

Bethany House Publishers is a division of
Baker Publishing Group, Grand Rapids, Michigan

Printed in the United States of America

Library of Congress Cataloging-in-Publication Data
Names: Musser, Elizabeth, author.
Title: From the valley we rise / Elizabeth Musser.
Description: Minneapolis, Minnesota : Bethany House, a division of Baker
    Publishing Group, 2025.
Identifiers: LCCN 2024043340 | ISBN 9780764243493 (paperback) | ISBN
    9780764245084 (casebound) | ISBN 9781493450855 (ebook)
Subjects: LCSH: World War, 1939-1945—Jews—Rescue—France—Fiction. | World
    War, 1939-1945—Children—France—Fiction. | LCGFT: Historical fiction. |
    Christian fiction. | Novels.
Classification: LCC PS3563.U839 F76 2025 | DDC 813/.54—dc23/eng/20241024
LC record available at https://lccn.loc.gov/2024043340

All Scripture quotations are from the King James Version of the Bible.

This is a work of historical reconstruction; the appearances of certain historical figures are therefore inevitable. All other characters, however, are products of the author's imagination, and any resemblance to actual persons, living or dead, is coincidental.

Cover design by Dan Thornberg, Design Source Creative Services
Cover image © Mark Owen / Trevillion Images

Baker Publishing Group publications use paper produced from sustainable forestry practices and postconsumer waste whenever possible.

25 26 27 28 29 30 31   7 6 5 4 3 2 1

This story is dedicated to
two of my wonderful grandkids:

Quinn Collins Musser, our young philosopher who loves mammals, reptiles, and all things outdoors. Your kindness, depth of character, hard work, and good humor bring joy to your Mamie and so many others.

Cori Lucille Musser, our beautiful little pistol. Your love of life spreads the delight that only a toddler can to all of us, especially your Mamie.

And they shall build the old wastes,
They shall raise up the former desolations,
And they shall repair the waste cities,
The desolations of many generations.

Isaiah 61: 4

LEXICON

La Résistance—The French Resistance was a collection of groups that fought the Nazi occupation and the collaborationist Vichy regime during World War II. Resistance cells conducted guerrilla warfare and published underground newspapers. They also provided firsthand intelligence and escape networks which helped Allied soldiers and airmen trapped behind Axis lines. The Resistance's men and women came from many parts of French society, including émigrés, academics, students, aristocrats, Roman Catholics (including clergy), Protestants, Jews, Muslims, liberals, anarchists, communists, and even some fascists. The proportion of French people who participated in organized resistance has been estimated at one to three percent of the total population.

Maquis—Rural guerilla bands, typically working class young men who escaped into the mountains and woods to avoid the *Service du travail obligatoire*—the compulsory work service set up by the Vichy government that sent men to provide forced labor for Germany. Eventually, they became organized into a strong resistance, with approximately 100,000 maquisards throughout France.

Maquisards—individual members of the Maquis.

F.F.I.— *Forces françaises de l'intérieur* encompassed all organized French resistance groups, including the maquisards, once they were unified under the Free French government following the Allied landings in Normandy.

Milice—the *Milice française* (French Militia), generally called *la Milice,* was a political paramilitary organization created by the Vichy regime (with German aid) to help fight against the French Resistance.

Boches—a shortened version of the word *alboche,* a blend of *allemand* (French for German) and *caboche* (slang for head). It was used mainly during the First and Second World Wars and directed especially at German soldiers.

androns—narrow and often steep covered passageways between or under homes in Sisteron.

PROLOGUE

AUGUST 14, 1954

I am sitting in an Adirondack chair high above the Durance Valley, soaking in the beauty of the starry sky, listening to the cicadas' chirping, and breathing in the fresh lavender that spreads its lavish fragrance from the mustard-colored Anduze pottery beside me. Then I turn my gaze past the newly planted almond and olive trees, past the tall cedars so familiar to the Basses-Alpes, and peer down into the valley to the town of Les Mées.

And they are there. The Penitents, spot-lit, regal, telling their story.

Tomorrow I'll drive down from my secluded perch above the valley, wave to the Penitents with a catch in my throat, and wind alongside the Durance River until it leads me to the neighboring town of Sisteron. I'll drive to the cemetery and stand with the others—the mayor, the dignitaries, the citizens, the children—and pay homage to those who lost their lives in the bombing.

Afterward I'll drive a short ten kilometers to the stone village for another ceremony, paying homage to people who never once wanted credit for their courageous service. But it is time to break the silence, let the secret out, to recognize the ones who saved my life, our lives. Again and again.

I wish desperately that he were here with me. I see his laughing eyes, feel his hand in mine, lift my fingers as if to trace the scars

11

on his arm, barely perceptible. I remember. All of it. The sounds of gunfire, the explosions, the terror in his eyes. His voice calling out over and over for me . . .

Then I blink back tears. I cannot remember the next part, so I turn my thoughts to the legend, the one he told me about those craggy formations that are glowing far down in the valley.

I tilt my ear. Are they calling to me? Or is that the wind winding its way through the cedars? My heart squeezes, pinches, a pain that causes me to wince as if it is real when I know it's not a physical injury but a deep wound in my heart.

I blow a kiss to the stars and then down to the valley below, and I wait for tomorrow to come.

PART I

1

ISABELLE

SISTERON, FRANCE
JULY 21, 1944

Isabelle shivered despite the almost debilitating heat of the late July night in the Basses-Alpes of Sisteron. She pulled her lightweight shawl over her shoulders and entered Café de la Tante. A glance at her watch. It was time. One naked lightbulb hung above the bar area, and Jacques offered her a weak smile. He raised his thick black eyebrow, the left one, and gave an almost imperceptible nod.

She lifted her chin and walked slowly across the room, past tables with uniformed Germans drinking schnapps and playing cards, certain of their eyes on her formfitting, sapphire-blue dress, her smart feathered hat, the way the high heels accentuated her long, shapely legs. Ginette had carefully drawn the black vertical line down the back of her legs to simulate stockings. No one in the Resistance wore stockings. No one in the whole once-lazy city of Sisteron except the traitors, the women who opened their arms and more to the *Boches*.

Purse in hand, she sauntered to the far table where Tomas sat nursing his drink. When he saw her, he gave a tight smile. "*Quel plaisir, Mademoiselle* Geraldine."

Her fake name, like her fake stockings, must seem real. She nodded to him. "May I?"

"*Bien sûr, ma belle.*"

His accent was atrocious, but his blue eyes were mesmerizing. He removed his SS cap, revealing his shocking white-blond hair— thick, neatly cropped, carefully slicked back from his forehead. He stood, towering over her, and kissed her hand as she held it out. Her heart beat so frantically she was sure Tomas noticed as he looked her over approvingly and motioned for her to sit down.

"A cigarette?"

"*Non, merci.*"

Her German was worse than his French, so they had decided to stick with her native tongue. *Keep smiling, keep talking, keep him interested.*

For two weeks she'd made her way to Café de la Tante every evening in preparation for what she must do tonight. *Distract him.* She would have preferred Jean-Yves's job and imagined him now, dressed as a gendarme with his *Maquis* friends, hustling the French prisoners up the long steep hike to the Citadel, the pride of Sisteron. This thirteenth century fortress perched on a rock that overlooked the town, and the river, and the entire Durance Valley.

She closed her eyes and imagined for just a few seconds the view from the top as she followed Papa from the ramparts on the north all the way to the southern tip. *"You can see it all, Papa—360 degrees! A perfect view of the French countryside!"*

Papa had patted her head, twisted one of her black braids around his finger, and smiled. *"Yes, ma chérie. It never gets old."*

A child's attempt to make her father proud. Oh, it had worked then, when the consequences teetered only between a smile or a frown. But tonight, no children walked the ramparts of the Citadel, and her father . . .

She swallowed hard and pinched herself to concentrate on what Tomas was saying.

"You look lovely tonight, Mademoiselle Geraldine. Your eyes are always so brilliant and blue. They match your dress." His eyes traveled down from her face to the rest of her body.

She shivered internally.

When they had first met two weeks ago, Tomas had commented, *"I've never seen such crystal-blue eyes, like a translucent sapphire. It is too bad your hair is black—lovely though it is. Were it blond, you would be a perfect Aryan sample."*

"May I offer you a drink?" he asked now, his right hand reaching over to cover her left one.

Don't flinch! Smile! Look at his sharp nose, his tight mouth, not those cruel blue eyes, not at the revolver in its holster, not at the swastika on his uniform.

"Of course. I'd love one."

When Jacques, the bartender, brought her a cognac, she thanked him with a dismissive *merci* as if she didn't know him, hadn't grown up side by side with him, playing hide-and-seek in the school's recreation court.

Pay attention, Zabelle!

She sipped her drink and continued the banter, the innocuous questions she had practiced, complete with the flirtatious lift of her pencil-thin eyebrow that her roommate Ginette had highlighted with their last piece of charcoal.

"Try again, Zabelle! You're an awful flirt!" Ginette had snickered. But Isabelle had read the fear behind it.

"It doesn't come naturally. You should be the one!"

"You know I would do it for you, but Tito insisted . . ."

Why had they chosen her for this role when, at twenty-five, she'd never even had a boyfriend? Not really. Only for a few months when she was a gangly teen. She'd thought he cared. How wrong she'd been.

And this handsome young German with the sardonic smile and the broad shoulders, she knew he didn't care.

"Shoulders back, legs crossed." Ginette's voice in her head. *"Look bored and enticing, Zabelle!"*

Somehow she must have been successful. Night after night

Tomas asked to meet her at the café snuggled in the heart of the old city. Night after night she blushed when he asked to accompany her back home. Night after night she refused. Instead, she lifted her head, closed her eyes, and received his kisses, feeling the confusion of desire and disgust. And night after night she bade him good-bye.

But now . . .

Now she must lead him back to her apartment and somehow gain the courage to invite him inside.

Tito's voice rang in her memory, the plan daring. *"We will be disguised as gendarmes and claim to be bringing back escaped prisoners . . ."* Instead, the *resistants* would enter through the first and second military enclosures of the Citadel and master the guardhouse.

Master the guardhouse. Isabelle shivered again. Kill the Boches, that was the truth. And free the prisoners, eleven of them. Political prisoners whom the Gestapo had yet to execute. Papa . . .

What would Papa say if he knew of her involvement now? Surely he would understand.

He had not frowned upon her joining the Resistance. For two years now, they had been coconspirators. But flirting with the Boches? Inviting one of them to her apartment and worse? He would prefer she blow up train tracks. *"You have the shape and the face to draw attention, Zabelle. A dark-haired beauty,"* Ginette assured her. *"And you're absolutely no good with explosives and guns. But you have the biggest imagination. Tell that German stories while we set the traps and free the prisoners."*

Later, glancing at her watch, Isabelle feigned a yawn, and Tomas picked up on it. "Your bedtime, ma belle?"

She gave the coy smile she had practiced with Ginette. Most girls could do it easily. "*Oui.* Time for bed." She lifted the eyebrow, rose from her chair, picked up her purse.

Tomas came by her side and took her elbow. "I'll escort you home."

They strolled by the Durance, its slow-flowing waters catching the light of the moon, highlighting the faint ripples on the surface.

Above them loomed the Citadel, rising from the jutting rocks like an elegant ship chiseled into stone.

Tomas's hand came around her waist as they meandered along the banks of the Durance, then crossed the wide avenue and turned back toward *centre ville* and the street where she lived.

"If the apartment is dark, you must invite him up. If there is a light, one light, I am there, and we have succeeded." Ginette's instructions.

She fingered her crucifix and silently prayed, *Let there be a light, let there be a light.* Ironic that she was almost reciting Scripture.

Around the corner and across the street she could make out the apartment she shared with Ginette on the second floor—in complete darkness. Isabelle quelled the fluttering in her stomach. Could she do this? *In the dark.* That meant the mission had failed. The prisoners still imprisoned.

Tomas's hand gripped tighter around her waist, and he pulled her to a stop by the alley. She saw a fierceness in his eyes that had not been present the previous evenings. "What is this game you play with me, Mademoiselle Geraldine?"

His tone was at once teasing and harsh.

Isabelle forced a laugh. "Game?"

"You tempt me, my dear."

"Tell me what you want?" She knew all too well what he wanted, and all too well what the Resistance required.

At his hungry look, she laughed again. "Or perhaps you don't want to tell me a thing." She stood on her toes and kissed his cheek. Tomas grabbed her with a power that took her breath away, then began to kiss her with a vigor that terrified her.

A siren broke the calm with its loud shrieking, and Tomas dropped his hold. "I-I must go."

She grabbed for him again, feigning desire. "What is it?"

"I don't know." He turned and ran down the alley, back toward the town and the Citadel that towered above them.

Weak and shaken, Isabelle stood riveted to the cobblestones, unsure of what to do. Then out of the corner of her eye she saw a flicker of light in a second-story window.

PETER

NAPLES, ITALY
JULY 22–23, 1944

The waiting seemed interminable. Soon 80,000 men would be spread across five battleships—three American, two French—twenty cruisers, and nine escort carriers, all making up the US 7th Army. Day after day they sat in the ports of Italy while the higher-ups planned Operation Dragoon, as bold as the Normandy Invasion, this time starting in the South of France.

How to wait well? Peter thought. *How to help these soldiers, while waiting, prepare to live or die?* For years he had trained and prepared. And then the unthinkable happened. One terrible mistake and . . .

But he was ready now, in a different position and in a different role. In fact, it was a completely different life.

He watched the soldiers lazing in the shade after their rowdy game of "real football," as he'd dubbed it. "Good game," he said, shaking the hands of Sergio, the Italian captain, as he caught his breath.

Back in his tiny room, Peter got out the roster for the soccer tournament. Nestled in the port of Naples with hundreds of recently liberated teenaged Italians who grew up playing real football, Peter had encouraged the Americans to try the game. For two weeks now, the twelve different teams had competed, the Americans always defeated soundly by the far more experienced Italians. Still, the competition had been friendly, with the Italians sharing with the Americans their precious commodities of wine and bread and olive oil and parmesan after the most recent victory. And today was the quarterfinal game between the 7th Army's second-division team and the Italians' local team.

"Hey, Ginger!"

He smiled at the nickname the soldiers gave him with his permission. Chaplain Peter Christensen, first lieutenant, was such a mouthful. And even with his carrot-colored hair cropped so short that none of the unmanageable curls were left, he couldn't hide the freckles dotting his nose and cheeks and chin.

He preferred this moniker to the one Helen had used. "My fiery friend," she'd whisper with a wink. But he could not bear to hear those words now. He wondered if the wound would ever heal.

The sea in the port of Naples was quiet on this day, the clock ticking, ticking, every man on alert for the "time to board" command. Which did not come. Not yet. But it would. And then the question would not be how to wait, but how to be ready.

He watched as hundreds of soldiers gathered the next morning for the Protestant church service he would lead, along with fellow Chaplain Danny Clark, four years his senior and four inches his junior. Nearby, Chaplain Rabbi Abe Horowitz led a smaller group of Jewish soldiers in worship. At forty-one, stocky with dark hair and beard, round gold-rimmed glasses, and shorter than Peter by half a foot, the rabbi soared above him in his calm demeanor and wisdom. Chaplain George LeDuc was the Catholic priest, thirty-five, serious with a deep kindness in his dark eyes, and his service always drew the biggest crowds.

"Let us open the Word of God to . . ." Peter began. That was something they all had, every soldier. A Bible. Tucked in their packs with their rations. He was thankful for good ol' FDR's insistence that the military have access to chaplains on every ship and port and base. And Bibles available.

After the services and lunch in the mess hall, Peter joined hundreds of men gathered for the 7th Army's volunteer choir. At first, they sang hymns—it was the Lord's Day after all.

"Many of you responded to my request for suggestions of songs." Peter held up a fistful of paper scraps. "Thanks to the talents of Privates Ward and Harrington, they'll lead us in a few of the most popular . . ."

He had known the favorite long before he'd passed out the papers. Every man old enough to serve had seen the film *The Wizard of Oz*, some countless times, when it first came out in 1939. Then in 1943,

Judy Garland had serenaded American troops live with "Somewhere Over the Rainbow," and because of its immense popularity, a special recording with the Tommy Dorsey Orchestra was released and sent to soldiers everywhere as a promise of better days to come.

Peter stepped back as the privates, one on a violin, the other a flute, played the hauntingly familiar melody, and hundreds of voices crooned along, "Somewhere over the rainbow skies are blue . . ."

Chaplain Horowitz came beside Peter. "Thank you, Ginger," he said. The Star of David on his uniform wasn't the yellow emblem of Hitler's insanity, but a symbol of purity and care. "You keep things light. The boys need it."

"Aw shucks, thanks, Rabbi," he kidded, overplaying a Southern drawl. He could almost feel the freckles dancing as he smiled.

"You know I mean it." The rabbi placed his thick, comforting hand on Peter's shoulder. "How do you say it? You have a 'laid-back way of looking at life'?"

Peter shrugged. "Most things aren't much of a big deal to me. I mean, God and country and family are, but so many other things just don't matter."

The rabbi removed his glasses, stretched his thick arms onto the railing, considering this. A rare smile crossed his lips. "God, country, family, *and* soccer."

Peter acquiesced. Yes, he was fiercely competitive. Growing up in the desert of North Africa with his missionary parents and all the time in the world to kick a soccer ball with the French and Algerian kids, he'd honed his athletic skills.

"If you ever end up in a POW camp, Ginger, you'll make a game of it. You'll teach us all how to survive." How often had he heard that from one of the soldiers? He always grinned outwardly. Inside he shuddered. *Please, no, Lord.*

But it hadn't been a game in North Africa when the bombs were whistling overhead, and he and the rabbi and the other chaplains were praying for the dying, pulling bodies off the field and carrying them on litters to the medical tents. It hadn't been a game to sit by Henry, nineteen, face ashen, eyes dulled with shock, and whisper the Lord's Prayer and hold his bloody hand, feeling it gradually lose its grip until it dropped listless from his fingers. Henry was the first soldier he had accompanied at his death two years ago, but there had been so many since then.

War wasn't a game, but Peter was darned if he wouldn't do everything in his power to keep these brave young boys playing and praying until victory came.

RENÉ

Near Sisteron, France
July 26, 1944

"Delphine, come back now! It's dark outside! What are you doing running around the farm at six in the morning?"

Delphine turned and stared at René. "Breathing fresh air! We've hidden here for two years. I'm tired of hiding! Let's go."

"We are not going anywhere."

"Then I will simply breathe. Do you have a problem with that, my dear *big* brother?"

"Petulant girl," René whispered to himself. She meant it as a taunt. At almost sixteen, René looked as if he were barely twelve, and when just-turned-thirteen Delphine stood tall, she matched his height.

Pigtails flying, Delphine twirled around, hands over her head as if imitating a ballerina. Then she took a deep breath and whispered, "Life!" dramatically.

That was Delphine, all right. Dramatic. But also confusing, mysterious.

René watched as she skipped over the small hill and disappeared into the grassy valley below. René could not see her, could not make out her form in the deep gray before dawn.

Pat-a-pat-a-pat.

At the sound of distant gunfire, René froze. Then he took off running in the direction she had gone and bumped straight into Delphine, whose wide eyes were the only thing visible in the dark.

"There are a lot of men," she whispered. "A very lot of men. I think they're Germans. I think they're coming here."

René grabbed her hand and swung her around. "Come on!"

They tore down the hill, slipping on the loose pebbles, and ran across the meadow where corn used to grow hearty and plentiful. But in the fourth year of an endless war, the stalks hung bare and wilted.

"The Boches! Here!" René cried out as they entered the farmhouse.

Dominique and Frédéric, the two young *maquisards* who were staying with them at the farm, spun into motion. Maman took a sharp breath, then did what she always did. She squared her thin shoulders and ran her hands through her blond hair, hair that used to be long and lovely and the color of the corn silk, but now was as thin and drab as the wilted stalks. "You know what to do, René."

René nodded, but as he led Delphine toward the wine cellar, the young girl stopped. "I can fight too! I'm not afraid. Let me fight."

René swallowed hard, a piercing ache in his stomach. He knew she could fight. Delphine was a survivor.

"There are not enough guns," Maman said. She took Delphine into her arms, held her tight, kissed her forehead.

"There are so many of them," Delphine whispered.

"It will be all right. We have Domi and Fred, Jean-Paul and Sébastien too." Maman nodded to the two older teenagers, who entered the room with rifles in hand. "And the other *Maquis* will come soon."

Out the small farmhouse door, René led Delphine to "the cave," opened the door, and hurried down the makeshift ladder. The small room smelled musty, and the air was cool, even in July. Where once an array of Papa's best wine bottles had been stored carefully, the shelves were now barren except for a handful of jars of peaches and three wine bottles filled with water. René emptied his pockets of a slab of hard cheese, a small roll of *saucisson*, and a half-day-old baguette.

"You know what to do." He placed the food in Delphine's hands. "Twenty-four hours. You wait." He unfastened his watch, the one from Papa, and slipped it around her thin wrist.

"I can't take this from you."

He paid her no attention. "After twenty-four hours, if I have not come, you take the documents hidden behind the peaches, you climb the ladder, and you open the hatch. You go to the Bernards' farm, just like we practiced. Understand?"

He watched as rage and fear battled on her face, so pale and thin, where rosy cheeks once bloomed under deep brown eyes. Then he saw it. A nod. Acquiescence.

Delphine threw her arms around René. "Please stay with me. Please!"

Gently, he pulled away. "I can't. You know that, sis."

He climbed the ladder, replaced the wooden door, dragged the hay across it, and wiped away the footprints. They had practiced. She could lift the door on her own.

If she had to.

"There are three columns of Germans and the French *Milice*—hundreds of men, I think—headed this way," Dominique said as he threw open an old wooden trunk filled with guns. "We've heard from the two Maquis on Ile Verte and on the Ganagobie plateau. They've seen the progress of the column coming from the south toward Les Rousses and are trying to create a diversion. They're the ones who have been opening fire so that our Maquis can have time to fall back."

"Fall back? The Maquis here are leaving?" Maman's voice, usually calm and soothing, sounded high-pitched, tight.

"The four of us will stay with you and René, Mme Amblard," Jean-Paul assured. "The Germans will not attack this farm."

But René could smell the fear in the room, as heavy as the stench of stale tobacco.

"Mme Amblard, you go to the cave with Delphine. Please." Frédéric's eyes softened.

25

René knew his mother would refuse. She had opened the farm to the French guerillas, the Maquis, the young untrained men who hid out in the elements and spent their energy destroying train tracks and causing confusion for the enemy.

"I will stay."

"So will I," René added, coming beside his mother. "Papa would want it, *n'est-ce pas?*"

Maman nodded, and they gathered their weapons, the ones the Maquis had captured throughout the endless occupation.

"We will kill the French Militia too," Fred spat. "Traitors one and all."

Rifle in hand, René took his post at the side window. He knew many of the maquisards who hid out in the woods and mountains nearby. Rural guerilla bands, young men of the working class who had escaped into the mountains and woods to avoid the *Service du travail obligatoire*—the compulsory work service set up by the Vichy government, a mandatory conscription that sent them to provide forced labor for Germany.

For two years now he had watched his older neighbors and friends leave their farms, disappearing into the wild. And finally his big brother, Antoine, had left. Little by little they had become organized into a strong resistance. Dominque bragged that 100,000 maquisards were hiding out all throughout France.

Perhaps they were, but on this farm, as the dawn broke in bloodred streaks, there were only four maquisards, along with his mother and himself. And a young girl hidden in the cave.

2

⟡

ISABELLE

JULY 26, 1944

Numbly, Isabelle fingered the crucifix around her neck and swiped at the tears trickling down her cheeks. She clutched at her stomach, doubling over with excruciating pain. Then she grabbed the gold-framed photograph from its place on the hutch and threw it with such force that the glass splintered into hundreds of pieces when it hit the floor. Her toothless smile beside her parents' beaming faces stared back at her from the broken frame as she sobbed, "Are You satisfied now, God? Are You?"

She felt her body shaking with fury as she slid to the floor, her knees pressed against her cramping stomach. She tried to take a deep breath, but instead she gave small, staccato hiccups.

"It will be known as one of the most spectacular escapes in the history of the Resistance. Just you wait and see!" Ginette's pale blue eyes had shone when she proclaimed this news five days ago.

"And Papa?"

"Safe."

"Where?"

27

Isabelle could picture the way Ginette's face had fallen, how she'd brushed her blond bangs off her forehead, the worried look, the wrinkled brow, her pale eyes somber.

"He's safe. They all are. But we fear reprisals, of course. So no one can know their hiding place. Any of our hiding places."

She remembered how her body had begun to tremble, how she had crumpled on her bed in tears. *"I'm so grateful. I was afraid, Ginette. Terrified. Tomas was . . . was forceful tonight."*

"Did he . . . ?"

"I was about to invite him up. He would have come at any rate, so determined was he . . ."

"Little Zabelle. You're brave. Rest now. All will be well."

Isabelle shook her head to erase the memories. She did not feel brave. She felt both numb and furious, terrified and bereaved. Huddled on the floor beside the bits of glass, she shivered in the heat of another late summer night.

All was not well.

Yesterday, five days after the stunning rescue of the prisoners at the Citadel, the prisoners had been gunned down. How foolish to ever think they would escape the Nazis' cruelty. How could she ever forgive herself for what Papa had done—going to prison to save her? In that moment, she felt as if she had held the gun that killed him.

Papa was dead.

Tito had brought the news late last night. When he realized Ginette was still away, he had not wanted to leave Isabelle alone in her grief. But already he had risked discovery by coming to the apartment, and she had begged him to leave.

Isabelle was terrified that Tomas was watching her. He didn't know which building she lived in, but he knew the street name. He did not know that her father was one of the prisoners, he did not know her real name, but he knew some things.

It had been six days since the rescue, but she had not had the courage to venture back to the café. Ginette thought her a good actress, yet Isabelle did not trust her face to hide her knowledge of the truth. And now with her father dead . . .

No, she could never face Tomas again.

"Tito says I have to go back to Tomas." She thought of her confession to Ginette that same night the prisoners escaped. How she had swallowed bile and twisted the bright blue material of her dress in her hand.

"I can't go back. Even if he suspects nothing about my father, he'll be furious that the Maquis outsmarted the Germans. He'll kill me." Eyes down. *"Or worse."*

Ginette had reached for Isabelle's hand and met her eyes. Ginette's, a lovely pale blue, looked worried, almost fearful. And her friend rarely looked fearful.

"But if you don't go back, Zabelle, he'll know that you were somehow involved, won't he?"

"Perhaps." Even so, she could not do it.

"Of course, I understand. It is all so horrible."

For the past six days, Ginette had been out with other resistants, creating diversions while Isabelle had remained hidden in their apartment. Ginette was braver than she was. Every time Isabelle had ventured out of the apartment, ration card in hand, she had plotted her route to the *boulangerie* and the *épicerie*. She knew the *vieille ville* of Sisteron as well as she knew her dear, lifelong friend Ginette. And the *androngs*, those narrow and often steep covered passageways between or under the homes in the village, why, they *were* her friends. She and Ginette had played as children in every one of the dozens of passages that cut between the wider streets, their pebbled stairs worn smooth from centuries of citizens going about their daily business.

And they knew the history, how the mazes of stairs and small arched streets that followed the natural and picturesque contours of the city finally reached the lofty Citadel, which the sixteenth century king, Henry IV, called "the most powerful stronghold of his kingdom."

On Monday, Isabelle had left her apartment, twisting down the dark stairwell and out into the blinding sunlight, passed through Rue de la Coste, and hurried down the androne known as the Pardenrière, wide stone stairs that led her to Rue Mercerie and the Long Androne, her favorite.

In happier days, she would skip down the steep steps of the Long Androne, steps paved with the pebbles from the Durance River. As a little girl, she had learned to count when she and Maman had walked up daily from le Bourg Reynaud into the centre ville for the *marché*, seventy-eight steps in all. How she had loved this open-air passageway with its stone-vaulted arches. She would run her hands along the smooth stone walls on either side with the thick wooden doors leading into the homes of villagers, their friends. Maman and Papa knew everyone in town.

But on Monday she had simply cried with relief to descend into town without encountering a German.

On Wednesday, she had not been so lucky. Just as she was half-way down the seventy-eight steps, she had seen a group of Germans marching along the Rue Chapuzie below, the soldiers erect, staring straight ahead, their faces cruel. Or perhaps they were scared, just like her. They were all so young. She was backing up carefully onto the stairs, her face flushed, when she saw Tomas farther down the line. Flattening herself along the stone walls, she wept again with relief that he had not seen her.

The Germans had destroyed the charm of her village. No longer did the andrones afford Isabelle an escape into her imagination, making up stories of days long ago when peasants led their donkeys along the cobbled roads, bowing before royalty. Instead, every turn brought fear of encountering the enemy.

And now the enemy was harder to spot. Had someone else, one of the resistants or maquisards, done the unthinkable, betrayed the hiding place of the freed prisoners to Tomas and the other Germans?

Ginette entered the apartment, stepping around the shattered glass and the photograph lying on the cracked linoleum. When Isabelle lifted her dull eyes, fists clenched, Ginette sank down beside her and took her into her strong arms. "I'm so sorry." With her uninjured hand, she brushed the tears from Isabelle's cheek. "It's so horrible about your father. How can Papa Jean-Pierre be gone? *Mon parrain*. He was . . . so good. And he loved you so much, Zabelle." She cleared her throat unsuccessfully.

"He loved you, too, his *favorite* goddaughter." Isabelle felt her lips curl up as she pronounced the words. Once when Ginette was four or five, she bragged to her friend, *"I'm Papa Jean-Pierre's favorite goddaughter."* To which Isabelle retorted, *"You're his* only *goddaughter."*

Ginette had loved her father too. Now her friend whispered, "I hate this war. I hate it so much."

Isabelle peeled herself out of her best friend's arms and noticed Ginette's bandaged arm. "You're hurt."

Her friend cursed and said, "I about bled to death installing the 'diversion' on those train tracks. This will leave a fine scar!" She met Isabelle's eyes. "But it's nothing. A stupid mistake. A flesh wound. Nothing like a heart wound."

Taking a breath, Isabelle said the next words so softly that Ginette squinted to understand. "Someone betrayed us." At her friend's startled expression, she added, "I feel sure."

Ginette shook her head, frowning. "Surely not." But then, "You really think so?"

"I do."

"But who could it be, Zabelle? Who would do such a thing?"

Isabelle shrugged, then shivered. "Could it be Maurice?"

"Why do you say this?" Ginette bit her lips, her cheeks flushed. She whispered, "You say it because he knew about where they were hiding the escaped prisoners. He worked with the Maquis from Bayons."

"Yes."

But surely not Maurice, the gentle man who was indeed a gentleman with laughter behind his eyes, always thinking of others. Was he thinking of the Germans? Was he helping the French Militia, the Milice?

All Isabelle knew was that ten of the escaped prisoners had been massacred right outside the village where they were hiding, even as the maquisards were heading to take them to a safer location.

Dead. Her father was dead, and so were the others.

They could have died in prison or in a prison camp. It didn't matter, she told herself. One way or another, they were gone. But it *did* matter. It niggled in the back of her mind, until she had finally spit it out to Ginette. It was obvious there was a traitor among them.

Tito, the leader. It couldn't be Tito. Jacques, Jean-Yves, Amandine, Maurice, Lucy, Bertrand, Ginette, herself . . . Isabelle mentally listed the names of their small *équipe* of resistants. A team. A community. A brotherhood and sisterhood. A traitor?

No!

She stared at the faded wallpaper in the *salon*, the way the pale pink roses wrapped around the wooden trellis and the rip in the far corner, where her younger cousin René had scraped it away accidentally with his dark green army tank. If only they were still playing war instead of living it.

With Isabelle sitting on her bed, Ginette began slowly brushing her hair, removing the tangles. "It's terrible, Zabelle, but I won't let anything happen to you. I promise you that."

They'd always cared for each other like sisters, a fierce bond, established as neighbors and schoolmates and best friends, weathering family tragedies and celebrating childhood victories. They'd climbed trees together, vacationed together, attended the same camp, and whispered about boys in the night. And two years ago, clutching each other's hands, they'd each enlisted in the Resistance in Sisteron.

Ginette set down the brush and said, "Try to rest. I'll wake you when it's time for the meeting."

Tito stood in the dimly lit room, his shadow huge, his voice, that booming voice of an opera baritone, tight with grief. All nine of them were gathered in their meeting place, a concrete silo on the outskirts of Sisteron. As with the silos in the nearby towns of Manosque and Oraison, this one was empty of grain but filled with essentials for the resistants. They'd even made an acronym of it for their name: *Site inaperçu des loyalistes d'opposition.* Every time one of them pronounced the word *silo*, it was done with a cynical nod toward resistance.

Unnoticed Site of Oppositional Loyalists.

Isabelle glanced around at the small group huddled in a circle, seated on a mishmash of wooden chairs, the smoke from their cigarettes floating silently up and up and up the tall empty tower. She closed her eyes briefly and thought, *Dear Silo, you at least are faithful.*

Indeed, the silo held no wheat or other grain, but she had opened her doors to the resistants as a safe place to meet, as a mailbox and miniature post office, as a weapons cache and as a bank. Occasionally, it had even served as a concert hall for a lone opera singer, as Tito would belt out a segment from *La flûte enchantée* or *Carmen* or most often just a verse of the French national anthem. The other Silo members would join in, using their voices to sing out their fierce resistance.

But tonight the silo served only as a place to grieve, and Isabelle could almost smell the despair that clung to clothes like days-old tobacco.

Tito was explaining, "Sometime between six and six-thirty in the morning, the German forces quartered at Sisteron progressed southward toward Bayons and passed through the town unnoticed. At the same time, two other German columns from the neighboring towns were already in position. Together the Germans began to methodically spray the entire sector with machine-gun fire and mortars."

Tito glanced toward Isabelle, then looked heavenward. "Our resistants were awakened by the sound of bullets and caught in the crossfire. The German detachments quickly sprang into action. The liberated prisoners were hiding by the edge of the road and awaiting their imminent evacuation."

He shrugged his broad shoulders, dropped his cigarette, and ground it out with his tattered boot. "They didn't have time to flee." He cleared his throat, wiped a thick finger under his eyes. "They were massacred on the spot."

"How did the Germans know to come to Bayons? We were so

careful!" This came from Jean-Yves, slightly built with large soulful eyes amid a thin face with a wiry, blond mustache.

Tito looked up, surveyed the room. "The Germans are clever. They knew the Maquis of Bayons was involved in the liberation of the prisoners. And the Boches never leave unpunished one of our acts of bravery."

True, Tito, but that doesn't tell us how they found the prisoners and resistants. But Isabelle kept quiet.

Everyone kept quiet.

They sat in silence. Only for a moment. Just enough time to catch their breath and hear about the next mission. *Quick grief,* thought Isabelle, hunched in her chair, head hidden in her hands. *No time to grieve.*

Then she felt a soft hand on her shoulder, and another, and another. Someone reached for her hand, wet with tears, and gripped it. She sniffed and sat up. One by one, her colleagues came and placed a kiss on each cheek, a squeeze to her shoulder, a knowing nod.

Desolés. We're so sorry.

She had lost Maman and her baby brother long ago, and now Papa.

But here in this dank room, she had a family.

And she prayed that none of them was a traitor.

3

PETER

Peter watched the boys as they slowly filtered into the mess hall. Men. They were called men. The closer they came to Operation Dragoon's D-Day and Provence, the ones who had already seen action stood tense, jaws steeled, eyes hardened. Most of the 80,000 men preparing to board the ships were seasoned soldiers, having spent time in North Africa, Sicily, or Italy. But some, those for whom this was their first mission, had a naive energy about them, an "innocence is bliss" on their young faces. Peter wanted them to keep that innocence for as long as possible.

True, the intense physical preparations required for the soldiers gave them an idea of what was to come. The training involved rigorous physical conditioning, individual combat training, and simulated amphibious landings as well as training on stress management. Still, there was a difference between those who had seen action and the newer recruits.

Sometimes, as on this evening, as lights-out approached, a soldier would come to his room. Tonight it was Andy. Mid-twenties, tall and skinny with hair only a shade lighter than Peter's, he'd served faithfully in North Africa.

"I'm scared, Chaplain. Terrified." It was whispered quickly, followed by, "Am I a coward?"

Peter didn't rush with answers to such a heartfelt question. They sat in silence for a long minute. Finally, he said, "You're not a coward. You're human." He motioned for the soldier to sit on the edge of the cot. Peter pulled a rickety chair over and sat facing Andy. "Cowards hide; they don't confess. Of course you're afraid. Terrified. We all are."

"Not all," Andy said, wringing his hands in his lap, head down.

"True. Not all the new recruits . . . and let them have their innocence. They're afraid, but it's a different kind of fear."

"Imagined. What they've read. But Rusty and Billy and Sammy haven't seen it, Chaplain." Andy glanced up at Peter. "They haven't tasted blood, salty and metallic, smelled death, seen the way a body . . ."

Peter grasped Andy's hands tightly to still their trembling. "No, your buddies will see it soon enough. But that is not for you to decide. What you decide is here." Peter patted Andy's uniform where his heart lay beneath the layers of fabric and skin. "You go on and admit your fear, your terror." He paused.

Silence.

"Go on, Andy."

And he did, as the others had done before him, each soldier who came in the night, confessing the dark, creeping terror that stole their sleep, dreading the horror that surely awaited them, convinced they were cowards or worse.

"You've told me. Now tell Him." Peter motioned heavenward with his eyes.

Sometimes, as with Andy tonight, the young man fell on his knees and wept, leaning against Peter's bunk, hands clasped in grief. Sometimes he sat silently, eyes closed, for long minutes, his lips moving as he voiced his prayer.

Often, after the silence and the tears and the prayers, Peter would take his worn Bible and read from Psalm 46, "God is our refuge and strength, a very present help in trouble . . ." in a soft, calming cadence, taking slow breaths until the soldier's breathing matched his own. Afterward, as he patted the young man's shoulder, Peter felt the soldier's sagging form lift slightly, until eventually he stood straight and sure.

"Thank you, Chaplain."

Sometimes a physical weight descended on Peter after they left, as if he had literally picked up the evil the soldiers feared and placed it squarely on his back. He knew it wasn't there to stay, but sometimes it took an extreme effort to hand it back to the God of the universe.

After the struggle, he'd slip to his knees, just as he did again on this night with the harbor smells of fish and diesel perfuming the night. And in that position, he whispered his own prayer: "You say it, Lord Jesus, 'Come unto me, all ye that labour and are heavy laden, and I will give you rest.' May it be so tonight. Rest for Andy's soul, for all their souls. And mine too."

The nightmare awoke him with its grim familiarity. He saw it again in vibrant Technicolor, and he felt the ache deep in his soul. The physical wound had healed, but the spiritual one, the soul wound, seemed lodged in his heart.

The fighting in Tunisia at its height, the wounded splayed before them. Peter rushing to tend to the injured, listening to one man's dying confession and praying with him to be with Christ. As he rose to drag the soldier from the sands, he heard another desperate voice yelling, "Down! Get down, Ginger!"

A grenade exploded, and the shrapnel wedged into his thigh. And then he was being dragged away, but when he looked up, it was a German soldier glaring at him, and the American's voice faded.

The dream flashed to the next scene with a German shouting in pitiful English, "Stand here!"

There Peter hunched against a wall as a group of Germans turned their rifles on him.

37

"Lord Jesus, into Your hands I entrust my spirit," he prayed, his heart ricocheting in his chest like a wild bullet as the soldiers raised their rifles.

It was always the same instant when Peter awoke, heart pounding, tears on his face, having called out loud to the Lord.

Breathing deeply, he reached for his canteen and took deep gulps of water. His heartbeat eventually slowed as he forced himself to remember the rest.

Where You showed up, Lord.

Because the nightmare had truly happened in the sands of Tunisia two years ago. Peter rubbed his eyes and massaged his thigh where the shrapnel's scar still taunted him as his mind's eye saw again the German firing squad and then heard that one word.

"Halt!"

The German officer fired over the troops' heads to stop them. Then the officer walked to where Peter cowered by the wall. "You are a pastor?" the officer asked in English, his eyes suddenly softer, his voice reverent.

"An Army chaplain," Peter managed to pronounce the words above the drumming in his head.

"Protestant?" and the officer pointed to the simple cross emblem on Peter's uniform.

Peter nodded, head swimming, vision blurred.

But he saw the German's lips curl upward, his eyes mist as he reached into his jacket and pointed to a Protestant medal pinned inside his uniform. While the German soldiers stood at attention, their faces registering shock, the officer brought out a photo of his wife and baby.

"We will send our medic to tend to your wounds and those of the American soldiers," he promised.

And he had. A miracle, the men had proclaimed when Peter hobbled back to camp, the shrapnel removed and carefully bandaged. Yes, God had been a very present help. But it hadn't erased the fear. Or the nightmare. The memory of that incident at once cursed and blessed Peter as he closed his eyes and fought his way back to sleep.

After lunch the next day, Frank Jamison, the stocky, fresh-faced lieutenant from Iowa, knelt beside where Peter sat with his back against the wall, head bent over his sketchbook. "Watcha drawing, Ginger?"

"Just what I see."

What I see now, Peter told himself, forcing the battle scene away, regarding the blond-haired lieutenant with the deep trust and respect he'd gained for this soldier.

Frank leaned closer to examine the sketch. "You're good, ya know. It's a right accurate likeness of them playing soccer." Frank liked to compliment Peter every time he caught him sketching.

"Thanks." Peter gave a grin.

"Nice game yesterday. You're good at soccer too."

"I don't know about 'good,' but *accro*, yes."

Frank lifted a bushy blond eyebrow. "Accro? Don't start speaking your French on me again! Need to know what you're talking about, especially once we get on the field."

Peter laughed. "Good point, Frank. It just means I'm rather addicted to the game." He felt his cheeks redden. "Maybe not the best thing for a chaplain to admit."

"Hadn't seemed to bother anybody too much. We're all mighty glad to have something to do, some way to spend a little of the pent-up energy. Mind if I join you?"

"Please." He winked at Frank. "My faithful bodyguard."

Peter liked the young lieutenant, who looked no more than sixteen with his ruddy cheeks and bright blue eyes that held a type of innocence despite the fact he was almost thirty and had served in Tunisia. Frank cared about his fellow soldiers.

And Frank cared about the chaplain. Which was important since he would be his assistant once they reached land. Chaplains never carried a gun, but the assistant did, charged to protect him, but also allowed to fight if he wasn't needed by the chaplain.

Frank literally embodied God's protection—he'd been Peter's

"very present help" on the battlefield in Tunisia, and he'd be the same on the beaches of southern France.

Frank settled beside him as they watched the game on the sandy field. With his team's next competition in two days, Peter had the chance to sketch the men in action on the soccer field today.

And the memory came.

He was sitting outside the cement schoolroom, his back against the wall, a sketch pad on his bruised and bloodied knees. He watched his friends playing soccer and quickly sketched their movements to quell the anger pounding in his temples. Mahid had fouled him, sending him crashing to the ground, a ground made of sand and stones that cut into his hands and knees as he fell. Mahid was always committing fouls. Problem was, no one refereed their schoolboy games at recess. Just Miss Trotter, the elderly missionary who often sat in a garden chair, straw hat tied securely with pink ribbons under her chin, the beating sun shielded by a taut parasol. She watched the children at recess and sketched them.

Every child knew and loved Miss Trotter. And in the mission compound, all the parents whispered to their children, *"She is the woman who brought Jesus to Algeria. She could have been a famous artist, but she chose to serve here."*

Yes, an aura of awe surrounded the tall older woman. Peter thought she had the most beautiful, penetrating eyes. She saw everything and translated it onto her sketch pad. A tiny flower caught in otherwise limitless sand dunes, a child strapped to its mother's back, one of the schoolboys, soccer ball at his feet, a mischievous smile turning his lips.

On that day, she stood over where he sat. "May I see it?"

Peter scrambled to his feet. "Oh, no, ma'am. It's just . . ."

Miss Trotter frowned. "Your knees, Peter! That must hurt."

He shrugged. "It stings. Mahid fouled me, and he gets to keep playing while I'm the one who got hurt."

Her blue-gray eyes twinkled. "That does sting the heart, doesn't it? But it looks like you've found something worthwhile to occupy your time."

She motioned again with a nod of her head, her gray hair pulled back in a tidy bun under the straw hat. "May I see it?"

Reluctantly, he produced the sketch pad. It wasn't the first time Miss Trotter had asked to look at his sketches.

Slowly she flipped from one page to the next.

"You draw well, young Peter."

"Thank you, Miss Trotter. I like to sketch." Peter felt the shy smile spreading across his face as he tried to stand tall before the old and saintly woman. "But what I really love is playing soccer."

Miss Trotter chuckled. "Of course you do. But"—and here her eyes met his—"you have a natural gift with the pen and pencil. It's from God. I encourage you to keep honing this talent."

Peter received the sketchbook and the compliment. "Thank you, Miss Trotter. I do like to draw. But I like to play soccer more."

The familiar tightening in his chest shook Peter from the memory. If only he were ten again, sketching his friends playing soccer in a sandy field outside of Algiers instead of a twenty-eight-year-old chaplain sketching soldiers kicking away their fears with a soccer ball on the shores of the Mediterranean and knowing that what they faced in a mere week or two would be much more than a skinned and stinging knee.

Peter watched from his position as sweeper as Marco, a young Italian kid probably half his age, yanked on his teammate. He'd tripped him twice and elbowed him once, always throwing his hands in the air with an innocent expression on his teenaged face. If there was one thing Peter hated, it was dirty playing.

Your job as sweeper is to protect the goalie and the goal. Your job as pastor is to protect your flock.

The thoughts scurried in his mind as he felt anger pulsing.

This is just a friendly match. Calm down, he reprimanded himself.

But he'd never been very good at keeping his temper at bay during a soccer match, especially when the opponent was pulling on his teammate's jersey.

When Marco dribbled the ball toward the goal, Peter was ready. The boy dodged around him before losing control of the ball. As Peter intercepted it, moving away from the goal, Marco grabbed Peter's jersey. And the reflex came.

His elbow smashed into Marco, and he felt the hard tick of bone. Then the kid was on the ground, moaning, holding his face. He wasn't faking it this time. His nose was spurting blood.

Adrenaline pumping, Peter shook himself to tamp down the anger. "Sorry," he murmured, reaching down to help the kid up.

Marco was in no shape to get up. His teammates gathered around Peter, eyes blazing, cursing in Italian, and the referee was running toward Peter with a yellow card held high.

Peter felt like cursing too. Anger still pumped inside, along with embarrassment. His face felt as though it were on fire.

"Sorry," he said to the ref, and to Italian teammates, "*Scusi, mi scusi.*"

And later to his own team.

Rabbi Horowitz found him after the game. "Maybe you aren't as laid-back as I thought," he said, lifting an eyebrow.

"A rotten temper, Rabbi. And the whole dang platoon got to see it in full display."

"I wouldn't worry about it too much. It's actually nice for the boys to know that we clergy are human. Makes it easier to relate."

Peter shrugged. "Maybe. At least it usually only shows up during a soccer match."

"When the opponents are playing dirty," the rabbi stated. "But maybe not only during a soccer match?" The rabbi rested a hand on Peter's shoulder. "What is so terrible in your past that you cannot forgive yourself, Ginger? You preach forgiveness to these men, you vibrate with love for God, but deep inside there is a wound, and you use a knife to continue to cut yourself and remove the scab."

Peter knew what that wound was. What brought out the anger. The fury. He closed his eyes as if he could shut out the memory, but it flashed brightly in his mind and sliced him to the core. Again.

A pastor's job is to protect his flock.

4

RENÉ

July 26, 1944

"I can't take another step," Delphine called out. She had a much-too-large-for-her knapsack, which held the almost-empty canteens of water, slung across her shoulders, and her eyes, which had taunted René just this morning, were now rimmed with grime and tears. He knew she had no more strength left. They had walked for hours in the dead of night, their shoes nothing but flapping leather with holes, her hair layered with sweat, and her voice, once so exuberant, now a mere whimper.

"The only thing that keeps me walking forward is seeing you in front of me. Please wait for me."

He stopped, set down his knapsack, and held out his hand to her. She grabbed it, squeezed it hard as if she could wring out the images seared in their minds, surely imprinted there forever.

"We're not far now. I'm sure of it."

"How can you keep walking! Look at you. Blood everywhere. Your arm . . ."

She motioned to the sling he'd made from Dominique's T-shirt to hold his shattered arm against his chest. Kilometer after kilometer, René wondered if perhaps the arm would simply fall to the ground at some point, detaching where bullets had caught it above the elbow. With his other hand, letting go of Delphine's, he pulled a canvas bag behind him, holding three rifles; one he had pried from Jean-Paul's fist, and the other two he had picked off the floor beside Maman and Frédéric.

"Almost safe," he moaned. His throat ached, and all he tasted was dirt and blood. Without warning, his knees buckled, and he stumbled to the ground, barely saving his injured right arm as he caught himself with the unharmed left hand, letting go of the canvas bag.

At once Delphine was beside him. "I don't know these hills! I don't know where to go. You said we are almost there. Come, I'll help you."

Awkwardly she tried to pull him to a sitting position as René winced. She retrieved a canteen and held it to his lips. He took one long sip, emptying the canteen, even as shame washed over him. He had to be strong for her, not the opposite. And yet—

Her eyes met his in the dark, and once again she read his mind. "You mustn't be ashamed! It's miraculous you survived." She pulled herself up and held out her hand. "Lean on me. Together we'll find strength."

With difficulty he managed to stand, clamping his jaw shut to keep from allowing the pain to explode through his parched mouth. Step by step, they trudged forward, following the dirt path until, in the distance, the full moon illuminated a river and a bridge, and beyond, the town of Les Mées.

"We're here. We made it. And look, there," René whispered, and he coughed from the effort. "There they are. Just across the river now."

"Who is it? Who do you see?"

"My friends, the Penitents."

With his good arm he pointed to a chain of craggy formations in the distance, looking to René on this night exactly as they had always been described: a group of hooded monks, frozen in time by the riverbanks.

"Oh, they are so beautiful!" Delphine cooed. "The moon makes them appear mysterious."

"We'll hide below the cliffs, and later I'll tell you their legend."

"Legend?"

"Yes, but not now. Now we must find water. And we must sleep."

One foot in front of the other, they crossed the wide bridge. And as his ghostly friends welcomed them into the shelter of their caves, René let out the breath he had been holding. For now they were safe. Only then did he allow himself to reflect on the battle from this morning, or perhaps from another world altogether . . .

René fired the rifle again and again from his perch at the window. Rows and rows of Germans marched forward as if oblivious to the gunfire.

When a grenade flew through the window and landed in the kitchen, Dominique rushed into that room, throwing himself on the grenade. The explosion rocked the house, causing the antique chandelier to crash to the stone floor.

Seconds or minutes or hours later, with all the windowpanes shattered, the ammunition almost gone, Sébastien and Jean-Paul gone too, René continued to fire into nothingness, despair blanketing the farmhouse. On and on the gunfire came, finally finding Maman, who fell where she stood, the rifle making a hard clattering sound against the floor.

How long could they keep fighting, just him and Frédéric? What would happen to Delphine if . . . ?

And then Frédéric was gone too.

Having no more ammunition, René stepped over the bodies. The Boches were waiting for him. He wondered if being riddled with bullets would hurt any more than the pain he was already experiencing from the bullet wound in his arm. Or should he run? If he waved a white flag of surrender, they might kill him, but would not search for Delphine.

Hands up, heart thumping, René opened the door and held out his rifle with a white cloth tied to its barrel, stained with Fred's blood.

Hundreds of men surrounded the farmhouse, their rifles aimed at him. German soldiers dashed around René and into the farmhouse while three men held their guns on him. The German in charge stood still, almost frozen in place, watching René, watching his men, his steely gray eyes hard, his medals flashing in the beating sun.

A minute. Two. Three.

The soldiers returned, shaking their heads, then looking at the commandant. "No one left. There were only four others and a woman. All dead."

One of the soldiers holding the gun on René walked closer. He was taller than the other men by a hand, his hair whitish-blond. And his pale blue eyes were cruel, proud, mocking. He lifted his pistol, held it inches from René's head.

René met his eyes, not blinking, only his heart hammering.

In one movement, the German commander stepped between the soldier and René. "Halt, Tomas." The taller soldier lowered his pistol, as the commandant's expression showed surprise. "This one is only a boy!"

René made his eyes hard, stood straight and stiff. "Oui. The only one left."

"It's unbelievable." A flicker of compassion registered on the commandant's face as he murmured, "You're brave, son."

A whistle, a shout, a sign from the commandant, and the Germans turned and left.

René waited at the farmhouse until the sun set in streaks of crimson as if mocking the butchery. When at last he opened the cellar door in the pitch-black night and whispered, "Delphine," she let out a squeal and clambered up the makeshift ladder, clutching the envelope with the documents.

"Oh, René! I was sure you were dead, that you were all de . . ." As her eyes adjusted to the night sky, she caught sight of his arm, which hung at an awkward angle by his side . . . and the blood. Everywhere, blood. "You're hurt! Where are the others?"

He shook his head.

A wail rose from inside her small chest, like the call of the wolves as they mourned a member of their pack and howled to the moon.

"Shhh, Delphine. We have to leave now. We have a long way to walk while it's dark." He took her hand. "Come. I've filled the canteens with water and packed all the food."

René wondered how he could change so quickly, could put on a different face, make his eyes hard and walk away from the farmhouse as if his mother was sitting in the chair peeling potatoes as she had been doing only yesterday. As if Dominique and Frédéric were knocking on the door, asking for a drink, and Maman was bringing them a glass of lemonade. Not as if four bodies lay bloody with bullet holes on the salon floor, and Dominique's torn body lay beside the bowl where the scrawny cat used to lap water.

And yet René knew he was right in every fiber of himself that if they did not leave this farm right now, neither he nor Delphine would be alive in the morning.

René woke with a start. A noise. He tried to sit up but winced with pain. The Germans! Where was he? Ah, yes. The Penitents. The deepest cavern in the bowels of the cliffs, the one where he and his buddies had smoked their first cigarettes.

"I found water." Delphine came to his side, her dark eyes alive again with expression. "You were right. The town square had a fountain and fresh water. Look."

She held out the three canteens, the ones they had filled with water before they left the farmhouse and emptied slowly on their hike through the night. Delphine put a canteen to his lips, and he gulped the fresh liquid. Then she gently removed the makeshift sling, soaked it with water, and began to clean his wound.

"Two bullet holes, René, but no bullets left inside. That's good. But it's a mess. It will become infected." She bent over him and wiped the blood from his face.

"How do you know? Who made you a nurse?" He sounded annoyed and immediately regretted it.

"You've said it before. I'm not a nurse. I'm a survivor."

Oh, yes, she is.

"And you're a survivor too."

"I'm sorry. Thanks, sis."

Delphine was busy ripping the bloodied T-shirt and using a swathe to wrap his wounds. Every movement caused agony, but he wouldn't cry out. If Delphine could find water in an unknown-to-her village in the dead of night and bandage his arm, he would not give her the satisfaction of crying out in pain.

"Tell me how to find the Maquis? Once it's dawn, I'll be afraid to leave the cave. But if I go now, perhaps I can find them. Tell me where they hide."

He surveyed their low-ceilinged hideaway, his favorite of the grottoes at the foot of the Penitent cliffs. This one showed no signs of having been used recently. Its depth allowed them to hide safely for a time.

He considered her question. Where were the maquisards? *"Partout."*

"Everywhere? What does that mean? That isn't one bit helpful. I'll bet there are Germans everywhere too."

"Yes, but we're safe for now, so we'll stay here. We don't need to find the maquisards yet."

René knew the names and whereabouts of others who were hiding in hills and farmhouses spread throughout the region. Later he would find them, would tell of the butchery, would convince them that he was brave enough to join their Maquis. But not now.

Now he must take Delphine to Sisteron, twenty kilometers away. There he knew someone who would keep her safe. If they rested all day, perhaps his strength would return. Then they could head for Sisteron as soon as it was fully dark.

"I still have some food." He grimaced as he said it, tried to wipe away the memories of stuffing the day-old bread, the saucisson, the cheese, and other remnants of food in his satchel, even as his mother and comrades lay dead.

"More food? Oh, I'm so hungry . . ."

But he could not keep his eyes open. He leaned against the damp cool rock, and as he faded into sleep, he thought of Delphine.

He'd not been able to figure her out. She said the strangest

48

things, and yet, each time up to this moment, she'd been right. That scared him.

He remembered that first night when she had come to the farm, a skinny eleven-year-old. Big brown eyes, almost black, staring at him as if she were reading his soul, as if she knew every secret in the universe. It made him shiver. There was something mysterious about her that made his stomach flutter.

During the first month she had come to their home, she pronounced in a sober little voice, "I need to leave you. If I leave, you'll be safe."

"Delphine," he'd answered, exasperated with her goodness, "don't you understand that's the whole point? We're hiding *you*, but we are not trying to be safe."

She had turned her head, looked at him, and said, "I know, but I care about you all now." Then, "We'll win this war, you know, but not all of us will live."

He thought it a very strange thing to say so matter-of-factly. He was happy to hear that she believed they would win the war, because it certainly did not appear that way at the moment. Not after the Nazis had taken over all of France, not when they kept hearing of the horrors of prison camps. But the other part, *"not all of us will live,"* that seemed like such a strange thing for an eleven-year-old girl to say.

Those first months he felt such an obligation to protect her, almost annoyed that Maman had made him responsible for her, but as the months went on, he grew more and more fascinated by this child with the chocolate eyes and the dark, shining hair. And then a few months ago, when she turned thirteen and he was almost sixteen, the fluttering in his stomach became something different—not fascination, not mystery, but love.

René loved Delphine, not as a big brother but as a teenager becoming a man. He loved her, and though he would never admit it to Delphine or anyone else, he swore that he was going to make sure that *"not all of us will live"* did not include her. Delphine would live. She would survive this war, this horror that had wrapped itself around their country and their farmhouse and their lives.

Delphine was shaking his good shoulder slightly. "It's almost dark. I slept a long time, but you've been sleeping forever. You're scaring me. Won't you please wake up?"

With difficulty he opened his eyes, pain shooting through every inch of his body although he had moved nothing but his eyelids. "Water, please," he mumbled.

Again she held the canteen to his lips. He drank greedily, but the effort exhausted him.

"I'll fill the canteens again when the sky is black," she said.

"Yep. Good." But his eyelids drooped.

"Don't sleep! I'm afraid you'll never wake up again if you sleep." She touched his face where it was bruised, and he moaned. "Tell me the story of the Penitents. You said you would. Tell me the real story."

Lethargic, unable to make any part of his body move, he succumbed again to sleep.

Moments or hours later, Delphine was shaking his good arm and saying, "Wake up! I filled the canteens."

"Merci," he said but he wondered if she heard him at all. Everything felt so heavy.

"Here. Eat something." She placed a thin slab of saucisson in his mouth. It hurt to chew, but he forced it down. Then a wedge of dried cheese on the stale bread.

Bit by bit she fed him bread and cheese and sips of water until finally he could think about something other than extreme fatigue.

"We'll leave now, but we must walk a long way in the dark. Can you do that?"

Delphine gave a solemn nod.

"Do you still have the watch I gave you?"

"Your father's. Of course."

She handed it to him. His best treasure from his father, a 1917 Elgin "General Funston" trench watch with the original factory strap featuring a compass.

"Good, then we have all we need. Come."

She helped him to his feet, and he bit his lip to keep from crying out in anguish.

Put one foot in front of the other, idiot! he cursed himself. *And drag the satchel with rifles and food.*

But he could not.

Seeing his hesitation, Delphine said, "I can manage both satchels." She pulled both the bag with the guns and the one with the canteens behind her. "I'm skinny, but strong. I used to carry stacks of heavy boxes for Papa at the *chocolaterie.*"

René was opening his mouth to resist when she added, "All you have to do is to tell me the legend. And take one step at a time."

Petulant girl, he thought with affection.

In the dark, the Penitent cliffs once again followed them, the moon highlighting their sharp, pointed heads and reflecting an eerie mirage on the Durance River. With the haunting rock formations on their right and the compass as an ally, they made their way north toward Sisteron.

"Now, please. The story! You promised, René."

With garbled speech, he whispered, "It's a legend. And of course, as with any legend, there are many interpretations."

"I don't care which one you give me." Hearing her sassy exasperation flooded René with relief. Just as she had declared, Delphine was a survivor. They were both survivors.

He perched himself on a boulder by the river, unable to ignore the throbbing in his arm and the way his legs were trembling. He couldn't make his mouth pronounce the first word.

Delphine's hand went to his forehead. "You're burning up!"

She held the canteen to his lips, and he drank deeply, then once again Delphine fed him pieces of bread. He stood, head swimming. Another kilometer, maybe two, they trudged along in silence, stopping often to rest, too often. Would they make it to Sisteron before dawn? René imagined Germans hiding behind every rock or tree.

Keep walking, one excruciating step at a time. Follow the compass due north.

Instead, he sank to the ground with the moonlight fading the sky to gray.

Delphine sat down next to him. "Please. You can do it. Give me your hand. I'm sure we're almost there."

But he knew Sisteron lay far to the north. Still, he nodded, tried to stand, and as the pain shot through his arm, he felt the tears fall. He couldn't make his body move. The fierce moan that escaped with the effort surely terrified Delphine, but he had no strength to hold it back.

Delphine was mumbling in some language he could not understand. Then she switched to French and whispered, "God of our fathers, good, benevolent God, we need help. Please. Help us."

And he was asleep.

A sound awoke him, so faint it might have been the wind. Another sound of twigs cracking, and then arms were coming around him, lifting him, lifting and walking, and somewhere in his mind he heard Delphine saying, "Sisteron. Somewhere in Sisteron."

Another voice was whispering, "I can only take you to . . . walk the last kilometers alone . . ."

Delphine was murmuring something excitedly, but then he had fallen back to sleep.

⊰✶⊱

"God answered my prayer, and the man appeared out of nowhere, just like the ram in the thicket. Do you know about the ram in the thicket? How Isaac was saved?"

On and on Delphine jabbered about the hulking man who had touched her on the shoulder as they slept, who had picked up René and carried him to the edge of Sisteron. "And he carried the rifles too as if they were feathers. An angel, René! I tell you, he was an angel."

René did not believe in angels, but his gratitude was great for whoever the benevolent stranger had been. Perhaps another maquisard?

Now Delphine held the bottom of her dress up to the canteen and poured water onto the fabric. She wiped the cool cloth across his brow, then his cheeks. "We only have a kilometer to get to the town. Then you will show me where to go, right?"

He nodded as he took another swig of water, pulled himself to sitting, scowling.

"Can you tell me the story now?"

"What story?"

"The legend! About the mountains."

"Oh, yeah. Okay." He blew out his breath. "This is my favorite version. It's . . . a bit racy." The heat rose in his already flushed cheeks, but the darkness hid it. "The monks from Montagne de Lure, right near here, were walking along the river, as they did daily, when they caught sight of a group of nuns bathing."

"Oh."

"Unable to resist, the monks sneaked a look at the naked nuns, and some saint—I can't remember which one—decided to punish them forever. Frozen right there on their journey, forever caught in their lustful look."

Delphine's eyes grew wide. She grinned. "Well, it was a rather naughty thing to do, but I feel very sorry for them. It's a tragic outcome of their—" she paused, searching for the right word— "indiscretion. But then I'm delighted for us, because not only do we see an enchanting rock formation, but we get an enchanting story."

There she went again saying such strange things. "I suppose you could call it 'enchanting.'"

He pulled himself to his knees, took Delphine's outstretched hand, and stood. He rested his back against a gnarly olive tree and then took a few tentative steps. They continued toward the road, his left arm resting on Delphine's shoulder as she lugged the heavy sacks.

"I like that story," she said. "I don't know much about monks and nuns. We don't have them. We have rabbis, and they dress very smartly, like the monks, perhaps. I like thinking that the monks are just human. They like to look at pretty girls too." She giggled, stopped, and turned to face him. "Like you, René. You like to look at pretty girls. I see it."

Her remark cut through the fatigue, and he snapped, "How do you see that I like to look at pretty girls when we are never with anyone else?"

Her eyes lit up. "Because you like to look at me. You think I'm pretty."

Heat rose in his cheeks. "That's ridiculous. You're my kid sister."

"But not really." Delphine pretended to pout. Then she walked ahead of him, calling back to him, "Say I'm pretty."

"Why should I say that?"

She waited for him and took his good hand. "Because Papa always told me, 'You will be a good Jewish girl. You will obey Torah, but,' and he would whisper"—which is precisely what Delphine did now, eyes twinkling in the moonlight—"'you're very pretty, my dear Sarah, so you must be careful with your beauty.'" She frowned. "Now no one tells me I'm pretty, and you're the only one I have. So tell me."

René grinned in spite of himself, then gasped at the pain shooting across his forehead. "You're my sister, and you're smart and feisty and kind." He tried to think of another word, any other word besides *pretty*. He wouldn't tell her that. He felt embarrassed—no, angry—that she had noticed how he looked at her.

She pouted. "I won't say you're handsome either, even if I think it. I'll say you're stubborn."

"That's a good thing to say," René muttered, cursing under his breath.

"You're stubborn and you're reckless and you're so mad." Her dark eyes looked on fire.

"I'm not mad. I'm tired, that's all."

Completely wrung out. Keep walking.

Her brow furrowed, and she said, "It's okay for you to be mad as long as you keep walking. And look, the Citadel is just there! We made it to Sisteron."

Indeed, the breaking dawn silhouetted the majestic fortress far in the distance.

Her whole countenance softened, and she brought her angelic face right up to his, her dark eyes looking into his. "But, please, don't call me your sister. Don't call me Delphine. Not here. Not now."

René reached over and held her hand. "I must call you Delphine now. But one day, when this war is over . . ." He cursed again and then managed a wink. "When it's over, I'll call you by your real name and tell you that you're pretty."

She beamed up at him. "Okay. It's a deal. And you know, I'm mad like you, but Papa always said to find a way to use my anger for good. So I'm trying."

René nodded, throat dry, but what he wanted to say was, *You've been my "good" for these last two years, and you're the reason we have both kept going until now. All I want is for you to be safe.*

5

ISABELLE

JULY 28, 1944

The knock on the door came at five in the morning. Isabelle felt everything in her go stiff. The Boches knew, and now they were coming back for her. Was it Tomas or someone from the Milice? Who would come before dawn? She struggled to calm her heart as she threw on her threadbare robe. She tiptoed to the front of the apartment, expecting to hear the gruff and angry voices of the French police. Instead, she heard the whispered cries of a boy.

"Isabelle. It's René. Open up, please."

Sucking in a breath, she peered out the peephole to see a young teen barely visible in the dark. She opened the door and found herself staring not only at her cousin René, but at a young girl with matted pigtails, a girl she recognized. Both of them were covered in dirt and . . . was that blood? And their eyes were so weary.

She tried to hurry them inside, only they moved with a lethargy that startled her. Then she noticed their bare and bloody feet and the makeshift sling that held her cousin's right arm tight against his chest.

"René! What happened?"

"He's hurt. He needs to lie down." The young girl gripped Isabelle's hand, her eyes glazed from exhaustion.

Holding René around his waist, Isabelle led him to the couch and settled him carefully on his back. The young girl followed, sinking to the floor beside the couch where Isabelle joined her. René's face was covered in grime, and blood stained the sleeve of his bandaged arm. When Isabelle looked more closely, she saw that almost all of his clothes were covered in blood.

René grimaced but made no sound. He had already fallen asleep. She turned to the girl. "You're Sarah, right?"

"Delphine, remember? I'm Delphine now."

"Yes, of course. Poor child."

Solemn brown eyes watched her as the girl told the story. "Germans attacked the Amblards' farm. The Milice were with them."

Isabelle felt her face go white, cleared her throat, and ran her hands through her hair. Perspiration soaked her blouse as she braced herself to hear another horror story.

"You and René were there?"

"René hid me in the farmhouse cave. He was fighting too. He only surrendered after the maquisards and his mother were killed and he had no more ammunition."

Hand to her throat, Isabelle could not stop the tears. Papa's sister, Tante Irène, was dead too, murdered only a few days after him? Perhaps her tears gave the girl—Delphine—permission to cry, for she moved into Isabelle's arms and began to weep. Isabelle held her trembling body, kissing her hair, gently wiping her tears even as they fell.

"I thought René would die before we got to you, Mademoiselle Isabelle. But I prayed, and an angel came to carry him. He's hurt badly. Please help him."

A conversation with her father two years ago, when the Nazis had occupied the French free zone, came floating back to Isabelle's mind as she hurried to fetch towels and water to clean René's wounds. She would never forget the way her father swayed in the doorway, his face ashen.

"I've heard from an Italian chaplain about what the Germans are doing to Jewish children in Russia. We must help save the children, Izzie." When her father called her by that nickname, she could never resist him. "When the Germans come—and they *will* come—we must be ready. There's a man I'll call Monsieur Martin. He's found homes where we can hide the children in this region. It will be dangerous. Some of us may be forced to give up our lives. There are stories. I will not tell you the details, but you know those who help, the resistants, if captured, are usually tortured and sent to camps."

"I know, Papa. I want to be ready. We must try to save those innocent children."

And so the Martin Network was born, in secret, with every child's name changed. And her father, Monsieur Jean-Pierre Seauve, the gentle intellectual, the town librarian who attended daily Mass, became a proficient forger with his stamp.

"A Catholic bishop here in Sisteron and another priest in Nice are helping to set up this network. Monsieur Martin, a Protestant pastor, is spearheading the operation."

"Do you know him, Papa, this Monsieur Martin?"

"That is not your concern, Izzie. What I can tell you is that he risks his life every day to save children, and now we will join him."

Papa had turned the musty wine cave into his office, and with his fake stamps, he became astute at forging documents for the children, as well as helping the clergy put together a campaign plan. Everything had been prepared to take between one hundred fifty and two hundred children from the French coast to the Basses-Alpes in the event of a catastrophe.

Of course, the catastrophe came.

When the Germans invaded the region, their manhunt began. In cities from Nice to Lyon, they arrested the Jews. Everywhere. In hotels, on sidewalks, dragging them into the streets, sending them to the camps, or at times, to their deaths right there on the pavement in front of their stores.

The time to act had come.

"I'm scared, Papa," she had said on that dark day two years ago. "I'm not brave like you. I'm not courageous."

Papa rested his hand on Isabelle's shoulder. "Remember that courage is not a lack of fear, my darling child. Courage is fear that has entrusted the outcome to God. We pray and we do what God Almighty asks of us."

When she looked unconvinced, he had added, "Remember what Saint Augustine said: 'Hope has two beautiful daughters. Their names are anger and courage; anger at the way things are, and courage to see that they do not remain the way they are.'"

"But what if I do it wrong? Papa, what if someone is hurt?"

She had seen then the extreme strain in his gray eyes, the deepening shadows beneath them, the way his black hair, black as midnight, black like hers, looked flecked with snow—or perhaps ashes. "People will be hurt, Izzie. People will lose their lives. It's war. But some will gain their lives too."

"It will be worse for you, Papa, if I accept this role to help smuggle the children. It's already dangerous with me helping the underground. And you won't be just forging documents in the cave. Someone might see me with children, and your work will be compromised."

Again the big, warm hand on her shoulder. His tired eyes nonetheless communicated that calm for which he was known. "I'm very proud of you, my Izzie. I know what God has asked me to do. If this is what God is asking of you, there is nowhere else I'd rather you be."

Isabelle sponge-bathed René, cutting away his soiled clothes and makeshift bandage, washing the wounds—there were so many from the bullets and glass—as tears fell onto her gray, cotton skirt. Her cousin—ten years her junior, sneaky and smart, wiry and strong, and so brave—had not awakened during the whole process.

Two years ago, when René had learned of the Martin Network, he had begged his mother, Tante Irène, to hide a Jewish child at the farm. Isabelle had heard him trying desperately to convince her. "*Maman, Papa is fighting with the Armée, and Antoine has joined the Maquis. This is our chance, my chance, to help . . .*"

And so they had taken in a Jewish girl. *This* Jewish girl. Delphine, who had bathed, and who now lay in Isabelle's bed wearing one of her nightgowns. Isabelle watched the slow up and down, up and down of her chest.

In her mind, Isabelle pictured the day Sarah came to them. The child had watched the Nazis break the glass in her father's store, Levy's of Lyon, rush inside, and drag away her parents, Theodore and Renata Levy. Theodore was known as the maître chocolatier of Lyon.

Sarah, at ten or eleven, seemed bright, fearless, determined, mysterious, proclaiming, "*I'm not afraid! We're going to win this war! And Maman and Papa will come back from . . . from wherever they are.*" Her little face had fallen only for a second. "*And we'll be reunited at our beautiful home in Lyon. Until then, I am very thankful to be here.*"

Isabelle remembered accompanying the same girl through another summer afternoon and her hesitation and fear when she came to Tante Irène and Oncle Tristan's farmhouse and rapped on the door.

Isabelle thought it was ironic how life repeated itself backward. Now the young girl, this Delphine, this child whose identity had been changed with a swift mark of her father's pen and a stamp, was once again on the run. And the Germans were still right here, right in this city, surely waiting for one misstep. She felt it in her bones.

Isabelle's only safety had been that Tomas did not know her true identity, did not know that it was her father who had been locked in the Citadel, her father who had been gunned down in the streets of Bayons. Perhaps the Germans were waiting for Isabelle to call out to Ginette or Tito or someone else in the Silo Network.

And if there was a traitor among the resistants, one who had betrayed the Citadel's escaped prisoners, did they also know the addresses where the children were hiding? Could that be why the Germans had attacked René's farm? What if someone, anyone among the resistants, found out Delphine was here?

René and Delphine slept, but Isabelle sat wide-eyed in the salon, staring out the window as the bright moon spotlighted the Citadel in the distance. She thought of all the other times she and Papa, and then Ginette, who had joined them in the Network, had been awakened by frantic knocking in the middle of the night. They'd open the door to find Jewish parents hugging their children close, fear and desperation drawn in dark circles under the adults' eyes. "*S'il vous plaît*. Please. Help us."

Sometimes, in the case where parents had been rounded up and taken away or shot in front of their children, other family members or neighbors brought the children—in a state of shock—the neighbors twisting their hands and saying, "We heard that you could help. The poor things—they watched their parents dragged away. Their father resisted at first and . . ."

After receiving the Jewish boys and girls, she and Papa became what he called "identity thieves."

"We cannot send these children to a new family until we have, in a sense, stolen their identity. We must hide the children until they have adopted their new names. It will take time for the little ones to understand. It's not hard to draw up all the papers, Izzie, but for the children to forget their identities and adopt new ones, it will be hard."

Oh, so hard.

Papa created the false documents, and she smuggled the Jewish children to safety behind the walls of homes of ordinary French citizens. Papers hidden in the fake bottom of her purse, she walked through the village in the bright morning or at dusk, holding the hand of the little one, chattering, stopping to inspect a wildflower, making it seem as if they were just any other family out enjoying a French evening.

Once she was sure no one was watching, they weaved in and out of the streets and the narrow, steep andrones, until they found themselves in the countryside, and she deposited the precious life with a family. She watched as the family took the Jewish child in, the child whose eyes were wide, who was trembling, the child who had seen her parents disappear. The family's mother smothered the child in her bosom, kissed each cheek, knelt to their level, and whispered, "Welcome. You're safe. We are glad you are here."

The families who sheltered the children needed help to feed them. Along with the fake identity papers, Papa made ration cards, knowing that he and the others could be caught at any time. For weeks, the Network worked at all hours to ensure that the children remained safe.

Three files were created per child. The first was hidden in the library underneath Papa's library cards and books; the second was given to the family who sheltered the child; and the third was sent to Switzerland to the International Red Cross. On each form appeared the name and date of birth of the child, the address of the parents, the name of any siblings, and the name of those entrusting the child to the Network. On the back of each form, each document, Papa wrote the new assigned identity.

Afterward, Ginette and Isabelle, with bright berets perched on their heads and dressed in pretty blouses and culottes disguised as skirts, biked across the region from family to family to check on the physical and psychological condition of the children. *"Dress as fashionably as possible,"* Tito had told them. *"It's another form of resistance."*

As their only link with the world "before," seeing those who had delivered them to their new family helped the hidden children to overcome the ordeal of being separated from their family and sent to a new home. When possible, Ginette and Isabelle brought small gifts, bars of chocolate or clothes or even letters to the children, along with hugs and kindness. And somewhere in the process, Isabelle had grown to love them.

Papa had often reminded her, *"We must be extremely careful. The whole Network could fall apart if one link in the chain is broken."*

Isabelle closed her eyes now as she remembered a morning last April. "Papa, it did fall apart," she whispered.

She had gone to check on Delphine at the Amblard farm and spent the night there with her aunt and cousin. She sped home on her bike to see Papa at the library after checking for news at the mailbox at the Silo.

No news.

But a few meters away from the library entrance, Jean-Yves stood, leaning against the wall, smoking a cigarette and nodding to Isabelle. The message was clear. *Stay away!* She pedaled for hours, terrified, finally daring to come back into town that night. Jean-Yves found her in the alley beside the library.

"They've just left. They arrested your father. If you'd come half an hour earlier, you'd have found them here, and they would have arrested you too."

She felt faint and sank to the ground. "What have they done to him?"

"They questioned him, but he was not tortured. He was taken to the Citadel. They found nothing except a few political newspapers that he had hidden poorly, expressly so they would be found if the Nazis came looking."

"I am very proud of you, my little Izzie. I know what God has asked me to do. If this is what God is asking you, there is nowhere else I'd rather you be."

Her father's special nickname for her brought comfort, and his words rushed over her like the refreshing waters of the Durance in late summer. He had known the danger and was not afraid. He had already lost so much . . .

Maman . . .

And suddenly Isabelle's memories were tumbling further back to happier times so long ago.

She could see her mother's stomach growing rounder, her joy deepening. How Isabelle had longed for another child in the family, and now, after eight long years, there would be a baby. Her mother's eyes were bright, her face, often so pale, had blossomed with pink cheeks.

And Papa's limp, the injury he sustained in that first war, the one that was supposed to end all wars, was less pronounced. Papa had served as a pilot when planes were just becoming useful in war. He'd been shot down twice, the second time sustaining an injury that all but crippled him. Papa could not walk far, could not work in the vineyards, but he learned from books. Every book. Any book. His love for Maman and for books had kept his eyes bright, almost as bright as before the war.

Isabelle had not realized during the many tellings of the story that her father's wound was much deeper than his withered left leg. That she did not know until much later.

When she had come into their life, the three of them were happy and bright and all was good, her mother cooing over her precious daughter, her father, the village librarian, always reading, always talking about airplanes and ace flyers.

His model airplanes sat on the bookshelf next to a signed copy of *The Aviator* by her father's hero, Antoine Saint-Exupéry. With Maman and Isabelle by his side, Papa lived his life through Saint-Exupéry, the great Frenchman, the great pilot, the writer, journalist, poet, and pioneering aviator.

Simple days, joyful days. They were free, there would be another baby, and there was food on the table. Maman was happy, Papa was happy, Isabelle was happy.

Isabelle shut out the next memory, slammed the door on it. She would not remember the rest.

What did it matter? They were both gone. She fell to her knees and admitted, "I am so mad and heartbroken and afraid, God. And alone. I don't have anyone else to love."

You are not alone.

She thought of the Silo friends and their understanding of her grief. She loved them, all of them. And she loved every one of those children she and Papa had helped to escape.

She touched the crucifix, crossed herself, and prayed, "God of the Jews, I'm afraid. Let me be strong for this child, for René, and for so many others."

And she heard the words as if from the loudspeaker that announced the arrival of the children's carnival: "You have been strong before, Izzie. You'll be strong again."

6

PETER

July 30–31, 1944

The Sunday services had ended, and now the volunteer choir was belting out a lively rendition of "Take Me Out to the Ball Game." Word had it that the St. Louis Cardinals had beaten the Brooklyn Dodgers soundly in both games of the doubleheader the day before, and the St. Louis contingent that would soon board the USS *Nevada* was busy with bragging rights.

Peter, with his sketch pad and tin box holding his Swiss Prismalo colored pencils, was perched on the rock wall that separated the land from the port. His pencil scribbled across the paper, catching the movements of the men as they swayed back and forth, laughing and swinging their arms in time with the music. Quickly he sketched cameos of the men in action, whether singing or playing soccer or writing letters to their sweethearts back home. For days on end, as they waited at the port, his pencil and pad caught them going about their duties or playing a game of cards or smoking cigarettes.

As with most evenings after dinner, Peter produced a comic

book–like page of the day's activities, complete with speech bubbles and conversation in each man's dialect.

Tall, skinny Andy, his self-appointed secretary, held up today's comic for all to see, shouting, "You men are gorgeous, singing in the choir. Too bad ol' Rusty forgot the words . . ." He bantered along as he passed the parchment paper around for the men to inspect. The mess hall reverberated with laughter, and the very air, so stifling and heavy, became lighter.

Later that evening, when the comic made its way back to Peter, he taped it to the wall in his room. His door was always open for the men to peruse the sketches. His goal was to sketch as many as possible before they reached the French shores, before his days and nights were filled with other duties. A goal he felt was worthwhile as he observed the easygoing kidding and banter between the men as they examined his work.

On the days when time and imagination were in short supply, Peter resorted to another of his favorite tactics. Brain teasers. Puzzles. Enigmas. The men gathered around whichever soldier Peter had chosen to burden with the task of, for example, removing a six-inch-long slice of wood attached to a string from the soldier's buttonhole.

"You have to think outside the box," Peter told them. Good humor and puzzling over brain teasers kept their minds supple, their fears at bay. That and prayer. Peter's tactics were simple: soccer, sketches, puzzles, prayer.

Pencil poised above the page, Peter thought of Miss Trotter again and her encouragement to use his gifts for good. She had given up a very prestigious career as an artist to be there in Algeria. Peter knew he didn't share her same talent, but he had learned to be observant like her. She noticed the tiniest detail of a flower or a plant. He noticed the young men.

So Peter sketched the faces in the volunteer choir, remembering Miss Trotter. And as he sketched, he prayed.

Day after day, the American battleships *Nevada*, *Arkansas*, and *Texas*, the British battleship *Ramillies*, and the French battleship

Lorraine were loaded with surface crafts, trucks and tanks and ammunition. These mighty vessels had already seen so much of the war. Everything about them was slow and calculated, heavy, important. The tugboats beside them in the harbor looked like miniature models that would be swept away with a few angry waves. But Peter knew the truth. Plain and sturdy, small but capable of guiding the battleships out to sea, tugboats were essential to the operation of the battleships.

Ever since he joined the chaplaincy after Pearl Harbor, he'd thought of himself as a tugboat, sturdy and dependable. He simply wanted to do his part to help the greater good. Like a small boat, he liked to be able to turn quickly, change plans, dock wherever he needed to. A big tanker moved slowly, whereas a tugboat could keep the tanker safe, could pull it out to sea or into a safe harbor. That's all he wanted, to be a tugboat, to keep the men safe. Maybe not physically, but in their souls.

Soon he would board the USS *Nevada*, along with two thousand officers and soldiers. He marveled at this ship, the only one that had managed to deploy during the attack on Pearl Harbor. But she'd paid the price, getting hit by a torpedo and at least six bombs as she steamed away from Battleship Row. Eventually the crew beached her on a coral reef before she sank to the harbor floor. But she'd been salvaged and restored and had crossed the Pacific to the Atlantic, from a harbor in Hawaii to one in Italy.

"You're a tough lady," Peter said out loud as he observed two jeeps entering her opened hull. "You've been all over the world, and soon I'll go with you to France."

Just pronouncing the word sent a physical pain through him.

It had been ten long years since he had been back to France, the first eight years spent in America after finishing high school at the International School in Algiers. Ten years ago, he had stepped onto American soil for college, stepped into his country, although it did not feel like his country. Still the passport said so, and yet how his heart had grieved for the desert in Algeria and the delicious cheeses of France, those two countries which had been his home for the first seventeen years of his life with only brief stints in America.

So he got his education, four years at an American university, and then because his heart was set on ministry, he went to seminary too. For three years.

Back when he had left for America, not quite eighteen, he had not imagined how hard it would be and that he would barely speak a word of French or Arabic in all that time. Oh, how he'd missed it!

He'd met Helen when he was finishing seminary at Harvard—she the stylish and sophisticated undergrad from Manhattan, he the awkward expat kid with clothes from the missionary barrel at a church in a little town south of Atlanta.

A blond-haired beauty, witty, smart, and devout—in her own way—Helen had captured his heart when she attended the cathedral where he preached one Sunday morning. In truth, she had lassoed him, pulled him in, knowing exactly how he would fit in with her plans.

"You know more about the world and general culture than any of your colleagues. Once we get rid of those dreadful clothes, you'll be perfect within a fine, established church in New York."

She'd never totally approved of his calling to ministry. She wanted him to have a lawyer's salary, like her father. But she loved him. And he loved her. And when, down on one knee, he presented her with a tiny diamond, she had said yes.

His first pastorate was in rural Kentucky while she finished her junior and senior years at Radcliffe. But in the middle of the second year, two disasters struck. Pearl Harbor catapulted America into the war. His personal disaster only had consequences on his soul and a small country congregation, but for Peter, it weighed as heavy as a sunken ship in the harbor.

He'd known then he would not stay in the pastorate. That the tragedy occurred around the same time as Pearl Harbor could not have been a coincidence. At least the seven long years earning college and seminary degrees would not be wasted. Chaplains were needed in the war effort. And he would be back again at Harvard for six weeks of training.

Near Helen once again.

As surely as the door to the pastorate had been slammed in

his face, when he heard about the need for chaplains, Peter saw another door opening.

Before Pearl Harbor, both the US Army and Navy were woefully understaffed. But in the wake of the Japanese attack, a new patriotism surged throughout America. Peter had felt it as well. His buddies from college rushed to volunteer for military service. But clergymen could not be drafted. Rather, the law required that the military rely upon the different denominations and ordination councils to do the recruiting.

Soon after the Kentucky debacle, Peter moved down to his grandmother's home in Georgia where his parents had been staying ever since they were required to leave North Africa when the war began.

"*Pete, son.*" His father had found him alone on the front porch of the farmhouse. He sat beside him on the swing, his heavy hand resting on Peter's bent elbow. Fire flamed his father's cheeks. Peter could not be certain if he read doubt or compassion in his father's hazel eyes. "*I'm sorry for this.*"

He never asked for an explanation. Instead, his father handed him a pamphlet. "The military needs chaplains, son," he said and pointed to a sentence on the pamphlet:

Based on the general requirements for the Armed Forces, the following quotas are required: United States Army—1 chaplain for every 1,000 personnel; United States Navy—1 chaplain for every 1,250 personnel.

The fact that he also fit the other requirements listed on the pamphlet had seemed more than coincidental, more than serendipitous. Almost predestined.

Except for one very big problem. The tragedy that had brought his short career in ministry to a screeching halt.

"*They won't recommend me now, Dad. You know that.*"

"*I'm not so sure, Pete. I believe the denomination will see the wisdom in giving you this new assignment.*"

And they had. No time to heal from the gaping wound, just a quick turnaround.

Let the higher-ups make the risky decisions. The disaster in

Kentucky had pummeled Peter to the ground. He never wanted a leadership position again. A minor role, that was all he wanted in this war. To do his duty. To be a tugboat.

Of course, he'd been wrong. Looking back, these past almost three years in the chaplaincy had been more challenging than anything he'd ever done before. More heartbreaking than what happened in Kentucky. If not for his colleagues, he would not have stayed the course.

Being captured and facing a German firing squad in Tunisia was not the only event that caused his nightmares. In North Africa, during the battles, he had gone sometimes three nights without sleep, after spending the day moving from unit to unit, praying with the men, offering brief words of encouragement as they stared off, bleary-eyed, in shock. He and his fellow chaplains had worked alongside the medics to provide emergency care to the wounded soldiers, carrying them to whatever makeshift shelter they had, praying by their sides, Peter knowing in his gut which ones would not last the night and crying in his heart as they wept in agony and passed away.

Late at night, on the battlefield littered with bodies, he'd helped identify and bury the dead. In North Africa, he performed his first-ever funeral. Ironic that the service in the desert heat had comforted him, provided a different outcome from the one he should have officiated in the small cemetery beside the white clapboard church in rural Kentucky.

Hard and heartbreaking, yes, but at least as a chaplain in wartime he knew the enemy clearly.

He'd been wrong about the chaplaincy, thank God. If he'd known the emotional strain and physical exhaustion entailed, he would not have volunteered. But now he loved this job. Here as a chaplain, once again he held the role of a pastor caring for his flock.

If only his first pastorate had worked that way. If only he had known how to spot the enemy inside the walls of the church. If he had not been so naive, if he'd known how to recognize betrayal. And worse.

But he had not. Only occasionally was the scab ripped off the wound. He blushed to think of his reaction during the soccer game a few days ago. He stuffed those feelings way down as he found a seat on a rusty bench. Staring out at the *Nevada*, Peter took out a piece of stationery and began a letter.

"Hey, Ginger."

Peter glanced up from his letter to see Andy, grinning. "Mind if I join you?"

When Peter said, "Sure," the skinny private perched beside him on the bench, removed a pen from behind his ear, retrieved his own piece of stationery from inside a novel, and said, "Gotta get this letter off today or Judy will be crushed."

"You write her every day?"

"Sure do. Gotta make sure she still wants to marry me once this stinkin' war is over." He grinned again. "You writin' a girl?"

Peter shrugged. "Technically, I guess so."

"What does that mean? Doesn't sound very romantic."

He set down his pen. "I'm writing my mom. She's a girl. A woman."

Andy punched him playfully. "That's very nice, writing your mom." Then, "Well, do you have a girl?"

"Nope."

"Have you ever had a girl?"

"Yep."

"Hadn't ever heard such short responses from you. Doesn't sound like a real happy ending. Wanna talk about it?"

"Nope." Peter took a deep breath. "But I'd like for you to tell me about Judy."

Andy's smile spread even wider across his face. "Ah, Judy. She's real swell."

Ten minutes later, Andy was still singing the praises of his fiancée. Peter would finish the letter to his mom tomorrow.

※

Peter lay on his cot, thinking of his fiancée and the way Helen's golden-brown eyes had flashed during their conversation in late December 1941.

71

"A chaplain! Say it, just say it. You *want* to go to war. A chaplain still goes to war! I'd rather you be a lieutenant commanding the troops. If you're going to war, then truly go to war! Be an officer. You would have authority and be protected from the front line."

How her comment had stung. He'd reached for her hand, watched how the small diamond caught and refracted light on the ceiling. "Sweetheart, I will be an officer. I'll be commissioned as a first lieutenant."

"You know that's not what I meant. You'll be in the middle of the war, with all the men."

"Exactly where I should be."

Helen swiped her finger under her eyes, as if she could hold back her tears. "No! You won't have a weapon. You're too kind, too good to go to war, Peter. You said it yourself—that the military can't draft clergy. Please, don't go. I don't want this for our life . . ."

Strange that she was using his rank as clergy as a deterrent to enlisting for war. Though she had not spoken it out loud, he'd seen relief in her expression earlier in the week when he'd explained he was leaving the pastorate. She had not even asked for the details of what had happened in Kentucky. Had she even cared?

"I know my becoming a chaplain is not what we planned, but with the war, with Pearl Harbor, it's my duty. And after Kentucky . . . well, it's what I want. What I feel called to."

"But I don't feel called to that! You promised we wouldn't live overseas! You promised not to go back to North Africa!"

"I'm not asking you to live overseas, sweetheart."

She took a deep breath, tears falling freely down her lovely face. "I know. But when you're there, it will draw you back. You've missed it so."

And he had. How could he explain it to Helen? "Yes, I've missed it, but I promised we wouldn't live there. I'm good for my promise. But this is war, and there's a great need for chaplains. It's like a fire in my belly, a conviction so strong. I believe it comes from the Almighty."

He'd only felt this strongly about one other thing in his life, yet she had never understood his call to ministry either.

And that had turned out all wrong.

"No." Helen's answer, short and sweet and spoken with conviction, shocked him. And then it didn't. She slowly removed the ring and whispered, "I will not be pitted against God! I know He'll always win with you. I've already given up so much with your choice to be in the ministry. Not this. Not now."

She swiped at her tears again, placed the ring in his hand, stood on her heeled tiptoes to kiss him on the cheek. "I'm so sorry."

Why did she invade his thoughts now when, in retrospect, she'd been right? They wanted such different things out of life. But love, at least in Peter's experience, did not run on pragmatism or logic. Love floated on the wind, catching one off guard and completely unprepared. And three years later, he still berated himself. *I fell in love with the wrong woman, Lord, but I think I still love her.*

7

ISABELLE

July 31, 1944

The young girl woke slowly, stretching her arms wide and yawning, almost as if she didn't have a care in the world. She sat up and then hopped out of bed. "How is he? Is René okay? Is he . . . ?"

"Shhh," Isabelle whispered. "Don't wake him. Good morning to you too." She smiled, and the girl returned it, planting the expected kisses on Isabelle's cheeks. "He had some difficulties in the night sleeping, but now he's resting more peacefully. Come, let's have breakfast."

She set a bowl with the last measure of milk in front of Delphine, then spread homemade blackberry jam on a slice of baguette and handed it to her.

Delphine moaned with pleasure. "It's so good! Thank you, Mademoiselle Isabelle! This bread is not as stale as the baguettes René kept feeding me." A playful smile turned up the edges of her mouth, then disappeared.

"Do you want to tell me about these past days, Delphine?"

Eyes bright, she said, "I will only tell you the good parts. We hid

74

in the caves at the foot of the Penitent cliffs! They are so beautiful." She stopped and laughed a little. "René says there's a legend claiming the cliffs are a procession of monks, frozen in time. They were punished for looking at a group of naked nuns bathing in the Durance River. I think it's both a funny and a sad story."

Holding a bowl of chicory in her hand, Isabelle sat at the antique cherrywood table Maman's mother had gifted them years ago. "I suppose it is." Isabelle felt distracted, thinking of what René and Delphine had just gone through.

Delphine's brow wrinkled. "Do you think that this war is God's punishment because we're Jewish? Like the saint who condemned the monks?" Before Isabelle could answer, the girl continued, "I learned always from the Torah that God is good and He punishes evil, but He doesn't punish those who follow Him." Solemn eyes, almost black, looked straight at Isabelle. "My family has always followed Him. And I love God. So why would He punish us?"

Isabelle stared out the curtained kitchen window to the ochre-colored apartment building across the way, tracing the ridges on the pale-yellow bowl with one finger. "I don't know why we must endure this war, this horror. But I love God, like you do, Delphine." She took a sip of the bitter liquid and admitted, "Though I'm angry at Him right now."

Eyes wide, the young girl whispered, "You are?"

"Yes. I'm heartbroken and furious that God's allowing this reign of terror, these massacres." She took one deep breath to calm her racing heart. "But I love Him, and I believe He is good, and you are His precious daughter. He's not punishing you."

"Maman Irène and Papa Tristan, your aunt and uncle, they were so good; they were Christians." She took another bite of the baguette. "Now Maman Irène is dead, and we don't know what has happened to Papa Tristan and Antoine. Only René is left. Did God punish them for helping a Jewish girl?"

"No! Of course not." Isabelle struggled to answer. "I know it's not God who is punishing. It's something else, something very dark and evil."

She reached across the table and grasped Delphine's hand.

Again the girl frowned, withdrew her hand, and said, "It's very confusing, Mademoiselle Isabelle. The Amblards are good, you are good, but I've heard that Christians follow Hitler. And he is evil."

How could this girl ask such difficult questions? Especially on this morning when the very air they breathed tasted of sorrow? Isabelle had no answer but the truth. "I am ashamed of some of us Christians. I think all kinds of people believed Hitler had good ideas at the beginning, and then when his evil plan became more apparent, many grew afraid, and so they didn't oppose him and his regime."

"You're not afraid! I see it! You're brave, Isabelle. You took me to the Amblards' farm to hide in the middle of the day. We pretended . . . do you remember?"

"Oh yes, I remember, my darling. But I was very afraid." She scooted her chair beside Delphine's and held the girl by the shoulders, brushed her fingers over her as if she could erase the worry. "My papa told me, 'Izzie, courage is not the lack of fear; courage is fear that has said its prayers.'"

Delphine considered this as she ate the crusty baguette, crumbs scattering on the table. "That's a good way to put it. Your father is wise and kind. René told me that he is locked up in the Citadel. I'm sorry."

How could Isabelle burden this child with another awful truth right now? She had not yet had the chance to tell René about her father either.

Delphine sipped her bowl of warm milk. "Is he afraid now? In that prison?"

"I'm sure he was very afraid. But he knew that we must do what is right before God, even if it's dangerous and scary and painful. When he was arrested, I know he kept praying for courage."

Delphine nodded. "God will help our fear be courageous. I like that. Courageous fear." She smiled again. "I remember he came home the first night I stayed here. And I wasn't supposed to see him because he was doing secret work."

Isabelle remembered that night well. Delphine had been the first child she smuggled. Afterward she and her father figured out a way to keep their lives separate when she brought children to the apartment. Ginette moved in to share the apartment with Isabelle, and often Papa spent the nights on the couch in his office in the town library.

And then Papa had been taken . . .

Delphine was still chattering. "He was surprised to see me, but I promised I would never tell anyone, and I haven't. He made those forged papers for every child you rescued, right? René has told me all about him."

Isabelle swallowed the hurt. Forced the tears away. "Yes." She studied the trail of dust and dirt the children's bare feet had deposited on the floor. After a moment, she raised her eyes and said, "I'm sorry to tell you that my dear father was also killed by the Germans, just last week."

Delphine's eye grew wide. "Your father too?" She reached across the table and grasped Isabelle's hands. "Your aunt and your father killed. It's terrible, Mademoiselle Isabelle." Her brow creased, and she nibbled her lip as two tears slid down her pale face. Then she looked up and said, "Your father called you Izzie. Now I will call you Izzie to remind you of how brave he thought you were, of how brave you are."

For two days, Isabelle and Delphine nursed René, cleaning the bullet wounds in his arm and the deep cuts on his torso, procuring the precious medicine from kind Doctor Niel, who never asked questions.

And always, Delphine sat by the window that overlooked the cobblestone street with the view of the Citadel far to the left and the huge rock of La Baume across the river on the right. The view used to bring such joy to Isabelle. Now Delphine watched to see if anyone—Germans or the French Milice—approached. Isabelle was thankful that Ginette had been gone all week, planting small bombs with the other Silo members, preparing for a bigger operation to help the Allies, who would soon be coming from the south to liberate them. At least that was the rumor.

On the third morning, René sat up from his makeshift bed on the couch. Though she had heard the story twice from Delphine, Isabelle listened as her cousin coughed out the words, slowly.

"They attacked the farm. The Germans and the Milice. Hundreds of them."

"René . . ."

"For hours we fought them, Isabelle. Maman and me and four maquisards. The other Maquis in the region were warned; they fell back. We fought with the weapons the Maquis had smuggled in until we had no more ammunition. The grenade killed Dominique, and then Jean-Paul and Sébastien were shot and Maman too . . . all dead!" He choked on the last two words.

"Then it was just Frédéric and me, and then it was just me, only me. Why, Isabelle? I think they fired more ammunition on our farmhouse than in a whole air raid. When I walked out, one of the soldiers aimed his pistol at my head. But then the commandant saw that only a kid had survived, surrendering with a bloody white shirt stuffed in a rifle . . ."

The first tear fell. Then another. Then his body began to shake. "He let me live. For once being a punk worked to my advantage," he spat out. "They left me there."

He closed his eyes, and Isabelle thought he had fallen back asleep. But after a few moments, René opened his eyes, chin raised, shoulders squared. "I'll fight." He looked almost fierce. "If we could hold off hundreds of men for hours, then I know the Maquis will want me. They'll let me join." His voice broke, and tears filled his eyes again. He blinked furiously but didn't wipe them away. "I'm going to join the Maquis. I'll fight those Boches. I'll get revenge for Maman. And *Tonton* Jean-Pierre. And my buddies."

What could she say except, "I'm so sorry. We'll find a way to keep Delphine safe. I believe I can find a safe place for you too."

"I don't want a safe place, Isabelle! Are you paying attention? I want to fight. I have nothing to lose. Papa is in a prison camp in Germany. Maman has bullets through her chest. Antoine is off with the Maquis, and we haven't had news from him in months—"

"Izzie!" squealed Delphine. "Come quickly! There's a German soldier walking the street below."

Isabelle hurried to the window, falling to her knees and peering down. She gasped, sucking in air, feeling fear clutch her throat. Tall, broad-shouldered, and that eerie whitish hair visible under his military cap. It was Tomas.

René crawled across the room and looked out the window. He moaned. "I know that soldier! He's the one who wanted to shoot me."

The three of them sat with their backs against the wall, as if their turning away from the window would make Tomas disappear.

At any moment, Isabelle expected him, or perhaps a whole troop of German soldiers, to storm the apartment. Or was this a different kind of mind game he was playing, slowly frazzling her nerves, patiently planning the impending doom?

René's voice was raw. "You have to hide Delphine, *cousine*." He closed his eyes. "That's why I finally surrendered. I thought if I surrendered, they wouldn't look for her. And they didn't."

"Of course," Isabelle answered, trying to calm the terror that grabbed at her heart. But to herself she asked, *What will I do with Delphine?*

Later, when both René and Delphine napped, when no Germans patrolled outside, Isabelle knelt beside the rough-hewn oak chest in the salon. Lifting out layer after layer of priceless family keepsakes, she stared at four stacks of envelopes, each neatly tied with twine, that sat at the bottom of the chest. She picked up the first stack and fingered the colorful array, held them to her heart, and winced with a physical pain as palpable as René's wounds.

My personal treasures.

Papa had never known she'd hidden them here.

I'll just read one, she told herself. Then, as if she held fire in her hands, she dropped the bundle, set it back in the chest, and quickly replaced the heirlooms on top.

Stop it! You won't punish yourself. Think of something else.

She knew what *something else* would be. The Penitents and Delphine's childish rendering of the legend. Once, when Isabelle was a young teen, she and Ginette and a few other teenaged Scouts had walked from a camp near Sisteron through the night to find those beautiful craggy rock formations so that they could pray, could *be penitent* like the poor monks.

She tilted her head as if she could still hear her friends' voices, could still smell the fragrance of that evening in Haute Provence, its lavender and pine and wild thyme inebriating her.

The summer she turned fourteen, she joined her Scout troop at The Camp Between the Hills, which was a tiny remote village near Sisteron built out of limestone from the region. Except many of the buildings were in complete disrepair. Every day at the camp and for the following two summers, the Scouts helped build back the old village, stone by back-breaking stone. In the evenings they sang songs and roasted the chipolata and Merguez sausages over a campfire while the cicadas made their loud yet comforting racket. At night they slept outside under millions of stars, or if it was raining, on musty mattresses on the floor of a dilapidated barn. Spiders and spiderwebs and rat refuse abounded, but so did laughter, so did some kind of enigmatic and contagious joy.

But late one night during that first summer, she and half a dozen other campers broke their strict curfew and sneaked away. They huddled around a grove of olive trees, whispering gossip as they passed around a bottle of wine, the nicotine smoke from their cigarettes curling around them like friendly ghosts.

How she had jumped when a hand had touched her shoulder. Then screamed. Perhaps the ghosts weren't friendly.

Eight sets of wide white eyes watched as that American giant of a man who ran the camp stepped into the circle where they sat. He towered over them.

"Kids, *les enfants*," he said. She could even almost hear his deep bass voice and his perfect French. "What have we here?"

He was always doing that—asking questions when it was perfectly obvious what they were doing. Disobeying—breaking curfew, drinking and smoking—but the real problem was the gossip, especially since that had been the American pastor's subject for their Bible study earlier in the day. He seemed larger-than-life, a giant indeed. But they weren't afraid. He had the biggest heart, the biggest vision, and the most outlandish ideas about God and faith and life. He asked questions like Jesus did in the Bible. To make them think.

What she thought of was walking to the Penitents to do what Isabelle had called "Protestant penance" for their disobedience. This camp was run by a Protestant pastor, so she wouldn't have an opportunity to do real penance, confessing in private to her Catholic priest and receiving absolution. But she'd wanted—no, *needed* to do something. So Isabelle decided to make a trek to the Penitents to join her "fellow" Penitents at the cliffs and spend time in prayer, asking God for forgiveness like the Protestants did.

She had been the one to suggest it after the giant had left.

"Let's go, everyone. We'll walk there, and we'll pray and ask God to forgive us."

The other campers who had been part of the gossiping circle frowned, doubt in their eyes.

"That's a long way to walk!"

"If we go now, and in the night, it will be cooler."

Somehow, in her young adolescent mind, she did not realize that sneaking out of camp in the dead of night was a much worse offense than gossiping among the olive trees.

In the end, only four of the eight guilty Scouts made the trek: Isabelle, Ginette, Paul, and Jean-Marc. They trudged through the black night, using electric torches to light the way, slapping at mosquitoes and gulping water from their canteens, emptying them long before they reached their destination. Even as Isabelle remembered it, she could feel the way the thick, muggy night had clung to them, and their desperate thirst, the way the boys had run ahead when the Penitent cliffs came into view and filled the canteens with the icy spring water from the fountain in the center of the town of Les Mées.

By the light of their torches, they climbed up the narrow, steep path to where they stood above the cliffs, looking out over the black valley, then staring at the starlit sky, and finally asking forgiveness in the company of the ill-fated monks.

When dawn came, the whole camp was there at the foot of the Penitents, everyone looking for them because of course the other kids told the gentle giant, Monsieur Christensen, and they came looking.

"You are my lost sheep, Isabelle, Ginette, Paul, Jean-Marc," Monsieur Christensen said, eyes twinkling, "and we will leave everything to come find you."

Ginette was indignant. "We were only saying our prayers, asking forgiveness like you always talk about!"

Isabelle would never forget the laughter, the way it exploded out of the gentle giant's mouth, and how his whole body shook with it.

"I suppose, then, young ladies and gentlemen, that you are forgiven."

Isabelle sat up straight, as if literally struck by a flash of lightning. No! This was a flash of brilliance. She knew what to do with Delphine. She would take her to The Camp Between the Hills, that ancient stone village that even to this day had not been completely restored. No camps had been held there since the beginning of the war, but hopefully Mme Nicolas still lived in the stone cottage just down the road from the village-camp, and hopefully, though elderly, that wizened woman still had plenty of tricks up her sleeve.

Isabelle would hide Delphine at The Camp Between the Hills. The mountain peaks of La Baume and St. Michel would watch over them, and twenty kilometers down the road, the Penitents would be praying.

8

PETER

July 31, 1944

"We've gotten word. The date for Operation Dragoon is set. We'll be loading soon, Lieutenant Christensen. What is your take on the men's morale?" Major General Alexander Patch stood with Peter as they watched the huge vessels rock back and forth in the port, preparing to carry the lives of thousands of men from the ports of Italy across the Mediterranean to the beaches of southern France. The goal of Operation Dragoon was to secure the ports of Marseille and Toulon and then march northward, freeing the southern half of France.

Operation Dragoon would finally happen. The meeting in the fall of 1943 in Tehran at the Russian Embassy had settled that, with Stalin and Roosevelt in favor of a southern invasion of France, and Churchill staunchly opposed, claiming that Russia would later use this as a benefit.

The Americans and Russians won the argument, yet the operation was stalled for months because of a stalemate in southern Italy. Until Rome was taken, D-Day in the south of France could not be scheduled. Finally, on the 4th of June, Rome was liberated, and now General Patch commanded the 7th Army. The assault force was the 6th Corps, whose 80,000 men belonged to its three infantry divisions—the 3rd, 36th, and 45th. Peter knew that the planning of Dragoon had been complex. *Mind-boggling*, he corrected himself. The coordination of all kinds of surface crafts, ships, and vehicles for transportation was staggering.

But soon . . .

Peter always felt intimidated by the tall, lanky, taciturn general who had graduated from West Point, who served in France during the previous war, and who began in the South Pacific in the current war. Known for his fiery temper and aloof manner, Patch surprised Peter occasionally with a friendly comment—like today.

"My take, sir," answered Peter, "is that the men are feeling antsy. They're ready to begin. Too much free time leaves one's mind susceptible to worry. And fear."

"You chaplains are a tough bunch. Thank you for keeping their minds *occupied*." He emphasized the last word with a tight smile as he patted Peter on the back. "Who do you favor in the final match on Wednesday?"

The major general wants to talk about soccer?

"The Italian's Risotto Rivals are strong, fast, and clever. But I have confidence in our men, the Burger Boys."

Each of the dozens of teams bore the name of a favorite food from their country. As the tournament had continued, the American teams had inevitably lost and moved into the second and third brackets. Only the Burger Boys continued to advance to the finals.

"I believe you are on this star team, are you not?"

Peter felt the blood rush to his face. "I don't have to play, sir, if you think it inappropriate."

Had the general seen his temper tantrum on the field a few days ago?

"I think no such thing!" came Patch's quick reply. "I've rarely seen a more gifted sweeper. With you in that position, and with Jasper as goalie, we've only given up, what, five goals in the whole tournament?"

Peter cleared his throat. "Four, sir. Just four goals."

And one broken nose. Poor Marco.

"Impressive. Where'd you learn to play like that?"

"Algeria, sir. I grew up playing soccer in the courtyard of our mission compound."

"Ah, makes sense." He tugged at his mustache. "Well, don't you dare think of sitting out. I'll be in the front row cheering you on come Wednesday."

The soccer tournament had been a roaring success with intense training that kept the men alert. Most of the Americans were much less familiar with the sport but had caught on quickly. Truth be told, they were getting pummeled in every game. Except for the Burger Boys. Nine out of the eleven main players had grown up overseas and, like Peter, had played. They'd begged him to make one American team competitive. So he had.

Still, Peter missed his North African buddies. Now *that* tournament in the desert sands had been a lifesaver, as they had called to each other across the field in Arabic. The equivalent of an intense and intimate World Cup that had helped them to recover from the devastating battles in Tunisia and Morocco.

"Good luck, Chaplain. You bring our team to victory here. After that, we'll be taking these beauties across the sea." General Patch nodded toward the battleships. "And keep up your sketching, Lieutenant. Soccer and sketches are good for the men's morale."

"Yes, sir."

Peter slid the sketch pad from under his arm as the general walked to the battleship, his mind straying to another vessel: a crowded ferry, when two decades earlier he had left the Port of Algiers to cross this same sea, heading to the Port of Marseille with his father, a trip for just the two of them.

They kidded with each other as the ferry neared the calanques, those white high cliffs that descended perpendicular into the Mediterranean. At eight years old, it wasn't Peter's first visit to France by any means, but it was the first time he had traveled alone with his father, away from his pesky younger sisters and his mother.

He thought of his mother's worried expression and her green face—Mom got seasick. She could not take the rough waters; she could barely stand the calm water when in a boat that was docked.

Mom had looked tired in those days, though he reckoned she had good reason, what with the blistering heat and the desert sand so fine it seeped into every part of their apartment. What with the news of the Great Depression in America, and with Miss Trotter on her deathbed. Mom would stay close to Miss Trotter's side, Peter knew. And so she let her son and her husband float away on the Mediterranean while she stayed back in the village with her daughters and did what she loved doing: teaching the children about Jesus.

Each summer, the mission sent their missionaries to France for a time of rest, to escape the brutal North African heat, to attend a conference where they enjoyed the freedom of singing hymns out loud and worshiping with no restraint. But this trip was different. Dad was going to buy a village!

His father, at six-foot-four and weighing two hundred forty pounds, most of it pure muscle, looked formidable. When he preached, his voice rose, as did his arms, and fire burned in his hazel eyes. With his father, Peter never knew what the next idea would be, but he knew it would involve adventure.

"I've found a village that we'll turn into a camp for children," he'd confided to Peter that morning as they neared the Port of Marseille.

Instead of their usual stay with their French friends, the Moulins, in the teeming city, eating fresh fish from the marché and munching on the baguettes bought at his favorite boulangerie, they borrowed the Moulins' old Peugeot and headed northeast from Marseille up into the rugged terrain of the Basses-Alpes. They passed by the towns of Aix-en-Provence and Oraison and Sisteron until the paved streets ran out and he and his father were bumping along a narrow, winding dirt road with two huge mountain peaks rising like giant friends on either side.

"When will we be at the village?" Peter had asked, impatient to see what his father had dreamed up.

"Soon, son, it's just up there between the peaks of La Baume and St. Michel."

And so it was named The Camp Between the Hills.

But when they arrived, Peter's heart fell. It was nothing but a few old homes and a rubble of rocks. "You bought this?"

His dad, eyes blazing with joy, turned and said, "Yes, isn't it marvelous, son? Think of all the possibilities!"

All Peter could think of was that he certainly would not find a boulangerie in this abandoned place. He felt a gnawing anger, like hunger pains, at his father, who had once again led them on a wild goose chase.

But Peter had been wrong.

For years, every summer he and his family traveled to France to attend the conference for all the missionaries who were working with North Africans as well as many working in France. These conferences were held in an old *château*—beautiful on the outside, crumbling on the inside—and they were filled with his best childhood memories, playing hide-and-seek, laughing with other children who spoke perfect English and French and Arabic as they switched between languages, poking fun at one another.

After his father bought the old village, every summer following the conference, his family and a dozen others would traipse to the village made of stones, all fallen. The families camped out under the stars or in tents, and during the blazing days, parents and children alike helped realize his father's dream to build back the village, to make it a place where tired missionaries could come and lay their weary heads far from the heaviness of Islam in North Africa and the encroaching secularism of France. It was a place to relax, to retreat.

After a hard day's work, with sore muscles and dirty hands, they washed in the chilly stream and grilled saucisses over the campfire and sang hymns. Sometimes the parents prayed long into the night, their happy voices lulling the children to sleep. Already The Camp Between the Hills had become a haven.

Almost twenty years later, much of the village had been restored. And weeklong camps were held each summer for Scouts and church youth groups and families needing a break. His father, larger than life, would often lift his hands toward the hills and toward heaven and quote from the prophet Isaiah, *"'They that shall be of thee shall build the old waste places: thou shalt raise up the foundations of many generations; and thou shalt be called, The repairer of the breach, The restorer of paths to dwell in. . . .'"*

That all seemed like a lifetime ago, and far away. Peter had never returned to The Camp Between the Hills, not in all his years in American school. But he had wanted to, had meant to, to help his father and mother and younger sisters.

To see *her* again. There, he admitted it.

But he had not returned, even when his father had begged and had offered to buy the boat ticket. Peter covered the open wound of his life overseas with soccer games and chess tournaments and sketches and then with Helen.

No camps had been held at the village since the Germans invaded France in the spring of 1940. And his father . . .

Why was he thinking of that village today?

He turned to his sketch pad, twirling a bright red pencil in his right hand, but the inspiration had fled, literally run away as if the young man he had sketched earlier had walked right off the page. *"Build the old waste places . . . raise up the foundations . . . restorer of paths to dwell in . . ."*

The village had been built back, but so much else from his past was still debris that Peter didn't have the courage to uncover, stone by stone by stone.

"Hey, Ginger, you got a package today."

Andy tossed Peter a brown box across the crowded mess hall. Peter caught it with one hand and looked to see his mother's lovely cursive written in ink across the brown-bag wrapping.

Mom's cookies, he thought, smiling. She sent them whenever he was at port long enough to receive something. He always shared what she sent with others, saving her letters to read in private with a knot in his stomach. Mom was in Georgia, living with her parents. But where was his father?

His parents had been forced to leave Algeria when the war began in 1940. But sometime after his father had convinced Peter to join the chaplaincy, Peter had suspected that his father had returned to Algeria in secret. The letters and packages that his mother mailed never held letters from his father.

For as long as Peter could remember, beginning he supposed when his parents first arrived in Algiers with him as a toddler in 1920, his father had typed a weekly letter on his old Smith Corona typewriter with the carbon paper inserted in the roll, sending those carbon copies out to family and friends, relaying news, asking for prayers. Every week. Since 1920. When Peter left Algeria for school in the States, he too became a recipient of his father's carbon-copied letters.

He cherished them.

They had moved overseas to Algeria as missionaries with the North African Coalition shortly after the First World War. His father had been a Marine in that war, come home determined to fight a different war, for the souls of men and women and children. And he had.

But his father's letters had stopped abruptly in the summer of 1942, a few months before Operation Torch, the Allied invasion of North Africa. Peter had guessed that his father returned to Algeria. He'd known it deep in his soul, had heard the whisperings of a ragtag group of missionaries who were now working undercover as spies for America.

His father, a spy. He believed it wholeheartedly. He thought back to his father's facility with languages—French, Arabic, Berber, German, and Spanish—and his love for brain teasers, puzzles, and codes. All giftings that would serve someone working as a spy.

Peter opened the box, inhaling the sweet smell of home-baked cookies, the butter and sugar—and was that cinnamon?—that his mother somehow managed to scrape together with her rations. He closed his eyes and saw himself in their minuscule kitchen in Algiers, him sneaking cookies as quickly as his mother and his sisters, Janet and Beth, removed them from the oven, their faces red and plastered with perspiration as they slid the cookies from the baking sheet onto a plate.

His mother had laughed at him, swatting away his hands.

But Janet was indignant. *"You have to wait. You never help. You just come in and gulp down all our hard work!"*

He'd laughed too, but now he felt a cramp in his stomach as he munched one of the cookies his mother had baked with his grandmother in his grandparents' big farmhouse kitchen in northern Georgia, the home that in years past had held Peter's whole family when they returned to the States for their mandatory furloughs.

All is well, his mother wrote. *Janet and Beth are busy working for the USO.*

He imagined his sisters tucked away with his mother and grandmother, working on the home front while their husbands fought in the Pacific.

Nana and I are doing our part too. And your father is caring for all the crops—so many different crops this year. We're grateful they seem to be healthy.

He felt his stomach tighten and reread the letter. For the first time since he'd deployed, his mother had inserted the family code into her letter, the same code they'd used for decades when they were in an area hostile to the gospel. "Crops" were people. "Healthy crops" meant successful campaigns. Before this war, those campaigns had been evangelistic, but now it meant that his father, always wild and adventurous, was off somewhere serving someone secretly, many "someones" who did not live in America.

At times Peter feared for his father, a force of nature, wild, impetuous, with an exuberant but perhaps misguided faith. He anticipated his father's response whenever he voiced concern. *"Doing the Lord's will, Pete! I'm ready for whatever He wants."* Eyes twinkling, the receding copper hair interspersed with gray, his laughter deep, almost boisterous. And then his father would quote a passage from one of St. Paul's epistles to make his point.

Peter had been right about his father being in Algeria. When Peter had been deployed to North Africa in the fall of 1942, he'd gone to their home in Algiers and found his father there. Peter recalled his attempt to convince his father to leave Algeria then, his father in his signature worn trousers and Peter dressed in his chaplain's uniform, both standing in the same little kitchen where cookies had been baked.

It had been unsuccessful, just as he knew it would be.

It was the last time he had seen his father, and then there had been such fighting in Morocco and Tunisia. Battles in Algeria too, but when the Allied troops marched into Algiers, the German troops saw they were outnumbered. Perhaps his father had escaped without injury.

He missed his father—the robust laugher, the larger-than-life personality, the natural-born evangelist, the man who loved life and kids and adventure. Family friends had often commented, *"The apple doesn't fall far from the tree, Peter,"* along with a wink. And it was true: The way his father looked at life had influenced him. Yet Peter didn't share his father's reckless nature, the tendency toward risk and danger.

What he knew was that his mother sent cookies and prayers while his father scurried around in some hidden passageway of some war-torn town, not typing on his old Smith Corona, but most likely scribbling out a secret message in code or solving one with the ease that many solved a simple math equation.

Peter took another bite of the oatmeal-raisin cookie, his favorite, and smiled . . . then frowned, then silently prayed, *Keep him safe, Lord, whatever he's doing.* "Safe" did not mean physically unharmed. "Safe" meant something deeper, in the soul. *Keep us all safe in Your loving hands.*

He held up the box in the mess hall. "First come, first served. Dotty Christensen's cookies!"

With a shout of joy, the soldiers hurried to where he stood, a rush of arms reaching toward him. Peter distributed the goodies into their outstretched hands, saving three for Danny, Abe, and George, his chaplain buddies, when they met for prayer later that evening.

When the last of his mother's cookies had been distributed, Peter found that she'd tucked another letter in the bottom of the metal tin. Now he sat hunched on his cot, his door closed, where he read it for the second time.

> *Your father is planning a surprise party for all the kids at the recreation center. Evie is preparing the food for the event. She is also making gifts for the children. She wanted to know their names. Here they are. Could you please send them to her in the usual way?*
>
> *The party is coming very soon. Unfortunately, one of the counselors who was going to help her got sick and had to cancel. Your father hopes a few other counselors will join Evie. He has been a little under the weather lately and so is resting up for now. No need to keep any of this after you let Evie know.*
>
> *Sending all my love,*
Mom

She had included five pages of names, listed in columns.

Peter read his mother's letter a third time. She'd used the family code again, but the message was startlingly different. What was she saying? What was she asking? He scratched his head. It was jammed with volatile words, words that made him nervous.

He got out a red-colored pencil and scribbled the real words beside the coded ones:

Surprise party = rescue mission
Recreation center = Camp Between the Hills
Evie = Yvette Nicolas
Gifts = the children need saving
The usual way = not using the family code, but the camp code
Coming very soon = send immediately through a courier
Had to cancel = betrayed them
Under the weather = identity compromised
Resting up = laying low
No need to keep = destroy all evidence

He studied the decoded letter. He'd been right all along. His father was a spy, and his job was rescuing children—Jewish children, no doubt. But someone had betrayed him, and so now it was up to Peter to convert these lists of names into a pigpen code and mail them off to the little village in the Basses-Alpes.

Okay, he needed to get busy.

But there was one other thing. Yes, his dad was a spy, but it looked like his mother—his easily seasick, sweet-as-molasses mother—was one too.

9

RENÉ

August 1, 1944

Leaning over the porcelain sink in Isabelle's *salle de bain*, René splashed water on his face with his uninjured hand, relishing the chill that momentarily replaced the throbbing in his right arm. Finally, after five days of rest and cleaning and taking medicine, pus no longer seeped from the wound. He could flex his fingers without crying out.

"The infection's gone," Isabelle had pronounced when she changed the bandage the night before.

This morning, he felt antsy. One more day and he would be strong enough to join one of the many Maquis spread throughout the region. They wouldn't refuse him this time. By now, every Maquis in the area would have heard of the slaughter at the Amblard farm, just as they had learned of the slaughter of the prisoners who escaped from the Citadel. How Isabelle had wept to learn of her aunt Irène's death while telling René the news of her father's.

Leaving Delphine hurt what was left of his heart. What had

not been ripped up and shot through became a tender spot for Delphine, his little sister only on paper. Could he leave her? He trusted Isabelle, of course. She was nothing short of a saint.

Every summer, before the war, the two families spent a month camping by the sea. René and Antoine loved to tease their older cousin when she was left in charge of them. The brothers would rush into the sea and scream bloody murder as if they were drowning and then tackle her every time she came running into the water, pushing her under so that she came up sputtering and shivering. She never revealed their pranks to the adults.

A saint.

As they grew older, René and Antoine developed an almost fierce protection of Isabelle, especially when older boys tried to flirt with their beautiful, quiet cousin who hid behind a book as she lay on the beach.

He knew all that she and his uncle had done to save the Jewish children, his uncle forging the papers and Isabelle delivering the children to farmhouses and apartments throughout the region.

Isabelle was courageous, yet he still questioned himself. Should he have brought Delphine here? He had not learned of the massacre of the Citadel prisoners until his cousin shared the details, including her role with the German soldier, Tomas.

Now they knew that the Germans, including Tomas, were watching this building. Had he put Isabelle in even greater danger by bringing Delphine here?

"Don't worry, cousin. I have a plan" was her answer to him.

When he came into the *salle à manger*, Delphine sat at the table, her back to him, her dark brown hair, which she sometimes wore loose, now twisted into pigtails as if she were six instead of thirteen. He sat down across the table from her.

"Look at you. You look fresh and clean and strong." Delphine hopped to her feet and went to the small kitchen. "And guess what? Isabelle got fresh bread and milk today with her ration card. Enough for all of us to have a little."

René doubted that. One ration card would not provide enough to feed all three of them, but they dared not use his card or Delphine's for fear the Germans would learn their whereabouts. Fresh bread and milk were luxuries.

"She must have gotten in line at five a.m."

"She did. Of course, she knows the *boulanger*, Bertrand. I remember when I stayed with her before I came to your farm, she said Bertrand sometimes found extra bread for her. He knew she was helping hide Jewish children, and it was his small form of resistance. And now she's at the *bouchérie* to see if there is any meat today. But look what she brought up from her wine cellar—a jar of blackberry jam that she made last summer."

Delphine's eyes sparkled as she placed a plate in front of René with half of a fresh baguette and the jar of jam. "I already tasted it, and it is so yummy. We picked the blackberries last summer that grew wild and abundant in the hills beyond your farmhouse, remember?"

Of course he remembered.

"We were so hungry that we ate the whole batch on the way home, and then we kept going back for more, every day. And your mother made the jam. She is the best cook . . ." Hand to her mouth, Delphine's eyes grew wide. "I'm sorry. I wasn't thinking. I shouldn't have mentioned Maman Irène."

"It's okay. That's a good memory." He wished he could feel the anger course through him as it usually did. Or at least feel annoyance at his little sister. Instead, he felt only concern and love.

Earlier, he had told Isabelle, "Delphine has no one now."

"I have no one either," she'd replied. "We'll be a little family."

He spread a thick layer of jam on the crusty bread. It would be months before he tasted jam again. "You know, I'm getting stronger, and so I'll leave soon. Isabelle will take care of you."

Delphine nodded.

"As she did before."

Another nod.

"But I'll come back, I promise. When it's over."

The sparkle had left her eyes. "Will it ever be over?"

"Sure, it will. The Allies have liberated the towns in the north, and there's talk of a big operation in the south coming soon."

"Not soon enough for your mother, or for Isabelle's father, or for my parents . . ."

"No, but soon enough for us." He brushed her cheek with his hand. "Remember, later I'll find you and tell you you're pretty. Not now, not yet. Now you'll be fine with Isabelle."

She gave him a weary smile. "And are you planning to sneak out in the middle of the night? Where will you go? What if the Germans are waiting for you?"

"They aren't waiting for me or afraid, but they should be. I'll make my brother proud, my father proud . . . my mother too, God rest her soul. They aren't coming for me, but I'm going to find them."

René awoke to the sound of a door squeaking open. Then he heard it close. He pulled himself upright in bed. Every unexpected sound caused his head and heart to throb. He looked at the empty bed across from his.

Where was Delphine?

"Ginette! You're back!" His cousin Isabelle's voice drifted from the salon to the bedroom. She sounded excited, cheerful, relieved. In the five days he'd been with his cousin, he'd not heard such lightness and hopefulness.

"Is that pus leaking from the bandage on your arm!"

"It looks bad, but it's healing fine. Don't worry. And the whole mission was successful." Ginette spoke quickly, equally excited. "The train tracks, the maps, the explosives."

"Such good news. Thank God you're back. You're safe."

Ginette lowered her voice and asked, "What's wrong?"

Isabelle must have motioned for her roommate to whisper, for the words were barely perceptible. "It's my cousin René. He's here."

"René is here?"

"Yes, the Amblards' farm was overtaken. Only René survived."

The young women's voices quieted, and there was silence for a moment, punctuated only occasionally by sniffles and sobs.

At last, Ginette spoke, her voice strained and throaty. "We heard there was an attack on a farm and that the maquisards were terribly outnumbered. I didn't know it happened at the Amblards'."

Isabelle began recounting the story he had shared with her. "Yes, Tante Irène and the four maquisards, Jean-Paul, Sébastien, Frédéric, and Dominique . . ."

René heard the sharp intake of breath from Ginette. "Dominique was there?"

And his cousin's reply, "You cared for him, didn't you?"

"Yes, he was a good friend."

"More than a friend?"

"Yes, I thought . . ." A long pause. "I thought that maybe he would be."

Silence, deafening as René imagined his cousin comforting her friend.

Then Ginette asked in a subdued voice, "But René is here?"

"Yes. He was wounded." Voices were lowered again, and René caught only snippets: ". . . for five days . . . stronger . . . wants to leave . . . determined to join another Maquis . . ."

Then came more sobs, followed by Isabelle's voice rising until he could hear her clearly. "I don't want him to go. My aunt is dead, and so are my parents. And now he wants to run headfirst into danger."

"I hear you. I'm awake," René called.

Ginette and Isabelle entered the bedroom.

"It's beyond awful what you've been through." Ginette bent her large frame down and pecked him on both cheeks.

René had known his cousin's best friend his whole life. Ginette had also been privy to Antoine and René's mischief when she'd joined Isabelle for summer vacations. He liked her no-nonsense personality and frank kindness. As feminine as his cousin was, Ginette looked sturdy and strong, short-cropped hair giving her a tomboyish appearance.

"I'll leave you two alone to talk," Isabelle said, turning and closing the door behind her.

Ginette perched on the bed across the room, her arms cradling her bent knees, as René explained the terror of that day. She begged for every detail, but he skipped over the grisly way Dominique had perished. "He sacrificed himself for the rest of us. He was very brave." He stared down at the tiled floor as Ginette's stoic face crumpled. "He spoke very fondly of you," he added, glancing up at her. "I'm sorry. Desolé. You're right, the whole day was *affreux*."

Ginette nodded, cleared her throat, and came to René's side. "Thank you for letting me know."

"I wish it had turned out differently."

Kneeling by his bed, her expression hardened, and her light blue eyes came alive again. "The BBC just informed us that the Allied invasion in the south is coming. We're drawing maps and showing the Allies every route. They're pleading for our help."

"I'll be joining a Maquis soon," said René. "They'll take me now that they know I can fight."

Ginette clasped his hand. "They've always known you can fight."

By moonlight, Ginette, René, and Isabelle hurried along the streets outside Sisteron until they came to the formidable building his cousin called the Silo. The cool interior replaced the night's stifling heat, and the enormous room smelled of grain and dust. Eight grim-faced young men and women sat in a circle, each rising to greet the three newcomers with the *bise*, a kiss on each cheek.

René recognized Tito, the swarthy opera singer known for his baritone voice. Isabelle had confided that Tito was now recognized as the leader of the Resistance movement in the Basses-Alpes, who coordinated with the various groups of resistants in the region. Tito was also familiar with the different Maquis, as well as the Martin Network.

Tito shook René's left hand and looked him in the eyes. "It's horrible about your mother. She was brave like your father. We let your brother know."

"You know where Antoine is?" René asked and caught his breath. He hadn't heard any news of his older brother for many months.

A nod from Tito.

Heart hammering, René stood with his bandaged arm held close to his chest. "Where is he? Is he well?"

From the shadows a young man emerged, dressed in the typical attire of the maquisards—beret, green chambray shirt and pants, with *F.F.I.* printed on white cotton fabric and attached to the sleeve of the left arm.

"Antoine!"

Four years René's senior, Antoine was everything René was not: dark hair and eyes and built like their father, muscular and compact. Everything about René's appearance came from their mother—petite, blond-haired, blue-eyed.

"*Frangin!* Brother!"

When they embraced, a sharp pain shot through René's right side. "Thank God, you're alive."

Isabelle rushed over and kissed Antoine on each cheek, then mussed his hair. "Yes, thank God! Both my cousins here together."

His brother motioned to René's wounded arm. "How bad is it?"

"I'll be all right. Isabelle's a good nurse," he said and gave his cousin a nod.

"We heard about the attack. Our Maquis was too far away, near Montélimar, and then they said the whole German contingent surrounded the farm." Antoine's dark eyes pooled liquid. He held his brother at arm's length, then embraced him again.

"It's Maman. They killed her."

"Shhh. I know."

René did not follow the other conversations as the Silo resistance fighters whispered tactics among themselves. The meeting dragged on as the smoke from their Gitane cigarettes circled the room and rose slowly. Lost in his own thoughts, he repeated over and over, *I'm here with my brother and joining his Maquis. I'll fight and get my revenge.*

René broke from his reverie when Tito asked, "And the Jewish girl who was staying with you, René, at the farm? Where is she?"

"They came for her. We hid her, but they found her and took her away." He stared at his shoes, forcing tears in his eyes to make his lie convincing enough to protect Delphine.

When the meeting ended, the Silo members slipped into the night, one or two at a time, leaving a few minutes between each departure.

Antoine caught him before leaving. "If you're going to join our Maquis, we've got a lot to do in the next four days. They say the Allies are coming soon. You'll fight with us, little brother."

Pride, that's what René read in his brother's eyes. Antoine looked hardened, strong and supple and determined.

Antoine continued, "Meet me back here tomorrow at midnight. Make sure no one sees you. Bring any provisions you have."

Walking home, Isabelle and René stopped beside a field of lavender, their deep purple stalks swaying gently in the night air. She reached over and plucked a few stalks of lavender, inhaling, and sighed. "The Germans can't steal the beauty of the lavender fields, their startling violet rows against the bright blue sky during the day—" she paused to take more deep breaths—"and their fragrant perfume at night. Lavender heals my soul, but it's also helpful to treat wounds. I've been using it when I clean yours."

Silently he ran his fingers along the stalks, removing a fistful of the buds, inhaling their soft, woodsy, sweet fragrance.

"That's right, cousin. Breathe it in. Let it heal you."

If only healing came that easily.

Still, his brother was alive. That was great news. "I'm sorry I lied about Delphine. I don't trust anyone but you, Isabelle. I won't tell them about her."

"You're wise not to speak of Delphine to the others. I haven't told anyone either, not even Ginette."

"But where is Delphine? I went to sleep last night, and when I awoke this morning, she was gone."

Isabelle gave a half grin. "You don't need to know."

"But I want to tell her good-bye."

"You already told her you'd be leaving soon. I trust you, René, but I won't tell you where Delphine is hiding. It's safer if no one knows. But she's fine."

His uninjured arm came around his cousin's waist. "Thank you."

Again and again, he inhaled the sweet lavender as they made their way home. Then he tucked the buds into his pants pocket. Just in case.

At midnight the following day, René found Antoine smoking a cigarette behind the Silo. After a quick embrace, Antoine surveyed his brother's knapsack, which held a few articles of clothing, the jar of jam, a canteen, and his father's watch. Then he lifted the canvas sack and studied the three rifles René had brought from the farmhouse.

"Good. We're always short on supplies, ammunition and guns. *C'est bien*, René." Antoine broke into a smile, the kind that lit up his face.

In that moment, years slipped away, and René was ten again, on a camping trip with his big brother who loved the outdoors, loved nature and animals and adventure.

As if reading his mind, Antoine asked, "Ready for an adventure, brother? There's so much to tell you. What do you know of the *Forces françaises de l'Intérieur*? The F.F.I.?" Antoine pointed to his armband with the initials.

"I know you've been working with the resistants, bombing railroad tracks and creating diversions in all different ways." He glanced away. "And freeing prisoners."

Antoine nodded. "We heard of the tragedy in Bayons—for our men and the liberated prisoners. It often feels like one step forward and two steps back, but we're going to win this war, and the Maquis will continue to play a vital part. Are you ready?"

"It's all I've wanted ever since you left two years ago. I knew Maman wouldn't have approved, but now . . ."

"Come. We've only got about ten kilometers to walk tonight." He started at a fast clip, then slowed and turned back around. "Is your arm okay? Cousin Isabelle made me promise to take care of you."

René grinned. "That sounds like Isabelle."

René sat by the campfire, joining the group of ill-clad men who called themselves the Durance Maquis.

"We're swift and silent as the river," Antoine had told René.

René recognized Antoine's childhood friends, who walked to school together and played soccer in the fields between their farms—Didier, Etienne, Samuel, Bastien, Gilles. And the leader of this Maquis, René recognized all too well.

Gabriel—the name of an angel, the heart of a devil! That was his moniker when René was in grade school, and Gabriel had indeed made his life miserable.

"Hey, runt! Poor Antoine's always having to defend his little weakling brother. Gonna have your brother take care of you all your life, or do you think you'll grow up someday?" Gabriel shoved René, then grabbed him by the collar. *"You'd better be careful. Someday I'll find you when your big brother isn't around for you to cry to."*

And he had, several times. Gabriel and his buddies had taught René many lessons during grade school. Or maybe just one. *Always watch your back.*

The image of Gabriel taunting and teasing turned René's stomach. He glanced at the proud young man squatting before him. He had the same handsome face, though a bit haggard, with the same golden, hard eyes. And he looked none too pleased to see René.

Antoine rose and motioned for René to come beside him. "Most of you already know my kid brother, René. And you all heard what the stinking Boches and Milice did at our farm." Hands shoved deep in his pockets, Antoine stared at his boots and kicked at the dirt. "My brother fought alongside the maquisards and Maman. He was the only survivor." He looked up and gazed slowly around the circle of men. "They killed our mother and Dominique, Jean-Paul, Frédéric, and Sébastien. We weren't there for them. No one was there . . ." His voice caught, but he continued. "I told René we would be happy to welcome him here. He's quite able to fight with us."

René circled the fire, holding out his left hand to shake each of theirs. Some grunted, gave a rough smile, and said, *"Bienvenue, gars.* Glad to have you." Others only looked at him, their eyes red-rimmed, which spoke of fatigue and hunger and sorrow.

When he held out his hand to Gabriel, the leader's piercing eyes focused on René, but he didn't extend his hand. Instead, he shrugged and muttered, "*Bon sang,* Antoine, you're bringing us a wounded child."

Gabriel sat on his haunches with the rest of the Maquis, cigarette hanging from his lips, pointing to the map Antoine held by the campfire.

"We and the other southern Maquis are tasked to blow up all the bridges on the Durance River—from Aix to Sisteron, almost a hundred kilometers. While the Normandy landings were a huge success, the Allies are now in desperate need of a major southern port to bring in the dozens of divisions waiting in America to fight in Europe. The southern ports will give the troops an easier route toward Germany. They're hoping to take Marseille and Toulon."

Gabriel nodded to Etienne. René remembered him well. A skinny, freckled-face prankster who enjoyed coercing Antoine into minor truancies, like stealing candy from the *tabac.* But he always returned it. He looked the same with his intelligent eyes. A sharp mind lay behind the goofiness.

Etienne took a drag on his cigarette. "We need to take stock of all the ammunition and supplies before we head out tomorrow, early morn. Retrieve everything you have, and meet back here in ten minutes."

As the men filed toward their knapsacks, René observed them, most wearing a mishmash of green shirts—T-shirts, short- and long-sleeved, all with one distinct feature, the white armband worn on the left bicep, printed with the letters F.F.I.

The meeting continued late into the night as the supplies were divided and tactics discussed. René's arm ached, and his stomach growled, and yet his heart pounded with excitement. Tomorrow. Action.

Gabriel had given instructions for the following day. "Okay, time to turn in, men. Remember, the Allies are depending on the F.F.I. to provide photos and detailed maps of the agriculture in southern

France. We all know that knowledge of the geography can play a deciding factor in battles. That's our job tomorrow. *Bonne nuit.*"

Gabriel stopped René as the other maquisards left the campfire, his hand fiercely gripping René's injured arm. René stifled a moan as pain ripped through his body. Leaning in so that their noses almost touched, Gabriel whispered, "I am perfectly capable of making your life miserable again. I don't want you here, kid, so stay out of my way."

When he let go and walked off, René felt the anger pulse right alongside the physical pain.

Etienne found him a minute later. "Glad to have you among us, Amblard." There was no mockery in Etienne's eyes, but instead fatigue and determination . . . and something else. "Sorry for the way you were left at the farm."

"Thanks."

He headed toward Antoine, then he caught sight of his brother with Gabriel.

René backed away, hearing Gabriel's jab. "I won't be responsible for him. He's young and small. He'll cause trouble, I guarantee it."

Antoine was shaking his head. "You're wrong. Are you too proud to admit it? To see what he did?"

"That's just it. I didn't see what he did. All I know is that there are four dead maquisards, our best, and your mother. And somehow he's still alive."

"He fought. You can see the wounds, his arm."

"Fine. You're in charge of him, and if he can't keep up, you'll find him somewhere else to go," Gabriel hissed, the glow from his cigarette flickering like a lone firefly in the night.

Antoine turned and saw René. He quickly shifted so that Gabriel did not see him. "He won't let you down."

Gabriel cursed, threw his cigarette on the ground, stamped it out, and said, "Antoine, you're so naive. Everyone lets you down in war. And this is war." He disappeared into the darkness.

10

ISABELLE

AUGUST 1, 1944

Isabelle stood in line at the bouchérie, hoping for a scrap of beef and instead accepting the chicken liver. She came out of the small shop, head down, tucking her ration card back into her purse and walking toward the intersection.

"Mademoiselle! Is it you, Mademoiselle Geraldine?"

She froze. That voice. *His* voice. She had no time to react, to plan for what had become her greatest fear. She pasted a smile on her face and slowly turned.

Tomas towered over her, his blue eyes sharp, the medals on his uniform gleaming, his mouth a tight frown. He removed his army hat, his white-blond hair slicked back, perfectly in place.

"Monsieur Tomas. How good to see you!"

"Is it?" His brow wrinkled, his eyes turning icy. "You disappeared."

"Yes, well." *Think, Isabelle, think!* "I-I saw that you were very busy, and I heard about some p-problems. I did not want to distract you." Every word came with difficulty, her mouth as if full of cotton.

He grabbed her right arm, and she dropped the basket of provisions.

"Problems, yes!" His face was a few inches from hers, his eyes vicious. His grip tightened. "Perhaps you are part of these problems, mademoiselle! Prisoners escaping, Jewish swine being sequestered in homes. We know of these things. We have resolved the prisoners' regrettable escape." A smile quivered on his lips.

Breathe. Think.

"They deserved their fate. So many bodies littering the road." He shrugged, then gave her arm a twist. "But the Jewish children! This is not yet resolved. We know they are hidden with families, in farmhouses with boy soldiers. I was there when we raided one. We were there to wipe out the Maquis in the region. We weren't looking for children. But later I received other information, and so I went back. Sure enough, a Jew had been there. I could smell it!" He jerked her arm. "Do you know about this? Perhaps you can help us with this problem?"

"Je . . . Jewish children?"

Ginette's voice was strident in her ears. *"Be coy, Zabelle! Act flippant!"*

"You are hurting me. Let go!" She took a step back and met his eyes. "How dare you accuse me." Then she leaned toward him and whispered, "I was not a part of those problems, but I will gladly help you solve them. What do you need to know about Jewish children?"

Tomas's hand remained firm around her arm. "Many things." He frowned. "Perhaps we can meet again and continue where we left off. And I will give you an assignment."

His smile did not look kind or even pleasant. She felt her knees go weak and could not think of one thing to say.

"Meet me tonight at the café—like old times?" His voice was mocking.

"Tonight?"

Not tonight—she was taking Delphine to the camp, Delphine who now for eighteen hours had been hiding, huddled in the wine cellar in the bowels of the apartment building. She hadn't been able to tell René *au revoir*. Thank goodness, René had left last night with Antoine. And Ginette . . . would she be there? Surely Tomas wouldn't intrude if Ginette was there.

Oh, what could she do? She tried to pray, but Tomas lifted his eyebrows, and a menacing look flashed in his pale blue Aryan eyes.

"What do you say? Tonight?"

His hand slid down her back, pressing her toward him. She tried to step back, heart beating wildly, and said, "Tonight . . . I have plans."

"Is there someone else?" Now his hand grasped her waist, holding her close.

"Someone else?" The thought was so ridiculous that she laughed. But then relief washed through her. Yes, let him believe that. "That is a very personal question, Monsieur Tomas."

"Nevertheless, I'd like an answer."

"Well, I didn't expect him back so soon." She felt her face go red. She hoped he would think she was embarrassed when in truth all she felt was terror. What could she say? "Yes, he came back a few days ago when he heard of the problems." She averted her eyes. "But he will leave again, I'm sure of it. He's just an old beau from school."

"*Flirt, Zabelle.*" Ginette's voice came to her again. "*Act indifferent. Raise your eyebrows. Flirt!*"

She gave a shrug and touched his shoulder. "It was just a fling, but you know men. He thought it was more serious and, well, I couldn't possibly disappoint him tonight. But tomorrow night or the next. I will find a way to send him on his way." She stood up straighter. She was amazed by her calm demeanor.

Tomas's grip loosened, and his jaw twitched. "So he's a Frenchman."

"Yes, but he's with the Milice. He's very fond of the Germans."

He pulled her close. Emboldened, she stepped back. "Tomas, I will not have this show in the street! Do you know what villagers think of women who are with the Germans? Tomorrow—no, Saturday—I will meet you at the café. Like old times." She managed a wink. "And perhaps I will have information to help with your problem."

He stood back, tilted his head. "Why should I believe you?"

"Believe what you want, but right now I have to go." She picked up the basket, turned, and felt her knees give way, felt herself wobble, but then she heard Ginette urging her, *"Remain poised. Don't show your fear. You can do it, Zabelle. You can do it!"*

Isabelle collapsed onto the couch, her sobs so loud she wondered if she would wake the whole building. Thank goodness René was gone, and Ginette had left for the morning. Isabelle had twisted through the vieille ville until she was sure Tomas had not followed. She shivered remembering his hand pressing against her, harder and harder, inching her forward, ready to rape her or kill her, she was certain.

Had he believed her, or did he already know of her part in the rescue of the children? One thing was sure—someone had revealed information about the Martin Network. He had never mentioned anything about Jewish children before.

She had to escape with Delphine now. They'd both hide at The Camp Between the Hills. She felt a stab of doubt. Surely the Germans hadn't invaded that haven? And what about the other children?

I don't know what to do, Papa.

She threw cold water on her face to wash away the tears, then scrubbed her hands with a scrap of soap. She felt dirty, or worse, corrupted by an evil that had seeped under her skin. She went and opened the oak chest, reached down low until her fingers touched the envelopes. Once, long ago, she had shivered with pleasure when a man's hand had brushed hers.

A boy.

It had been pure and good, that feeling of love, and how she had missed it, had ached for it until the weight of it became too heavy, and she stuffed the emotions into an old chest along with the letters. But now she needed to remember it so that Tomas's cruelty didn't suffocate her with fear.

She closed the lid of the chest, relishing the memory of the fluttering in her stomach every time a letter had come. But too soon, a crushing heartache had replaced the fluttering, and she had closed her heart to protect her soul.

Stop remembering.

She hurried to prepare the bread and cheese and the livers and the *pommes de terre* for Delphine. On shaky legs, she left her apartment and descended past the *rez de chaussée* entrance into the dark basement where each apartment had a small wine cellar, where Papa had forged the papers before . . .

When Isabelle opened the door to the cave, Delphine leapt up from where she'd been huddled on the ground. "I was so afraid. You didn't come back. I-I thought I would be here forever."

"Shhh. I'm sorry, Delphine. It's all so complicated. We have to leave tonight, after I let my friends know."

"Why must I stay down here now? It's so tiny and cramped. I was in your apartment for five days, and you weren't worried."

"My roommate, my dear friend, Ginette is back. She knows about René but not about you."

Delphine gasped. "You don't trust Ginette? You think she will turn me in?"

"No, of course not. But I don't want anyone, even our friends, to know you are here. To know you're alive. We've let them think the worst."

"But why?"

"The less each of us knows about the others, the better. Then if one of us is caught . . ."

"You're afraid someone will be caught and tortured and reveal too much. That's it, isn't it?"

Isabelle set the tray of food down on the ground and hugged Delphine close. "My dear child, I wish you didn't have to know such terrible things. Tonight we'll leave, and you'll need to be brave." She knelt, and the cool dirt in the cave penetrated the skin of her bare knees. "I promised René I would take care of you. And I will. Do you believe me?"

She nodded. "Oui, Mademoiselle Isabelle." Her face, so serious, relaxed as she said, "I believe you, Izzie."

They were all at the Silo again, together, no one missing, no one wearing a guilty face. Her comrades. Her colleagues in this war. Could she trust them? But then, what else could she do?

Trembling, she thought, *I can only tell the truth.* "Tomas met me in the street today." Her voice squeaked even as she pronounced the words. Her heart began to beat erratically just recalling the encounter.

Ginette gasped; Lucy raised her eyebrows.

Jean-Yves's large soulful eyes met Isabelle's. "*Ooh là là*, this is not good. Not good at all."

Tito gave a grunt. "And?"

"And he was unhappy. I was so shocked to see him and then terrified . . ."

"What did he want?" Tito sounded accusatory.

Isabelle looked up. "You can't figure it out?" She gathered her arms across her chest as if protecting herself. "He accused me of helping with the prisoners' escape and of sheltering Jewish children. He knows something about the Network. He was at the Amblard farm when the commandant let René go. Tomas went back later, found the cave, and suspected it had been used to hide Jews."

The Silo resistants began to curse and talk among themselves.

"Zabelle, how did you get away from him?" Ginette had come by her side, arms around her friend.

"I listened to your voice in my head. I acted offended and told him I would help him." She hung her head, took a deep breath. "He wanted to meet again tonight, but I told him . . . I made up a story."

"What story?" Tito's baritone voice was harsh.

"I told him that an old lover had come back."

Ginette laughed, then covered her mouth. "Good for you."

"I said he was with the Milice and that I needed a day or so to make him leave."

Even Tito wore a smirk. "And did he believe you?"

"I don't know. But I promised to meet him at the café on Saturday night." She glanced at Jacques. "I'm sorry—I hope he won't
suspect you."

The bartender shrugged. "*Ne t'en fais pas.* I'm not afraid."

"I told Tomas I would find out information about the children."
She folded herself into Ginette's arms and began to shake. "I didn't
know what else to do. I was so terrified. I've got to leave Sisteron.
Now. Tonight."

"Yes. Leave Sisteron," Tito agreed. His voice was gruff, his
eyes angry.

Was he mad at her? "I'm sorry it happened, Tito. I've tried to
avoid him."

Tito calmed. "I know."

"You were brilliant to think of the Milice lover," said Amandine. Of all the Silo resistants, she was usually the most critical
of their plans.

Isabelle's hands were knotted into fists. She loosened them
from her skirt, staring at the ground. "I'm afraid the Germans
may know about the other children. At least they know there are
children hiding in the region. Tomas as much as admitted this."

"Yes," Maurice agreed. "But how do they know?"

Her lips trembled, and she swallowed again and again. Her
mouth went completely dry. "I don't know. Tomas said he had gotten more information after the raid—about the children. Someone
must have told him."

Ginette stood to her feet. "Isabelle's right. It could have been
someone in this room."

Gentle Maurice pulled at his bushy eyebrow and said, "Perhaps
one of the maquisards who were gunned down with the prisoners
had already betrayed us."

"You were friends with the Maquis from Bayons, Maurice!
Perhaps it was you who betrayed us." This came from petite
Lucy.

The ambiance in the room changed from comradery to hostil-
ity in one short minute with each resistant making an excuse and
an accusation.

"Stop this!" Tito said. "The enemy would like nothing more than to have us fighting each other. I don't believe it is one of us. I trust you all. But you're right, Isabelle. I too have wondered about the incidents occurring at the same time." He lowered his voice. "In light of these things, I believe it's safest for us to discontinue our meetings here. Instead, the messages will be placed in the mailbox in Isabelle's building. Always coded."

"Too risky! That's how Jean Moulin was caught! Surely you remember this?" Tiny Lucy, eyes fierce, stood while shaking her head.

"I agree with Lucy," said Maurice.

Isabelle shivered, remembering the way everyone in the French underground grieved last year when they learned that Jean Moulin, the revered leader of the French Resistance, had been betrayed by one of their members, who had told the Gestapo about the coded messages concealed in a mailbox in a secret passageway in Lyon. Poor Monsieur Moulin was caught and tortured but revealed nothing before he eventually died.

"That is precisely why it will work, Lucy, Maurice," Tito explained. "The Boches will not think us stupid enough to use the same tactics again."

The arguing continued until the sky outside turned black, but at last they agreed on the way to send and receive messages. As Isabelle prepared to head home, Tito held her back.

"A word, please," he said.

Fresh tears burned her eyes. "Why were you so angry with me, Tito? You were the one who had me flirt with Tomas, the one who wanted the distraction with the German officer! I only did what you had asked."

His face fell, his eyes softening. "I'm angry because I *care*. I don't want anything to happen to you. We've lost so many, and I can't have anything happen to you. I care about you, Isabelle."

He reached for her small hand with his large one, his grip strong. But the look in his eyes scared her. No, he couldn't care. Not about her. Not this brave, talented man who risked his life daily. And she couldn't care about anyone else, couldn't bear to have her heart shattered again.

"Merci," she murmured. Then she and Ginette slinked off into the inky night together.

"Tito cares for you," Ginette said as Isabelle hurriedly packed a few clothes into a suitcase.

"He mustn't. It's too complicated. I don't want his love. There's no time for that. Look at me—I'm a complete mess."

"You're nervous. We're all nervous."

"Terrified is what I am." Hands on her hips, Isabelle circled the bedroom, distracted, then went into the salon. She grabbed the picture of her childhood self with her parents that sat on the hutch. The gold frame was repaired but still missing its glass. She returned to the bedroom and inserted the photo between two blouses.

Ginette tucked a piece of hair behind her ear and nodded. "You're right, of course. Caring for someone only makes everything worse when—"

Isabelle spun from her suitcase and grabbed Ginette in a fierce hug. "I'm so sorry about Dominique. I've been caught up in my grief, but yours is awful too."

Ginette sat back and shrugged, pretending indifference. But Isabelle knew what that cost her friend. "Best not to care because we don't have time to grieve."

"Exactly."

What was love anyway? She thought of the framed photo. Isabelle had known love with Papa and Maman, but after Maman's death, she hid away between the pages of a book or on the floor beside her father as he managed the library. Until one day she had sat beside him as his assistant. Books would not betray her.

But a boy? Only once had she allowed herself to care in that way. Isabelle had given her heart wholly to a boy at the camp all those years ago. Just one conversation, a couple of nods and friendly hellos, their eyes meeting, and that was enough. She had known it would be love.

How foolish!

Maybe foolish, but the letters are real.

What was it that caught in her throat? Fear. She was afraid of Tomas, afraid of the Nazis, afraid of bombs, afraid of the evil that was seeping into every pore of the country. Terrified. But deeper down, if she dared look, she knew what the real fear was.

She was afraid to open her heart, to let in any more love. She loved René and Ginette, and she cared deeply for her colleagues and the rescued children, especially Delphine. She would keep risking her life for all of them—to serve her country and to honor her father's memory. She'd do it so she wouldn't hate herself when all this horror was over. If it was ever over.

She thought of Maman, how painful, how anguishing it was to lose her and the baby. And then Papa. They had been a family, and now it was just Isabelle. Safer, then, to close off her heart. Tito said that he cared about her. She had seen it in his eyes before, and she chased it away.

She would not let herself love anyone else.

You have to love, came a soft internal whisper. *It's what makes life worth it.*

No! was her unspoken response. *I won't. It costs too much.*

She knew she was lying to herself, lying because of the terror in her soul. But she wouldn't let herself care about a man. Not even Tito, whose voice could inspire an audience of thousands. Or just one.

11

PETER

For the second night in a row, Peter locked himself in his room, the room that always stood open, ready for anyone to enter to pray or peruse his daily comic-strip-like drawings taped to the wall. Now he finished transcribing the last name into what was known in his family as the "camp code."

Peter tried to recall the return address on the brown paper wrapping, now discarded, in his mother's handwriting. He had paid no attention to it. Had it actually come from the US, or was she somewhere in Europe or North Africa?

He yawned and rubbed his eyes.

His mother's letter had been written in her handwriting in the family code. Then at the top of each page of names, his father had included the same short message in his own unmistakable penmanship, although he had called himself by a different name.

Network compromised, children to be rescued and taken to Camp Between the Hills immediately, Monsieur Martin.

And his father's hand had written the lists, which he'd since transcribed into a pigpen code. Like all those years ago at The Camp Between the Hills.

"Okay, Pete, I need to see if you can break this code. Work quickly. If it is too easy for these kids, they will lose interest. But if it is too difficult, they will lose heart."

His father was sitting at the round oak table in the salon of the home at The Camp Between the Hills. Tomorrow, forty-five preteens would invade this space for two weeks, Scouts from the nearby towns of Sisteron and Oraison and Dignes-les-Bains. These were children raised by faithful Catholic parents, those who looked suspiciously at the American Protestant missionary setting up shop in the hills beyond the cities.

There were few Protestants in this region of France. The descendants of the Huguenots, French Protestants resided farther south. Philip Christensen did not worry about a minor detail like the centuries-long animosity between Protestants and Catholics in France. This camp was for all.

Peter, already an adolescent, followed his father's orders. Philip Christensen had a sharp mind, and he loved to use his training from the Great War to tease and prod the minds of youth. Now Peter studied the symbols, easily deciphering the code. He enjoyed the challenge and especially his father's deep laughter and the pat on his back when Peter solved it quickly.

"It's another cipher, another pigpen code, Dad!"

"Good, Pete. You're older and brighter. These kids will solve it, I believe, but not so easily." His father held up the sheet of paper, where Peter had written the letters under the symbols. "And if they cannot, I'll let you give them a few clues."

Peter had shrugged and replied, "Sure, Dad." But a few days later, when a bevy of bright-eyed girls rushed to him for help, his face turned crimson, no doubt matching his hair. He had heard their whispers.

"It's the director's son. Isn't he cute?"

Peter shook himself back to the present, his eyes heavy. All those years ago, he'd become adept at writing in the camp code, and it had come back easily. He studied the sketchbook one final time before setting aside the transcribed papers. Tomorrow he'd pack the sheets into a manila envelope and send them to the camp. The family code had specified that he send them by courier, and he knew just who to ask.

Marco.

"You sure know how to pick 'em, Ginger," Frank had said a few days ago. "Just learned that you broke the nose of the fastest kid in the Italian resistance in Naples."

Peter smiled as he struck a match and watched his mother's letter, and the lists, burn in the little metal trash can.

"Good game, Ginger." Rusty, the Burger Boys' team captain, slapped him on the back as Peter made his way off the field.

The last game of the tournament had highlighted the Italian Risotto Rivals' superiority, soundly beating the Burger Boys with a score of 4-2.

Peter gave an uncharacteristic frown. "They were solid, stronger. But I shouldn't have let those two get past me." Laid back, perhaps, but Peter did not like to lose, even to a much better team.

"Yeah, tough break. You were almost there both times."

He shrugged as the broad-shouldered center jogged over toward the Italian team.

Exactly. Almost there.

Peter had given up two of the four Italian goals. His job was to tackle the opponent before that opponent got to the final barrier, the goalie. Defense. Everything in him spoke of defense. Not attacking, but defending.

Protect the goal. Protect the flock. Protect the men.
Protect the children.

It had been four days since he'd entrusted the coded message to Marco, who had assured him that his team of resistants could deliver the message from the bottom of Italy to a little village at the base of the French Alps in only two days.

Protect the children.

As they shook hands after the match, swiping at the sweat that ran down his face and taking gulps from the canteen, Peter replayed those goals in his mind to distract him from worrying. He'd been too slow to react. Twice.

Just a game, yes, but still. And tomorrow the games would be over as 80,000 men boarded the 7th Army's fleet of ships and his job as chaplain called for a different kind of defense. He wasn't keeping an opponent from dribbling a soccer ball around him and into the goal. His duty was keeping the men safe in their souls. Reminding them of how to defend themselves in the secret places of their hearts with the weapons of faith and prayer and trust.

I couldn't protect her, Lord.

He shook the thought away as he prayed for the soldiers' physical protection, for victory over the enemy. But much more often, he prayed for an invisible protection of their souls. And no matter what, he would be there to defend them from the ultimate enemy—death. That goal he would never give up.

Marco jogged over to where Peter was talking to the captain of the Risotto Rivals. The kid's grin almost touched the wide, white bandage across his nose. "Delivered," he said in heavily accented English and held out his hand to Peter.

Peter felt his face relax and his body calm as he shook the boy's hand, looked him in the eyes, and said, "*Grazie.*"

The Mediterranean Sea

"You're looking a little green there. You okay?" Peter eyed his assistant as the ship swayed and rocked in the deep blue of the Mediterranean. For two days, the men on the *Nevada*, the *Oklahoma*, and the *Texas*, and countless other convoys had sailed west to a rendezvous point on the coast of Corsica. Now the whole invasion fleet was heading north to France.

Frank grimaced. "You know good and well that this isn't my best moment. I'll be fine once we get this baby anchored and my feet hit solid land." He nodded out to sea. "Pretty impressive, ain't it? We got a dang-blasted armada around us."

Peter looked skyward. "My favorite are those blimps floating up there. I know they're big, but from here they look like tiny, personal protective clouds."

Frank glanced up, then screwed up his face. "Sorry, Ginger. Nature's calling," and he proceeded to vomit over the side of the ship. "I think I'll go lie down."

"Good idea."

Uniform billowing in the wind as he leaned on the railing, Peter closed his eyes and pictured his view of Marseille from the sea all those years ago with his father. The white calanque cliffs rising stark to the west, the water that blinding, shimmering blue, the way the red tiled roofs in the distance split the blue of the sea and the deep azure of the sky, the gulls swooping in and out, and the boats, all shapes and sizes, sails flapping in the wind.

Although seizing the ports of Marseille and Toulon was the final goal of Operation Dragoon—the Allies desperately needed these ports as a place to unload their tanks and munitions for their push to the north—the battleships' destination was to the east, with the men debarking near beach towns with names such as St. Tropez, St. Maxime, and St. Raphaël.

Peter's father had told him, "*When Torpès, a Roman officer under the reign of Nero converted to Christianity through the influence of the apostle Paul, the cruel and infuriated Emperor Nero had Torpès decapitated. And the town honored him as a martyr and named the town after him.*"

Would there be more carnage on the beach of St. Tropez soon?

Leaving the railing, Peter walked the deck of the ship, zigzagging in between soldiers who sat, stood, and played games. He walked to pray, to remember, to look ahead, but mostly he walked to trust.

"'He will hold me fast,'" he sang to the sea. He loved that hymn, the one embedded in his soul, the one his parents sang in whispers in Algiers when they were afraid, when it seemed the devil himself was surrounding the house.

"'When I fear my faith will fail . . . He will hold me fast,'" Peter whispered the words again. He imagined what awaited them on the shore in just three days. Yes, veterans like Andy and Frank knew, but Rusty and Billy and Sammy did not. Their eyes were bright, hopeful.

He shook his head to shove aside the images, but they came anyway, in living color. In Tunisia, troops blasting each other in the desert, bodies strewn across the sand that was stained with blood, the explosion, the shrapnel, him being dragged away, the firing squad, the miracle . . .

He took another lap, nodding to each soldier as he walked.

"Praying again," Billy called out. "Good old Ginger, he's taking care of us all."

And it felt that way to Peter. Oh, they knelt and prayed, confessed their fears to him, but in their eyes, he saw trust. They believed that Peter had a direct line to the Almighty. And they trusted him to comfort them.

Amid the ceaseless, piercing gunfire, he held Henry, lifeless in his arms, and felt anguish and terror. Then there were two hands on his shoulders, and Rabbi Horowitz was calling out God's blessing and mercy and love and comfort. Peter felt it, almost like an electric current zipping through him. The love from the Jewish rabbi who had seen much worse than Peter was comforting him, speaking truth.

Somehow the rabbi had known instinctively the fear and crippling grief that Peter felt. The rabbi whispered, "You will be able to love them and give them hope, my friend, when the time comes. I am giving you hope now, and you will give it to them."

And he had. They each had. Time and time and time again.

With a sigh, Peter made a final lap, then took a seat on the deck and removed his Bible from his pocket. The small book was ragged, the leather smooth and crinkled. He kept it in his vest pocket, ready to pull out at any moment to read to a fearful soldier.

He loved life and yet, time and again in North Africa, he had sat beside a young man with the life draining out of him. He no longer asked why because the *why* had become so evident, the evil all around palpable, painted in blood in the sands of North Africa.

Peter took a slow breath, swallowed the lump in his throat, and opened the Bible to where a faded envelope had, years ago, become a bookmark smack in the middle of the prophet Jeremiah's lengthy prophecies. The envelope marked the verse that had first brought the holy conviction that he was meant for ministry.

"Then I said, I will not make mention of him, nor speak any more in his name. But his word was in mine heart as a burning fire shut up in my bones, and I was weary with forbearing, and I could not stay."

It was that fire he had felt in his belly and in his bones as he watched his father preach to a roomful of devout Catholic youth at The Camp Between the Hills. It had been an epiphany for Peter and a calling all those years ago.

But during his last summer at camp, something—actually *someone*—had almost derailed him from his calling. The envelope marking the Bible verse held a letter from this girl.

He removed the letter from its envelope, scanned the letter until his eyes read *Tu es doué*, Peter. *Vraiment doué. Tu dois être un pasteur.*

You're gifted, Peter. Really gifted. You should be a pastor.

She had seen it and encouraged him in his calling, having no idea that she was ironically the one who was causing him to question it. It had all gone wrong, and yet, he still kept that letter in his Bible.

Why?

Because sometimes I doubt my calling. I couldn't protect that little girl in Kentucky. Will I be able to keep these men safe, Lord?

Peter lifted his head and inhaled the salty aroma of the sea. Back when his family sailed from Algeria to France, preparing for the summer camps, he used to look across the wide Mediterranean and feel the excitement, imagine the enthusiasm and momentum

122

of the youth. The adventure. Now, out in that same blue sea, Peter did not feel ready.

Hold me fast, Lord, he prayed. *Hold us fast.*

Peter tossed and turned, wide awake, thinking of his mother's cookies and her coded message. Was she back in Algeria? And where in the world was his father hiding out? He left his room and again paced the ship deck, now with the moon high and a zillion stars lighting the universe.

"Hey, Pete! You care for those soldiers. That's your calling. But don't forget all the Jewish children spread around France."

It was a snippet from that strange conversation with his father in 1942 in North Africa. Had his father been helping hide Jewish children for the past two years? The lists had been successfully delivered to Mme Nicolas. Were some of those children even now huddled in that vast cave he had helped his father reconstruct in The Camp Between the Hills?

Often, thinking of children brought crushing grief, bringing that dark tragedy in Kentucky back in harrowing color.

He tried to push it away, but Peter saw in his mind the small casket as young men carried it into the white-steepled church in Kentucky. He had stood and watched from afar, tears streaming down his face, wishing Helen were there to comfort him. But there was no comfort on that day. He felt a stab of pain with the memory.

I couldn't save that sweet, innocent little girl back then, Lord. I tried to help, and it all backfired. A disaster. A tragedy that had disqualified him from the pastorate and almost from life. *Thank You for the chance to help these children now.*

12

ISABELLE

AUGUST 4, 1944

"He's still there," Delphine whispered from where she hid behind
the stone wall. They'd sneaked out the back entrance of the apartment building and through the old town, down the Long Androne
to the river. But now a German officer—not Tomas, thank goodness—stood guard at the footpath that led out of the city and
toward the camp.

It was well past midnight. They couldn't wait much longer
or dawn would break before they reached the camp. Isabelle felt
rooted in place by fear, shivering in the balmy night.

"We need another angel to show up and protect us," Delphine
whispered.

Isabelle started to answer when she looked over at the child,
whose eyes were closed. She wasn't addressing Isabelle, but the
Almighty.

Lightning streaked across the sky, with thunder rumbling in
the distance. Another bolt, a deafening roar, and then the heavens
opened and the rain came down in torrents. The soldier left his

post at a brisk trot, heading back to town, perhaps only to fetch rain gear, but now was their chance.

Delphine held on to Isabelle's skirt as they stooped and jogged along the path, the downpour forcing them to proceed much more slowly than Isabelle had hoped.

But Delphine looked up at Isabelle and grinned. "It wasn't an angel the Lord provided, Izzie, but it worked! He is merciful!"

"Yes, of course." Yet the thick clouds and rain hid the moon and Isabelle's hope of seeing something familiar in the environs.

She had never walked the eight kilometers from Sisteron to The Camp Between the Hills. She'd ridden in an old bus, crowded with energetic kids, along the bumpy unpaved roads, twisting in and out of the mountain ridges until the camp opened before them. On one side was the limestone peak of the formation called La Baume, and on the other, the rounded, gentler peak called St. Michel.

The pelting rain drenched her, but she didn't know if the goose bumps on her arms were from true chill or the fear that at any moment another German soldier might step onto the path.

Delphine saw everything as a blessing, but all Isabelle felt was a tumultuous mixture of fear and grief and anger.

She remembered her father's words: *If this is what God has called you to do, I don't want you anywhere else.* And she remembered one other thing that giant of a pastor, Monsieur Christensen, had said in his deep bass French: *"Bad things will happen, kids. But don't let that derail you. God causes it to rain on the good and the evil. And life is not easy. But He will not leave you. Ever."*

It was certainly raining on both the good and the evil right at this very moment. But the rain had helped them escape, had protected them. Gratitude washed over her along with the rain, and Isabelle began humming a refrain from a hymn she'd learned at the camp.

Delphine looked up at her, eyes wide. "Could we sing, Izzie? With Mama and Papa, we would sing the Psalms of Ascent, just like the Jews going up to Jerusalem at Passover. Do you know them?"

"I don't know them, and we mustn't sing out loud. But we can whisper them together. I'd love for you to teach them to me."

Softly, Delphine said, "'I will lift up mine eyes unto the hills, from whence cometh my help. My help cometh from the LORD, which made heaven and earth.'" She turned to Isabelle. "Papa loved that psalm."

"It's beautiful. Let's pray and trust God to help us as we lift up our eyes to the hills."

An hour later, as the young woman and the girl walked and whispered the psalms, the rain stopped, the clouds dispersed, and a snippet of moon broke through.

Isabelle could not stop herself from laughing out loud. "There they are, Delphine! Look, can you see them—the two peaks? We're here. We've made it!"

Delphine tightened her grip on Isabelle's hands. "We praised our way to our new home," she exclaimed. "We're going to be safe here, Izzie. I just know it."

The minuscule village looked virtually unchanged from nearly a decade ago. In the fading dark, as streaks of gray and pink cleared above them, a stone arch with an ivy-covered room above separated several interconnected apartments on the left from other buildings on the right.

For three summers, she had attended the camp with other Scouts. There they lifted rocks from the ditches to help build back the ancient village, one stone at a time, one backbreaking, wheelbarrow-filled push across the broken terrain, the majestic peaks of the Basses-Alpes rising on either side. The village nestled in the valley had enamored the Scouts as they listened, young and impassioned and filled with faith, while the giant man shared his vision. It was a place of retreat for young people to stop and listen. A place of quiet with only the gurgling stream and the tempered mistral singing in the background. And butterflies who whispered a silent magic around the Scouts as they dug the trenches and sweated through their Bermuda shorts.

Back then she was fresh-faced and naive and generous. Back then she listened with empathy and compassion and a wisdom beyond her years.

Her heart hurt in a good way with the memory. She could almost forget that she was in the middle of a war, that she and Delphine were hiding from madmen bent on their destruction.

Walking through the archway, Isabelle said, "This was where the camp was held, and the director, Monsieur Christensen, stayed here in this house with his wife and children."

With him.

Don't think of him.

She pointed to a two-story structure on the left with ivy trailing up the stones, the heavy wooden volets painted what looked to be a deep green in the dawn light.

Isabelle tilted her head as if listening for the director's booming voice. "The Christensens were only here for the summers. The rest of the year they lived in Algeria." In her mind's eye, she was holding an envelope with an Algerian stamp. Why was she sharing this information with Delphine?

She stopped in front of the thick wooden entrance door and knocked. The village was obviously abandoned, she reprimanded herself. When no one answered a second knock, she tried the door, and it creaked open.

A bat flew out, wings flapping wildly, brushing Delphine's hair. She screamed, as did Isabelle. Then they looked at each other and began to laugh.

"I guess they don't live here now," Delphine said. "But something does." She scrunched her nose and shrugged as Isabelle took her hand, and together they stepped inside.

Isabelle scanned the room with her flashlight, surprised at the cozy feel, relieved to see that the furniture had not yet been upended by German troops. They backed out, closed the door, and walked to the left of the house, around to where Isabelle remembered helping to dig a trench for some sort of electrical wire. The stone porch on the second story was covered with a parasol, and beyond lay what had been a garden, with terraced levels for tables and a sandpit.

"Pétanque!" cried Delphine, running to the sand. "Oh, my papa was very, very good at this game."

Isabelle smiled. Every French child and adult knew the game where teams tossed heavy metal balls toward a smaller wooden ball, the closest ball gaining a point.

"Wouldn't it be lovely if we found some pétanque balls!" Delphine removed her shoes. "I'm thankful you found these for me, but being barefoot is luxurious now!" Her toes sank into the wet sand. She spun around, then bent and picked up a fistful and let it drop in clumps through her fingers.

The leather boots were three sizes too big, but they were all Isabelle had found to replace the torn ones Delphine had worn when she'd arrived at the apartment, the leather soles hanging by a thread. Even in the dim light, Isabelle could see the blisters on Delphine's feet. But she'd not complained once during their journey.

Isabelle walked up the stone stairs to the next tiered level, where the backyard opened into a field of brambles. "They're here! Look," she said, holding her flashlight to the rambling bushes. "Blackberries everywhere."

"Real blackberries!" Delphine squealed.

They picked the black fruit, ignoring the prickling thorns, gathering handfuls and stuffing them into their mouths.

Delphine began to cry. "I was remembering with René about picking blackberries last year in the bushes around his farm." She gathered them in her skirt. "They tasted so perfect, soft and tart, and they gave us hope. We were hungry, and the blackberries were wild, untamed. The Germans could not defeat them, could not steal them from us, because they belonged to no one but God."

Isabelle listened, touched by Delphine's excitement. She pressed her lips together to keep from smiling. Delphine's eyes were dark, serious, but around her mouth was smeared the juice of blackberries.

⁂

From where they stood high up in the tiered yard, Isabelle could barely see a light burning in the small farmhouse just across the gravel road and down the hill from the camp. Oh, if only Mme Nicolas were still there!

"Come, Delphine. The Christensens are not here, but I think their friend is."

They left the blackberries and the pétanque pit, walking under the arch and past the rocky area where cars and vans parked during camping season. Crossing the road, they started down a steep gravel driveway and stepped onto a tiled patio. When Isabelle lifted her hand to knock on the wooden door, Delphine squeezed her hand, stopping her.

"You are sure there will be someone friendly in this house?" she whispered.

Isabelle took one deep breath, bent down to look into the child's dark eyes. "I am not sure, but I'm trusting."

But before she could knock, the door opened, and a round, bright-eyed woman of at least seventy clapped her hands together, crossed herself, and murmured, "God be praised, you're here! We've been waiting for you."

"Madame Nicholas! *Bonjour!* I know you don't remember me, but . . ." Then the woman's comment registered, and she asked, "You've been waiting?" and Isabelle realized she'd said *we*. "Who is here with you?"

The woman gave a jolly smile and a shrug. "I got word."

"Got word from whom?" Isabelle felt fear grip her stomach. Another traitor? No one knew she had come here with Delphine. Had someone followed them?

But she didn't say this, and Madame Nicholas was laughing. "Yes, I heard," and her eyes went heavenward.

"Surely you don't mean that God told you I was coming," Isabelle said.

Madame Nicholas laughed again. "Believe what you want, my dear, but you're safe. Only I and my Lord know that you are here in this little village right now. I'm happy to have you. Isabelle, n'est-ce pas?"

Could this older woman possibly remember her from a decade ago when she was a teenager?

"Oui, madame."

"And this child?"

"I'm Delphine." She held out her hand and added, eyes serious, staring at Mme Nicolas, "But I'm not Delphine."

Whyever would Delphine admit such a thing to a stranger?

"Oui, of course," and Madame Nicholas nodded. "Well, my dear not-Delphine, it's good to meet you." Then she said, "Ooh lá lá! *Vous êtes trompées, toutes les deux*—you are both drenched! Come inside, quickly."

Isabelle stepped into the farmhouse, and a flood of memories followed. This woman, a recent widow when Isabelle had first attended The Camp Between the Hills over a decade ago, had just become the cook for the camp. An amateur chef, she had delighted in serving simple French family meals with little touches of extravagance. And after the whole debacle with the broken curfew and the gossiping and the Penitents, Isabelle had been assigned to kitchen duty with Mme Nicolas for three days.

Now, the older woman procured a pile of towels. "Dry off, you two." Then, "It's so good to see you again, dear Isabelle. I've always thought of you as 'Isabelle of the Penitents.' A girl with such a pure heart. So of course, when I heard what you're doing, what you've done—"

"You know why I'm here? But I only just had the idea to come, to hide Delphine here."

Mme Nicolas simply smiled, motioned for her visitors to take a seat at the kitchen table, and brought them glasses of water and a baguette.

"Fresh bread!" Delphine gasped, tearing off a crusty chunk with the soft center and taking a bite. "It's even warm!"

Mme Nicholas smiled and nodded. "Oui, bien sûr. I baked it just for you. As I said, we've been expecting you." Mme Nicolas motioned to the violet stain around Delphine's lips. "I see you found the blackberries."

Delphine swiped at her mouth, embarrassed, then grinned. "I was hungry. We walked from Sisteron, and God cooled us off with the rain!"

"I will find you some dry clothes shortly." Mme Nicholas's face sobered as she stood and retrieved a large manila envelope from a long shelf stuffed with cookbooks, a black rotary phone, and an old transistor radio. She handed the envelope to Isabelle. "This is for you."

Eyes wide, she stammered, "For m-me?"

"Oui. It came by courier last night. I believe it's a message from M. Christensen."

"Why would he write to me? I haven't seen him in many years."

"Perhaps it has to do with your work?"

"My work?"

"I think you're involved in something . . . *délicat*."

A flicker of doubt made Isabelle take in a breath. Surely she could trust this woman who seemed to know so much about her. But she kept silent.

"I believe you will find the answers to your questions in there," Mme Nicolas said, and she nodded to the envelope.

Delphine scooted her chair beside Isabelle's, peering over her shoulder as she unfastened the envelope and pulled out several sheets of thick ecru paper. When she did, Isabelle caught her breath. Strange symbols were scribbled on the first page, and suddenly another memory assaulted her. Each year, Monsieur Christensen made up a secret code and used it to write messages for the campers to decipher. The camp code! How it had delighted and exasperated them.

Slowly, Isabelle thumbed through all five pages and gave a funny little hiccup. Sure enough, they held scribblings as random and incomprehensible as the first.

"The camp code," she said, this time out loud.

Delphine looked up at her quizzically.

"When we got to camp the first day, the director, Monsieur Christensen, would present each camper with a notebook. He liked to tease our minds, that man!"

Mme Nicolas gave a soft smile and a nod.

Isabelle stared down at the pages, remembering Monsieur Christensen's eyes twinkling as he produced a small blackboard with the strangest configuration of symbols scribbled across it.

"He loved to teach us code because he said it might come in handy one day. He'd used codes as a soldier during the Great War, but for us, he had another reason. Each year he wrote different Bible verses in code, and the code changed each year. In the day, we built back this village, and at night we tried to break the code. As we searched, we naturally memorized the verses, word by word, phrase by phrase."

Delphine grinned. "That sounds like fun."

Isabelle nodded, a lump in her throat. She could still recite those verses—if she cared to, which she did not.

"And now this man has written a new code for you?" asked Delphine, taking the pages from Isabelle's hands. "Pages and pages of code." Eyes shining, Delphine looked up at Mme Nicolas and asked, "Are these messages just for us?"

The woman nodded.

Isabelle shook her head. "Surely not. *C'est impossible!*"

"Nothing is impossible with God, Izzie. My papa always said this. Mme Nicolas just told you that she knew we were coming. Right, madame?"

"Yes, my dear. You are very clever."

"It can't be, Mme Nicolas. No one knows we're here. I've told no one at all." She grabbed the girl's hand and stared at Mme Nicolas. "To keep Delphine safe."

Mme Nicolas seated herself beside them, her gnarled hand covering Isabelle's. "You have been working with Monsieur Martin, n'est-ce pas?"

Isabelle froze, her hand tightening around Delphine's, hopefully squeezing her quiet. Mme Nicolas referred to the code name for the man who had organized the rescue of Jewish children. Could she trust this dear woman? Everything was clandestine, yet somehow she knew.

At her silence, Mme Nicolas continued, "He of course knows who you are, even if you are not aware of his true identity."

Isabelle's eyes flew open. "M. Christensen is M. Martin?"

Mme Nicolas merely gave her hand a squeeze.

Delphine looked impatient. "Well, I think we should try to

solve the code, Izzie! If this M. Martin knew we were coming even before you knew we were coming, and if he wrote a message for you in a special code, well, we must solve it!"

Isabelle swallowed, trying to comprehend this new information. "Yes, of course." Distracted, she fingered the pages. "I was never any good at the codes." Isabelle frowned, recalling her frustration as she tried to solve them. "But we would get others to help us. Monsieur Christensen's son was quite good at solving them."

Stop! Do not think of him.

But her mind strayed to the tall, fun-loving teenager, three years her elder. He had bright green eyes, as green as a fresh leaf of mint, and had incorrigible hair, thick with loose copper curls. The girls giggled at him, only to hide from one another their teenage crushes on Monsieur Christensen's son.

Peter . . .

Her stomach cramped, and she swiped at a tear that threatened to slide down her cheek. Peter had helped her with the codes that first summer. *And he used to include the codes in his letters.* The letters she had touched only yesterday.

"Izzie?"

How long had she been lost in thoughts of Peter?

"Yes, you're right. We need to solve the code. We'll change into dry clothes, and then we'll get to work."

As the sun rose over the mountains, Isabelle yawned, rubbed her eyes, and set down her pen. She'd solved the first page of the code.

"It's not too hard, Isabelle, once you get the hang of it. It's a cipher. You know, a pigpen code. Here, let me show you . . ."

Peter had sat down beside her at camp, coaching her. By her third year at camp, she'd become proficient at deciphering the pigpen codes, even though the boy no longer sat beside her.

Exhausted as she stared at the decoded message on the first page, Isabelle felt as if a handful of those old stones used to build back the camp had settled in her stomach:

*Network compromised, children to be rescued and taken to
Camp Between the Hills immediately, Monsieur Martin.*

Underneath his note was a grid. In the first column, in alphabetical order was a list of the names of the families hiding the Jewish children. Beside each family name was a number, which Isabelle knew referred to how many children were hiding in that home. The third column held the names of the villages where the families lived: Sisteron, Dignes-les-Bains, Oraison, Salignac . . . And the final column held one word: either *lost* or *found*.

ALAIN	2	lost
AMBLARD	1	lost
BALAGUER	1	found
DUCLERC	2	found
BILLOUD	3	found
FERAR	2	found
GUIRAUD	1	found
ROCHER	1	found

The next pages held similar grids that Isabelle was sure, once decoded, would list the other families where the children were hidden.

Her eyes filled with tears as she looked up at Mme Nicolas. "The Alain family was compromised? The children were taken? It says they are lost."

Two years ago, Nathan and Marthe Alain, who lived just outside of Sisteron, had taken in two sisters, Lucie and Marie Feyrard, ages three and four. Isabelle thought now of those little blond-haired cherubs and how, for three days, she had worked to "depersonalize" them before sending them to the Alain home. *Depersonalize* was the term they used in the Network. For children like Delphine, older and more aware, they had easily understood that their names must be changed for safety's sake.

But the little girls did not understand. Again and again, Isabelle had repeated, "*Your names are now Michèle and Laure Alain. If someone calls you Lucie or Marie, you must not answer. If anyone asks if you are Mademoiselle Feyrard, you must not recognize that name."* Over and over, she would explain this for their first names and then their last names. Over and over, tiny Marie would turn her head and smile when Ginette came into the apartment and called her by her given name.

But after three days and many tears, Isabelle had taken them to the Alain farm. And until now, she had believed them safe.

"Where are the others? This list implies that ten children have been found. But Delphine was at the Amblard farm—she's not lost."

"No." Mme Nicholas held out her hand to Isabelle and the other to Delphine. "Follow me."

The rain had stopped, and the dawn had broken as they walked back through the village to the arch. Stopping in front of a wide garage, where the Christensen family had stored their old ramshackle bus, Mme Nicolas produced a key. The thick wooden door creaked as she folded it back against itself and motioned for Isabelle and Delphine to step inside. An old silver Citroën was parked inside, and the rest of the space was jammed with tools and machinery and several rusted bicycles. On the right wall hung metal shelves that ran from floor to ceiling, and several boxes sat on each shelf.

"We'll need to move these," Mme Nicolas said, and slowly she began transferring the boxes from the middle shelf onto the concrete floor with Isabelle and Delphine joining in. Then Isabelle and Mme Nicholas dragged the now empty shelf to the side. Behind it a small door had been concealed. Producing another key, Mme Nicholas opened it.

"You must bend down. Careful of your head," she said as she flicked on a switch, and light broke the blackness.

One by one, they descended five wooden steps into a voluminous cave.

Isabelle gasped as they entered the first of two huge rooms with high vaulted ceilings, cool and smelling not musty or humid but of fresh bread. In the room on the left, shelves were lined with jars of canned food. Tomatoes, jams, jellies, green beans, even fresh eggs and lard.

It was a miracle. There was no other explanation. For some reason, God had whispered in her spirit about The Camp Between the Hills, had pushed her along out of necessity to this place where someone else had planned for them to be sheltered. Her eyes misted over as she thought of the coded letter. Monsieur Martin *was* Monsieur Christensen. And he and others were bringing the children to the camp, where Mme Nicolas had been storing food in the enormous cave for just this purpose.

God had been preparing a place for them.

"In My Father's house are many mansions. . . . I go to prepare a place for you."

The verse she had memorized all those years ago at this very camp rose to the surface as she stared at the abundance of food. "I can't believe it, Mme Nicolas. But how did you know to get this ready for us?"

The old woman laughed a deep, healthy chortle and said, "Our God provides. He told me you would be coming and that I needed to get ready. I've been preparing for months now. And not just for you, my dear."

"Is he here now, Monsieur Christensen—Monsieur Martin?"

"No, not now." The way she said it, with an enigmatic smile, made Isabelle's stomach do a little flip-flop.

"He hasn't been taken captive, has he?"

The old woman shook her head. "Now is not the time to ask questions. Now we'll celebrate that you have brought this precious child, and then you'll go. There are so many more Jewish children to save."

Mme Nicolas led them down two steps into another dark, open room filled with cots, perhaps the same ones Isabelle had slept on with the other campers. On two of those cots slept children. And poking out from under the covers, Isabelle saw two heads with blond curls.

"You see, my dear, the Alain sisters are not lost. They arrived not long before you two."

Isabelle brushed a tear that trickled down her cheek. "Who brought them?"

"That is not your concern. Someone I trust," Mme Nicolas whispered. "And now you have brought another. You need to finish deciphering the codes, so you'll know which children to fetch." Eyes twinkling, she added, "Monsieur Martin decided to have one more measure of security. He asked me to list the children who were safe as 'lost,' and the children who needed to be rescued as 'found.' We must get to work. Later you can take the red bicycle from the garage and find the others. As I told you, we've been waiting. Now this child will help me with Michèle and Laure, and you have work to do."

13

RENÉ

Dawn had not yet broken over the valley. Once again gathered around a dying campfire, Gabriel was giving his daily report to the Durance Maquis. "Remember that the great General Patton has proclaimed to the heads of state that the rapid advance of his army through France would have been impossible without the fighting aid of the F.F.I. in the north."

The men nodded. Etienne slapped Antoine on the back and handed René a cigarette.

The information wasn't new, but René felt a growing pride as Antoine attached the white armband with the letters F.F.I., the *Forces françaises de l'Intérieur*, to his left arm. In reality, the F.F.I. wasn't an army at all, but mostly composed of resistance fighters who used their own weapons, wore civilian clothing, with the F.F.I. armband their only distinguishing trait. Many F.F.I. units included former French soldiers. But not this one.

Gabriel's cigarette hung from the left side of his mouth, his eyes bright with that devilish gleam René knew so well. "Now it's our turn in the south. We keep getting messages from Radio London."

The men murmured among themselves, excited.

Gabriel continued, "We believe the landing in Provence will happen within the week!"

Soon. Very soon.

Gabriel dispatched his men, some of whom were to join another Maquis in the hills to the east of Les Mées. He slapped René on his wounded arm and handed him a pair of binoculars. "Your job is to be our eyes. Keep watch from atop the Penitents. You can see the whole region from up there."

As the sky lightened, René walked with Antoine the five kilometers from their campsite to Les Mées. "I don't need to be protected," René complained to Antoine. "He's just sticking me way up high to get rid of me because I'm small. Same ol' Gabriel." He felt the tightness in his chest, combined with restless energy and anger.

"Everyone is hiding in the hills. We each have a job to do, and your arm has not completely healed. Leave the past alone and concentrate. Every one of our roles is vital. You know the code, right? Send it to me if you see the slightest movement of the Boches."

"He won't even let me carry a gun! How can I protect myself?"

Antoine turned and threw his rifle, which René caught in his left hand. "Do you want this? Take it from me, little brother, if you need a weapon so badly."

Ashamed, René shook his head, trying to shake the anger from his mind. "Sorry." He handed the rifle back to his brother. "I'll do my part."

What he couldn't tell his brother was how fear landed in his gut at the thought of watching helpless from on high as his brother fought on the ground a hundred feet below.

I watched Maman fight and die, Antoine. I cannot bear to think of watching you too. Please, no.

A cloudless day in August, the sun was brutal as René snaked up the well-worn path, scurrying across the limestone. He cursed his size, still hearing Gabriel's taunts from long ago and just last night, as he easily scaled the steep cliffs of the Penitents, his only weapons a pair of binoculars, an electric torch, and a canteen. *Concentrate on the present,* he reprimanded himself. But letting the anger from past cruelties fuel him also protected him from the collision of thrill and terror as he watched Antoine shrinking little by little in size.

He paused by the ancient chapel and stared out over the red tiled roofs of the village of Les Mées, the Penitent monks standing tall and erect to his left. He climbed slower as pebbled limestone crumbled under his feet. At last he was perched over the first monk, the scruffy pines, and timeworn holes in the cliffs, making the monks resemble unshaven old men with acne-pocked faces from their teenage years. This one, a limestone arch, attached like a huge round earring to the monk, allowed René to peer far down into the valley below.

Leaning over the edge, he perched himself on what he imagined was one of the monks' noses. Binoculars in hand, he stared down at the valley, feeling a wave of dizziness wash over him. *Not too close. Watch your step. Don't give Gabriel a chance to berate you for stupidity.*

He swallowed hard and continued until he arrived at the point where, with his binoculars, he could look down through the twisting pines and past the limestone peaks to see the road from Sisteron.

There he waited. And waited.

Then . . . from his perch high above, René spotted two trucks coming from Sisteron, escorted by German soldiers. He signaled down to Antoine.

René could barely make out the figure of Antoine signaling to the other maquisards on the road below. He watched them disperse in different directions. Then, as Gabriel and Etienne halted the first truck with their rifles, the other maquisards hurried around the back.

The German column was approaching from the rear, and René watched again through the binoculars as the *pat-a-pat* of machine guns and bright red blasts from gunfire echoed through the valley.

Heart in his throat, René lowered the binoculars. One of their men was down, and the Maquis was retreating. He did not know which maquisard had been shot; he only knew it wasn't Antoine. Thank God! Even from his perch so high up, he recognized his brother's stocky build and his distinctive gait.

Throughout the long afternoon, René observed the progression of the Boches, continuing their advance to the east. Again through his binoculars he saw the Mallemoisson Maquis opening fire on the German column, and the Durance Maquis rallying.

Resistance fighters, posted on the hills overlooking the valley on all sides, were taking advantage of their dominant position to go on the attack. René would have preferred to be down there fighting with them. Instead, sweating, standing, sitting, pacing, he watched the battle continue for two hours.

As the sun set, casting its eerie glow on the cliffs, René stared out at his panoramic view of the rocky formations that had inspired stories and legends. He inhaled the scents of pine and wild thyme, touched the buds of lavender in his pocket, and watched the way the enormous ball of fire sank in the sky until it became smaller and smaller and finally disappeared. He questioned, as he often did, how such beauty could exist alongside the brutality and horror of war.

Much later, around the campfire, the mood was tense.

"We lost Gilles." Gabriel's face was drawn and hardened, yet René saw the grief so close to the surface. "After two hours of fighting, the Germans managed to escape toward Bléone, but they lost two men, and they abandoned their weapons and vehicle." A long drag on his cigarette. "So we have more ammunition and this stinking German truck."

As the men headed to their spots under the Penitent cliffs, the same grotto René had shared with Delphine only days earlier, Antoine touched his brother's shoulder. "You did a good job up there, René. You were the first to see, the first to warn us."

"But Gilles . . ."

"Not your fault. We know the cost. We live with it every day." Though Antoine's tone was stoic, his face looked as pale as the other men's.

Language was a strange thing, René thought. Gilles wasn't lost. They'd all seen his bullet-ridden body, splayed on the ground by the German truck. Just as he'd seen Dominique's, Frédéric's, Sébastien's, Jean-Paul's, and Maman's.

Lost was a euphemism meant to comfort, but it didn't. It only brought that same feeling of rage. He had been powerless to save any of them. But oh how he'd tried.

Before entering the grotto, Antoine motioned for René to stop. Then he fished in his pocket. "This just came in." Antoine looked almost apologetic when he handed a folded piece of thick paper to his brother. "Gabriel thinks it's a good job for you."

The anger simmered. *Trying to get rid of me again. I'll show him! I'll show them all!*

But when René read the message, the anger fizzled, replaced by something else. Hope. On the sheet of paper were written strange symbols. Underneath the symbols, the translation read, *Network compromised, children to be rescued and taken to Camp Between the Hills immediately, Monsieur Martin.*

The message in French was followed by names and the villages where the children were housed, along with the number of children at each location. Tiny villages he knew well where maquisards and resistants played their part, where Jewish children had lived, hidden in plain sight—like Delphine, who had been safe until now, until someone had betrayed the Network at the Amblard farm.

René swallowed the lump in his throat as he reread the message directly from the head of the Martin Network. He had heard of this camp from his cousin, had heard stories of Scouts and broken curfews and these same Penitent cliffs. He smirked. Maman and her brother, Isabelle's father, Tonton Jean-Pierre, liked to tell the story of a young Isabelle at this camp and her "penance at the Penitents" when René was much too young to attend the camp. He had visited the stone camp once and had hoped to attend one day. But the war had come when he was only ten, and the camp had closed.

He looked down again at the wrinkled paper. No, that was wrong. The camp had not closed. The camp was once again a refuge, built back over decades, now opened not to Catholic Scouts, but to Jewish children.

"I don't mind this task," René told his brother. "I'll leave immediately."

Antoine lifted an eyebrow, surprised. "You'll be far away from any action again."

"It's a way to help."

René knew Gabriel saw it as a punishment, but perhaps, just perhaps it was a blessing. And another way to see Delphine again.

The sliver of moon and the light of his torch were René's only companions on the first leg of his journey from Les Mées. The Penitent cliffs rose, now looking not like friendly, oversized monks, but like ghostly apparitions jutting their malformed heads into the sky. Was a German soldier watching his every move from above as he had watched for the Germans just this morning? His arm ached, and his stomach grumbled, but at least he had a pair of socks and solid boots.

Merci, Gilles.

He swallowed bile as he thought of Antoine removing them from their fallen comrade. He too thought of that other night, with Delphine when he was injured. When he wondered if he might collapse and die before they reached Sisteron. He was stronger in body, all the wounds healing well, but still he felt lethargic.

Throughout the night, while his fellow *maquisards* prepared their continued acts of sabotage, René followed the snaking Durance River back through Peyruis, Montfort, Voronne, and Salignac, the tiny towns where the children were hidden.

He arrived first at the darkened farmhouse on the outskirts of Peyruis and rapped on the door. *Three loud knocks, separated, count to ten, then three more.* He knew that code.

143

A sleepy-eyed woman, her frizzy gray hair poking from beneath a bonnet, opened the door. Sleepy-eyed, perhaps, but not surprised. The knocks were their warning.

Danger, someone from the Network is coming to help!

"René, *mon pauvre garçon!*" She took him in her arms.

He stiffened. He did not want pity.

"I've come for the children, Mme Geist," René whispered.

"Yes, of course, I know."

As she went to wake her husband, René leaned against the wall, arm throbbing, throat parched. She returned a moment later. "M. Giest will prepare the children. Come, you're famished. Thirsty."

She lit a candle, then set a tin of sardines and a piece of bread on the kitchen table and nodded to René to sit. He collapsed in the chair, devouring the food while she refilled his canteen.

"Merci," he whispered, feeling strength return. "And we've just heard. The Allies are coming to the beaches soon—in a few days."

She paused, her back still to him, the canteen in her right hand. He heard her clear her throat and saw the way her left hand gripped the sink. A sob resonated throughout the kitchen. She then breathed deeply and turned to face René. "God be praised!" she said, crossing herself. "Soon we will not have to hide the children. Soon we'll all be free."

A few minutes later, rubbing their eyes and yawning, two children entered the kitchen behind the old farmer.

"Annlise, Stephane, this is René," Mme Giest said. "He's going to take you on a small adventure." While she helped them into their shoes, M. Geist handed René the false documents for the children.

"Maman Giest! I don't want to leave," the child called Annlise whimpered. She could not be more than five, René thought. Would she be able to make the remaining fifteen kilometers to the camp? She clung to Mme Giest until the woman stooped down and, holding the child's face in her hands, whispered, "Remember, you are brave. And Stephane and René will take good care of you."

Mme Geist was right. Both children, though fearful, were brave. They had seen atrocities, they knew hunger, they also knew safety.

In silence the three walked, Annlise between the boys, the seven kilometers to Montfort, where René repeated the knocking, where another weary but not wary mother greeted him. She offered him water and bread while the husband fetched the child. He whispered again the hope of the invasion, then met another child, Gaëton, eight years old, clutching his canteen as René stuffed the false papers in his shirt.

When the small group reached the farmhouse outside Voronne, René was relieved to be greeted by an older boy, Henri. Tall and solemn-eyed, his lips trembled, and his eyes filled as he stood, shoulders back, and said, "Au revoir" to his foster family. He cleared his throat and stuck out his hand to René. "Bonjour, I'm Henri. I'm thirteen."

They shook hands, and René felt an immediate bond form. A boy nearer his age.

"Can we sing?" Henri asked. "It helps us to sing. We pretend we're going to Jerusalem and sing the Psalms of Ascent. Do you know them?"

René shrugged. "No, I don't know them. And you can't sing. But you can whisper them to each other, if it will help the kids' morale."

He thought again of their long pilgrimage from the destroyed farmhouse to the grotto of the Penitents, followed by the exhausting hike to Sisteron. Delphine's faith, her sweet voice, had kept him going.

Now Henri whispered, and the younger children joined in.

"You all know the same songs?" René asked.

"Of course, we're Jews. We band together."

They whispered their psalms, and René listened in wonder. He was fueled by anger and revenge, but these children spoke of hope and love and a God who was protecting them. So strange.

It was only a short three kilometers to Salignac, where the group added three siblings—Lydie, Mathieu, and Jacques—and then, by miracle, they arrived at their destination, the Baume Mountain guiding their way. Annlise on Henri's back, four-year-old Lydie on René's, and the four boys walking silently behind. The psalms were hushed as they came to the village, and René searched for a gravel driveway that snaked down a hill with a wooden mailbox painted a provincial blue, where a woman called Mme Nicolas was supposedly expecting them. Those instructions had been penned below the columned list of names.

Using his torch, René located the blue mailbox and the farmhouse below, in total darkness, his little flock following close behind down the winding gravel driveway. René rapped as before, and a plump gray-haired woman opened the door without a sound, her face somber, hurrying them inside, peeking out as if to assure herself that no Germans were nearby.

Without a word she motioned for the children to sit on the floor. The house remained in pitch-darkness, and she shook her head when René lifted his torch.

Hot milk and delicious jam-covered baguettes were served, the children holding out their hands as Mme Nicolas wiped them clean and placed first the tins of milk and then the baguette in theirs. Only the whites of the children's eyes showed their astonished faces. Then their smiles and their soft giggles.

Half an hour later, the small band of children trekked behind Mme Nicolas under the cover of night. She opened a huge garage door, ushered them inside, where an old Citroën sat amid what looked like tools and bicycles. Then she motioned to René and Henri to help her push aside a metal shelf, and finally, lighting her torch, she led them into the wine cellar, holding her hand out to steady the little ones as they walked down the rickety steps.

When the door was closed, René gasped. It felt like a chapel, a sanctuary of light. Votive candles gleamed along the shelves of an enormous, vaulted room, casting warmth and welcoming shadows. Down two steps led to another room, equally as large, with cots filled with sleeping children—except for a young girl who sat on her cot, reading by candlelight. René felt the blood rush from his face, his heart hammering as Delphine hopped off the cot and ran to his side, engulfing him in a fierce hug.

"You came! And you brought the others!"

Blond and brunette and black-haired heads shook themselves awake, a redhead too.

"Praise God," Mme Nicolas said.

"Isabelle is bringing more tomorrow, we pray," Delphine confided, now gripping René's left hand while she touched the soft bandage on his right arm. "We'll all be safe."

René let out a long breath and steadied himself. *Safe. Delphine was safe.*

"I was hidden in Isabelle's cave for two days, René. There was no light, only a candle and the food Isabelle would bring, and it was scary. But it was okay because God was with me, and then I prayed for an angel to come like the one who carried you. Instead, God sent a thunderstorm that chased the Germans away as Izzie and I walked to the camp. I call her Izzie now because that was her father's nickname for her. It rained and kept us hidden and then it stopped so that Izzie could see the moon and the mountains and find our way here." She leaned close. "To Mme Nicolas and this cave."

All the other children slept while Delphine continued to whisper her story.

"Monsieur Martin left secret codes for Izzie to solve so she could find the children. Mme Nicolas had been preparing for weeks to keep us. At first it was only me here with Michèle and Laure, but then Izzie and Ginette were bringing more children each day. And now you are here, just like I prayed."

When Delphine took a breath, dark eyes still shining with excitement, she asked, "Do you like codes?" But he could not answer. "Because they are very important to the work, and Izzie is teaching me. I can show you if you want." She stopped and frowned at him. "René, you aren't paying me any attention. Aren't you glad I am here?"

He cursed in his mind, cleared his throat, and said, "I'm very glad you're here, Delphine."

14

⟞⟝⟞

ISABELLE

AUGUST 9, 1944

M. Martin *was* M. Christensen. For the hundredth time, Isabelle absorbed this truth as she bumped the red bike along the dusty countryside road toward her next destination, the small hamlet in Bevons on the outskirts of Sisteron where families housed Jewish children.

She almost wished she didn't know the real name of the man who had organized the Martin Network. She shouldn't know, for truly that would be safer. But it made sense. Of course, the unconventional Protestant pastor who ministered to Catholic kids at camp would be championing Jewish kids during war.

Reaching inside the hidden compartment in her purse, she removed the list of the children she needed to rescue, the list she and Delphine had deciphered.

ALAIN	lost		2
AMBLARD	lost		1
BALAGUER	~~found~~	lost	1
DUCLERC	found		2

BILLOUD	~~found~~	lost	3
FERAR	~~found~~	lost	2
GUIRAUD	~~found~~	lost	1
ROCHER	found		1

In the middle of the night for the past four days, Isabelle had made her trek on the red bike, from farmhouse to farmhouse, apartment to apartment across the region. Six families, ten children. She would perch the youngest child, holding her torch, on the bike and walk beside it, with the older children gripping tightly to her tan culottes.

And it had worked. These children were all safe at the camp.

Ginette, too, had spent the last days going from town to town. Soon all thirty-one of the Jewish children hidden in their immediate region would be at the camp.

The children would not be lost.

No, the lost children were really found. Lost and found. Sometimes language was so confusing. And even more so when the words were twisted to be a code.

And there were other confusing words.

Traitor, colleague, enemy, friend.

I don't know who broke the link in our chain, Papa, but now you are dead, and the children are in great danger, and we're trying so hard to save them.

And by now Tomas knows I'm involved. Perhaps he will have others searching for me. Why am I risking being caught by returning to Sisteron at night? Because I love these children. Because we will all resist until the end.

Twice she had opened the wooden mailbox in the entryway to her apartment building, hoping for a message from someone in the Silo, only to find it empty. Ginette, she knew, was sneaking to villages just as she was and bringing children to the camp. But the others? Were they truly creating distractions so that ammunition and trucks could be stolen from the Germans? Were they planting explosives on the train tracks, weaving the coils in and out of the

rails? Were they drawing detailed maps of the region to send to the
Allies? Were they hiding in another basement, printing contraband?
Yes, of course.

Or was one of them carrying a list of Jewish children very similar to Ginette's and Isabelle's, only with the desire not to rescue
but to capture?

"Pay attention, Zabelle." She could hear Ginette's admonition
as she approached the village. The Maquis were notorious for
changing the road signs to confuse the Germans. She wondered
if René was doing that very thing now with Antoine.

She knew the way to these homes by heart. How often in that
first year had she gone, late at night, to visit the families, to check
on the Jewish children to be sure they were well. Still, she needed
to be sharp—especially now. The word *compromised* reverberated
in her mind, and her hands grew moist on the handlebars. But the
voices of Ginette and Papa coaxed her on.

"You can do it, Zabelle."

"You are brave, my little Izzie."

The door to Mme Duclerc's home stood open, and a scrawny
cat was weaving in and out of the overturned furniture. Isabelle
stepped inside, caught herself on an armchair still upright, her
heart beating out an incantation of fear. Was she too late?

She stumbled into the kitchen, where a tin of sardines had been
licked clean. Broken glass littered the counters. Flies circled some
unknown liquid. It looked as though the Germans or the Milice
had already been here. Or one of the Silo members.

Compromised. Betrayed.

Lost?

Found?

And then she saw it, a note scribbled on a file card, sticking out
from the recipe box.

*Chéri, I've put the canned peaches in the cave. Leave the
fresh fruit out. Much must still be picked.*

Merci, Maman

A message—not the camp code, but a coded message nonetheless. She and Ginette had invented it, though every participant in the Network knew banal messages must be interpreted. And this one . . .

She rushed through the hall and down the stairway that led to the basement with its caves. The code was clear. Children—the canned peaches—were in the cave, and the family—the fresh fruit—had left, and there were many other children to be picked up.

The ancient, blackened door was not padlocked, this too planned. The Germans would of course check the cave, so the doors were to be left unlocked as a confusing deterrent. But somewhere . . .

Please, God, let André and his little sister, Roxanne, be hidden.

She walked into the cave, a dank room made of stones and smelling of urine and animal refuse. A rat scurried into a dark corner. Except for the rat and a lone small table, the cave looked empty.

Isabelle found the concealed trapdoor behind the shelves that were stacked with jars of conserves. Pushing it aside, she opened the door and shone her flashlight into a smaller cave. "Children, are you there?" Then she remembered the words to say to assure them it was safe to show themselves. "I'm just looking for the canned peaches."

Four bright eyes appeared, then their small bodies, then arms were holding her at the waist, and the children were weeping. "We knew you'd come, mademoiselle! We knew it."

When Isabelle rapped on the farmhouse door, Mme Nicolas greeted her with a kiss on each cheek and sparkling eyes. "*Entrez.* How wonderful! More children."

"Roxanne, André, I'd like you to meet Mme Nicolas."

Once again, the older woman hurried them into the farmhouse, directing them to the kitchen table, saying, "Have a seat. I'll be right there."

As with Delphine, their eyes grew round with surprise when

Mme Nicolas placed cups of warm milk and fresh baguettes in front of them.

"And for you too, Isabelle. You must keep up your strength." The older woman nudged her to sit down and brought milk and more bread for her. Wiping her hands on her apron, brushing a few stray gray hairs from her face, she added, "This makes nine little ones who've arrived in the past twenty-four hours."

"Is Monsieur Martin bringing children too?" Isabelle asked, looking up from her milk.

"No, just you and your friend Ginette. And now the young boy, Delphine's friend, has brought us seven during the night."

"René is here?"

"Neither are here now. Just the children."

But René had been here.

"How many?"

"Twenty-nine now. But we have room for more. And don't worry. Where at first they were frightened and shy, now they laugh among themselves and whisper what the young boy told them— 'The Allies are coming. Soon we will be free.'"

Mme Nicolas lifted her eyebrows and *tsk*ed. "I'm afraid he's getting their hopes up. They are bouncing off the walls! Fortunately, your Delphine has kept them busy, deciphering and memorizing verses from the Psalms. She found the codes in some of the old notebooks Monsieur Christensen left here."

Isabelle blinked back unexpected tears, a feeling of deep gratitude washing over her.

Delphine flew into Isabelle's arms. "René came, and he brought Annlise and Stephane and Henri and Gaëton and Lydie and Mathieu and Jacques. And your friend Ginette brought Jesse and Quentin and Alexandra and Lina and Coralie." Her eyes danced. "Of course, those aren't their real names. Mme Nicolas has given us good food, more than any of our ration cards could supply, and we aren't lonely. And at night we sneak out and pick blackberries."

Before Isabelle could comment, Delphine's face fell. "But René couldn't stay long. He's working with the Maquis to confuse the

Germans." She screwed up her face and asked, "Are all the children here now? Are they all safe?"

No, not all the Jewish children were safe. But the thirty-one children from the Network in this region, those for whom she felt responsible, most of them now lay on cots and mats in the cave.

"Almost, Delphine. Almost."

Isabelle tossed and turned on a skinny mattress in the cave. Although she could not conjure up a recollection of her father meeting M. Christensen long ago when he came to pick her up after her second summer at The Camp Between the Hills, a different memory from her first summer there kept her wide awake.

"I hear you walked to the Penitents last night. *Pas mal*, do you often run away from camp? I never took you for the rebellious type."

Isabelle jerked her head up from where she had been poring over the camp code and getting nowhere. It was the pastor's son, the redheaded boy, speaking to her. She felt her cheeks flush as she glanced at him, unsure of what to say. Was he making fun of her?

"You mean about the curfew . . . and the other things?"

"Yes, exactly."

"It wasn't my best moment." She went back to work. If he was going to tease her, she could not look at him for fear she might cry.

"No, but you were brilliant. Doing 'Protestant penance' at the Penitent cliffs."

She frowned, not looking up. "I don't care to talk about it if you mean to humiliate me."

"Not at all. I'm sorry. I like to tease."

She looked up at him again and saw that he was embarrassed, his face almost matching his red hair. He reached out, and when he touched her arm, she shivered. Her face was burning. Peter, the director's son, three years older, was speaking to her. She tried to think of something to say.

I've been watching you every day. You are handsome and gentle and kind and fun . . .

But she could not say these things.

"I felt bad about the broken curfew." She winced. "I felt bad that we were gossiping. Your dad had just done that study from the book of James on the dangers of the tongue." She stared at her shoes. "I wanted to do something."

He lifted his eyebrows, red, like his hair. "That's a long way to walk just to say you're sorry."

She peeked up at him through her bangs. "Well, I knew your Protestant father couldn't lead each of us in a private confession, so I decided we'd join those poor old frozen monks in prayer and ask God for forgiveness."

At this he threw back his head, red curls bouncing against his shoulders, laughing. "That's great, praying with the monks."

She was sure her face was purple with embarrassment. She wanted him to leave. Instead, he came and sat down beside her.

"Having a little trouble with the codes?"

"Yes, I'm quite stupid," she snapped, and closed the notebook.

"I'm sorry. I'm an idiot. I'm not making fun of you. I think you're quite . . . intriguing. I've been watching you."

She turned her eyes up to his. Mesmerizingly green. And freckles!

"You've been watching to see how many other stupid mistakes I would make—breaking the rules, gossiping, having the ridiculous idea of Protestant penance, and being so dumb I can't solve a simple code."

His smile vanished. "Could we start over? I'm Peter."

"I know who you are. Everyone knows who you are."

"I'd like to know who you are."

"Can't you guess? You've been watching me. Surely you've figured out my name." She couldn't quite believe how sassy and sarcastic she sounded.

"You're Zabelle."

Now Isabelle really blushed. The beautiful boy with sea-green eyes knew her name and was talking to her. "No one calls me that except my best friend, Ginette. I'm Isabelle." She pronounced it slowly, Is-a-belle.

"Well, Is-a-belle, I was not trying to make fun of you. I truly think you are gifted with people."

"What good is that? I need to be gifted with rocks and codes."

"Are you kidding? You could lead the whole Scout camp with your personality. You're kind. You're a peacemaker. It's a . . . a really good trait." If possible, his face darkened even more, and she realized he truly was trying to compliment her.

"Well, it's not going to get me anywhere with this code."

And he was sitting beside her, his arm brushing hers. "It's not too hard, Isabelle, once you get the hang of it. It's a cipher. You know, a pigpen code. Here, let me show you."

Heart hammering, she tried to concentrate as he explained the way the code worked, but all she could think about was the way his hand kept brushing against hers as he wrote.

"Merci. For helping me," she said later, not wanting him to leave.

"Of course. And my father really liked your Protestant penance." He cleared his throat, looked out toward the mountains, and said, "Anyway, my father loves to break the rules, to shock people with his outlandish ideas. You've heard him preach."

"Yes, he's quite different from our parish priest. I was surprised Papa let me come to this camp, but since all the other Scouts were attending, he figured it would be a bunch of Catholic kids against one Protestant pastor."

They laughed together.

"He wants this place to be for everyone, to be used all year long. In Algeria, we all get along well—Catholics, Jews, Muslims, Protestants . . ."

Peter! She had lain awake every night for the rest of the camp, dreaming of him. *Like I'm doing right now.* He had found her during the day and worked alongside her. And twice he had asked to take a walk with her after the evening vespers. They had shared interesting conversations, strolling along the road or standing by the gurgling stream or sitting on the ground by the pétanque pit.

It was the first time in her fourteen years of life that she had felt that fluttering in her heart, that breathless excitement and maddening obsession that her friends called puppy love.

They had exchanged addresses and for several months had written long letters back and forth to each other. How her heart had soared when she saw an Algerian stamp on an envelope, covered in a comic strip he had drawn. Peter wrote of school, of soccer, of faith, and sometimes, he even wrote in a code she understood. Instead of signing his name at the bottom, he would sketch a comic likeness of himself, with wild curly red hair and a silly grin on his face and a bubble off to the side with the words, *See you soon, Zabelle.*

She'd shared her first poems with him and confided about the hard things in life—about her mother and baby brother, about her questions. She had even tried to write a few phrases in English. Even now she pictured the brightly colored envelopes she had fingered only days ago.

Stop remembering before you get to the painful part.

But it rushed on her. How after four months of constant letters back and forth, of his sketches and her simple poetry, his letters had stopped. Abruptly.

When five of her letters went unanswered, she agreed with Ginette that he was a cad, convinced herself that Peter had found someone else. Still, throughout that year, she had hoped and prayed for a letter, then hoped and prayed she would see him the next year. But he never came back to camp. Away at college in America, his father had said, and how disappointed she'd been. Heartbroken. Eventually she had totally forgotten about him, his dancing green eyes, his quick mind, his kindness, their night walks by the stream, his letters.

Well, not totally forgotten, she admitted to herself. Just stuffed way down somewhere inside, along with all the other disappointments and sorrows in her life.

15

PETER

Peter made his way to the sick ward on the *Nevada*. He greeted several soldiers as he passed them on their cots, then sat beside Frank's bed.

"Hey, buddy. Sorry you're feeling so poorly."

Frank didn't even manage to smile. "Yeah. Not in the best shape."

Usually his assistant radiated youth and strength, but now he looked almost emaciated. As the orderly checked his vitals, Peter asked, "Is it a fever?"

He shrugged. "No, but it's the worst case of seasickness I've ever seen. He's dehydrated, Ginger. Don't look like he'll be getting off the ship with you tomorrow. He's been upchucking for three days. We got an IV in him. Hopefully that'll help."

"I can hear you," Frank said, his voice barely a whisper. "All I need is to step onto solid land."

"You need rest, buddy. Just rest," Peter said.

In a voice that was starkly unconvincing, Frank said, "Don't

157

you worry, none, Ginger. I'll be good to go real soon. You ain't getting off this boat without me."

Peter hoped that was right. He trusted Frank. They'd been to-gether in the thick of battle in North Africa. He knew Frank's reactions, knew Frank's wordless signals, could recall half a dozen times when Frank's cunning had saved his life.

"I know you'll be there for me. You just rest now, you hear? And lay off the heavy alcohol for a while."

Frank was a Baptist teetotaler, but even Peter's obvious joke didn't get a reaction from his assistant.

Hundreds of men attended the joint service the chaplains held on the night before D-Day. Peter, George, Danny, and Abe each took turns reading from the Scriptures and speaking of courage overcoming fear, of hope amid seeming defeat, of faith holding steady as God watched over them.

As Peter watched the men's faces, eyes eager and intent, he thought about the power their words held to imbue the strength the soldiers needed to step out of the boat and onto the beaches of war, more power than the rifles the soldiers carried.

Throughout the night, the chaplains listened and prayed with the men. A long line of Catholic soldiers waited patiently as Chaplain LeDuc heard each confession and granted absolution. When Communion was served, Peter watched his soccer teammates, fierce competitors like him, kneel down with their hands out to receive the bread and wine, nodding when Peter said, "The body and blood of our Lord Jesus Christ."

Young men, in perfect physical condition, men he had come to care deeply for, humbly knelt before him and prayed. Andy's hands shook slightly as he took Communion. Rusty bowed his head. Billy cleared his throat before eating the wafer.

Observing the men in that position of humility, Peter knew they were ready for the challenges of war.

It flashed in his sleep, reel after reel, a movie of memories played out in his mind. He stood before the German firing squad, but the German commander's eyes were soft, kind, excited, pointing to his cross, then reaching inside his pocket and bringing out the photo of his wife and child. Was this man who had spared his life and who loved God and family, was he the enemy?

Then the reel skipped forward to a little girl's face staring into his, smiling, laughing, giggling, big brown eyes looking into his with such delight. The reel shifted, and her eyes were sad as she held out her wrist and he saw the scars and bruises there.

Another reel played faster and faster with Andy on his knees, confessing his fear. Then Frank gripped his rifle, his eyes searching. "Don't you worry, Ginger. I'll protect you."

Now his father was patting him on the back, handing him a sheet of carbon paper on which were printed not words but symbols. Bold, black symbols. His father was yelling, "The children! Don't forget the children!"

Peter jerked awake, his heart ramming against his ribs. He took a few deep breaths to clear his mind and shut off the alarm. He fumbled until he found his flashlight.

He had slept for just this hour, a little bit of peace before all hell broke loose tomorrow. One hour until he was due up on deck.

Peter knelt by his bed and prayed, pronouncing the names out loud of the soldiers who would be stepping out of a boat onto a beach renowned for beauty and tourists and wealth.

But what would the beach be known for after tomorrow?

16

RENÉ

The explosion spewed fire and water into the night air as René watched the bridge crumble, the whole thing tumbling into the Durance River. He squatted along the riverbank, congratulating himself on his third successful bombing in the past two days. Somewhere close by, Antoine and Etienne were waiting for him.

The Durance Maquis had spent the last four days bombing bridges south of Sisteron. Little by little they were working their way up the Durance Valley. And with each bomb he planted, René felt satisfaction, the anger and need for revenge quelled even if for a moment.

"You're good at placing the explosives." Antoine had winked at his little brother when the first bridge came down. Two years ago, before Antoine had joined the Maquis, the brothers went out in the middle of night, just the two of them with their flashlights, huddled in the cave at the Amblard farmhouse, practicing with pretend explosives on pretend bridges.

160

Before Antoine joined the Maquis. Before Delphine came to the farmhouse.

Gunfire joined the cacophony of the bridge's destruction, interrupting René's thoughts. He watched bullets skim the water's surface nearby like skipping rocks. His head buzzed with noise as he struggled to climb the steep embankment. More bullets ricocheted around him. He slipped, grabbing at a tree root that broke away from the bank. With a splash, René landed in the river as more bullets rained down all around.

He dove underwater, forcing himself deeper toward the bottom of the wide river, then swimming until his lungs were burning. Even then he didn't dare emerge as bullets sprayed above him.

Finally, he grasped onto more roots by the bank and came up sputtering and gasping for air. Again he clambered up the embankment, but the algae and moss and wet ground made the steep surface impossible to climb.

Then he heard Antoine screaming above the gunfire. "Not here! Swim farther downstream. It levels off, and you'll be able to get out."

He plunged underwater again, his strokes frantic as he pushed the heavy water to the side and kicked with all his might. When he finally emerged again, the riverbank jutted out into a tiny peninsula. He pulled himself up on the rocklike surface, gasping, his chest heaving.

Antoine signaled with his hands while Etienne screamed, "Come on, René, you can do it!"

He crawled along the rock, grasping at the air, finding one hand and another as his brother pulled him back into the wooded area beside the river, and they disappeared into the pitch-black night.

An hour later, when they arrived back at the campfire, Antoine told the others about René's narrow escape. Didier, Samuel, and Bastien congratulated him as they passed around a bottle of rancid alcohol and met René's eyes with respect in their own. René took a swig from the bottle, trying to ignore the continued ringing in his ears and the way his legs shook.

Gabriel had not looked up from the map he was studying.

He fiddled with the dial on their small radio and motioned for everyone to be quiet. They huddled together, listening, until the familiar voices from the French broadcast of the BBC came forth. All the Maquis across France had followed the same routine every night for the past months. A stream of seemingly meaningless phrases, read slowly, one after the other.

Then *"Nancy a le torticollis."*

"Nancy has a stiff neck!" proclaimed Etienne. At last, they were receiving the coded signal that the Allied invasion was indeed imminent.

"Shhh," said Gabriel as each man leaned in closer to understand the next spoken phrases, all innocuous. Then came a second message, *"Le chasseur est affamé."*

The silence was broken only by the heavy breathing of the men. Again, it was repeated: "Le chasseur est affamé."

The hunter is starving. That sentence, repeated twice, meant that the invasion would start early the next morning.

Gabriel was beaming. *"Enfin.* Finally."

Tomorrow was D-Day. Yes, finally.

17

ISABELLE

August 14, 1944

Isabelle woke before dawn, disoriented. Then she remembered. She had bumped along the roadside until she passed the familiar little metal sign announcing the village's name: *Sisteron*. She pedaled away from centre ville, climbed toward the wooded hillside area where she hid her bike in the shrubs surrounding the Citadel, sneaked down the steep embankment as the moon shone over the proud fortress, and fell asleep in the woods high up behind her apartment building.

She had spent two days at the camp, helping Mme Nicolas and Delphine with the other children, thirty of them now. It was time to venture into the old town of Sisteron, down the Long Androne. Just one more child to rescue, to bring to the camp.

She stretched, running her hands through her thick hair. When had she last bathed or washed her hair? The days had twisted together into one, long, desperate attempt to reach the children before Tomas and his Nazi colleagues did.

The last child. Anne.

The heart-wrenching process of "depersonalization" for four-year-old Rebekah Weinstein to become Anne Rocher had lasted for hours. *"You're no longer called Rebekah Weinstein; you're called Anne Rocher. Can you say it again? Your name is Anne Rocher!"* On and on, the child looked at her, baffled by what this woman was asking.

Only when the children had, in a sense, been stripped of their identities could the Network entrust them to families. Isabelle had given little Anne to Laurette and Yannick Rocher, a devout young Catholic couple who lived near the Long Androne in the center of town. They were fearless, eager to help.

But when Isabelle had visited them a day later to see if everything was going well, Laurette had wrung her hands, her eyes red with tears and exhaustion. "Mademoiselle, I can't take it anymore. Ever since you left this poor child with us, she has said only one sentence: 'Where's Mommy, where's Mommy, where's Mommy?' I don't have children yet. I don't know how to comfort her."

Laurette led Isabelle into the salon where the child was curled up in an armchair. Isabelle knelt beside Anne, stroking her cheeks and said, "How are you, little one?"

Anne lifted her little head, her eyes wide with tears, and cried, "Where's Mommy, where's Mommy, where's Mommy?"

But eventually Anne calmed down and stayed. Was she still there, still safe?

Isabelle headed to the Rocher apartment tucked at the foot of the Long Androne in the predawn. She swallowed, wiped her brow, welcomed the mix of chills and sweat. She preferred either of these to fear, but fear followed closely. Would it erupt in an explosion of terrified screams? Surely Tomas and the others were waiting and watching. They had been to the Duclerc home. Did they have this address too? She thought of the news of reprisals in other towns, a whole village rounded up and locked in a church that the Nazis set on fire, three young resistants executed beside a train station.

Her stomach cramped. How did the others do it? Bravery was

trying to push past her fear, but still the fear got in the way. No, Papa had said bravery, courage, was admitting the terror and praying.

"Dear God, help!" It came out as an anguished sob with only the dawn to hear. "Let me be brave like the other resistants and the families housing the children."

How she admired them all, these good-hearted townspeople who risked their lives doing what they considered their duty, nothing heroic. They were simply civilians, civil people fighting against incivility, knowing that if their acts of rebellion were discovered, their own chances of survival were slim.

She wound between the streets to the Long Androne and saw it. The door to the Rochers' home stood ajar. She felt terror slide up her back and surround her neck, choking her until she couldn't breathe. Should she enter? What had happened to the young couple keeping little Anne? Had they been taken along with the child?

Were the Germans still inside? Or nearby? Was Tomas waiting somewhere in the shadows, ready to grab her?

I am not brave, Papa! Help me.

Go inside, little Izzie. You must see if the child is still there.

Roxanne and André had survived in their hiding places. Maybe Anne . . .

She crept inside, gagging as the smell of human excrement accosted her. She imagined a terrified child soiling herself as the Germans broke in and grabbed her.

Where was Anne?

The rooms held overturned furniture, a slashed leather sofa, shards of porcelain littering the floor. Isabelle bent, and by the light of her torch she retrieved the broken piece of a blue-and-white plate. Turning it over in her hands, she saw what remained of the stamp, *Limoges.* Fine bone china, the very best.

She wandered as if in a trance from room to room, trying to imagine where a child might be hidden. The armoire doors stood gaping open, the clothes lying in messy piles on the floor. Room after room, eviscerated.

But no child.

And with each step, a voice warned, *Be careful! It's time to leave.*

When Isabelle saw the cave door open and entered the empty cellar, she knew. They had come and taken the child, had taken them all.

She vomited, then fled through the andro_nes as the sun peeked through the passageways, twisting and turning, confusing anyone who might be watching, confusing herself as well.

Isabelle forced herself to concentrate on one last task as she hurried through the empty streets of the old town, tiptoeing down the short androne called Sainte-Claire to the street behind the church where the town library was located. She took the key, opened the heavy wooden door to the ancient building, slipped inside, then closed the door and locked it. In the dark, she walked between shelves of books to her father's office, located at the back of the building. As she let herself inside with another key, she caught her breath, inhaling memories. Papa's office still smelled of old books, old leather, and kindness.

His huge wooden desk was piled with papers and books that gave the impression of disorder. But Papa had been meticulous, always planning ways to distract the enemy. On the floor to the left of the desk, she moved several thick encyclopedias, precariously stacked on top of several smaller volumes, and lifted the single floorboard underneath, which was a compartment where the data sheets with the children's information were hidden in a small metal box. With a tiny brass key, she unlocked the box and retrieved the stack of documents secured together with twine.

After placing the documents inside the hidden pocket of her satchel, Isabelle locked and replaced the metal box, the wooden floorboard and then the haphazard-looking stack of books. She opened the desk's lap drawer and took out one more thing—her father's copy of *The Little Prince*. She locked the office and the library and rushed across the cobblestones, the city still asleep.

At last, out of breath, she let herself inside her apartment building, pushing open the beautiful thick wooden door with the ancient knocker, entering the cool hallway with its wall of wooden mailboxes, unlocking the tiny lock to her box with trembling fingers, expecting nothing but hoping for something.

A single white envelope lay inside.

Grabbing it, she locked the wooden box and took the well-worn stairs two at a time up three flights, which gave way to six apartments. With the second key she unlocked her apartment door, the only home she'd known since Maman had passed away when she was only eight. Straight ahead, a narrow hallway led to four small rooms, and off to the left was the salon, offering a breathtaking view of the village and the Citadel.

The apartment looked the same. No evidence of compromise. She sank to the cool tiles, ripped open the envelope, and read the note scribbled in Ginette's hand:

Every one of the peaches was rotten, and the gardener was furious. He was determined to take the whole crop to market. He believes the strawberries are still in season, but they are not. I left a bottle of wine in the cave for you. I knew you would appreciate it.

Ginette

Isabelle swallowed hard. This was again the code that she and Ginette had perfected. Ginette had managed to retrieve most of the children on her list before Tomas or another German got there. But they were on the prowl and still hunting for other children. Ginette would fetch the strawberries, those last children on her list. And wine! Wine meant that a child was in their cave. Had Ginette already found little Anne? She must have felt it wasn't safe to try to bring her to the camp for some reason and hidden her in the cave.

She rushed down the steps, flashlight in hand.

Was this the last child from the Network who needed rescuing? She was doing Protestant penance again, asking God to forgive her for involving her papa in the Resistance, even though she knew he had willingly volunteered. Save the children, and then what? It didn't matter. The Allies were coming. Maybe the tide would turn, as they said. Maybe the war would end, the horror of it all.

She found little Anne, asleep, huddled in a corner of the cave, under piles of old blankets. Isabelle awakened her, half carrying her up the three flights of stairs and into the apartment where she tucked her into Ginette's bed.

Once again, she tossed and turned throughout the night, clutching *The Little Prince* by Antoine Saint-Exupéry, her father's hero. While at camp, Mme Nicolas had told her that Saint-Exupéry's plane had disappeared. The great pilot and author, the one who brought Papa back to life after Maman was lost!

She remembered her lovely mother's face, contorted with pain, her cries, deep, bloodcurdling, unnatural to her young ears. The midwife's voice, alarmed, shouting for more towels, her father pacing. At eight years old, Isabelle rushed in unnoticed, watching through her fingers as the baby, a perfect little boy, slid into the world. He was blue. And then her mother slid out of the world as silently as the baby entered. At the sight of her tiny lifeless son, Maman had died of a broken heart. This Isabelle knew, even though the midwife had said it was the hemorrhaging that took her mother.

The Great War had stolen Papa's soul, and Maman's and her baby brother's deaths had stolen his heart. But it had solidified the bond of love between her father and herself. They lost themselves in books and in each other and in Mass.

And her father lost himself in the writings of Saint-Exupéry.

Shut up in the library, Papa read and reread his philosophical musings, stories that had won awards, made Saint-Exupéry a hero for France, a literary star who was also a man of perpetual action. An intellectual with a pilot's drive to climb higher and higher and higher. In fact, he plummeted from the sky again and again during his lifetime, crashing and being reborn.

As a teen she had found his books confusing. But she too thanked God for Saint-Exupéry because his life and writings had given Papa another way to live.

And then only last year, Papa had received the thin, dog-eared volume she held in her hands. *Le Petit Prince.*

The Little Prince.

France had mourned their beloved pilot when he was exiled to America in 1940 as France came under the Nazi regime. His works banned in France, he spoke out freely in the US and Canada against the Nazis, calling for the Americans to enter the war. And at some point during Saint-Exupéry's three-year exile, he penned a children's story for adults and included his own watercolor illustrations. A French publisher in America had published it just last year, 1943, in English and in French.

Somehow, Papa had procured a copy, not an easy thing to do during wartime, when books were as much a luxury as meat and good wine. Papa had received it, smuggled in like contraband, from someone whom Isabelle now suspected was Monsieur Christensen, the American missionary who seemed in some ways larger than life, like the author Saint-Exupéry.

Papa read it over and over. *The Little Prince* fell from the sky, from his planet, even as Saint-Exupéry had often fallen from the sky in his many plane crashes. And survived.

But now the author had not survived. It was all over the news in between coded messages for the Resistance and the Maquis: *Beloved author and pilot lost at sea. Saint-Exupéry's plane disappears.*

Only ten days after Papa was gunned down, Saint-Exupéry fell from the sky for the last time. Where he fell was not known, only that he was on a reconnaissance mission in North Africa for General Eisenhower.

How could he be gone? Again and again, he had come back from the ashes of a crash, and this last time he had come back from exile in America to serve his country, this brave and battered man, forty-three years old, determined to continue his battle with the sky and the planets and the Earth and the enemies and the minds of men.

Thinking of Saint-Exupéry, Isabelle could almost see the deep compassion in her father's eyes, could almost feel the comfort of his arms around her, embracing her, warm, loving; could smell that familiar odor of books and ink, could hear his soft voice encouraging her. *"You can do it, Izzie. You can."* He was not gone; he was with her still, whispering in the wind and in the pages of a well-worn book.

Isabelle thanked God for Papa and Maman and her baby brother and St. Saint-Exupéry and little Anne, sleeping in the bed across the room. Tucking *The Little Prince* under her pillow, she slept.

PART II

18

❖

PETER

D-Day—Provence
August 15, 1944
4:00 a.m.

Peter gripped the railing of the *Nevada*, trying to calm his stomach, which threatened to upend whatever had settled there the previous evening. D-Day. It was time. Somewhere in the distance lay St. Tropez, Ste. Maxime, and St. Raphaël. Peter knew the hope for this day on the "beaches of the Saints," as he thought of them, was to open a second front in France. In the Mediterranean. But first they must destroy the 19th German Army, which was defending the south of France. Then, after liberating the Saints, the Americans were to push toward the Rhône Valley while the French Liberation Army targeted the ports of Toulon and Marseille. How easily it could be summed up in a sentence or two. How hard it would be to implement.

He'd heard the plans for weeks now, explained by lieutenants and generals clad in their decorated uniforms. *"Ultimately, our men in the south will join the Allies coming from Normandy."*

He turned in a circle, and on every side, all but hidden in the dark, were ships of every type and size—French, American, British—bobbing off the coast of southern France. The whitecaps of the Mediterranean painted the surface of the sea in crests of cream not unlike the stars that shimmered above. And all night long, beginning at midnight, he had heard the steady drone of the planes filled with thousands of Allied paratroopers, swooping inland to strike the German ground troops who were moving toward the main assault areas on the beaches. Hundreds, maybe thousands of airborne troops parachuted to their predetermined drop zones, not far from the beach called Fréjus. Just pinpricks in the distance, they looked like giant flocks of birds, poised in flight, then dropping to the earth.

Soon the first Allied soldiers would set foot on the beaches of Provence in the first day of Operation Dragoon.

Dragooned, thought Peter. Originally the term stood for mounted soldiers, cavalrymen, of which this military siege would have none from the Allies. Now the word meant to pressure or coerce, and General Patch had explained the name with a lift of his eyebrow and a tilt of his chin.

"That stubborn oaf, Churchill! He opposed the operation till its last breath, finally conceding by muttering that he'd been dragooned into the operation."

Yes, well, thought Peter, *haven't we all?* All these precious lives, coerced to continue the fight to free Europe from a madman. And the main invasion force was the 7th Army, led by General Patch, with the goal of getting the men, all eighty thousand of them, to the Saints' beaches.

Pray for us, dear saintly beaches! Pray for us, mothers and fathers, lying wide-eyed in your beds in a farmhouse in Iowa, in Georgia, in New York. Pray for us, resistants, hiding in the hills, watching, waiting. Pray for us! Pray for General Patch and pray for Lieutenant General Truscott, who is leading the 6th Corps infantry to the beaches.

And pray for Frank, who is still in no shape to get off the boat.

Peter felt a flicker of fear in his gut. As much as he had longed to get off the boat at dawn with the first debarking soldiers, now, without Frank, he had no desire to leave the ship, period. He prayed again for the soldiers who would soon step off the ship.

Have mercy, Lord. Hold us fast.

19

RENÉ

5:00 A.M.

The Allies are coming. Destroy more bridges to prevent the Germans' retreat.

After only a few hours of sleep, early on the morning of August 15, the Resistance had received messages from the BBC and gave the order for general mobilization. Thousands of maquisards along the southern coast and farther inland had watched the parachutes descend.

"They were floating like heavenly umbrellas from the sky," Gabriel reported, that devilish smile on his face. "But we know they're delivering weapons and explosives to blast the gates of hell."

René felt the energy pumping around the small circle of men. D-Day!

Gabriel was smoking and pacing as he listened on his radio to the communiqué and then spat it out to the men. "Word coming in from the other Maquis is that our acts of sabotage have been successful in distracting the Germans. Massive railroad interruptions, many bridges damaged and now impassible. The Boches' communication network has been disrupted.

"The Allies are going to avoid the Rhône Valley and head directly this way, east, because it's less fortified by the Germans. You've done your work well, men. The Germans are confused.

"Two more bridges to destroy this morning. Les Mées and Château Arnaux. As you found out yesterday"—Gabriel nodded toward René—"we know there are many Germans patrolling, and it will be difficult to maneuver. Cramped spaces. I'm going to need you to put the explosives under that bridge. Antoine and Etienne will go too.

"They're asking us to demolish them before the Allies land on the southern beaches. Every escape route for the Germans must be cut off. The Allies have already started their aerial flights with paratroopers. If we cannot destroy these bridges on foot, they will do it by air. But it may destroy a lot more than a bridge."

René felt a combination of excitement and terror. Yesterday's close call left him literally gun-shy. Driving a German truck into enemy territory, climbing on a bridge, and planting explosives no longer sounded like an exciting adventure. More like a death threat.

But although Gabriel could not bring himself to admit that he appreciated René's size and cunning, his instructions made it clear.

The men watched as Gabriel continued pacing. Calculating. Fire in his eyes. "The bridge in Les Mées first. Go now. Immediately."

The sun was rising, peeking over the Penitents as Antoine, Etienne, and René rushed out of the grotto, hurrying to the first bridge only minutes away in Les Mées.

René wiggled through the tunnel and climbed under the bridge, attaching the explosives by light of the torch Antoine held. Hanging by his hands from one of the steel partitions, then crawling through the claustrophobic space with only a railing above and the river below, René worked feverishly to plant the explosives while Antoine and Etienne kept watch. Hanging upside down, he saw a German guard at the other end of the bridge.

Heart hammering in his chest, he wriggled under the partitions, attaching the explosives, hearing Antoine yelling, "Get out!"

177

Hand over hand he climbed as if on monkey bars to the east end of the bridge and landed with a splash in the shallow water at the edge. He paused, listening for the sound of gunfire, like yesterday. Nothing.

He clambered up the incline, grabbing Antoine's hand, even as their eyes met, terror and resolve in both.

As daylight broke, they raced down the avenue to where the recuperated German truck was hidden in the bushes. René glanced back as Etienne pushed the lever and the sparks flew. The explosion lit up the bridge and the faces of the Penitent monks who looked on mournfully from just beyond.

20

PETER

6:00 A.M.

Peter watched as thousands of soldiers slowly, methodically descended the rope ladders from the *Nevada* onto the smaller boats that would take them to shore. They looked alike, each in uniform—the helmet, the heavy knapsack, the rifle.

Troops.

Individuals. Precious souls.

As each soldier stepped off the boat onto the rope ladders, the chaplains touched their uniforms and prayed over them, "Lord, have mercy" on their lips. Many of these soldiers had attended the midnight mass or three a.m. prayer vigil the chaplains had led just hours earlier.

On and on, the men continued disembarking the ship, climbing down the ropes into the small vessels called Higgins boats, which allowed for fast troop deployment on beaches during amphibious landings. The firing went on from shore and from the battleships as the scuttles carried the men to shore in a haze of smoke. The difference from the Normandy invasion, Peter had heard, was that here on these beaches, the Germans did not have the advantage of cliffs.

As dawn broke over the Mediterranean, Peter thought of the euphemisms used to describe war, such as "troops lost" and "casualties suffered." He had been good at riddles, math and statistics, and in his mind, after every battle, he calculated and compared. But here on the *Nevada*, as the hours passed and his hands rested on each "troop," as he murmured each name, his eyes meeting those of the fresh-faced young men who had just days earlier knelt in tears by his side and confessed their feelings of terror, Peter could not think in terms of statistics or percentages.

He thought only one by one.

For each individual, he breathed a prayer, "Lord, have mercy." For each frightened soldier, a touch of kindness, a meeting of the eyes to imbue courage. And when the last soldier had stepped onto the rope ladder, swinging briefly above the sea before descending into a Higgins boat that dipped and floated toward the distant shore, Peter felt the weight of it all descend on his whole self. Until that very moment, he had been buoyed up by the Spirit, strengthened by the urgency of the moment, carried along by that power that was greater than the evil in the world.

But now he sank to his haunches, his body and soul heavy with the souls of a thousand men in grave peril. He watched and waited with binoculars trained on the shore, all the while praying, *Lord, have mercy. Hold us fast.*

21

ISABELLE

7:00 A.M.

Isabelle watched out the second-story window of her apartment as the sun cast a golden hue on the imposing mountain of La Baume, looming like a giant friend just outside the window in the salon, across from the Durance River. She moved to the window, opened it, and looked to the left, where the beloved Citadel sat proud and silent in the distance, perched on the rock directly across from La Baume.

These two rock formations had marked her childhood, had given her such comfort when Papa had found this refuge and moved the two of them here after they lost Maman and the baby.

She loved the stories Papa had recounted, that many millennia ago the rock of the Citadel and the Baume were all one. But as the ice melted and expanded, the mountains were cracked in two and left the wide Durance River between them. How the rock of La Baume, with its vertical limestone strata and folds, was famous throughout the world. How geologists came from far and wide to study this curiosity.

And she had studied it every day.

They never moved, always greeting her every morning when she was a child, as she slathered butter and homemade blackberry jam on her baguette and sipped the *chocolat chaud* from a big bowl, leaving the telltale dark mustache above her lips. She would lean out the window and greet her monumental friends, then wave down to the red tiled roofs in the village.

"Bonjour, bridge," she whispered to the Pont de la Baume, the wide stone bridge that permitted passage from La Baume's eastern side to the west, where the center of town stood with the Citadel watching over them all. Every view of Sisteron pleased her.

Tall cedars stood in the foreground, just across the street, and the steeple of the cathedral peeked above the trees. She loved the old Romanesque church, considered it a friend as well, a friend she visited with Papa every Sunday for Mass.

How she had loved running through the narrow streets, up and down the steep androges, zigzagging from one street to another, playing hide-and-seek with Ginette and other children of the neighborhood.

Now Isabelle stared out the window and let the tears stream down her face. Time to leave, before the city woke up. But even as she thought it, her heart raced. A young German walked in the street below. She cowered to the side of her window as he turned to stare up at her building.

Tomas!

Why didn't he just come up and arrest her or do something worse? Why did he keep baiting her, teasing the hope and courage out of her soul? Perhaps it was to confuse her. She sank to the floor. Now the tears were of fear. Once again she was playing hide-and-seek, only the consequences now were life and death.

She woke young Anne and silently slipped out the back of the apartment, bidding it farewell. But instead of uncovering the hidden bicycle, setting the child in front of her and peddling as fast as she could away from Sisteron, she slipped down the cement stairs with the child and into the cave.

"I'm sorry, but you must hide in here again until it's dark outside. Then we can escape."

Eyes round, the child nodded, brown curls bobbing on her face. Hunted like an animal, she had not said a word, clutching at Isabelle until she fell into a restless sleep. As she sat in the cave, where only days before Delphine had hidden, Isabelle thought she could see through the child. Anne was trying to be invisible.

"I'm coming back. Soon."

22

PETER

10:00 A.M.

The men crowded around the radio on the ship, listening to the first reports. "Landings on time. Enemy opposition light. Beach operations going better than expected for a daytime assault . . ."

The general looked pleased. "The men are getting to the beaches to secure them. It's time to send in what's left of the equipment and supplies, to reorganize and advance north."

Three chaplains had already been deployed with the troops, but the general's command was that one chaplain remain on the battleship until late afternoon.

Peter didn't mind doing so. It would give him time to get to know his new assistant, who stood before him.

"Lieutenant Lee Johnson reporting for duty, sir." The young man saluted. Instead of Frank's blond hair and blue eyes, Lee's hair was black and his eyes dark, brooding. He cleared his throat. "I mean, Chaplain Christensen."

Peter held out his hand. "Good to meet you, Lee. You can call me Ginger—that's what all the other boys call me."

Lee's brow furrowed, and he tilted his head for a brief second with a frown.

"The men call me Ginger," Peter clarified, "because of the hair." He lifted his hat. He couldn't tell if Lee even glanced his way.

All through the morning, Lee stood stiffly, his eyes darting around the boat, as if the enemy were hiding right behind them.

Peter tried to generate conversation without much success. Lee was twenty and came from Idaho. When he asked, "Where have you served?" Lee's face darkened. "This is my first mission, sir. Chaplain." He took a deep breath but stood erect. "But I've been through the training program for protecting chaplains back in the States. Lieutenant Jamison has instructed me too. I'll look after you, sir. You can trust me."

Peter gave a weak smile. "Of course."

But how could Peter trust someone he didn't know? Never had Lee come to his room to ask for prayer, share fears, or look at comics. He hadn't played in the soccer tournament or sung in the men's chorale. Peter had had no interaction with him at all.

"Keeps to himself a lot," Andy had confided.

He was young, serious, aloof. Doubtless a good soldier.

This is his first mission.

Peter felt that flicker of fear again. He knew everything about Frank, and Frank about him. They could read each other's body language. They'd laughed together, cried together. He'd been excited to get to shore, to be with the men, but now he doubted.

Now was not the time to be afraid.

Hold us fast, Lord. Please.

The good news kept trickling in all day.

Two German divisions entirely crippled. More than 2,000 POWs taken. Allied casualties relatively light.

By midmorning the gliders corps had arrived at the Le Muy area, the tanks for the infantry had arrived on shore, and they too began their push forward as others cleared the quick access routes from the beaches north for the passage of infantry, artillery, and armored units.

As the afternoon progressed, General Patch issued a special order. "Keep advancing. The enemy is perplexed and stunned. They're being kept off-balance by artillery fire. They're becoming disoriented. The opportunity for decisive results is just ahead of us."

23

ISABELLE

NOON

Throughout the endless morning, Tomas and another SS officer patrolled in front of her apartment. Where was Ginette? Had she been captured and tortured? Would the Germans at any moment rush up the stairs and find her?

Stomach in knots, she waited.

Finally at noon she risked going to the mailbox to see if there was more communication. When she opened the little wooden box, she stared at a single piece of paper as if it were a hallucination, then grabbed it, locked the box, and ran up the stairs again. Only when she had bolted the door did she dare read what Ginette had scrawled, surely only a few hours ago. Two identical phrases: *Le chasseur est affamé. Le chasseur est affamé.*

It was happening. The signal. The invasion was happening. All would be well. Soon.

She glanced down from the apartment window. No sign of Tomas, of anyone at all on her street. But beyond, she saw people strolling the cobbled streets. She was amazed by the calm of the city when her heart was racing. She did not have a radio here, but the rest of the city would be huddled around their radios, and they'd hear the announcement that the Allied troops had landed near St. Raphaël. She could almost hear their collective cheers: *The saints are with us! And soon the Allies!*

She imagined the whispered conversations at Café de la Tante. *It's a lovely summer afternoon. We've heard about Normandy, and now the rumor—O God, let it be the truth!—of an Allied landing in Provence.*

How that would revive spirits. After the fatigue of war, people were regaining hope, courage to take a stroll in the countryside. Some teenaged girls were even bathing on the outskirts of the Buëch River, just as she had done each summer as a child.

She felt it, fear mixed with joy. On this magnificent summer day, finally there was joy. A beautiful summer day, like those of her childhood, yes, but this day was different. After all they had been through, the citizens of Sisteron, the citizens of France—today's sun would bring not only warmth to bodies and hearts, but hope.

Hope! An imminent liberation.

All she had to do was keep out of sight today and then, tonight, with the child on the handlebars, she'd peddle to The Camp Between the Hills.

24

RENÉ

2:00 P.M.

Antoine looked up from where he was crouched by the radio, concern on his face. "News is that the Allied planes are on the way. They will be carrying out a systematic bombardment of the bridges over the course of the Durance and the Verdon Rivers. In Sisteron they are hoping to destroy the Baume bridge, the Buëch bridge, and the railway viaduct, which will block the retreat of the Boches."

High on the rocky incline on the east side of the Durance River, René absorbed his brother's report, admiring the Citadel fortress across the valley and below the thick ancient ramparts of La Porte du Dauphiné.

Ici un pays finit, un autre commence. Here one country ends, and another begins. He had grown up hearing this phrase. The Gate of Dauphiné separated, symbolically and literally, the passage between Dauphiné to the north and Provence to the south, between the Alps and the sea. On this side of the Durance, La Baume rose to his right. René could almost reach out and touch the limestone wonder with its vertical striated indentions. Sisteron boasted two wonders, the Citadel and La Baume. And the Pont de la Baume, the ancient bridge that connected the two, provided passage across the wide river.

In the shadow of La Baume, Antoine and Etienne were perched above la Route Napoléon, the infamous road that Napoléon Bonaparte had taken in 1815, a road that passed straight through Sisteron. René had heard the story countless times. The exiled emperor escaping from the island of Elba and riding toward Paris with a thousand of his men, his greatest worry being the Citadel in Sisteron, its fortifications, its army. But the authorities of Sisteron, though Royalists for the most part, had surprisingly given Napoléon the equivalent of a blink and a shrug and let the emperor and his men pass through without opposition.

But the Allies would not blink and let retreating Germans follow in the footsteps of the emperor. The bridge must be destroyed.

René recalled Gabriel's warning from that morning: *"The Allies have already started their aerial flights with paratroopers. If we cannot destroy these bridges on foot, they will do it by air. But it may destroy a lot more than a bridge."*

Could he slink down the mountainside and onto the bridge in broad daylight?

Buoyed by the successful downing of the bridges in Les Mées and Château Arnaux earlier that day, René said, "I'm going down."

"No, you're not. These bridges aren't our job," Antoine countered. "Our job is to create roadblocks on this side of the river in case any Germans still make it across."

"Anyway, we can't blow up the bridges in the middle of the day," Etienne said. "Too many people milling about. Too risky for many reasons. The Boches have eyes, and it's a sunny day."

René gave a nod and observed the red tiled roofs of the city, the church steeple, the cream-colored buildings, all ancient and beautiful. From his position they rose, some of them five or six stories high, like miniature towers, while others were square and block-like, tucked side by side or stacked, as they appeared from his position—row upon row, one behind the other, rising in a gradual pitch across the city.

René watched through his binoculars as the townspeople moved about like tiny toy figurines, insouciant, enjoying a lazy summer afternoon in Sisteron. Children bathed by the riverbank of the Buëch, the tributary of the Durance. And beyond that, the Buëch bridge.

"Another message," Antoine said. "The Allies are on their way. We need to find cover. Now." He grabbed René's arm. "Let's go."

As the three boy-men shrank into the crevices of La Baume, they heard the deep droning of airplanes before they saw them. René felt impending disaster in every part of him as the American planes drew closer and closer.

25

PETER

3:00 P.M.

Peter sat in the Higgins boat with Lee Johnson, the young assistant, who peered toward the beaches. It was finally time to join the men onshore. The enemy firing had quelled, and small fires could be seen all along the coast, though he couldn't tell if they were the soldiers' campfires or the result of the day's battle.

"Ready, sir?" Lee asked, grabbing his thick backpack and rifle as they prepared to debark.

Peter nodded. His assistant looked confident, but Peter felt his gut cramping.

Calm down. You can trust him.

All was quiet except for the low humming of the engine as the small boat brought them to shore. Peter's boots left prints in the wet sand as he followed Lee across the beach, searching for cover. Lee motioned for him to squat down and follow him as he listened to the walkie-talkie.

Everything was quiet. So quiet.

Would a German appear from behind a dune? Would one of them step on a land mine?

Rifle fire rang out in the distance. They crouched together, finding cover behind the shrubs and dunes. "Sir, move along. That's right. Watch where you step. Follow me. Hurry."

Frank, what am I supposed to do?

Trust.

Peter heard gunfire nearby. He threw himself onto the ground, hands covering his helmet, heart racing.

"Sir, come on! We gotta move, and fast." Lee reached for Peter's hand, pulling him up.

Peter couldn't make his body move.

"Sir, we need to get to the dunes over there. I've got you covered."

Lee was beside him on the ground on his belly, firing off a round of ammunition as he screamed, "We can't stay here on the beach!"

Move, Peter. Trust!

But Peter felt frozen with fear.

Lee shouted, "Ginger! You're okay. I promised Frank I'd take care of you."

Something broke through his terror at the sound of his nickname, and Peter scurried in front of Lee into the dunes and then behind a line of trees.

Lee seated himself in the sand in front of Peter, checked his compass, and took out the walkie-talkie. "Our guys are two hundred yards up and to the east, sir. They're sending men down to cover for us."

When Peter didn't react, Lee reached over and shook his shoulder. "Ginger, you're okay. Our boys are coming for us. Take some deep breaths. That's right . . ."

Minutes later, as several GI's motioned them forward and stayed to throw grenades, Lee ran ahead of Peter, glancing back every few steps to make sure he was following. As they weaved in and out of the trees, Peter saw them.

Two corpses. Both German.

Then Peter heard moaning nearby. He called to Lee, "Someone's injured. I need to check it out."

"You can't go over there. If it's the enemy, he may still be able to use his gun."

From the ghoulish sounds he was making, Peter imagined the injured soldier was near death. "I'm sorry, Lee. I have to."

He found a German boy propped against a tree, his chest soaked in blood. Peter knelt beside the injured soldier. "Don't worry, son. We'll take care of you," he said in French.

"Merci," came the feeble reply.

Lee came beside him. "Gotta leave him, sir. He ain't gonna make it."

The German officer had his men carry Peter to the medic tent, where they treated his wounds and sent doctors to help their wounded.

"He might," said Peter.

Peter splashed water from his canteen on his face. "Thank you, Lee. You saved my life. I'm sorry about that. Don't know what caused me to freeze up like that."

The young lieutenant blinked and nodded. "Just doing my job, sir." He ran his hands over his face, covered in sweat, and took a long breath. "Trying to calm my heart down." He took long gulps from his canteen. Finally, Lee said, "It was brave what you did too—saving this German."

Peter shook his head. "I don't know if I was brave, but like you, I was just doing my job."

"It's a hard job. Going into battle with no weapon."

"I trust my assistant." He met the lieutenant's eyes. "You did fine out there, Lee."

A tiny smile wavered on his lips as he said, "Thank you, Ginger."

Together they carried the wounded German two hundred yards to where thirty-three men from the platoon greeted them and the dying enemy.

26

ISABELLE

4:00 P.M.

When the sirens sounded precisely at snack time, four p.m., Isabelle stiffened, then felt relief. Another alert, just like the many that had sounded in Sisteron for the past few months. Just practicing.

She heard the drone of airplane engines and hurried to the window, peering up at the sky where, far in the distance, hordes of them were flying north toward the city. Not practicing, for today was another D-Day. Like the one in Normandy just two months ago.

The protocol after a siren sounding was that the city's inhabitants must limit their movements and stay close to the shelters. Isabelle rushed through the apartment, gathering a few belongings and her father's copy of *The Little Prince*. Once again at the window, she glanced up and saw them: countless American planes, heading their way.

The Allies were coming. How often had Tito reminded them that Sisteron possessed a strategic interest for the Allies. The RN85, the main national route from Cannes to Grenoble, passed precisely through the narrow streets of Sisteron. Tito had said just the other day, "*Once the Allies have landed on the beaches, it will be up to the aircraft and to us to cut off access so that the one hundred sixty Germans stationed here in Sisteron can't retreat, and so the thousands of other Germans approaching from the south can't get through either.*"

Soldiers like Tomas. She shivered and thought of him being captured. How she longed for this.

"*We'll do what we can on the ground, but the Allied bombers will do much of the work. With the help of the Maquis, they'll destroy the three bridges in the city,*" Tito had told them during their last meeting.

Isabelle shaded her eyes as the planes drew nearer, like enormous black geese heading south for the winter. Yet these geese were heading north. Friendly geese. The Allies were finally here!

Their dull roar sounded louder, more insistent as they flew closer. And then something was falling from the sky. It looked like the huge black geese were dropping enormous white eggs on the city!

Isabelle blinked, then clutched her throat.

Non! It couldn't be!

Bombs falling, hundreds of them, an avalanche of bombs raining down on Sisteron . . .

The sound! The cacophony!

Isabelle's hands flew to her ears. She watched, stunned, from the second-story apartment as across the way she saw the bell on the church tower blown off.

"*Non!*" she screamed.

They kept coming for what seemed like hours. More and more bombs, right outside the window. She could reach out and touch them, grab one, grab a hundred.

Help! Stop! You've missed the target. Not the town . . .

On and on the geese flew as Isabelle watched in dismay, frozen in place like the Penitents, cursed to watch the destruction of her beloved city.

The same view, so peaceful and calm only an hour ago, now resembled a horror film. Her screams were piercing, her hands waving high in the air as the Citadel, the king's best fortress, shuddered, and she watched in disbelief as a massive portion of the fortress was blasted away, crumbled, and came crashing to the ground far below.

People were out in the streets now, though their screams were muffled by wave after wave of bombs, again and again, pounding the city. Not destroying bridges but decimating the city. In a daze she watched the bomb that fell on the church.

Leave the apartment! Get Anne out!

The people's shrieks were drowned out by the explosions, but the shrillest of them, piercing, continuous, racked her mind, and she covered her ears. Only then did she realize that the sound was billowing up from inside her soul.

Isabelle stood numb, staring across the way to La Baume with its high, craggy cliffs that knew stories of both glory and tragedy. Today would be its worst story yet. She had no strength left to even sob.

Move! Why would her feet not move?

In the distance, the smoke rose like the last whiffs of a smoldering campfire, extinguished by a group of rowdy Scouts. But it was no Scout that had caused the blazing flames that leapt above the wisps of smoke, nor was it Hitler's men. It was those great black birds from the Allies, dumping bombs on the poor city of Sisteron. First the church, then the Citadel crumbled in pieces, like the tiny clay buildings that populated the *crèche* in every French home at Christmastime.

Go!

On wooden legs she left the apartment, tripping down the stairway and then through the door into the cave, where little Anne cowered. She threw herself over the child, holding her, rocking and crying out for mercy.

Fifteen minutes, twenty, on and on the bombing continued, the explosions reverberating in the cave. Would it also crumble on top of them, trapping them forever?

Finally, silence.

She waited precious minutes. No sounds, no sirens, no light. Nothing. And Anne, huddled in a ball, never made a sound, as if she had literally been frightened to death.

27

RENÉ

4:00 P.M.

The skies, so clear and blue earlier, suddenly grew cloudy. One minute René was watching girls bathing in the river, and the next, bombs were falling from the mass of planes filling the sky. The sound was all-encompassing, numbing, rebounding, again and again, so that he threw his hands over his ears.

Across the way, the Citadel was struck, and one side crumbled. Then the spire on the church toppled to the ground, fire and smoke surrounding it. René did not know when he started screaming, but he knew when he stopped twenty minutes later when the sky, black with smoke and fire, grew quiet. He looked beside him, dumbfounded. Etienne was shaking, Antoine crying. Then the three of them ran toward the Pont de la Baume. The Allies' bombs had struck the bridge, yet it was still passable. But across the river, the massive Port of Dauphiné was gone. That ancient gate between two regions was completely destroyed.

They sprinted across the bridge and into the city. Would they be shot down by the enemy or shattered by another Allied bomb?

When they arrived at what had been Rue Saunerie, they stared at great heaps of wreckage, the houses totally leveled.

René's head ached, and his eyes swam. At first they were greeted by silence, the city stunned beyond words. But then people emerged from buildings, all of them with the same shell-shocked looks on their faces, trembling, white ash covering them so that they resembled ghosts. Amid the buzzing in his ears, René read lips.

"*Au secours! Help!*"

"*Aidez-nous*, s'il vous plaît."

"Maman, where is Maman?"

René had been prepared for death. It had knocked him down, terrified him, broken his heart, but he knew it, had experienced it with Maman, Dominique, Frédéric, Jean-Paul, Sébastien. Gilles. All dead. But each of them had known the danger, had counted the cost of resistance.

René was not prepared for what he saw before him. Total devastation, the blue sky with its stifling summer heat now filled with smoke. Fires everywhere. And endless screaming. On autopilot, Antoine, Etienne, and René began to clear the passageway. They joined others who wandered in the rubble with a dazed look on their faces, as if just leaving the cinema after a horror film, only to step into a horror scene in real life.

He knew that Isabelle had returned to Sisteron yesterday to retrieve one last child. Was she still here, somewhere in the catastrophe that was once a road which meandered peacefully up to the Citadel?

28

ISABELLE

5:00 P.M.

Everywhere there was smoke and fire as Isabelle stumbled through the wreckage. The Porte du Dauphiné, that wide, old, thick vestige, had simply disappeared. Several children huddled in the debris, hands plastered over their ears. It looked as though the whole city lay in ruins.

"The wedding!" sobbed a woman. "They were in the church when the bombs fell. The wedding, the bride and groom . . ." She was heaving and hyperventilating, not even realizing that her head had been gashed.

Among the rubble, Isabelle caught sight of Ginette. Her friend stumbled toward her, walking through the remains of a bombed building, her face covered in grime where tears had mingled with the soot.

"Zabelle!"

They fell into each other's arms, speaking words that were muffled as their ears rang and hummed, deafened by the exploding bombs.

"Anne?" Ginette mouthed.

Isabelle nodded.

Ginette stared at Isabelle blankly, tilting her head. "Our apartment?"

"Untouched. Anne is okay."

But that truth, while comforting, did nothing to abate the immensity of the destruction around them. What was one child amid such suffering? How many citizens were buried in the ruins?

Ginette said, "Tito is here, as is Jean-Yves. We'll find someone to take her to the camp."

All afternoon the friends worked in the shadow of the Citadel, now in jutting pieces, the broken heart of the city. Isabelle had rarely seen her dearest friend cry. Ginette was sturdy and as true as they came. But as they stood at the head of Rue Saunerie, where Ginette had grown up, and observed the flattened houses, Ginette sank to the ground and wailed.

A silent fog of disbelief hovered over the citizens of Sisteron as they worked removing the injured, carrying them to a first-aid tent set up by the river. There, women improvised, using their nursing skills, stitching, bandaging, calling out for buckets of water when there was none to be had. Already the city's one hospital was overrun with the wounded.

Men and women of every age picked their way through the destruction, helping in any way possible. Ginette and Isabelle found lone children and walked with them to where nurses had set up another tent as a temporary station in the middle of the square where the town bell had welcomed all. Now it lay in a heap beside the tent.

Once again there would be orphans. Precious children who had witnessed their parents buried under tons of rubble would be alone.

"The smoke, the thick black smoke rose up," a girl of about nine or ten was saying. "That's when we realized what was happening. Papa was working at the paper mill, and the whole staff was called on to rescue the injured and clear the town."

A young boy held on to Isabelle and screamed. An older boy, his cousin, shook his head. "He doesn't understand. I cannot understand. We saw it, we watched the bombs, but it was surreal. Before this day, the only view we had of the war was of a German soldier guarding the access to our road."

Another little boy cried, "Why did they want to kill us? I thought the good guys were coming. I thought it was their planes. They killed Maman. Maman!"

She found him standing barefoot and bloodied beside a pile of rubble that had been his home.

Even as she worked alongside others to clear the debris and search for survivors, Isabelle found herself glancing up toward the Citadel. If only she were a child again. She closed her eyes and recalled attending her first opera with her father at the Citadel's theater when she was ten. "We watched *Carmen*, Papa and I," she whispered to no one.

During the war years, the theater was used only for the Boches, and the actors were prisoners who once wrote and taught and sang about freedom.

"And now, my beautiful Citadel, along with Maman and Papa and so many I love, you too lie in ruins."

29

RENÉ

6:00 P.M.

Bent over a corpse, trying to dislodge the boulder that blocked the door to an apartment, René heard a hoarse cry.

"René. René!"

Covered in ash, the whites of the eyes lighting up what was surely a face, Isabelle engulfed him, held him. She was trembling. Then mouthing words with no sound. Then stumbling into René's embrace, she spoke in disjointed, nonsensical words. Nothing made sense. Her tears made rivulets in the white ash on her face. She kept repeating, "The child, the child. Anne . . ."

Finally she calmed enough to say, "Anne. In the cave below our apartment, untouched. I watched it from the window! Fire and brimstone, hell coming down on us!"

She clutched his shoulders, and he welcomed the physical pain obliterating for only a few seconds the tragedy before him. He could feel his cousin slipping away. It was impossible to tell if she was wounded, the way she trembled, but he saw blood. "Are you hurt?"

"Only my heart."

"There's blood."

"I wish it was my blood. I wish, but it was . . ."

She tried to clear her throat, but no sound came out.

"Whose blood?"

She shook her head. René let out a sigh. Someone's blood, but she did not know the name. Surely that was better.

But then her eyes met his, that glassy numb stare. "Children's blood. The Dumont family . . ." It caught in her throat, and then she retched and sobbed again. "Ginette and I found the whole family. Mother, father, and three children. Only one child survived."

30

PETER

8:00 P.M.

The sun set in bright flames over the sea as Peter and Lee watched with the other soldiers farther inland. The men were hunkered down in pockets across the beaches, and in the group they joined, the soldiers were grimy but uninjured, almost in a state of shock at the minimal resistance they'd encountered by German troops.

They sat or lay in the sand behind tufts of seaweed or dunes, spent but buoyed up by the success of this first day. The Germans had been surprised, caught off guard, ill-equipped. Many other words, more derogatory, were used. But Peter cared about only one.

Zero.

On the first day, word came across the lines that none of the soldiers from the *Nevada* had been "lost." Even the wounded German was expected to survive.

As the darkness fell, he crouched around the fire with these boys. Not boys. Men now. Even the newer recruits had been transformed in one long day from boys to men. They had prepared and waited and prayed and stepped off the boat into the dark sea, and now they were onshore, the day was done, and there were so few casualties.

Peter felt deep gratitude. He could have been one of the casualties. Lee had talked him out of feeling frozen, panicked.

They all knew the statistics from the massacre at Normandy. Operation Overlord had been successful, but oh so costly. Peter supposed that was the baseline for life. Success cost a lot. Lives. Hope. Courage. It demanded everything, and the soldiers had given everything on this day.

Count the cost. Carry your cross. These metaphors for the Christian life were lived out in the colors of army fatigues and sea waves and cloudy skies today.

Thank You, Father, for holding all of us fast. Just for today.

31

ISABELLE

10:00 P.M.

For the Silo members who had been near Sisteron on D-Day, their sabotage acts were halted as they had rushed into the city. In the long hours after the bombings, Isabelle recognized them by their eyes, their faces as white and covered with ash as hers.

Maurice, Jean-Yves, Jacques.

"We were outside of Les Mées when we saw the bombs falling, and we rushed this way," Maurice explained. "Amandine and Lucy came with us and immediately changed from resistants to nurses. And Tito is here too. Somewhere."

For hours, they continued sorting through the destruction until late into the night. Though the bombs had long stopped falling, Sisteron continued burning all through the night as they and hundreds of other citizens worked around and between the flames that leapt up from pockets of the centre ville.

Numbly they toiled beside neighbors and police and old men and women, the sporadic comments of the citizens all echoing the same disbelief:

"An avalanche of bombs has turned our city into a field of ruins."

"Nothing will ever be the same again."

"Men and women, children and babies, dead. Our friends killed not by the enemy, but by the Allies."

"The soul of our city will forever be marked by this tragedy. The Allies have destroyed our city."

Isabelle, Maurice, Jean-Yves, Ginette, and Jacques now worked side by side. When Isabelle had first found René, she clung to him, forbidding him to leave her sight. As if she had control of anything.

"Why? The Allies bragged on the accuracy and precision of their new bombsights." This came from gentle Maurice.

"Shhh. Stop. You'll only drive yourself crazy," whispered Jean-Yves. "We've had a vision of the apocalypse, but we aren't the first city destroyed by war. We'll follow the example of other cities. We'll be like the phoenix, arising from the pyre of death to be reborn."

"You are such an idealist, Jean-Yves!" Jacques spat. "We don't have time for idealism. The war isn't over. The Germans are retreating from here, but we're needed farther north."

René nodded. "Gabriel is asking the Silo resistants to join us as we move north."

"But how can we leave?" Isabelle could hardly make out her own voice. "It will take days, months to clear . . ."

"That is not our role," Jacques said. "But yes, some must stay. What is the situation with the Jewish children?"

"They're safe in hiding," answered René.

"All but Anne. She's in our cave," Ginette said.

"Then hide her too. For now. See if there is room in this hiding place of yours for the other children who are now—" Maurice paused and cleared his throat—"orphaned."

"I'll go," Ginette offered.

"No, I'll take her," René said.

"I'll join you later." Isabelle's tone was strangely stoic. "But first I'll find Tito and tell him."

An hour later, the smoldering ash burnt her eyes, and Isabelle coughed and choked, the fires in the village their best light as the town searched for their own.

Ginette's scream pierced the quiet, and Isabelle made her way through the smoke and dust to where her friend stood. "Go away, Zabelle. Go away!"

Ginette had a crazed look in her eyes, and she was covered in blood.

"Ginette, you're hurt. Let me help!"

"Go!" she shouted.

Ignoring her friend, Isabelle moved toward her. Then she saw it —Ginette was standing over a body.

"You can't see this! Go away!"

Slowly, Isabelle stepped closer . . .

It was Tito. His large body lay there broken, his deep, beautiful voice forever silenced, his massive hands cradling a small child whom he had sheltered from an explosion with his own body. The child was unconscious, a girl with black curls that were matted against her face.

Isabelle fell to her knees beside Tito's body and wept.

PART III

32

PETER

D-Day+2
August 17, 1944

One.

Peter knelt by the coffin, removed his helmet, placed a hand on the wooden box that was covered with day lilies and end-of-summer roses, fresh flowers placed there by local villagers, plucked from their weary gardens.

He did not know this soldier, but Peter would ensure he received a burial service as Frank and Lee helped him load the coffin onto the jeep.

But there would be no funeral. Not yet.

On D-Day plus two, the platoon was on the move, even as the rumor spread among them, "The enemy is on the retreat!"

Still. One.

A lone coffin, lying on the dirt road on the outskirts of St. Raphaël, had halted the men in their tracks. They removed their helmets, covered with moss and branches of camouflage, their faces streaked black with camouflage paint, and knelt.

213

A soldier from a different platoon had lost his life here, and the villagers testified to their deep appreciation of his sacrifice.

Even as they mourned, General Butler, their new commanding officer, talked about an intercepted message from the German High Command, the code broken in a mere few hours by British cryptologists. The message revealed Hitler's orders for the German army's retreat from southern and southwestern France. Only those forces defending the ports were to stay put.

The first two days of Operation Dragoon had been overwhelmingly successful. The messages and radio announcements resounded throughout the beaches and villages along the coast of southern France. So few casualties. The Germans confused.

The soldiers, on their knees only an hour earlier, let out shouts of delight. "We've got 'em on the run! The Boches are gonna run instead of fight!"

Only yesterday, D-Day plus one, Peter had been appointed one of the chaplains with Task Force Butler, the group named after Brigadier General Butler who would be heading up the division.

"He's a good man," Peter said to Lee. "Frank and I worked alongside him in Tunisia."

"Good to know," Lee said.

Frank had recovered completely and took back his role as Peter's assistant, but Lee had also been recruited for the Task Force.

Peter wondered at this brand-new division, seemingly created overnight by Lieutenant General Truscott, the commander who had led the 6th Corps infantry onto the beaches.

"New information," General Truscott had informed his men. "Since that hard-nosed French General de Gaulle has ordered that we send all the French armored brigade back south to liberate Marseille and Toulon, we've got to round up an all-American mechanized exploitation force of our own to move north."

Though General Truscott sounded none too happy, he assured the men that his deputy, Brigadier General Butler, a West Point engineer who had very recently been involved in the grueling combat in Sicily and Tunisia, was perfect for the job.

General Butler explained, "As I said, Hitler has ordered all his troops to retreat except those guarding the ports. So it's up to Task Force Butler to hightail it toward Lyon, bypassing the Rhône Valley and instead heading east through the Basses-Alpes. Our job is to capture the enemy as they attempt to retreat. We shouldn't have to worry about counterattacks from the east. We've been given priority for vehicles and fuel. Orders are to intercept the fleeing Germans."

Task Force Butler drove forward along the road from St. Raphaël heading north toward Draguignan. As the jeeps bumped over the cobblestones and turned into the centre ville, both sides of the street were lined with cheering women and children and old men, all waving flags.

A young woman rushed up to Peter and kissed him smack on the lips. "Thank you! Thank you!" she cried in her heavily accented English. "Merci!"

The cheering and clapping were unexpected. Peter watched as the villagers rejoiced. It was a celebration of life, of resistance, of newfound freedom. Of hope.

"It's something, ain't it, Ginger? Really something!" Frank slapped Peter on the back. "After North Africa, after Sicily and Rome. This, well, this makes it feel as though the fighting was all worth it."

"It's inexplicable. The feeling. And the look of glee and gratitude on their faces," Andy said, his cheeks turning crimson as he too received a forceful kiss on the lips from a blond woman waving an American flag. He glanced over at Peter. "I'm not telling Judy about the kiss."

Peter winked at him. "No, best not to give your fiancée that news."

One older villager trotted by the jeep and handed Peter a bottle of *eau de vie*. Another lifted a squawking chicken toward them, calling in heavily accented English, "For dinner!"

The stark contrast assaulted Peter, like the piece of shrapnel that had ricocheted through the air in Tunisia, implanting itself in his thigh. Deep pain and great relief. The shrapnel was removed, but for weeks he had walked with a limp. Celebration amid death.

Cheering amid destruction. Joy covering sorrow. Such was the price of war as the Task Force moved north, its jeeps carrying not just living troops but sixteen coffins—the one they'd just retrieved today and fifteen others.

The Allies had watched from the beach in St. Raphaël two days earlier as a lone German plane circled nearby. Only one. Surely there was nothing to fear. But that single plane had dropped one bomb, a bomb which hit its target: a landing ship tank. The LST had been loaded with artillery and ammunition. The explosion rocked the whole beachfront, and the ship burned and smoldered for so long that it took several hours to retrieve the dead. No one on the LST survived.

Yesterday, Peter had explained to General Butler, "The men tried to dig graves in a cemetery we opened there in St. Raphaël, but digging shale rock was all but impossible. We needed TNT to blast the graves, but TNT is reserved for battle. With your permission, sir, we want to ask French officials for their aid in finding a suitable spot for a cemetery. We're bringing the bodies to Draguignan."

Butler had granted permission for Peter to follow the Army's protocol to find or create a cemetery in which to bury the dead. "The Allies have just liberated Draguignan," the general said, hefty eyebrows raised and a rare smile forming. "You speak perfect French. Will you talk with the mayor?"

"Of course."

As the men in the Task Force soaked in the glory—crowds lining the road and cheering the Allies, tossing confetti, singing and dancing and breaking open bottles of champagne—Peter entered the *hôtel de ville*. The town hall was amazingly untouched by the bombs and mortars. He greeted the mayor of Draguignan with a handshake.

"Bonjour, Monsieur le Maire."

The short, stout man with graying hair and bloodshot eyes pumped Peter's hand up and down, then grabbed him by the shoulders and placed a wet kiss on each cheek. "Merci! Merci! We are so grateful!"

Peter resisted the urge to swipe his cheeks and instead nodded, remembering how shocked he had been as a boy when French villagers, both men and women, had greeted him with kisses on the cheek. "Yes, we are grateful as well." He then locked eyes with the mayor. "But I'm afraid I must discuss an urgent matter with you. We need to purchase land for a cemetery so that we can bury our dead."

Thick eyebrows shot up, and the little man's face fell as he expressed his sympathy. "*Mais bien sûr! Toutes mes condoléances!*" He thought for a moment and said, "You can bury them in our own cemetery, sir. It would be an honor to have American soldiers buried beside the French." His eyes glistened with what looked to Peter like a mixture of sorrow and pride.

"Merci, Monsieur le Maire. I deeply appreciate the gesture. Unfortunately, we have too many dead."

The mayor's bloodshot eyes registered surprise and then understanding. "Then my secretary will help you locate a field that will accommodate the number of fallen men."

The mayor motioned to a young man, who rushed up to Peter and grasped his hand, pumping it up and down. "Lieutenant, sir, thank you. Yes, an honor. Of course. Follow me. I am Cyril."

Cyril led Peter to his jeep, jabbering with enthusiasm. "The Allies were fighting here just this morning. Two or three hours ago, they drove those filthy Germans out. We're finally free. *C'est incroyable*! Liberated! *Liberté, Égalité, Fraternité*!"

Peter smiled weakly. Celebration and mourning. Life and death.

By late afternoon they had found a field that would provide easy digging and was surrounded by trees, perched on a hill where silence was broken only by birdsong. When Peter and Cyril returned to the mayor with the necessary papers to purchase the land, the mayor said, "There is no need. The French locals have taken up a collection to buy the land for the cemetery. It is my honor to present this land to the American Army to bury her dead."

The following day, another ceremony began, not with confetti and French flags but with solemn American soldiers standing at

217

attention and a crowd of grateful villagers, who draped the coffins
with flowers and promises to tend the graves.

Frank found Peter sitting in the field, sketchbook in hand, his
opened tin of colored pencils beside him. He was staring past the
newly turned soil, now covering sixteen caskets.

"Beautiful service, Ginger."

Peter nodded, though in his mind he heard:

Sixteen.

Great success.

Germans retreating.

So few casualties.

Sixteen. It did not feel like success on this broiling afternoon
with the sun beating down on them like fire from Hades. He continued sketching the parched field, the raised mounds of dirt, the
wreaths of flowers lying solemnly on each of the fresh graves.

Frank kicked at a loose stone, cleared his throat, ran his hands
through his short-cropped hair, and said, "There's been an unfortunate incident farther north."

This was an unfortunate incident. These graves. A byproduct
of war.

More euphemisms.

Peter closed his eyes and took a deep breath, then turned to
face Frank.

"General's been hearing rumors among the units that a town
was bombed by us. Many civilian casualties."

Frank pronounced the words with care, as if they themselves
could wound the chaplain. Peter considered his youthful-looking
assistant, his friend, and saw a new sadness in his blue eyes, as if
the color had faded.

"They're requesting we send a few jeeps and men and a chaplain
immediately to help out. The rest of the Task Force will arrive in
two days." Frank cleared his throat again and looked directly at
Peter. "I believe it's a town you used to visit. Sisteron."

Peter felt the lurch in his stomach.

Sisteron.

"My father started a retreat center ten kilometers from there. Yes, I know the city well. Beautiful."

Almost as lovely as The Camp Between the Hills.

Frank put one hand on Peter's shoulder and gave him a sheet of paper. "I think you might want to see this report from the general."

Peter took the paper and started reading:

At 16H00 on August 15, 72 B26 Marauder bombers of the 42nd American Bomber Wing flew over Sisteron with the aim of cutting off the retreat of the Nazi enemy by destroying the 3 bridges of the city. 36 American planes arrived via the Durance Valley for the 1st and 4th wave, and 36 French planes descended the Buëch Valley for the 2nd and 3rd wave. The entire fleet headed back south at 4:40 p.m. There was a miscalculation. In 23 minutes, 240 bombs fell on the city, causing many civilian casualties. . . .

Peter staggered over to a scrawny pine tree and sat down, leaning against the trunk, breathing deeply, head in his hands. Sisteron destroyed? Demolished? By the Allies? American and French bombers?

"Ginger?" When Frank received no response, he knelt beside Peter.

Nothing.

Frank stayed beside Peter for silent minutes that felt like hours, then offered him his hand and helped Peter to his feet. "I'm sorry to have to give such terrible news, especially now." He nodded to the field of new graves. "General wants us to leave pronto. Word has it they've been working through the night and are still rescuing survivors from the rubble."

Frank's hand felt heavy on his shoulder. His vision blurred as he murmured, "Okay, Frank. We'll leave right away."

Andy, waving from a jeep, drove up beside them and stopped. Grinning, he said, "The men have been busy clearing a massive roadblock that engineers from another of our units set up to halt the retreating Germans." The grin on his face widened. "You'll

219

never guess what we found while we were hauling away all those boulders and mines and cables. A German corps commander perched on a park bench with a bottle of brandy and a pistol in his hand, crying. And around him were a bunch of furious French villagers. We saved him from their wrath. Thought you'd be glad to know."

Peter nodded, barely registering the words.

"Ginger, what's the matter? You look pale."

"'Course he's pale. He buried sixteen men today," Frank said, "and I just gave him some pretty rough news."

Peter had removed his cap and ran his hand through his hair while sweat traced lines through the grime on his face.

When Frank explained the latest tragedy, Andy lost all playfulness. "Mighty sorry to hear it," he said, patting Peter on the back.

But all Peter heard was *"many civilian casualties."*

⚜

Three jeeps headed out of Draguignan toward Sisteron as villagers once again hurried to them, handing out Camembert cheese and bottles of the finest red wine retrieved from their caves. The cities were only 125 kilometers apart, but Peter expected they would encounter more roadblocks and perhaps retreating Germans as they made their way north.

With the hot wind in his face and Frank driving the jeep, Peter stared at the destruction along their route and thought of his parents and the camp code he'd created and sent via Marco to The Camp Between the Hills. He thought of the Jewish children who were supposedly hidden in that humongous cave he and his father and so many others had dug. Safe from the Nazis maybe, but had they been safe from friendly fire? The whispered reports of the damage to Sisteron used words like *apocalyptic*. The Port de Dauphiné had been annihilated. And the Citadel, that majestic symbol of strength and safety, now lay in ruins.

All along the rutted roads, Peter allowed himself to remember his boyhood visits to Sisteron with his father to purchase supplies for the camp. Once, with his mother and sisters, he had watched

The Misanthrope, Molière's famous play, in the theatre that sat at the base of the Citadel, high above the town. That night when the lights were shut off after the production, he'd marveled at the way the stars seemed so much closer, and he'd wanted to reach up and grab one of the twinkling dots.

At last he let himself remember the girl, a woman by now. She'd attended one of the camps his father had held for the Catholic Scouts the summer before Peter's senior year of high school. His last summer at the camp.

She was striking in so many ways, with jet-black hair that fell almost to her waist in a long French braid, her eyes a crystal blue. She was different from the other young girls who giggled and batted their eyes at him. When he learned of the gossiping incident among a half-dozen Scouts and then this girl's hike to the Penitents to do penance, he'd laughed.

But he wanted to know more.

Isabelle.

He'd called her Zabelle, the nickname her good friend had given her years earlier.

Beautiful Zabelle.

He'd helped her with the camp code—she was hopeless with it—but she was brilliant with conversation. She'd softened to his teasing, yet they had also discussed things that mattered. Usually they spoke in French, the language used at the camp. But she had been keen to learn English, and as they'd spent more time together, she'd asked him to practice with her.

Did she still live there with her father? He remembered one night she had told him the sad story of her mother's and baby brother's deaths and of her father's quick descent into despair. She had felt responsible for him.

She had a calm personality, reserved and smart and devout. He'd looked for occasions to talk with her. One night, with the moon high and the cliffs of La Baume and St. Michel their only companions, they had strolled down past the village and the tents set up alongside the stream. They had walked and talked, switching from English to French, then to English again. That evening her hair flowed freely, thick and shining in the moonlight. He liked the way her eyes lit up with passion for helping anyone in need and with a budding faith in a God she did not really understand.

And he had wanted to continue conversations with this girl who dared to ask pertinent questions about faith and God and life. Sometimes, before he had met Helen, he would fantasize about returning to the camp and meeting up with Zabelle. He would close his eyes and feast on their midnight stroll, how he'd broken the rules of camp to be with her, how they had sat and talked for hours by the stream.

She had kidded him. "Would you like a cigarette? I have some in my tent. And I can tell you the latest camp gossip."

He'd narrowed his eyes and said, "Really, after all the trouble that brought you last time and that hike to the Penitents?"

But she was laughing, eyes dancing. "I'm just pulling on your leg!" she'd said in English, almost getting the idiom correct. "I cannot break codes, but I can tease too!"

And then he remembered the rest. Their flurry of letters back and forth from France to Algeria, and Algeria to France. Back and forth, back and forth.

He smiled, remembering the pleasure he felt as he decorated every envelope with a comic-strip collage, and in a bubble drawn from his mouth, he'd write her address in Sisteron. And the joy he felt every time a letter arrived with a French stamp and his name on the envelope.

Until not only her letters arrived but temptation too.

Maybe he would stay in France after graduation, return to the camp to be with her next summer, even stay in France for his schooling and visit her in Sisteron.

But no! Impossible. He couldn't abandon his calling to the ministry. His mother had been so pleased that for once he'd taken life seriously enough to plan ahead—an education in America, what she had always desired for him. And his father, as wild and reckless as he was, nonetheless rejoiced at his son's call to ministry.

He removed his Bible from his pocket and fingered the envelope that bookmarked the verse in Jeremiah and contained Zabelle's letter that had encouraged him to pursue his dream of ministry.

"You're gifted, Peter. Really gifted. You should be a pastor."

And give her up.

He couldn't disappoint his parents, abandon everything for a teenage girl, all for, dare he admit it, love?

No! Love was a game he was not ready to play.

Now the shame washed over him. Beautiful young Zabelle had kept writing to him. They were deep, soulful letters, occasionally including her simple yet lyrical poetry. But he never answered them. And he never returned to the camp the following summers. He'd pushed her away. Far away.

He'd been miserable in America. At least at first. He didn't fit in. But gradually, studies and soccer and sketching and getting to know other young men with the same fire in their bellies—all of this had helped him to lock Zabelle in a compartment deep down in his heart.

Oh, occasionally he'd open that compartment and peek inside, especially in those first days and weeks of dating Helen. He'd remind himself of the way Zabelle's presence had fed his soul, whereas Helen's presence merely made his heart beat faster with something he could not tame.

Ironic that he had fled a pure and lovely temptation for something that was much more dangerous to his soul and his calling.

Arrête! Stop it! Stop this remembering.

Zabelle.

Sisteron.

Sixteen graves.

Many civilian casualties.

33

ISABELLE

D-Day+2
August 17, 1944

One hundred.

One hundred dead.

So far.

There was no time to mourn Tito, whose body had been carted off along with so many others to be buried later.

Isabelle continued the mind-numbing tasks of clearing the huge stones and rubble all around, praying that they would hear the cry of a child underneath. Twice in the past six hours it had happened, and the fire that lit the sky was one of rejoicing, not destruction. For this moment, a firecracker launched so that all the rescuers could see.

Another one found alive!

Two days of searching, clearing, lifting. In some twisted way, it reminded her of those summers long ago when they were clearing the village at the camp, loading rocks of all shapes and sizes to be repositioned into a residence or a barn or a cave. A cave where the children now huddled. Safe from this horror.

What had Monsieur Christensen said as they lifted the stones at camp? *"We're building back the ruins. All will be used for good. Every stone . . ."*

She didn't believe it. Bitterness crawled up inside and ate at her soul even as she wept and cleared. No more would Tito sing in the Silo, the acoustics reverberating off the cement walls, causing hope to fill the minds and hearts of the resistants as they listened, enthralled.

His life. Wasted. And the child he had sheltered? Had she lived? Isabelle did not know.

All she knew was that the whispered rumors continued to prove true. After those twenty horrific minutes of the planes dropping bombs on their city, Sisteron was two-thirds destroyed, a gutted city mourning over one hundred civilian victims, many of them children, with more than two hundred injured and two dozen still missing.

In her mind, Isabelle heard over and over the words they had memorized as children, words good King Henry IV had said: *"The Citadel is the most powerful stronghold of my kingdom."*

And now it lay in ruins.

The Germans have the stronghold now. They are the most powerful, she seethed to herself, then stopped, frozen. No, the Germans had left. Surely Tomas was gone, retreating or perhaps captured. It should be cause for celebration.

It wasn't German bombs that had destroyed the Citadel and the city of Sisteron. It was the Allies' bombs. Americans.

They hadn't even destroyed the bridges, their intended targets. The Baume and Buëch bridges had been hit but were still passable. And how many bombs had fallen on the Citadel? The area below the Citadel, not far from her apartment, was pulverized. On the other side of the Durance River, in the southern district of La Baume, all the houses had been blown up. It was a miracle that René and Antoine and Etienne had been spared, for they had escaped to the shelter of the Baume's crevices.

"The pipes on the north slope of the Citadel have been cut," Jean-Yves said as he passed Isabelle, his arms laden with debris.

"*Et la chapelle n'existe plus,*" he added, confirming the rumors that the Citadel's Gothic chapel, as well as many other of the fortress's buildings, had been destroyed.

No more bad news! I can't stand it, Isabelle repeated in her head. But it kept coming regardless. Throughout the past forty-eight hours, the villagers had each shared their version of the continuing nightmare.

"We have no more water in the city."

"The east part of the Coste district is gone."

"All the houses in the center of the rue Droite are on the ground."

"North of the town hall square and around the crossroads with the impasse Paul Arène, leveled."

"The town hall was blown up."

"No telephones."

In a few hours, the city had become a pile of stones under which were buried men, women, and children.

What could she do with her rage, her bitterness, her grief, her shock, her heartbreak?

Keep digging.

34

RENÉ

D-DAY+3
AUGUST 18, 1944

Forty-five.

Forty-five children huddled in the cave that had seemed so enormous just three days ago. Now it was overcrowded with the children of war, sleeping on cots, tucked on mattresses on the ground with blankets retrieved from the camp's apartments gathered and wrapped around them.

The Jewish children hidden in the region had all been rescued and brought safely to the camp. But before there had been time to rejoice, fire and brimstone had rained down on Sisteron, and for the past two days, René had made the trip back and forth from Sisteron to the camp, on foot, eight kilometers he now knew by heart, to bring more orphans, children whose parents had been killed in the Allied bombing. So many children.

The ones he brought to the camp were uninjured physically, but what of their souls? René wondered if a human soul could be extinguished even if the body lived. Did he still have a soul? He cursed the Americans just as he did the Germans. Perhaps he had a soul, but if so, he was walking through hell.

An accident. Yes! An accident that resulted in death. And orphaned children. And destruction. His head throbbed with hate, anger, and repressed rage.

But then there was a young girl's hand on his shoulder, and a voice in his mind whispering Delphine was safe.

"Can't you stay for a little while, René! You're so tired! And we need help here. Mme Nicolas will never complain, but we're running out of food. I've seen the rations. There is only enough food for another three days at most." Delphine had perched beside him on the floor in the upper level of the cave. She held a wet rag in her hands with which she had been washing the chipped and cracked plates they had gathered from the camp's empty apartments.

"Ginette will be here tomorrow to help. I can't . . ." He could not tell her that they were still searching for survivors in Sisteron.

But somehow she knew.

"They need you more in Sisteron," she said. "I'm only speaking my heart because I want you here. But you must go." She motioned to his right arm. "It hasn't healed, has it?"

"Don't worry, sis. I just need to rest it a little." How could he rest his arm when, with one more lift of it, a life could be spared?

"It's bleeding through the bandage. Is it infected?"

"Shhh. I can take care of myself. Don't worry! You have a cellar filled with orphaned children to care for with Madame Nicolas. Worry about them."

She turned her eyes away. "You sound mad."

He sounded mad? He was furious. What did she expect?

"I am mad! Why must we first be destroyed by the enemy and then by our allies? Our allies, Delphine! It wasn't enough for a regiment of Boches to attack our farm and murder Maman and the others. Now the Americans must swoop in with their filthy bravado and destroy not just many more lives, but the entire town. They have done this." He swept his wounded arm around the cave where the children were sleeping. The sharp pain with the movement at least quelled the fury momentarily.

Calm down.

"But it was a mistake!" She touched his hand, and he flinched. He would not look into those innocent yet wise eyes. "A terrible accident. Just think how awful those American and French pilots must feel. They'll live with it for the rest of their lives. We must forgive them."

"What do you know?" he snapped. "You're just a kid with lofty ideas and a soft heart. I'll never forgive any of them!"

At the look of shock on Delphine's face, he melted. Then he saw her lips tremble and a lone tear sliding down her cheek. "I'm sorry."

She didn't meet his eyes. Instead, she fingered the dust on the cave floor and blinked furiously.

He touched her hand, took it in his. "I didn't mean it."

Finally, she turned her head up, her eyes brimming with tears. "But you did mean it."

Her words cut him.

"I'll always try to forgive," she said, staring straight into his eyes. "So of course I forgive you. And I know you're sorry. But I also understand something else—that so many things said in jest or in anger are laced with layers and layers of truth. I'll not be able to forget what you said. That I'm just a kid with lofty ideas and a soft heart."

She stood, still holding the washrag in one hand, climbed the rickety steps, and exited the cave.

Stupid, stupid boy! René reprimanded himself over and over. *You've wounded her as deeply as if a bullet went through her chest.*

The anger pounded in his head while something much harder to control settled in his heart.

35

PETER

There was no rejoicing as the three jeeps entered Sisteron. Instead, they were greeted by bitter stares and shell-shocked expressions. And total desolation. The citizens' silence screamed at the soldiers:

You didn't hit the Germans. You didn't destroy the bridges. You just destroyed our town! Our lives!

We heard you boasting of the accuracy of your new bombsights! What accuracy? You killed our citizens and not the Germans!

Slowly, the townspeople were digging their way out of the rubble and burying their dead. These were not soldiers trained for combat, hardened by years of war, but innocent men, women, and children, mowed down when they'd had hopes of imminent victory.

The city was nothing but piles of wreckage made up of stone, cinder blocks, and bodies. Peter watched as the people sifted through broken furniture, twisted appliances, pieces of automobiles. What were they uncovering, stone by stone? His thoughts swirled in the smoke to a group of Scouts lifting stones in the ancient village. He could almost feel the stiffness in his back as throughout each day he and the others picked up stone after stone, his father right there beside them. But back then, there was no fear of finding the body of your neighbor underneath.

He shuddered as he surveyed the horror and the suffering before him. The look on the citizens' faces showed grim determination, shock, terror, and disbelief all melding into glassy-eyed stares as they labored together amid all the debris.

Throughout the day, Peter joined the dozen soldiers from Task Force Butler, turning over stones, pulling out bodies, holding a hysterical woman in his arms, begging God to somehow let this simple gesture bring comfort. Their jeeps helped clear away the rubble, and old cars became makeshift ambulances.

"Sure feel sorry for the fellas who did this," Frank said. "They'll have to live with this for the rest of their lives. Killing the enemy is one thing, but killing innocent civilians who had already suffered so much, killing kids . . . How will they ever get over that?"

Peter heard it again and again. A mistake. A terrible mistake— the Allies had misjudged their target. The clouds, the height. Standing in the midst of that terrible misjudgment, the scene flashed in his mind, too quickly, before he could force it back, block it out, as he often did.

The fresh-faced child, Libby, came into his little room in the clapboard church in Kentucky, the room which served as his office.

"I'm—I'm afraid, Uncle Pete." Beautiful, wide eyes stared up at Peter, a trembling lip, a trembling chin. Slowly, she pulled up the sleeve on her right arm. It was covered with bruises.

Peter stared, speechless. Finally he managed to ask, "What happened, Libby?"

"Sometimes . . ." She turned her eyes to the floor, looking at her bare feet. "Sometimes my father is not well, and he scares me."

Peter felt his stomach drop. "Did your father do this?"

Her nod was barely perceptible.

"Oh, Libby."

"And sometimes he does other things, late at night." Now her whole body was shaking. A tiny voice. Still staring at the floor.

"Can you help me?" Then, looking up into his eyes, hers filled with terror, she pleaded, "But please don't tell my father I said anything. He said it was our secret. He said only bad little girls betray a secret."

Even now, standing in the rubble of Sisteron, Peter could feel the dread and horror in his gut. Could see the results in his mind.

How foolish he had been. How naive.

"I misjudged it, Lord," Peter said out loud. "I didn't know how to handle it. It was a terrible mistake. I didn't know what to do."

He was like those pilots, bombing citizens instead of bridges. No, they would never get over it. But perhaps they, like he had done, would bury the guilt deep in their souls so that they could live in the present, at least until another tragic mistake brought it all to the surface again.

The rest of Task Force Butler was on the road, hoping to join them the next day, but General Butler sent them a warning. "Tell the townspeople to leave! More air raids are planned!"

Where could they go? All the able-bodied citizens were caring for the injured, walking miles to fetch water, setting up makeshift hospitals in other parts of town.

Two days after the bombing of Sisteron, the airplanes were still flying above them, dipping wings toward the three bridges that, though damaged, were passable. "We must block all possibilities of retreat for the Germans" was the reply whenever the soldiers in Sisteron tried to communicate the depth of suffering in the city.

And at every plane that flew by, the people who were clearing the debris would cringe, cover their ears and duck, expecting disaster to strike again.

"We're moving the wounded to a neighboring suburb," the mayor had told the soldiers as soon as they entered the city, his face stalwart, but his eyes betraying him, as if saying, *This is all your fault!* "There's no more room in our hospital."

Three women approached Peter, covered in ash and grime. They were carrying a little girl with brown ringlets, her face smeared, bleeding. "We pulled her out from under the church," a heavyset woman said in French, her eyes that same glassy stare. "Two days buried, and she's still alive." Then in broken English, she asked Peter, "Help us, please."

He was carrying Libby's lifeless, bruised body, weeping . . .

Stop! Come back to the present.

He took the child into his arms, cooing, "*Ça va aller, ma petite.* You're going to be okay."

As he laid the girl on the back seat of the jeep, a firework fizzled in the sky to announce the good news, but no one reacted. Instead, the townspeople froze at the drone of planes overhead. There were shouts as once again the civilians covered their heads and clung to the ground.

We will be killed, all of us. Help!

The stocky woman shuffled to the jeep and climbed in beside Peter, her eyes now burning with fury as she cursed the Allies. Somewhere during her diatribe as she directed Peter with finger-pointing and grunts, when she realized he understood French, she calmed down and said matter-of-factly, "The former nunnery in a village five kilometers away has been turned into a hospital. Castel-Bevons."

The countryside is so calm, thought Peter as he left the ruined city and drove toward the neighboring suburb. Strange how the landscape was unblemished between the two towns, the craggy mountains puncturing the sky on the periphery, the fields and scrub trees, lavender and sunflowers nodding to them, all while an injured child moaned in the back seat.

He steered the jeep up a steep incline to an L-shaped building, four stories in height, with abundant windows, a red tiled roof and a burnt yellow exterior. Cars and trucks were crammed into the square in the center of the L, people running back and forth, carrying supplies. Others were making their way up the incline on foot with the injured carried on planks or sagging mattresses. A red cross marked one car.

"*Suivez-moi,*" the woman said as Peter lifted from the jeep the unconscious child. He carried the little girl in his arms, following

From the Valley We Rise

his guide into the entryway, where nurses hovered around a bleeding man.

When a woman dressed in civilian clothes with a bloodstained
kitchen apron tied around her waist came over, he said, "She was
just rescued from the city center in Sisteron."

His French was perfect, but she eyed his American uniform and
took the child in her arms.

"Merci," she said curtly.

Peter turned and walked outside and heard it again—the droning, on and on, of airplanes.

"*Vite!* Hurry! Find shelter!" a doctor shouted above the noise
of the planes, his white lab coat billowing in a gust of wind the
planes produced.

A young woman was kneeling beside a stretcher, where an elderly
woman lay.

Then everything blurred. Peter watched as if in slow motion,
hearing the low-flying planes and the spit of machine-gun fire,
the glint of the sun reflecting from the shiny metal exterior, the
screams, the doctor lifted up by the force of the bullets, then falling to the ground, as did a woman beside him.

The woman bending over the elderly woman looked up, shad-
ing her eyes, then gasped, screamed, and draped herself across the
stretcher to protect the injured one as the plane dropped closer,
strafing the courtyard.

Almost without thinking, Peter rushed toward the two women,
arms out, yelling, "No! Noooo!"

As he threw himself on top of them, he felt the first bullet hit
his shoulder. He felt the second pierce his side. Then he slumped,
blackness descended, and he didn't feel the third.

36

ISABELLE

The mayor, disheveled and harried, had announced it yesterday and repeated it several times afterward, and the word spread that another makeshift hospital, the third, had been set up in Castel-Bevons.

Now Isabelle rode beside Jean-Yves as he maneuvered through the wreckage toward the nearby district. Poor Mme Lefort, who had worked tirelessly for the past two days to free those buried under the debris and bandage the wounded, had twisted her ankle and fainted, and Isabelle feared the elderly woman's leg was broken.

"*Pas la peine. Je n'ai pas besoin de l'hôpital. Quelle bêtise!*" Again and again, the woman moaned that she didn't need a hospital, that she was stupid to have fainted.

To which Isabelle soothed, "We'll just have your leg checked out. And don't you want to visit the lady you rescued yesterday? I heard she's awake now and doing well."

As they left the desolation of the city and drove the few kilometers to Castel-Bevons, Isabelle imagined it was all a twisted, horrible nightmare—the bombing of Sisteron, the death of Tito, of Papa, the rescue of the Jewish orphans, the whole incomprehensible war. Just a terrible figment of her imagination.

Please let it be so. Let us go back in time, rewind the clock, rewind our history. Please . . .

Then Jean-Yves maneuvered the truck up the steep driveway to the nunnery-turned-hospital. He parked beside an American military jeep, shut off the engine, and retrieved an ironing board from the back of the truck that would serve as a stretcher for Mme Lefort.

People were hurrying inside the building, glancing to the sky. With difficulty, Jean-Yves and Isabelle slid Mme Lefort onto the stretcher and set it on the ground.

"I'll get help," Jean-Yves called over the roaring sound around them and dashed toward the hospital entrance.

Isabelle recognized the same cursed sound from before. Planes approaching. Doctor Niel emerged from the building, followed by two women, all three shouting for everyone to take cover.

Clutching her throat, Isabelle knelt beside Madame Lefort. "Let's get you inside. Ne t'en fais pas! We're all right. We're almost there."

The plane flew closer, and she heard rapid gunfire. Isabelle watched in horror as bullets hit the doctor and women. They fell just feet from where she sat beside Mme Lefort.

She did not know what to do except throw herself over the injured woman. She felt the first bullet, then something else, heavy and strong, engulfing her, covering every part of her. She heard the raking of bullets again, but she didn't feel them.

And then it was over.

As the planes flew on toward their next target, Isabelle tried to scream, but it came out as a whimper. Something, *someone* was crushing her. Yes, someone. A body, pinning her down.

Protecting her. Protecting them both.

Was this person dead? Below her, Madame Lefort was motionless. Panic seized Isabelle as she lay sandwiched between the two bodies.

"Madame Lefort?"

"I'm here," came the weak and raspy voice, but nothing from the one who was holding her. Then hands were pulling the body off her, lifting her up, lifting Madame Lefort, carrying them.

But what about the one who had saved their lives?

She tilted her head to see a man in an American soldier's outfit sprawled on the ground. Excruciating pain shot through her body, and she fainted.

37

❖

RENÉ

D-Day+3
August 18, 1944

Confetti floated from the sky and landed on the hood of the German truck that Antoine now drove. Mildewed tricolor flags that had been hidden in trunks and wine cellars waved from windows along the cobbled street. Old men and women, children, and young women lined the sidewalks, cheering, the girls dressed in their finest skirts and blouses and hats, surely treasures that had also been hiding in a trunk somewhere. Their lips were painted with bright red lipstick, their eyes lit with celebration.

"Freedom! Liberté!" rang through the town of Oraison, forty kilometers south of Sisteron, as the Allied troops passed through the city. True to the rumors, these same girls rushed into the street, embracing the soldiers and kissing them full on the mouth.

Antoine and Etienne and René followed behind the American troops in the German truck, now adorned with French flags. The shouts of joy continued, though René again felt anger.

"Stop here!" René commanded. "Antoine, right now! Arrête!"

Antoine looked over at his little brother, cocked an eyebrow, and said, "Really? What's your deal, René?"

"Just stop!" René leapt out of the vehicle before it had completely stopped. He headed toward the boulangerie they had just passed.

Etienne ran into the bakery behind René, who was yelling, "How can you celebrate when you know what happened to Sisteron? It's in ruins! We need help. We need your bread."

The middle-aged woman behind the counter cocked an eyebrow, just as Antoine had done, and said, "Of all the nerve. What in the world are you talking about?"

"You haven't heard what happened to Sisteron two days ago?"

The woman frowned. "Here," she said and handed him a crusty loaf. "Yes, we'll help. Of course. How horrible. *C'est terrible. Inimaginable.*" Yet her voice was light and happy.

Antoine entered the boulangerie and grabbed his brother by the scruff of the neck. "René, what are you doing? Leave her alone." He turned to the *boulangère* and, red-faced, stammered, "*Excusez-moi, madame.* My brother. He's . . ."

Her eyes softened, and she shook her head. "Don't worry," she said, then handed Antoine another baguette.

Back on the street, René twisted in his brother's hold and seethed, "The people of Sisteron are suffering. They have no water and very little food. We must do something!"

"Of course, little brother, but scolding that poor woman isn't going to help."

René ripped off a piece of bread and held it up to his brother. "This is at least something."

All around, firecrackers exploded and confetti rained down, carpeting hats and shoulders and the cobblestones. More flags waved, and the shouting turned to singing as the townspeople belted out the French national anthem: "Allons enfants de la patrie, le jour de gloire est arrivé!"

After all the trucks had passed by carrying the Allies, girls standing on running boards, the jeeps' doors flung open, the people rushing en masse toward the troops . . . René stood in the middle of the deserted street, the bread crushed in his fist, and bawled like a baby.

Later, when René entered the next boulangerie two blocks farther down the street, he wore his kindest smile, brushed the tears from his face, and said, "*Chère* madame, I doubt you've heard the news with everything going on here, but Sisteron was bombed two days ago, and there are many civilian casualties. Men, women, and children. Other children are orphaned. We're collecting food and water and supplies. Can you please help?"

Just as Antoine had predicted, this tactic worked much better than threatening the joyful and celebrating townspeople. Soon he and Antoine and Etienne were headed back to the ruined city, loaded down with food and supplies and bandages and water. These things they could do. Back and forth, the French-flag-covered German truck shuttled provisions and even nurses and doctors to Sisteron from the neighboring towns.

Late that evening, René left Antoine and Etienne in Sisteron and drove the truck to the camp, as always careful to ensure no one was following him. Surely with the towns being liberated, none of the Jewish children were in danger now. And yet those ugly words *traitor*, *betrayed* haunted his thoughts and kept him wary.

When he cut the motor and stepped out into the night, he took out the crushed buds of lavender he kept in his pants pocket and breathed in the calming fragrance. He listened to the chirping of the cicadas. No smoke stung his eyes, no smell of burning flesh infiltrated his nostrils and made him gag. No endless moaning and cursing and weeping.

Silence.

He stood in the courtyard and gazed at the stars and at the outline of the Baume and St. Michel, which looked unchanged in the distance. If he stood still too long, he would fall asleep on his feet. He reached into the back of the truck and retrieved a satchel, which overflowed with the last baguettes and chocolate bars that he'd saved for the children.

He trudged over to the garage, opened the door, and removed the shelves that revealed the entrance to the vast cellars beneath. Then he stepped down into another type of bedlam.

Children laughing and crying and singing, each one of these dozens of small humans seemingly needing to shout louder than the others.

When Delphine spotted him, she let out a joyful cry, ran up to René, and hugged him. "I'm not mad at you anymore. I know you care about me. I know you think I'm smart and brave." She peeked up from where she was smothered into his chest. "And pretty."

René, shoulders slumped, wrecked with fatigue, nonetheless managed a grin. "Think what you want, silly sister," he reprimanded.

How he longed for her to hold him like this forever, fiercely. Instead, he peeled himself out of her skinny arms. "If you're so smart, show me what you've been up to. *This* is what *I've* been up to—I've brought food for everyone."

He hoisted the linen bag stuffed with fresh baguettes onto a table, and the children squealed with delight.

"Merci, René!" the children cried in their high-pitched voices.

Henri walked over to René, hand outstretched. "*Trop bien, mon pôte,*" his thirteen-year-old voice cracked, and René was not sure if it was from puberty or emotion.

Ginette appeared then, dusting her flour-covered hands on a worn apron. "There you are, René. And you've brought bread! God be praised. I'm wearing the only flour we have left." She winked at René, then confessed, "It's great to see you. Thank you for rounding up food."

"Bread!" Delphine declared, holding up a baguette in one hand, high over her head. Eyes flashing, in the other hand she produced three paper-wrapped bars. "And chocolate!"

The children cheered again, and René, Delphine, Henri, and Ginette spent the next several minutes dividing the baguettes into thick slices, inserting pieces of dark chocolate into the soft center of the crusty bread, and placing a slice into fifty outstretched hands.

Little Anne took her chocolate-stuffed chunk of bread and cooed, "It's like before the war. At four o'clock we have our *goûter*, our *pain au chocolat*." She giggled. "Except it isn't four o'clock. It's nighttime."

"It's bedtime," Ginette corrected. "Come now. Let's all get ready."

The bedlam had quieted, and the youngest children were now asleep. Ginette, Delphine, Henri, and René left the cave and walked into the cool night air. They made their way down the road to the little creek.

"Where's Mme Nicolas?" René asked.

Ginette raised her eyebrows to Delphine before the child could answer and replied, "She's resting in her house. Doctor's orders."

Delphine snickered. "Ginette is our self-appointed doctor."

"She is unwell?"

"She's exhausted. She was unstable on her feet. I thought she was going to faint, or worse. I begged her to rest."

"And she agreed?" René asked.

"Well . . ."

"Ginette spun a story. She made it sound like the children wouldn't sleep if she didn't leave. It was a long and complicated story, until finally Mme Nicolas rolled her eyes and said, 'I see what you're trying to do. I'll go now. Please wake me if you need anything.'"

Ginette shrugged. "Delphine and Henri and I have work to do. And since you're here, René, so do you. Tomorrow, each of the children will receive a canning jar." She pointed to where the jars once filled with Mme Nicolas's canned tomatoes and peaches glistened in the moonlight, washed clean in the creek. "It was the easiest way to wash them. Wasting no water. Grab a handful now and bring them back to the garage to dry out."

Obediently they slipped fingers into the open jars, piling others in their arms as they walked up the moonlit road to the camp. Back in the garage, Ginette explained, "Tomorrow morning, we'll each take a group of the little ones and have them pick blackberries.

The shrubs behind the houses are filled with them. But tell them to be careful—picking blackberries can get you all scratched up."

Delphine's eyes sparkled, and she grabbed René's hand. "Just like we used to do, picking blackberries."

Just like we used to do at our farmhouse, which now sits abandoned, and Maman . . .

As they walked back to the camp with only the moon to light the way, Delphine tugged on René's sleeve and whispered, "Guess what? Mme Nicolas has found the notebooks with the camp code!"

"How nice," René said, too tired to admit he didn't know what she was talking about.

Back in the cave, with the jars arranged on the shelves, ready for the children in the morning, Delphine pointed to another shelf and reached up to retrieve a school satchel, from which she fished out a small notebook.

Delphine asked, "Do you know about the camp code?"

"No. I never went to this camp. The war started before I was old enough to attend."

Delphine let that register before continuing, "That really is a shame. *Dommage.*"

Then he remembered the message Antoine had handed him with the strange symbols: *Network compromised, children to be rescued immediately and taken to Camp Between the Hills.*

Ah, yes. That was *the camp code.*

Delphine prattled on, "Anyway, we have all these notebooks that were used long ago when Isabelle was a camper. The camp director used to get the campers to learn Bible verses by deciphering codes. And I'm going to see if the children can figure them out. The older ones will help the younger ones, and we'll be memorizing the Psalms." She shrugged. "The Jewish children already know a lot of Psalms, but maybe not the ones in code."

René crossed his arms over his chest. "I've never learned a Bible verse. I've never even opened a Bible. But if you think this will help keep the children busy, calm them down, then go right ahead."

"You'll see. It will. And then Isabelle will come and help and then you can go with Antoine to chase the Germans away."

Delphine glanced toward the sleeping children, then motioned with her eyes for René to follow her out of the cave and into the garage. She stopped once they were outside and again whispered, "Gathering blackberries and solving cipher codes are just part of the plan we've made to help calm them down. The kids keep hearing the explosions. They saw more bombs being dropped on Sisteron today. They're rowdy and scared. So we have to think of things to keep them busy."

"Codes and blackberries should do it."

"And they won't be thinking about the bombs. We'll be safe again, and Isabelle will come soon to help us."

René thought of his cousin in Sisteron just yesterday, liquid pooling in her eyes as she talked about Tito, as she carried a rescued child from the wreckage, as she worked beside other citizens. Her eyes had held sadness and despair, and something else. His cousin was angry just like he was. Fury had fueled her tears.

It was after midnight, and an eerie silence permeated the countryside as René drove the German truck to where the Durance Maquis was hiding.

All was quiet now.

For three days, the air had filled with celebration and cheering as town after town was liberated by the Allies. Then the air became heavy with smoke and the smell of death when he headed back to Sisteron. At the camp, the air filled with both the laughter and cries of orphaned children.

But here it was quiet again, his comrades smoking cigarettes and listening to the cicadas and plotting the course for their next assignment, joining the 7th Army and something called Task Force Butler.

Gabriel's eyes had that familiar haunted look, but he smirked when René showed up. "Figured out how to drive that truck, petit? You're growing up fast."

René ignored the insult and joined the rest of the Maquis huddled around the campfire, listening to the latest news from Gabriel.

"Americans are begging us to keep moving north with them to catch the fleeing Germans. We've got to leave Sisteron."

"All of us?" asked René.

"Oui, petit," Gabriel spat. "All of us. The Allies are worried about an enemy retreat at the Montélimar gap. We're supposed to keep up with the Task Force."

Bastien gave a chuckle. "The Task Force was moving pretty good until they got to Quinson. Their jeeps got stuck in a creek bed. But the townspeople joined us, and we formed a nifty little fire brigade. Should have seen us passing flagstones along. Built a ford for the Allies."

Samuel reported, "Allies took a thousand prisoners in Digne-les-Bains, bunch of Boches wandering around, coming down from Grenoble. Germans were trying to block the Route Napoléon. Didn't work. Nice to see all of them prisoners after the carnage in Sisteron."

"Wasn't the Germans who destroyed Sisteron," René muttered, and no one dared to challenge him.

"You've done a good job, men," Gabriel offered. "I've heard the only thing that is slowing the Allies down is lack of fuel."

"That and getting lost because of the road signs we jumbled to confuse the Boches," said Bastien.

Antoine nodded. "Made me shed a few tears to see all our old frenchmen in their worn Great War uniforms, saluting by the roadside as the Allies passed by. And all those mildewed tricolors the women took out of their hiding places in the caves."

"And all them beautiful gals rushing out to kiss the soldiers!" Didier, only seventeen, was blushing.

"Wish they'd kiss me. Not like we didn't do most of the work." This came from Samuel.

"Yeah, well, I imagine you'll get some ladies soon," Gabriel said, drawing them back to the reason for the meeting. "US 7th Army is progressing north at a fast clip. No fears of reprisals from the east. They want as many of us to join them as we can spare. They've even given the different Maquis code names: Chloroform, Novocaine, and Ephedrine."

"Drugs. They want us to deaden the pain with our names," said Etienne.

"Something like that, I suppose." Gabriel managed to smile.

"Catch the Boches. They're running for their lives, the cowards. That's the order now. Capture or destroy them." This came from Didier.

René felt a quiver of excitement replace his fatigue and anger. Finally, a mission that was offensive. They'd been desperately defending for so long. At last, they would make the enemy tremble and fear for their lives.

In the distance, a light flickered. Gabriel frowned and motioned with his hand for silence. The men started stomping out the fire. Surely the Germans had left the region, surely . . .

They raised their rifles, then quickly lowered them as Jean-Yves entered the circle of men, breathing hard, face pale. "Thought I'd find you here." He leaned over to catch his breath. "I'm afraid there's been another incident. Another *mistake*. More innocent victims over in Castel-Bevons where they set up a third medical center." He took a deep breath. "This afternoon, a doctor and four others were machine-gunned by our own French planes . . ." He hesitated and looked over at Antoine and René. "I'm afraid your cousin, Isabelle, was one of the victims. Wanted you to find out from me."

The bile rose so fast in René's throat that he gagged and vomited.

Tears in his eyes, Antoine whispered, "Is she . . . ?" But he could not pronounce the words.

"All we know is that she was shot. Sorry, men. I don't know anything else."

René reached out for Antoine, tried to stand, felt dizziness overcome him, and fainted.

38

ISABELLE

D-Day+4
August 19, 1944

"I have to get up. Please. I'm fine. I'm not hurt." But the nurse was looking at Isabelle with doubt and pointing to the bandage that covered her midsection.

"A bullet grazed your side, and you have two broken ribs. You'll stay put, young lady."

How could she stay put when all around her, people were swarming, trying to fix the unfixable, to stave off more death. Were they keeping themselves busy with nursing so that their minds didn't go crazy with fear, with hate, with exhaustion?

All through the days and nights, explosions could be heard in the towns that surrounded Sisteron. Explosions that caused the villagers of Sisteron to cry out, to seek cover, even when they knew the neighboring towns were celebrating their liberation, sending rockets and firecrackers into the sky to announce victory.

When had life stopped making sense? Was it when Papa was wounded in the Great War? Was that the first sign that her family,

247

the Seauve family, the family name with the word *save* in it, would meet disaster after disaster, heartbreak after heartbreak?

She could not lie in this bed with her thoughts as her only company. She bit her lip as she pushed herself to the side of the cot, gasping at the pain of her broken ribs.

"Don't cough, don't sneeze, and for heaven's sake, don't laugh," the nurse had warned.

That last command she would obey forever. Isabelle could not imagine ever smiling again, let alone laughing.

"Well, look at you, Miss Disobedient!" Ginette strode into the room lined with cots on which lay the wounded. "I just talked to the nurse, who said you're forbidden to get out of bed."

"I have to. It's much more dangerous for me to stay here with my wretched thoughts. Please, help me."

"I'll help you by beating you at cards. I've brought a deck. Now sit!" Ginette placed a soft pillow behind Isabelle and sat cross-legged across from her. As she began dealing cards, she said, "It's a little intimidating, playing with a hero. They're gonna give you a Croix de Guerre or induct you into the Legion of Honor, Zabelle!"

"For what?"

"You saved Mme Lefort's life. Took a bullet for her. Or did you forget that little detail?"

"It was just a reflex."

"Well, Mme Lefort appreciates your 'reflex,'" said Ginette with a wink.

"How can you make light of everything? You act as if it's all a simple card game we either win or lose in the end! But, Ginette, it's the in-between that is killing me, that's killing us all. What does it matter if we win the war if we are too broken to ever heal?"

Ginette leaned forward, elbows on the cot, her pale blue eyes defiant. "Sorry, Zabelle. I guess we each have different ways of dealing with the horror."

Isabelle studied her best friend. Her cheeks were streaked with grime, her yellow cotton dress was ripped, her arms covered in scratches, her wrist bandaged, and her hands raw from sorting metal and broken glass and bodies. "Thank you for being here," she murmured.

"I'd just come from the camp this morning to get supplies and stopped by our apartment. Jean-Yves found me and told me the news. You gave us quite a scare." Ginette patted Isabelle's hand. "I'm so thankful you're going to be okay. And just for now, for just a few minutes, let's lose ourselves in a mindless game of cards."

"Okay. Let's play piquet. It's the only game I can ever beat you in."

Ginette shrugged and dealt the cards to France's favorite card game while commenting, "I'll drive back to the camp later. I want to make sure they hear you're okay before any rumors reach them about yesterday's air strike."

"Thanks. How are the children? And Mme Nicolas?"

"The kids are fine. Mme Nicolas looks exhausted but remains her no-nonsense, cheery self. And that Delphine. Are you sure she's only thirteen? She has the mind and heart of a saint. Between her and Mme Nicolas, they're running a Scout camp."

Isabelle glanced at Ginette. "A Scout camp? Like before?"

Ginette grinned. "She has the children working on the camp code. Mme Nicolas dug out all the old ciphers that Monsieur Christensen once used. The kids love it. And they all pitch in with food prep."

Isabelle laid down a queen and asked, "Have they enough food?"

"Thanks to René, there's food. He's relentless. He rides with Antoine in that German truck from village to village, collecting food and water and milk for the children. And chocolate. He can be demanding at times. I heard he put the fear of God in the villagers in Oraison." Ginette mimicked René's scratchy, adolescent voice. "'How dare you celebrate when Sisteron mourns. When the children are hungry. Help them first, then celebrate!' Evidently, he was very convincing."

"I'm not surprised." Isabelle picked a card, made a face, and laid another down. "And . . . have the Germans left? Is Tomas gone? Or perhaps they were captured?"

"They're definitely gone. On the run is what I hear. But the Allies will catch them. Or the Maquis will."

"Thank God." Yet her voice rang flat.

"You don't sound very pleased, Zabelle."

"I'm afraid there's still a traitor among us."

Her friend's countenance changed. "Yes. I've wondered too. But surely—"

"Surely whoever he is will suddenly turn into our ally again?" Oh, the cynicism in her tone. When had she become such a skeptic?

"I don't know. Surely with the Germans gone, with the villages liberated, no one would dare do more harm." But Ginette didn't look convinced.

"It is all one horrific jumble to me. I'm numb, then I'm enraged, and then I burst into tears. Nothing makes any sense. I wish I had your courage, your ability to move forward. To forget."

Ginette leaned forward, her face within inches of her friend's. "I don't know anyone braver than you, Zabelle. You're so strong. But you have to rest for now. Please?"

Isabelle dared one more question. "The soldier who saved my life—I think he is American—could you find out if he . . . if he survived?"

"I promise I'll find out. But I won't tell you if he didn't. I won't burden you with that."

"Your silence will tell me."

"Then let it."

⟡

Isabelle glanced up from her cot at the American soldier who stood in front of her, wheat-blond hair slicked back, boyish face, and earnest bright blue eyes. He looked like a wiry teen wearing an army uniform. He removed his hat and nodded. "Sorry, miss, about your town, 'bout your injury too."

She managed a nod back. "It was awful," she said in English, and he looked surprised that she could speak his language.

She wanted to scream at him, *It's all your fault!* She almost enjoyed his extreme discomfort and said nothing to relieve it. She simply stared at him.

The soldier cleared his throat. "I'm Lieutenant Frank Jamison,

US 7th Army, Task Force Butler. One of the nurses sent me over here. I heard you would like to meet the man who—"

"Who life saved me," she said in English.

He frowned, his brow a ripple of wrinkles. "Pardon me, miss?"

"I want to meet the soldier who life saved me."

His mouth twitching, he glanced at the floor and said, "Yes, miss. The soldier who saved your life."

"Yes, saved my life," Isabelle corrected herself as heat rose in her cheeks. "Can I meet him? I heard he is alive."

Why did her voice sound so harsh, so angry?

The soldier lifted a bushy blond eyebrow, his round cheeks now crimson. "Yeah, the guy who took the bullets for you. But they say you took one too." He looked miserably embarrassed.

"Well, can I meet him?"

Calm down, Isabelle. For heaven's sake, don't bite the poor guy's head off.

"Well, the thing is, he hasn't woken up yet. He's kind of bad off. I'm sure he'll pull through. Don't you worry yourself none, miss. All in the line of duty."

The soldier's tone cut her deep. His sarcasm and disappointment matched hers, and she felt an unexpected prickle in her eyes.

"I'm sorry." She fiddled with the crucifix around her neck. "Of course I want to meet him. I want to tell him thank you." Meeting the soldier's eyes, she dared to ask, "His injury is bad?"

"Pretty bad. It's a head wound, and he's still unconscious. Twenty-one hours now." He glanced at his wristwatch. "That's a bit worrisome. He took a bullet in the shoulder too, almost punctured a lung. Two others, one in the arm and one in the leg."

"Oh! So many bullets. This is terrible." *Be kind, act grateful.* "He is a brave soldier. He has fought for a long time in this war?"

"Ginger? One of the bravest. He's been in the war since the Americans shipped over here. But he doesn't fight. He's a chaplain. He prays for us, buries us. That's all he does."

That tone again.

"But I guess occasionally he decides to save somebody's life too, not just their soul." The soldier met her eyes.

She looked down. "You say he's a 'shaplan'? I do not know this word in English. He prays? Is that like a priest?"

"Yeah, like a priest to the soldiers. Chaplains aren't allowed to carry a gun, miss. I'm his assistant. I go with him into battle, carry the weapons, and try to keep him safe while he cares for the injured and dying. Lord knows, I didn't expect him to get all shot up at the hospital. Awful sorry, miss. Real, real sorry."

"It is ironic, n'est-ce pas? Getting wounded at a hospital." She glanced around at the surroundings of the nunnery. "But I'm thankful to be here, and they won't let me leave just yet. So will you please tell me when the *shaplan* wakes up?"

He tipped his hat and gave her a half smile. "It would be my pleasure, miss."

She watched as he walked away, hat on head, shoulders back. *He cares about this shaplan. This chaplain,* she corrected herself again.

His name. She'd forgotten to ask the name of the chaplain. The soldier had called him Ginger. Wasn't *ginger* the spice she called *gingembre* in French? Was that his surname, Chaplain Ginger? Compassion for him stung her heart, and Isabelle welcomed that strange emotion. It had been foreign to her since the bombing. And another thought surprised her. She would pray for this chaplain. She would pray that he lived, and she would pray that she could turn her mind to the goodness of this one man who didn't carry a weapon but who had saved her life nonetheless.

He lay so still under the white sheet, this American soldier swathed in bandages. His head, both arms, and who knew what else was bandaged under the crisp-looking sheet.

"Has he awoken at all?" Isabelle whispered to Céline, a nurse who had been several years ahead of Isabelle in high school.

"I'm afraid not. He's not opened his eyes at all in thirty-six hours. But his fever's come down, and the infection in his lungs is clearing up."

"Then he'll survive?"

Céline placed a hand on her arm. "I can't promise you that. But I'm so thankful he . . . he did what he did."

"He risked his life for mine." *I am grateful, God.* "May I stay here for a moment?"

"Stay as long as you wish. I'll get you a chair. Talk to him if you can. The doctors say that people can hear even when they're unconscious. Might help him come back to us."

Céline produced a metal chair, and when Isabelle winced as she sat down, Céline added, "Broken ribs are horribly painful, aren't they?" Then she moved down the row of cots.

Isabelle grasped her midsection and began to whisper, "Hello, Mr. Chaplain. My name is Isabelle. I will try to speak in English, but I don't do it very good. I don't know what to say." She paused. "Well, yes, I know what to say first. Merci. You know *merci*, right? Everyone knows that French word."

She stared at the figure on the cot who made no movement, who gave no hint that he'd heard her.

"Well, in case you do not know, it means 'thank you.' Thank you for life-saving me. Non, I said that wrong. I mean, thank you for my life-saving . . . for saving my life. There. Yes, that's it. Thank you for saving my life." Her eyes filled with tears. "There's one more thing I need to say, monsieur. Please live. *Please!* So many people have died. Please don't die because you saved me. I will pray that you live."

Isabelle sat by his side for an hour, saying nothing more. And then she knew. She would talk with this chaplain as if she were talking to Father Duesy after Mass at the church that was no more, the church whose steeple she had watched crash to the ground from her apartment window.

Non!

She would not think of the church, of Mass, of Papa . . .

This would be a Protestant penance, like when she walked to those Penitent cliffs all those years ago. Yes. She'd share her heart with this soldier who looked as frozen and still as the monks, who could not answer, but would hear. And perhaps, if she bared her soul long enough, through a day and a night, perhaps he would wake up. But if he did not, if this brave chaplain took her rage and anger and heartache to the grave, perhaps that would somehow heal her soul.

She could not sleep. Every time she tried to lie down, the pain shot through her. There was no way to get comfortable, so she walked back and forth, down the rows of cots, through hallways, into another room with the wounded. Back into the chaplain's room.

The soldier, Lieutenant Frank, stood, back against the wall, smoking a cigarette. His face looked older in the dark. Haggard, sad. She felt sorry for him.

"Bonjour," she whispered. "You cannot sleep?"

He shrugged, flicked his cigarette. "Nope."

"You are taking care of the chaplain? Watching over him? That is nice."

"Just doin' my duty, miss."

"You care for him. I see it. This is good. You are good."

The soldier shrugged again and crushed out his cigarette, his gaze on the chaplain lying in the bed.

"He has not awoken yet, Chaplain Ginger?"

The soldier frowned, his brow creased. "Excuse me?"

"The Chaplain Ginger?"

He chuckled, then recovered. "Afraid not."

"You laugh at my accent?"

"No, no. Your accent is great."

"I have talked with him today. Talked *to* him. My English . . . I'm sorry."

"Your English is just fine, miss. Keep talking to him. Tell the rascal to hurry and wake up."

"The rascal?"

"Yeah, good ol' Ginger, the rascal. You know, he's a prankster."

"Prankster?"

"He likes to joke around. Only this time he's not joking, and we sure wish . . ." His voice broke, and he looked away, cleared his throat. "We sure wish he'd wake up and get better."

"You said he is brave. Is he a good man too?"

"Yeah, he's a good man. One of the best. He's been keeping up the men's morale."

"That is good. Important in war. War is so bad."

"Yeah. He's got a real knack for games and other stuff to distract us."

Isabelle thought about the card game she'd played with Ginette. "My friend Ginette is like that. She said it would help us take off our mind."

Frank let out a belly laugh.

She flashed her eyes, and he muttered, "Sorry, miss. Just a tiny mistake. Help you *take your mind off* how bad things are." He met her eyes. "Not making fun of you. Just thankful for something to cause me to smile."

"You mean my mistakes are good for your soul?"

Again the furrowed brow. "Well, the Good Book says that laughter is good for the soul, so I guess you could deduce that your little mistakes in English that make me laugh are good for my soul." He gave her a wink, and Isabelle felt warmth rise in her cheeks.

"Then I'll keep talking to him. About life-saving." She glanced up at Frank and smiled. "I'm sure Chaplain Ginger will wake up soon. I will watch over him for the rest of the night. I cannot sleep. I will talk to him, and you can sleep."

Lieutenant Frank tipped his hat. "Thank you, miss. I believe I will."

39

PETER

Everything hurt. Just breathing caused such unbearable pain. Sleep was a blessing. He was not really asleep, though. He heard the voices. Frank's, scratchy and soft, so unlike Lieutenant Jamison. And Andy's, trying to joke, talking about a good-looking nurse. Then Lee saying, "You're gonna be all right, Ginger." Their voices floated in and out of his consciousness.

And another voice. "Please live, monsieur. Please live. Thank you for life-saving me." The words were in English, but the accent was French, the tone pleading, fervent.

Peter prayed silently, echoing that voice. *Let me live, Lord. I want to live. I know You don't need me, but it feels like the men do. I want to be with them. Not here.*

In and out of consciousness he drifted. Or perhaps he was never conscious at all.

Somewhere deep inside, he kept hearing it. *"Please live. . . . I will pray that you live."*

"So, buddy, ya needed some action, I guess. Couldn't just sit back and be a chaplain."

Peter knew that voice. Frank's, he was sure. But he could not fully comprehend the words. He struggled to open his eyes.

"What? You wanted to take more bullets than anybody else in the whole dang-blasted platoon, Ginger?" Then Frank's voice lowered. "We were afraid you'd never wake up. Gave us a good scare."

With difficulty, Peter turned his head toward Frank and whispered the word, "Where?" It felt like cotton in his mouth.

Frank leaned in closer. "Did ya say somethin', Ginger? Try again. I'm listenin'."

"Whhhere"—he blew out the sound—"am I?"

"Where are you, buddy? Why, you're in a little nunnery-turned-hospital, outside your favorite town of Sisteron."

Sisteron. The bombing.

"Hhhurt?"

"Yeah. You got hurt, all right."

"How?"

"Trying to rescue a dame. A pretty little French gal."

Peter wanted to ask more questions, but the light! His head, splitting open. "Too . . . bright."

Frank glanced back at the window and blocked the sun's rays with his army jacket.

"Thank you." Two words. Hard to pronounce.

"You go on resting, Ginger, and I'll explain everything. Keep your eyes closed and just listen. They say you were bringing a little girl to this place when a plane flew over—a French one this time—in real bad cloud cover. They couldn't see a thing. Still trying for the bridges. As the plane sprayed the courtyard with bullets, you jumped on top of a French gal. Sorry if that sounds a bit indecent, but it wasn't. Was real heroic, actually. You saved two women—the French gal and the old lady she was trying to protect. You took four bullets. One to your head, one to your shoulder, which just missed your heart. One to your arm, and one to your leg."

"How long?" Peter asked.

"Two days you been scaring us half to death. Weren't sure you were ever going to wake up. But the bullets missed your lung, missed your brain, and just grazed your ear. They got the bullets out of your arm and your leg, and it looks as though the wounds are healing."

"Not in too good of shape, I guess," Peter mumbled.

Frank sobered. "Not too good, Ginger, but they think you'll be okay."

Yes, he remembered now. The horror of it all, the little girl lifted from beneath the stones, buried alive for two days. The drive to this place, the serenity, then the panic and the planes. And yes, the young woman.

Frank interrupted his thoughts. "There's someone who wants to meet you. That pretty French gal. She says you saved her life." Frank chuckled. "She spoke to me in English and kept saying how grateful she was for your 'life-saving' her. Of course, her English is a lot better than my French! Anyway, she's been talking to you while you've been sleepin'. Hope she'll come back. Mad as all get-out at this war. Not too pleased with the Allies right now. Can't blame her, though . . ."

Frank continued talking, but all Peter heard was, "*Thank you for life-saving me. . . . I will pray that you live.*"

40

RENÉ

AUGUST 20, 1944

When René arrived in Castel-Bevons early the next morning, he found Isabelle sitting on her bed in the infirmary. She looked thinner and more exhausted than even three days ago as they had picked through the ashes of the city. But she was alive and awake. For this he rejoiced.

"Another air strike?"

"It was so frightening, René. The doctor and others are dead. I should be dead, but an American soldier, *un aumonier*, saved me." She was staring at her hands, which were clasped in tight fists. "He saved my life, and now we don't know if he'll live." She raised her eyes. "Not another death because of me."

"Shhh. You saved the older woman too. How badly are you hurt?" He didn't care to hear about the wounds of an American, no matter that he had sacrificed himself for Isabelle. He hated the Allies and the Germans and everyone else connected with the war.

A young American soldier made his way to Isabelle, and René

felt himself stiffen. The soldier smiled at Isabelle and spoke to her in English.

"René," she said to him in French, "this is Lieutenant Frank. He's the assistant to the man who saved my life."

René gave a nod to the boyish-looking soldier but ignored his outstretched hand.

"René," Isabelle said, looking exasperated. When he still said nothing, she whispered in French, "Be polite. It wasn't this man's fault what happened to Sisteron, or to me."

René felt the boiling rage inside, even as he reached and took the soldier's hand and murmured, "Merci."

The soldier's face was scarlet as he left, tipping his hat to Isabelle.

"I'm sorry. I'm not in the mood to be polite," René admitted.

"I understand. Neither am I. I was rude to him yesterday. I'm trying to be more polite now." She changed the subject. "How are Delphine and Mme Nicolas?"

"Ça va. They're keeping the kids safe and fed."

"You're lying. I see it in your eyes. It's hard. They need help, don't they?"

René nodded. "But you can't come yet. Ginette's there now. She'll stay for as long as she's needed."

"Ginette is worn to the bone. She came to see me yesterday. She's like you, running back and forth from the wounded in Sisteron to the kids at camp to this place where I'm stuck. I can come soon. I'm fine, really."

"They say you've got broken ribs. I know what that feels like. Just breathing is painful. Stay here and get well, cousin. We'll get others to help."

"I'll be okay." But when she went to stand, she winced and cried out. René lifted his eyebrows and gave a half smile. "All right," she conceded. "But if I stay here, tell me who will help?"

"Don't worry, we'll figure it out," René said, then added, "I've been wondering if I could check with the families who housed the children, if I could go to the villages that have been liberated. I'll bet they would happily take the kids back. That'd ease the burden at the camp. Surely they'll be safe now that the Germans are gone."

Isabelle shook her head. "Ginette and I were discussing that, but someone was supplying information to the Germans. Even if the Germans are gone, I'm afraid no one is safe yet. I heard whisperings here at the nunnery yesterday that a priest was murdered in Nice just two days ago. The city had been liberated, the Germans had left, but someone in the Resistance there was a turncoat. They killed the good priest who had saved the Jewish kids—shot him in his bed in the middle of the night."

René made a face and cursed under his breath. "No one is safe yet. Well, do you know who the turncoat is?"

They talked through the possibilities from the Silo Network: Maurice, Jacques, Jean-Yves, Bertrand, Lucy, Amandine, Ginette. Also the Durance Maquis: Gabriel, Etienne, Antoine, Bastien, Samuel, Didier.

Impossible! All of this was unthinkable, and yet someone had betrayed them.

René corrected himself. Not someone. Not one person, but everyone. The Americans who had dropped the bombs on Sisteron. The French who had dropped them on Castel-Bevons. And trusted friends who had succumbed to hate and fear and sided with the Germans.

He wanted revenge for all of it. At least he could race after the fleeing Germans. Kill a few of them. That would help, wouldn't it?

No.

René knew his role. He wouldn't rejoin the Maquis yet. Instead, he would stay with Delphine and Mme Nicolas and Ginette. And the Jewish children, the children of Sisteron, and any others who came to the camp needing shelter. He'd make sure they had all the supplies they needed, and he'd watch for traitors among the ashes of Sisteron.

At nightfall, René left the infirmary in Castel-Bevons and went into Sisteron, where he found the Durance Maquis.

Antoine met René with a question in his eyes. "How is she?"

"Broken ribs and a flesh wound. But she's okay. She looks awful, though. And if the soldier who saved her dies, I think she'll lose her mind. She's a mess."

"And the camp?"

"I'll go back. And I'll get supplies for the kids. When I can, I'll join the rest of you."

"Keep the truck—you'll need it for the children. We'll hop rides with the Allies." Antoine tried to smile, but it didn't quite make it to his eyes.

Etienne had his arm draped around a young French soldier. They came to where the Durance Maquis had assembled after once again working through the ruins.

"René, Antoine, this is Michel. He's with the Marauders." The look in Etienne's eyes told them to keep quiet and listen.

Yes, keep quiet, René thought. *This man was in one of the planes that flew over Castel-Bevons. He probably wants to do penance for what they did.*

The young man wore deep grief on his face, and something else. Guilt.

"I told them we were too low. None of us wanted to drop the bombs. We knew the goal was to destroy the access routes, stop the Boches. We knew. We obeyed orders." But the hollow look in his eyes conveyed the rest. "I'll never forgive myself. Never."

René observed the soldier, and for a moment, the hatred and anger took a long breath. *At least I'm not dragging a lot of guilt around too,* he thought. Cursing the war, he headed back to the German truck, then back to the camp where fifty orphaned children were picking blackberries and pretending everything would be all right now.

41

ISABELLE

Castel-Bevons
August 20–21, 1944

All through another night, Isabelle sat beside the silent stranger's bed and talked to him

"Hello, Chaplain Ginger. I am back. My name is Isabelle. I will try to speak to you in English. I don't do it well, but your soldier friend said it was good for his soul. I hope it is good for your soul.

She continued. "But my soul is sad. When I close my eyes, I see horrible images, so I am going to keep them open and confess the truth. I hope you do not mind."

Nothing. No movement, no indication that he understood her words.

"I am so angry, Monsieur Chaplain. I do not understand life. I cannot remember when life has been simple. I have always looked too deep and then been afraid and then been so disappointed and mad. Now I am mad at the Germans, mad at the Americans, mad at everyone. But really, I will tell you this because you are an *aumonier*. You know this word? It is French for chaplain. I do not know if you are a priest. In France we have priests as chaplains, and they hear confessions and absolve us. I will tell you, I am mad at God."

She paused, almost hoping that such a sinful admission would rouse the religious man.

Still nothing.

"God took my mother and my baby brother and then my father and my aunt and my friends and my city, and I have nothing else to give Him, so He tried to take me! And sometimes I wish He had. At least the dreadful aching would be over. He is a mean God. I was even mad at you because you are working for God."

No movement. No reaction.

Even if this soldier did not awaken again, Isabelle felt some sort of relief at admitting the truth that, until this moment, she hadn't dared to speak out loud. Perhaps she had not even known where the anger was directed.

"I know life is precious. I don't want to hate. I don't want to be mad at God. But I don't know what to do. Except this. Tell you."

She yawned, then moaned with pain.

"Once, when I was a young girl, I went to a camp right near here. It was a wonderful camp for young people who loved God. I wanted to please God. And I have tried to please Him. But you see, Chaplain Ginger, I am still angry.

"Papa and I have been trying to protect the Jewish children, and many, many other good people have tried to help. But I am always so afraid. Do you think God sees my fear? I used to pray to Him, to ask for help. But it does not do any good. Or have I done it the wrong way? I tell the Jewish children that God loves them, that He loves us all, sees all. I tell them that this evil is not from God.

"But then I am so tired, and I am not sure. So I am telling you, and I hope that afterwards I will know how to move on. There is so much to do, but I feel stuck and angry and numb and wounded."

And tired. So tired. Every part of her body ached.

"Ginette, she is my good friend. She knows how to move on. I don't. Sometimes I live in the past. Ginette is like so many others, simply doing the next thing. It is hard and painful, but it is only what is expected. But will I be able to do the next thing? I need to get back to the children. Would you pray for me, please? Even if you cannot talk, cannot open your eyes, surely you can hear me, and you can talk to God. God will hear your silent prayers. I believe that. Please ask Him what I should do now."

She picked up a small Bible that sat beside the chaplain's cot. She felt the smooth, supple leather, and smelled it. It was a comfortable worn smell, like Papa's favorite chair at the library, the library that was no more . . .

"I cannot read to you from this Bible yet. It is too dark. But I will tell you some verses I learned from the Bible. They are in French. But maybe you would like that. I learned them long ago at that camp. The camp director always reminded us that we must not just talk to God. We must listen to what He says to us. The Bible is His letter to us."

Isabelle closed her eyes and concentrated, remembered reciting the Lord's Prayer at Mass, remembered deciphering the camp code and learning other Bible verses. She reached for the soldier's hand. "So even if I am mad at God and confused, I think you would want to hear His words."

Softly, she quoted the verses in French: "'Our Father which art in heaven, Hallowed be thy name . . .'"

"'The LORD is my shepherd; I shall not want . . .'"

On and on she whispered the verses that came back to her, one after the other. She paused, unwilling to recite the one that was Monsieur Christensen's favorite. The one he proclaimed at the beginning of each camp service. The one Mme Nicolas's son had engraved on a wooden plaque that hung in the Christensens' home.

"And they shall build the old wastes, they shall raise up the former desolations, and they shall repair the waste cities, the desolations of many generations."

That one was hard, for she did not believe it could be true for her or for Sisteron.

Then Isabelle remembered how Mme Nicolas had known she was coming and had stocked the cave with food. She thought about Monsieur Christensen being Monsieur Martin and how many

Jewish children had been saved. They were still safe. She thought how she was here at this moment because this chaplain had saved her. She had survived. And Monsieur Christensen had told them long ago that life would not be easy. She remembered him leaning forward at the campfire, drilling them with his eyes, and saying, *"But the things the enemy means for evil, God will use for good. We see this time and again in the Bible."*

They had built back the village, they had rescued the children, the Germans were running away . . .

She did not know when she fell asleep, but she awoke with a jerk and a moan as the darkness was giving way to dawn. She was still sitting by the chaplain. Sometime in the night, his Bible had slipped from her lap.

Holding her side, Isabelle carefully bent to retrieve the book, and when she lifted it off the floor, an envelope slipped out. Leaning further over, she groaned in pain and plucked it from where it had landed by her feet. She was about to put it back in the Bible when she noticed the recipient's address.

Monsieur Peter Christensen. Written in *her* handwriting.

Her breath caught, and her head started pounding.

No! Impossible . . .

Isabelle opened the Bible's leather cover and read on the first page:

The Holy Bible
Presented to: Peter Christensen
By: His loving parents, Philip and Dotty Christensen
On: July 10, 1934,
in celebration of his graduation from high school

Isabelle let the Bible and the envelope fall to the floor as she stood bent over the wounded chaplain. His face was bruised and swollen, the freckles across his cheeks the only hint that this was the boy from long ago. Then she lifted the bandage around his head. Amid the blood that had dried to a deep brown was copper hair, cropped short and bereft of curls. This chaplain was indeed Peter Christensen.

Isabelle gave a soft cry, then numbly shuffled away from the sleeping soldier.

She couldn't find her voice at first. But when she had left the nunnery and walked up the steep incline into the woods, she found it just fine. She screamed as a rooster crowed and the sun peeked over the ridge. Then she cursed. Cursed! Words she had never thought she'd say.

The wounded soldier, the soldier who had saved her life, was Peter Christensen!

Don't faint, don't cry out. Leave. Leave. This she had told herself after finding her letter.

It was a cruel joke. After all the heartbreak and sorrow and cruelty, surely this wasn't true. The man who had saved her life three days ago was the same man, only then a boy, who had broken her heart eleven years ago! That was impossible!

A sick coincidence.

Was this the way God was answering her prayers? Dragging her back into one more painful memory? She had never let herself care for any other boy or man since then. She'd had no time for another heartache.

She hated him! He had broken her heart.

But he had saved her too.

Why him, and why now? She blushed to think how she had sat at his side and confessed so many things that she had never said to anyone else except for this same Peter, eleven years ago.

Back then, she had dared to tell him about her anger at God, her confusion.

This was all too odd.

If she left now, it wouldn't matter. Simply an odd coincidence. Surely this Peter would not want to see her once he woke up, *if* he woke up. She had exasperated him years earlier with her questions, her babyish poetry, her long, heartfelt letters.

"You wounded me back then, Peter Christensen, and now you have made up for it by saving my life. That's enough."

"Ça va, mademoiselle? You okay, miss?"

Isabelle froze. Had she been speaking out loud to the trees nestled up beyond the nunnery? Who was talking to her now? How long had she been lost in her thoughts?

"Oui, yes, fine. Merci," she murmured to an older gentleman, arm in a cast, who smoked a cigarette and walked back toward the makeshift hospital.

It could not be true, this young soldier, the son of the gentle giant, of Monsieur Christensen—Monsieur Martin!—was in Sisteron. A chaplain?

She had to leave, now, before the sun warmed her and she lost her resolve. When Jean-Yves came to visit later in the morning, she'd have him drive her to the camp, to help Mme Nicolas and Delphine and René.

She found Lieutenant Frank asleep in the hallway and roused him. "I must leave, sir," she stated.

But she would do one last thing before the world woke up. She made her way to Peter's cot where he slept. Thank goodness he still slept.

She stood by the bed and whispered to him in French, "I'm leaving now, Chaplain Ginger. But I'll tell you one more story before I leave. It is the story of a girl who loved a boy with red hair. Of a moonlight walk, of jokes and kindness and codes. Of letters, of comic sketches and simple poetry, of her first true love. And then he was gone, and he never explained why he left. And she did not want to love again after that.

"And now this boy is playing another joke on her. It feels like a very cruel joke to come back in this way. The girl does not understand why. But she will say thank you, merci, to this same redheaded boy for saving her life. Because when he saved her, she was angry and wretched and grieving and so much more. But she is alive, and she knows life is a gift. And so that girl who loved a boy with red hair will tell this boy with red hair thank you. Au revoir, Peter. *Je m'appelle Zabelle.*"

42

PETER

He had heard her voice, the woman sitting beside him: *"Merci. You know what* merci *means, right?"* Talking in English, confessing her confusion and anger. Or was that the girl at camp asking forgiveness for her sins from the top of the Penitents?

Zabelle!

No, not the camp. Now. Last night. In the night.

This girl, this woman had told him stories and had recited Bible verses in French.

Peter tried to organize his thoughts. Could they honestly be that jumbled? He kept hearing over and over the words, *"Au revoir, Peter. Je m'appelle Zabelle."*

Good-bye, Peter. My name is Zabelle.

Her voice, that sweet, slightly sassy voice from the Penitents. The voice from the walk by the stream, teasing, the voice in a whisper confessing her anger.

All the same voice? Surely not.

No, Peter reprimanded himself. No, he had been *thinking* of Zabelle as they drove to Sisteron. He had let himself remember her, let himself remember so many details of their times together, of the letters. But that was before he was injured.

Yes, yes. Now it was clear. First the shock of hearing about the mistake of the Allies and the bombing of Sisteron, then Butler's admonition to get there quickly. Next, the twelve of them hurrying to Sisteron. The crowds in neighboring towns cheering along the way until they had arrived at pure devastation.

Yes, yes.

And along the route, he had thought of Zabelle. Because she had lived in Sisteron. Because he had addressed so many letters to her. Peter closed his eyes and saw the name of the road where she had lived written on the envelope.

But who was the voice in the night, the pretty French gal Frank kept talking about?

His head was splitting. The light. The voice. The silence. The pain. Then the nurse talking and Frank talking and then the girl talking, talking, talking all through the night. Urging him to listen to her secrets.

It must have been a strange dream melding with reality in his mind.

A French girl speaking in heavily accented English, wondering if a chaplain was like a priest. And then talking about the Penitents and her anger and the war and her father. And Jewish orphans. Quoting Bible verses to him in French.

How strange dreams were! And his wounded brain—a head injury—was apparently jumbling real events and conversations over the course of a decade.

"And now this boy is playing another joke on her. It feels like a very cruel joke to come back in this way."

In a dream, people do strange things, play cruel jokes. Or do they?

"Au revoir, Peter . . ."

Then, *"Je m'appelle Zabelle."*

The nightmare again, the dying soldier, the German officer, the firing squad, the Protestant medal, the airplanes drawing nearer, nearer, the way he threw himself over the young woman . . . it all blurred together.

And his head. The excruciating pain!

Then Frank was by his bed again.

"Hey, Ginger. Calm down, buddy. It was just a nightmare." Frank's hand on his forehead. "You're burning up again. I'll get the nurse."

Drifting in and out of sleep, people hovering over him.

He was so cold!

"Cold." Had he said it out loud?

A blanket. Sleep, blessed sleep.

The German, the medal, the plane, "*Je m'appelle Zabelle . . .*"

Peter jerked, reaching for something, whispering, "*De l'eau*, s'il vous plaît. Water. Thirsty."

A cool rag laid on his forehead, a woman saying something in French. "*Buvez*, monsieur." A straw to his lips. Parched lips. So hot. So cold.

Voices. Whispers.

". . . not looking good. The infection . . . so many wounds . . . hallucinations . . ."

Sweating, sopping wet, tossing, crying out. The pain, wrenching his head, his whole body. Shivering. He could not stop shaking.

"Hang in there, Ginger. Hang in there." Frank's raspy voice.

Fading, fading . . .

The sun was bright, glinting through the window. Peter winced and put his hand up to shield his eyes. The movement pierced him, and he moaned.

He heard scrambling and turned his head to see Frank straightening in a chair and rubbing the sleep from his eyes. "Ginger! Look at you! Got your eyes open!" His smile stretched wide, a smile that said relief.

"Hey."

"Glory hallelujah! You're back. You had us all on our knees earlier this morning, begging the Almighty for your life, Ginger. Fever broke a little while ago. Céline and me, well, we got you changed into some dry clothes. And then you slept all peaceful-like."

"Thanks." The only word he could manage.

"You had me practicing your prayer walking. Walked these halls again and again, half the night long."

Everything hurt. Even thinking hurt. But he was alive.

Thank You, Lord, for life.

"*Merci. You know what* merci *means, right?*"

"*Au revoir, Peter. Je m'appelle Zabelle.*"

"Frank?"

"I'm here, buddy. Right here." Frank's hand touched his own.

"Dream . . . angel came . . . can't quite . . . make it out . . . so confused."

"'Course you are, Ginger. I told you—we thought we'd be performing your funeral. You've got a nasty head wound. 'Course you're confused. You just rest now."

Peter drifted off again for a second or a minute or an hour. When he opened his eyes, Frank was still there, looking down at him, his brow knotted in worry. "What'd ya say, Ginger?"

Had he been speaking? Oh, yes. "Girl?"

"You want to know about the girl?"

"Girl. French. Here?"

"The girl you saved? She was here for several days—she was injured too. She left real early this morning. That's when you took a turn for the worse—when I replaced her. But she asked me to tell you *merci* again. You didn't expect a pretty little French gal to wait around for you forever, did you?"

No, not forever.

"My name, Frank?"

"What?"

"French girl . . . my name?"

"Did the French girl know your name? I don't think so. She called you Chaplain Ginger, or more like 'Shaplan Jeenjur.' She heard me calling you that. Never did correct her. Like I said, her

272

English was fine, but she fumbled around a little. And she was ... not in a great place. Really angry. Understandable, I guess. At least she's alive, though. But I didn't want to correct her. She had a bit of fire in her."

"Didn't . . . know my name."

Frank grinned. "Well, in a way she knew your name. Called you Ginger, like the rest of us do."

His eyes, so heavy. Closing . . .

Then Frank's voice again. Had he slept through their conversation? Had he asked a question?

"Remember, you came here a few days ago with the first part of the Task Force. There were twelve of us. The rest showed up yesterday. We came to help the villagers clean up the rubble. Sisteron has been liberated, not that they're celebratin' or anything." Silence. "You remember what happened to Sisteron, don't you?"

"Yes," Peter whispered. "How many lost?"

"Over a hundred, with lots still missing."

"What day?"

"It's August twenty-first. You've been here three days now."

Three days. He had to get out of this place, get back on the road with the men. "Troops. Progress?"

"Yeah, the troops are making progress. Those Germans are running scared. Most of the Task Force left Sisteron, heading toward Grenoble to block the Boches. But then early this morning an envoy showed up at General Butler's command post and had an urgent message from General Truscott to rush back west to Montélimar to block all routes of withdrawal up the Rhône Valley. It was a bit confusing, but Butler got 'em all turned around. Don't know how we'll fulfill that order—we're short on both fuel and vehicles. They want us to hightail it to Montélimar, but it's hard with so little fuel."

How could they find more fuel for the Allies? His mind spun as Frank continued talking.

"The Boches are congregating by the Rhône. We're supposed to block them to the north. Supposedly the 36th Army will come to our aid, but they're moving slow. Seems like the beach landing was so successful that a lot of the ammunition meant for the landings wasn't unloaded from the *Nevada*, and the fuel and vehicles are stuck down in the belly of the ship. I just got word that the Task Force has arrived in Montélimar. Good group of soldiers . . ."

Peter pictured the men hurrying, crowded on jeeps, some on foot, determined. How he wanted to join them as they pushed back the enemy.

And then he was sleeping again.

The nurse hovered over him, taking his vitals. *Céline*. She had told him her name earlier this morning.

"*Très bien*, Chaplain Christensen. Fever's gone. Heart rate nearly normal. Good to see your eyes open. You scared us all silly last night."

"De l'eau," he whispered as Céline held the straw to his lips. As the cool water trickled down his throat, he knew this wasn't a dream. It was real. He was alive.

"Girl?" he whispered in French. "Name?"

Céline cocked an eyebrow. "*Comment*? What, sir?" She leaned down over the cot.

"Girl. Name. Saved."

Céline's face brightened. "The young woman you saved? I'm so glad you saved her. And by saving her, you also saved Mme Lefort, one of the mayor's assistants, a lovely older woman. And the girl? Yes, I know her name. We went to the same high school. She's a few years younger than me. Isabelle Seauve. Eerie, isn't it? Her surname is like *sauver*, you know? You say 'save' in English. You saved Isabelle Seauve."

Isabelle Seauve. He closed his eyes and pictured the envelopes covered with cartoon images of Scouts delivering letters to France. Colored envelopes he spent hours decorating, complete with a comic strip. How he had smiled to pen her name.

Isabelle Seauve.

Ironic, yes. A cruel joke, no doubt. He had saved Isabelle Seauve. The beautiful teenager from camp. The girl he'd poured his heart out to—about living in Algeria, about his father's eccentricities, about his love of France, his fear of school in America, his deep conviction for ministry.

The girl who had tempted him to stay in France.

The girl whose heart he had sliced in two. Never again had he written her another word. After forty-three letters exchanged over the course of four months. Nothing but silence from him.

And he'd never told her why.

A cruel joke.

And now God or Satan or serendipity was playing a cruel joke on them again.

Céline was speaking. "She was here, talking to you all through the last two nights. I think I even heard her reading to you from your Bible." Céline glanced around. "I'm sure I saw her with the Bible." She knelt on the tile floor. "Ah, here it is under your cot. She must have dropped it in the night—when she fell asleep."

The nurse set the Bible on the chair by the cot. "Like I said, she was here most of the night. Oh, and hold on." She bent down again and came up with an envelope. "This must have fallen out of the Bible."

Peter squinted, and then his heart thumped as he fumbled with Isabelle's letter to him. Had she seen it?

"Au revoir, Peter. My name is Zabelle."

She *had* said his name. She knew who he was, and she certainly would never want to see him again.

But he wanted to see her. Of all the messed up things in this war, here was something messed up that could be used for good. Here was a chance to tell her that he was sorry for his silence.

He'd wanted to before. Throughout the years, he'd catch a snippet of a phrase and think of her. And remember. And then feel guilty. Why had he never apologized before?

Because life was complicated, and he was a coward. And years ago, he had decided leaving her alone would be the kinder thing to do.

Would seeing her again be kind or would it be cruel?

With the envelope clutched in his hand, he looked up at Céline and said, "I . . . would like to meet . . . this Isabelle."

Céline flashed a sympathetic smile. "I'll let her know. She's terrific." She then leaned closer and whispered, "She's been part of this rescue mission for Jewish kids for almost two years now. She's a resistant. One of the best. She hid the kids, and her father forged the papers. Father was gunned down by the Nazis, though. She's had a real rough time. So thankful she's gonna be all right, thankful you saved her." Looking around, Céline said, "Let me see if she's still here."

Isabelle was a resistant, saving Jewish children.

He had two thoughts—he was not surprised by her bravery, and he had to see her one more time. To say he was sorry.

43

❖

ISABELLE

AUGUST 21, 1944

When will Jean-Yves show up? Isabelle paced back and forth in the courtyard as she'd been doing for hours. She needed to leave this hospital!

She jumped at the sound of Céline's voice. "The American chaplain finally woke up."

Isabelle swiveled around and felt her cheeks redden and her heart began to thump in her chest, pulling at her broken ribs.

"He's awake, and he's asking for you."

"I . . . no . . . I can't."

And yet she wanted to see Peter again. Would she cry or smile? She certainly wouldn't slap him in the face, although that seemed the better option.

You broke my heart all those years ago. Why did you save me now? I don't want anything to do with you!

Oh, but I want everything to do with you, her heart answered back.

"How long will he be in the hospital?" she asked the nurse.

"Oh, my goodness, Isabelle. He's not going anywhere quickly. He may fall right back into a coma. To tell you the truth, we don't know if he'll even survive. Scared us something terrible just after you left this morning. But for right now, he's awake, and I think you should take advantage of it."

Jean-Yves arrived in the courtyard, and as Isabelle stepped toward the truck, before she could change her mind, she called out behind her, "I've got to go, Céline. Please tell him I am so thankful he woke up and that I'm thankful he saved me."

Dozens of children scampered into the sandpit. Others were busy picking blackberries. When a few recognized Isabelle and rushed up to her, Ginette used her hefty body to block their way. "No hugs, kids! Isabelle is injured."

But Delphine could not resist. She sidled around Ginette and grabbed Isabelle's hands. "I knew you'd come."

Isabelle took Delphine's face into her hands and gently kissed her forehead, her cheeks. "Ma petite. I hear you've been working very hard, helping Mme Nicolas and Ginette."

"We've picked blackberries and taught the children the camp code. René brings food from the surrounding villages, Ginette prepares it, and I help." Her eyes dimmed slightly. "But Mme Nicolas is tired, so she's forced to rest."

Isabelle glanced over at Ginette. "How's that going?"

Ginette gave a wink. "She's almost as stubborn as you, but not quite."

All day long, Isabelle helped prepare meals and told stories to the children and walked with them to the creek, assuring them the Germans had left the region and they were safe now. Yet she kept hearing her own words in her mind, *"But there's a traitor, and it isn't safe yet,"* followed by Céline's words, *"We don't know if he'll even survive. . . . But for right now, he's awake, and I think you should take advantage of it."*

Such thoughts taunted her as she slowly made her way to Mme Nicolas's house, exhausted, pain stabbing her side. Letting herself in, she found the older woman crocheting socks, rocking in her chair.

"You are unwell?" Isabelle asked.

"I am fine. But your friend, that wretched Ginette, thinks she owns the place and is insisting I rest. I refuse to traumatize the children further with them thinking I'm about to die. I've just had a few sinking spells. But Ginette insists I rest, so I've told the children I'm making them a surprise gift. I've already finished twenty-three pairs of socks. Almost halfway there. Then I don't care what Ginette says—I'll be back on the job."

The smile she gave Isabelle didn't quite reach her eyes. Mme Nicolas looked depleted.

"Now, that's way too much about me." She patted Isabelle's hand. "Tell me everything. I'm so sorry."

"It's all horrible. Tito is dead, so many dead. Everything destroyed. The Germans are gone. We should be celebrating with the other towns and villages. Instead, we keep searching for survivors. Four days now. There are no new survivors, but many still missing."

"And you were hurt?"

As Mme Nicolas crocheted socks for the children, Isabelle told her the whole story.

"Peter Christensen rescued you? That's unbelievable. He is here, in Sisteron?"

Nodding, Isabelle watched as Mme Nicolas put the pieces together.

"I had heard he was a chaplain in the Army. His father told me that." At Isabelle's raised eyebrows, she added, "Yes, you know I've kept in touch with Monsieur Christensen. Not lately, but sometimes I hear personal news."

"Well, I doubt he's heard the most recent news. His son is badly injured. Because of me." Unable to help herself, Isabelle lay her head in the older woman's lap and let the tears fall. "I should be dead, but I'm alive because Peter Christensen saved me. Please pray that he doesn't die."

※

Ginette stepped into the farmhouse and observed Isabelle and Mme Nicolas. Hands on hips, she proclaimed, "You look awful, Zabelle. We'll manage on our own. Go back to that nunnery."

"I'm fine."

"You're not fine. Nowhere close. What happened?"

"The plane, the bullets . . ." she said and sniffed.

"I know that story. But tell me the story that has wounded not only your body but your soul."

She shook her head. "You know me too well. I wish you couldn't read my eyes." She blew out a long breath. "I don't want to tell you that story. I want to help you fix dinner." She stood up with a grunt and squeezed Mme Nicolas's hand. "The socks are perfect. You finish them, and we'll present them to the children tomorrow."

Ginette took Isabelle by the arm, calling back to Mme Nicolas, "There are fifty-one children now." Then, once outside, she whispered, "If you think I'm letting you help without telling me what's going on, you're wrong."

"I'll tell you as we fix dinner. I promise."

⁎⋆⁎

With each bit of information Isabelle recounted about her rescuer, Ginette's eyes widened.

"That's . . . impossible. Surely it can't be Monsieur Christensen's son. Peter? The boy you wrote dozens of letters to? The boy you were in love with? Non."

"But it *is* him. And you're the one who understands why I can't go back to see him. It's like a fairy tale and a nightmare mixed together."

"Fairy tales are often nightmarish. Good and bad. Love and heartbreak. Try to forget about what happened so long ago and just tell him 'thank you' for now."

Isabelle shrugged. "You make it sound so easy."

"Give the man a chance. He saved your life. And he wants to see you."

"I can't separate the two." Isabelle set a few peeled potatoes in a pot. "It feels raw and confusing, between what happened way back then and what happened a few days ago."

"Of course it does, but you can at least try to forgive him."

"You've never told me to forgive Peter Christensen before," countered Isabelle. "You used to describe in vivid detail what you'd do to him if you ever saw him again." She gave a tiny grin.

"True. I was furious with the guy for breaking your heart. But he was just a foolish teenager then, and you were just a kid. If he's asking to see you, I think you should go. Who knows? If his head injury is very bad, maybe he won't even remember you from before."

That would be the worst of all if he didn't remember me. That would keep the poison in the sting.

"Go back. If not for Peter, for yourself then. You truly do look wrung out."

"He may not even survive."

Isabelle drew a deep breath, then another, and turned to leave. The distance between the camp and Castel-Bevons was not far, but the distance between her mind and her heart felt as far apart as the sea that separated France from Algeria. Tonight, she would sleep at Mme Nicolas's, and tomorrow, perhaps, she would return to the building on the outskirts of Sisteron and walk into that space where the past and present collided.

44

❖

RENÉ

August 21–22, 1944

In the middle of the night, René entered The Camp Between the Hills again. And again, silence greeted him. The moon hung low, a semicircle slice above which stars winked. He parked the German truck at Mme Nicolas's house, surprised to see another vehicle there. He was about to walk back up the rock driveway toward the camp when an arm grabbed him around his chest and a hand came over his mouth.

"Not a word." A man's voice, in French, a whisper. The man's grip tightened as René struggled. Heart beating fast, he twisted as a hulking form pulled him back. René kicked and squirmed, but he was no match for this stranger. Anger surged within at his helplessness. Was this the traitor they feared? Had he harmed Mme Nicolas, found the children, hurt Delphine?

Think, René. If you can survive three hundred Germans, you can defeat one man. Think!

After he was taken a short distance, the stranger commanded, "Go down. Not a word."

René descended seven steps into his musty prison, the heat heavy even in the underground space. Something was being dragged over the opening above him. As his eyes adjusted to the darkness, he found he was standing in the middle of a small room similar to other wine cellars. He climbed back up the steps and pushed on the metal that covered the cave's opening, but it didn't budge.

Find a way to use a lever to lift the door. Break a wine bottle and use the broken glass as a weapon. These were things every maquisard knew.

Was this stranger even now entering the cave where the children were hidden?

He needed to move fast, but how to escape?

He reached for a bottle and broke it against the shelf, dark liquid puddling on the ground at his feet. He grasped the broken neck of the bottle, expecting the stranger to return with a gun. Instead, he heard a soft voice whispering, "René!"

Delphine?

Then she was beside him, her arms thrown around his neck, her body shaking, heaving, though she made little sound. She whispered, "I'd hoped it was you. Prayed it was you." Her grip on him tightened. "Who was that?"

He set down the broken bottle. "I don't know—a large, strong man. He grabbed me from behind as I was leaving the truck."

He could make out the whites of Delphine's eyes, the fear and terror. "Hours ago, I left the big cave after the children were settled in their beds. I wasn't supposed to leave, but I wanted to spend some time with Isabelle. She came today—I told you she'd come. But as I was walking to Mme Nicolas's house, a car drove up and parked near her house. I saw a large man get out of the car and walk toward her house. I think Mme Nicolas was home, crocheting socks for the children. A light was on. And then there was no light and no sound. I didn't see where the man went, if he had entered the house or not." A sob. "I don't know what happened. Where is Mme Nicolas? What has he done? I ran here to hide." Her voice was rising, panicked.

"Shhh, Delphine. Talk softly."

She whispered, "Mme Nicolas had told me, 'If you must hide, go to my cellar. Stay away from the children. There are supplies in the cellar, where you'll be safe for a while.' She showed me how to enter. This is supposed to be a secret cellar, René. She said no one knew about it. So I came here to hide. It was like at your farmhouse, the way I opened the hatch and then closed it so that no one would know. I've been down here for hours! I didn't know when it would be safe to leave. And then I heard someone removing the hatch. I hid behind the wine bottles when he brought you in. And now we're trapped here!"

"*Du calme*," he whispered, trying to quell his own panic. "Shhh. He may be up there listening."

Delphine scooted closer, both her hands grasping his, head buried in his chest. "How did he know of this place? Mme Nicolas said it is more secret than the wine cave with the children." René felt the damp of her tears on his shirt. She was trembling, clutching his arm, repeating again and again, "No one knows except Mme Nicolas and me." A gulp. "But someone else does know."

"Try to calm down." He brought his other arm around her thin shoulders. "We need to think what to do next."

Lifting her tearstained face, she whispered, "We must pray. The Lord will show us what to do."

They had tried to remove the heavy slab of metal that covered the opening to the cave but without success. They then moved around the cave looking for food. True to Mme Nicolas's word, they found saucisses and cheese and bread and five canteens filled with water. And a pile of woolen blankets. After encouraging Delphine to eat something, he spread the blankets out on the dirt floor, where eventually she fell asleep.

By the light of his torch, René searched the shelves where he found wine bottles, canned peaches, jars of jam, hard little toasts wrapped in a dish towel, and another towel hiding a large chunk of cheese. No dust or spiderwebs were visible, so surely the provisions had not been there for very long.

Though René tried to stay awake, he must have fallen asleep, huddled on the ground beside Delphine, with half of the blanket covering him, the broken wine bottle clutched in his hand. The sound of scraping startled him awake. René shook Delphine, put his finger to his lips, and motioned for her to hide beyond the wine shelves. Perhaps the stranger hadn't figured out that she was here. René might be killed, but she would be left in the cave. And she could escape.

Just like before.

But his chest thrummed with anticipation and terror.

Keep Delphine safe.

He repeated it like a mantra or a prayer to the Penitents as the scraping continued and light flooded the cellar.

His shadow filled the wooden stairway, a giant of a man. René stood straight, prepared yet terrified. But the man held no gun or weapon at all. He wore a look of both relief and extreme weariness on a face that was covered in wrinkles.

When René scooted to a corner, the man descended and stood towering over him. "I won't hurt you. You are René?"

René swallowed. Surely this giant could see the way his heart thumped through his shirt.

"I'm sorry to have treated you this way. Let me introduce myself. I'm Monsieur Martin." He held out a callused hand.

Monsieur Martin? Surely not! René didn't trust anyone, and he certainly wasn't about to trust a man who had thrown him into a cellar.

"I'm afraid I had to hide you rather precipitously. I'm sorry. I was not thinking clearly when I saw the German truck. Yvette— Mme Nicolas—sent an urgent message to me yesterday, and I came quickly."

The older man, at least sixty, looked confused. René remained stock-still, eyes searching for a moment of weakness.

"René, your family was keeping a young girl. I know what you've done. Your bravery. I know about the ambush at your farmhouse . . . the butchery." His bloodshot eyes held sorrow, compassion. "I'm so sorry."

René kept glancing at the opening in the cave, the way the dawn was filtering through. Could he knock this man out with the bottle? "I don't believe you!" he spat. "I don't believe anything you're saying."

"You're wise to be careful. I'm sorry for this shock." The stranger sighed and glanced around the cave. "When we first heard the rumors of war coming, Mme Nicolas's son helped me build this cave as another hiding place. We had the camp and the big cellar where the children are now, but it seemed wise to build another smaller cellar just in case." He ran a hand over his face. "Your cousin, Isabelle, used to attend our Scout camp. She has been helping in the Network, as did her father. I'm sorry about your mother and your uncle."

His voice was low, commanding, his eyes pleading for René to believe him, but René could not. Every piece of information the man had shared could have been gotten from someone who had betrayed them.

Delphine emerged from behind the wine shelves, eyes blinking as the morning light broke through the darkness. Step by step, she crept nearer to the immense man.

"Delphine, stop!" René said, but still she walked forward until she stood before the stranger who towered over her tiny form.

Without a glance at René, she wrapped her skinny arms around his huge body and began to sob. "You came. You came for us all. And the light. Why, it shines like a halo over you." Still clinging to the man, she turned to René and said, "Can't you see the glow? This is the angel who carried you to Sisteron! He came back to help us now. Don't be afraid. He has come to save us all."

René tried to piece together the story as dawn broke across the horizon. Seated around the kitchen table in the farmhouse with Mme Nicolas and the man called Monsieur Martin, they spoke in hushed tones.

Mme Nicolas was twisting her hands in her lap. "I had to contact Monsieur Martin when I heard that Peter—that his son—had been injured and might not live." She nodded toward the rotary phone on a crowded shelf and glanced around. "I cannot tell you more."

"I don't need to know more," René said. "I trust you."

Isabelle had taken Delphine back to the large cellar after the child had promised not to speak a word about the events of the evening. Now his cousin entered the farmhouse and joined them at the table.

"Delphine will keep the secret. She can talk a blue streak, but she can also keep quiet when necessary," René reassured his captor.

"That's good to know," Monsieur Martin said. "She is quite a precocious girl."

René nodded. Then a fuzzy memory pricked his conscious. "You're the director of this camp. I came once with my uncle to pick up Isabelle after camp was over." His brow wrinkled as he put another puzzle piece together. "You *were* the camp's director, and you *are* Monsieur Martin."

The big man leaned forward in his chair, hands clasped together on the table. "Yes, one and the same. But you understand, René, that it is best never to say this to anyone else."

"Oui, bien sûr. I'll keep quiet about that, about all of this. As quiet as Delphine." Then he smirked as another memory came. "And your son was the guy who broke my cousin's heart. Right, Isabelle?"

She shrugged, her face betraying the truth. "That was long ago." She glanced at Monsieur Martin shyly. "I doubt his father even knew about our . . . our friendship."

The big man chortled. "Oh, I knew, Isabelle. I saw those envelopes that he spent hours illustrating and sending across the sea to France. I knew about you." He gave a wink. "And I was plenty pleased he was writing to a girl who knew all about Protestant penance." Another wink. "And now, amazingly, you have met him again in Sisteron in the oddest of ways. He was sent by the American Army to help with the rescue effort?"

"Yes, he was bringing a wounded child to the infirmary when the planes approached. He saved me from being mowed down by friendly fire." She stared at the tiled floor. "I'm so thankful to him, but I'm afraid he suffered many bullet wounds."

Mme Nicolas was nodding, fiddling with her crocheting, but

unable to stitch. "I hope I haven't risked the Network by sending for you, Philip."

His large hand reached for Mme Nicolas's hands, covered them, and said with a gentleness that pierced René, "Yvette, you know how grateful I am for the chance to see Peter." He turned to look at Isabelle. "Yvette thought that you could perhaps go with me to the infirmary, help me visit Peter a bit clandestinely. I'm known in the region. It would be best if very few people see me."

"Of course," Isabelle said.

Finally, Monsieur Martin turned to René. "I'm sorry I handled you roughly, son. I had to check with Yvette to be sure of who you were, but I had to wait for her to come up from checking on the children. We know there is still a real threat of a leak in the Network."

"I understand, sir."

"And I can't let the children here at camp see me. My underground efforts continue. Soon these children will be free, hopefully to return to their foster homes, but if ever they said a stray word, if they talked about 'the giant' who came to the camp, someone might overhear, and what I'm continuing with would be compromised." Monsieur Martin again gave that pleading look. "Sisteron is free, but the war is not over."

Gradually, René felt his body relaxing, felt a flickering of something inside. He stood and held out his hand to Monsieur Martin. "It is an honor to meet the head of the Martin Network, sir. I'll help you in any way I can."

Monsieur Martin stood too and grasped René's hand with his large callused one. "Isabelle and I will leave shortly." He looked at Mme Nicolas. "I've asked a young woman from the Network who lives in Nice to bring supplies to the camp. Sandrine is her name. She wants to stay and help you all with the children. You remember her?"

Mme Nicolas nodded. "Yes. God be praised. Sandrine will be a great help."

"Now that Nice is liberated, she wants to come here."

Mme Nicolas took both of Monsieur Martin's hands in hers,

held them tight, then placed her hand on his cheek. "We'll be fine with Ginette and Sandrine. You go with Isabelle to see your boy." Her voice broke, and René saw the liquid pool in the old woman's eyes. "Tell Peter I'm praying for him to heal soon. And be careful, Philip. I know your work isn't over yet, but hopefully you can go back to Dotty and the girls soon."

"No worries, Yvette. All will be well."

But his voice sounded flat.

Turning to René, Monsieur Martin said, "You're free to join your Maquis. You've done a good job, son. For your country, for your family, for us. Thank you."

45

PETER

D-Day+7
August 22, 1944

"Mighty hard to see Sisteron now, but you remember how we built back the camp. They'll do it here too . . ." Someone was talking and then quoting from the Bible.

He recognized the voice but couldn't place it. Deep. Familiar. Yet somehow different. Weaker. Scratchier. Long pauses.

Concentrate, Peter! Open your eyes!

But he could not.

Cold. Hot. The pain. The headache. The chills.

The voice.

". . . mighty proud of you, son . . . Lieutenant Frank has told me about your most recent exploit . . . amazing about the young woman you saved, Pete. What a coincidence!"

His father!

Pause. Throaty sound. "We never have believed in coincidences, have we, Pete?" Chuckling. "Still think about those Penitents cliffs. Memory always makes me smile."

Another pause.

"Sure wish you could open your eyes, son. You've got a job to do. Those boys need you out there with them, chasing the enemy." Now he was leaning close, and Peter could feel his breath on his face, could smell the scents of hard work and coffee.

"I guess you figured out that your mom is back in Algeria. She's been working with the Muslim underground to hide the Jews there. Staying at our house and baking cookies while I've been here in France."

A forced chuckle. A deep breath.

"And Yvette has been part of the underground for some time. She sends messages from the camp when necessary. She even risked a call earlier to let me know what happened to you. I got word to your mom, but I've begged Dotty to stay put. She's spittin' mad, but she knows I'm right. Still pretty dangerous around here. She says she won't send any more cookies till she hears you're awake. You know your mom and her threats. But her prayers are nonstop."

A sniff. Then he was blowing his nose.

"I've had to lay low. A priest in the Network was murdered in Nice. We still aren't sure if it was a member of the Milice or one of the resistants. I had a little skirmish there too." He cleared his throat. "Thank you for putting those names in the camp code. Yvette said an Italian boy delivered them in the middle of the night. The Jewish kids hidden in this part of the country are all safe. How kind of our God to provide the camp for them. Do you remember helping dig that enormous space all those years ago? We didn't know why, but we believed, and we dug. I was at the camp last night with Yvette and the young woman you rescued—Isabelle."

Silence. Another clearing of the throat.

"But turncoats abound, Peter. It'll be harder to spot them now that the southern villages are free. And there are many other children hidden farther north." His father's hand found his under the sheet, reassuring. "I'm heading that way." A sniffle. "Let's meet up when this war is over, back at the camp. Or somewhere else. You name it, son." A squeeze, the warmth of life soaking into Peter's cold fingers. Then his father whispered, "You hang in there for us. Your mom will never forgive me if you don't come home to her. Your sisters either. They always remind me I got you to sign up for the chaplaincy."

Now he was crying, unabashedly. Had he ever heard his father cry? Philip Christensen did not have time for tears. Peter tried to make his hand move, tried to reach over toward the voice.

"I can't stay. I just needed to see you, to tell you to hurry up and heal." The voice was scratchy, so unlike his jovial father. "I love you, son."

The hand withdrew.

Stay, Dad, stay!

Then Frank's voice, farther away, low. "Did he wake up at all? Open his eyes?"

"No. 'Fraid not."

"I'm sorry, Mr. Christensen. Don't you worry—none of us will say a word about your being here." A pause. "I'm sure he's hearing you, sir. He was awake yesterday. Pulled through a horrendous night and was awake. Last night was just as bad, but he's here again. He'll come out of it. We need our chaplain . . ."

Later—whether a minute or an hour, Peter didn't know—Frank was standing beside the cot. "Ginger, your old man was here. You heard him, didn't you? Brave man. Just like you told us. Big ol' guy." A pause, then, "Oh, I almost forgot. The soldiers in the Task Force have sent you get-well-soon cards. Tried to decorate them like you do, but none of us is too talented. But Andy got a pretty good likeness of you. You're gonna have to open your eyes to see it, though, Ginger."

Another pause, longer.

"We're getting good news from down south. The French General de Lattre informed us that Toulon is surrounded by the Allies. The Frenchies were helped by some monks who guided them around the terrain, and another battalion commander led his men through the night by marking the trail with toilet paper provided by the good ol' US Army." Frank forced a laugh.

Peter tried to open his eyes, tried to nod, to show some sign that he understood, but he failed.

"As for our men, I told you the Germans are on the retreat. Task Force has chased them up near Montélimar. Fighting started yesterday. I may have to head that way soon. Lee will stay here in my place. He took a likin' to you. Real serious kid, but he grins every time he asks about Ginger. Soon as you're ready to join us, I'll come get you." Frank cleared his throat. "There's someone else who wants to talk to you, so I'll say good-bye for now. You take care, Ginger. And wake up soon, please."

46

ISABELLE

AUGUST 22, 1944

It had been such a strange conversation with Monsieur Martin—
Monsieur Christensen—as she drove to Castel-Bevons with her
heart thumping, the heat of embarrassment climbing up her neck.
But the awkwardness had disappeared as they began to talk.

In some ways, he seemed diminished from the gentle giant of
a decade ago, his red hair streaked with silver now, his eyes still
green but heavy with fatigue, the skin underneath them a dark gray.
She wondered if the man ever slept. The loud, boisterous voice
she remembered, the one that echoed off the Baume, was calmer
now, more subdued. Yet his words held the same conviction, the
same fight for truth and for life.

"You remind me of my father," she told him.

"He was a very fine man, your father."

She sucked in a breath. "You knew him, didn't you? You met
him when he came to pick me up at camp all those years ago."

"Not only at camp, dear."

Her head jerked up. Of course! "You saw him when you were setting up the Network?"

Her father once explained to her, *"There is a man. We will call him 'Monsieur Martin.' He has found homes for the children. It will be dangerous, my child . . ."*

"Yes, dear. Your father was one of the first people I sought out."

M. Christensen had sought out her father, had invited him to help set up the Martin Network.

"He was a fine soldier. His reputation from the Great War was renowned. His injury kept him from piloting but did nothing to weaken his sharp mind. A strategist through and through. I'm indebted to your father for so much."

His words felt like a balm being rubbed into her wounds. "Did you send Papa this copy of *The Little Prince?*" She nodded toward the back seat where the book lay beside her satchel.

"You're very clever yourself, Isabelle. Yes, I did."

"Saint-Exupéry inspired my father, and *The Little Prince* gave him hope in the last year of his life."

"I'm glad to hear that. I found the book consoling too. We're all dreamers in this Network, aren't we? Believing there's a better world out there and fighting for it."

Isabelle nodded, unable to speak.

"Your father's work as a forger was essential. And of course, he helped me plan for . . . the future."

"We've retrieved all of the children's documents . . ." She hesitated, then felt relief wash over her as she asked the question she had wanted to ask her father. "Do you think it's safe now to return the children to their foster families whose homes were not destroyed by the bombing or by the Germans who were on the prowl? I'm afraid for the children to leave the camp. But surely the Germans are gone."

"You hesitate because you fear there is a traitor?"

She nodded.

"Do you have any idea who may have compromised the Network, Isabelle?"

"No. I trust all the resistants of the Silo Network. I know that somehow the Germans in Sisteron found out about the children, for they went hunting through some of the homes where the children were hiding. It's a miracle we got the children out. Ginette— do you remember her from camp?—she and René have done the most work."

"And you, my dear. How brave you've been, Isabelle."

His gentle voice wrapped her in a warm embrace, almost as if Papa were sitting beside her. "Thank you, sir." How she missed her father's wisdom. Tears welled as she glanced over at Monsieur Christensen. "You've lived through so much, and you never seem afraid. But I am very afraid. My father used to say that faith is fear that has prayed to God. I don't have such faith anymore, and I don't know what to do."

"My dear child, I'm afraid too at times, even after I've prayed. You all have been courageous, have risked your lives. Since we cannot know if there are traitors, we must assume it is possible. For now, the children are safe at the camp. And we can provide enough supplies for them to stay at the camp indefinitely. The children are strong. Let's keep them together for a bit longer."

"Merci."

"And with Sandrine coming from Nice to help at the camp, perhaps you should stay at the infirmary until you've healed?"

"You trust Sandrine?"

He nodded. "I do, yes."

"It's hard to imagine not being with the children."

"True. But Yvette and Ginette and Sandrine can surely handle the children for a short while. I believe you said that Peter was asking to see you?"

Isabelle felt the heat on her face. "Yes."

"Please visit him."

It almost sounded as if Monsieur Christensen were pleading with her.

But I have visited him and poured out my heart to him.

As Isabelle parked in the infirmary's courtyard, the same courtyard where she had heard the planes, where Peter had saved her and been injured, Monsieur Christensen admitted, "I haven't seen my son in two years. I haven't written. He only heard from me when I asked him to help at camp. And now . . ."

"And now you will see him. And he will see you. Even if he never opens his eyes, I know he can hear us," she had tried to reassure Peter's father as she walked him through the halls to Peter's room and left him alone with his son.

Now the older man came out of Peter's room, his shoulders slumped, a glassy look in his eyes when he turned toward Isabelle. "God bless you, child," he whispered and turned to go.

She wasn't sure what pushed her to do it. Was it compassion at the sight of another person's suffering? She came over and wrapped her arms around him as if he were her own father. She rested her cheek on his broad shoulders and let her tears dampen his coat jacket.

"Thank you, Monsieur Christensen. Please be careful. We need you. We're all thankful for your work. I hope I will see you again." She let go and backed up as she added, "I'm sure Peter is very proud of you too."

Slowly his arms came around her, and she felt the gentle shaking of a man broken with grief. And perhaps regret. "I must go," he whispered. "I cannot wait . . ."

"Go, Monsieur Christensen. Go." She unwound herself, stood back, and looked him full in the eyes. "I will watch over Peter for you, I promise. Since Sandrine is coming to help at the camp, I'll stay here until he gets better."

Isabelle felt perspiration break out everywhere as she watched Monsieur Christensen leave the building, and she made her way down the hallway to Peter's room. She stopped beside his bed, relieved to see that his eyes were still closed.

I don't have to face him just yet.

She stood there undecided. Should she sit down? Come back later? Then she saw Frank coming her way.

"Talk to him, Isabelle," Frank urged. "It's okay. He's just resting his eyes, right, Ginger? Right, buddy? She's here. The girl, the angel."

No response.

"His father was here. Perhaps I should let him rest, Lieutenant."
I promised I will watch over him.

Frank touched her arm. "I'm sure it did him good to hear his
father. It'll do him good to hear you too. I've got to leave—join
the troops heading north. Peter's been asking for you. Please. It
may be the only chance you get."

When Isabelle met his eyes with a question, he added, "He had
another rough time last night. Fever spiked. It's not looking too
good for him." He lowered his voice. "The nurse, Céline, she said
that with his injuries, sometimes it's like that."

Tears flooded Isabelle's eyes, completely unbidden.
Peter, please don't die!

"I'll stay," she promised again.

"I appreciate it. We all do." Frank handed her a heavy satchel.
"This is Ginger's, the chaplain's . . . his things. He may want it if
. . . I mean, *when* he wakes up. He likes to draw. He's real good
at it. Tell him the boys would like some more of his sketches."

Frank opened the satchel and pulled out a sketch pad and a tin
of colored pencils and handed them to Isabelle. He flipped to the
back of the pad. "The men have put get-well cards in here for him.
Be sure to show him when he wakes up." Frank met her eyes, his
bright blue and shining with tears. "Thanks for staying, Isabelle.
You'll see. He'll pull through."

But she wasn't sure he really believed that.

Isabelle repeated the same movements as before, holding on to
the back of the metal chair, wincing at the sharp pain in her side
as she took a seat by Peter's cot. She settled herself in the chair
and began to leaf through the sketch pad, filled with drawings of
soldiers playing cards or kicking a ball or smoking a cigarette as
they penned letters to their sweethearts and loved ones back home.

She felt the catch in her throat and forced herself to swallow.
This same Peter had sent her letters in envelopes covered with his
comic sketches. They were clever, funny. Even now she could feel

the elation, the delight when she returned from *lycée* and saw a decorated envelope waiting for her on the breakfast table. From him.

She had saved every one of them and had tucked them in that old oak chest.

Papa had not said too much. He was perhaps thankful that Isabelle was floating on air. But she knew that he worried. And when the letters stopped coming, Papa could barely contain his anger at the foolish American teenager who would dare break his only daughter's heart.

Stop it! she admonished herself.

How she had missed Peter's letters, where he talked about the French literature he was studying at his international school, where he wrote sweet notes to her using a pigpen code. He even talked about faith and God and the big questions of life.

And he made her laugh.

She fingered the comic-strip drawings depicting scenes from a soldier's life and felt a tiny movement in her lips. She set the pad beside his Bible and pulled one other book from his satchel. She gasped, then smiled, then chuckled. "Of course you would have this one too, Peter."

A copy of *The Little Prince.*

Later, as she sat beside Peter's bed, his head still swathed in bandages, Isabelle noticed his freckles, auburn pinpoints on his cheeks and on the bridge of his nose. Once, long ago, as they walked by the stream, she had touched them softly. *"I like these,"* she'd said. *"I do not know how to call them in English, but in French we say* taches de rousseur. *Red spots!"*

"Freckles," he'd told her as he took hold of her hand, just for a moment, and she had shivered with pleasure.

Now she reached out again and rubbed his cheek with the back of her hand. "Freckles. I like your freckles, Peter. Your taches de rousseur."

Once again, tears came unbidden. She said in French, "I know who you are, and you might as well know who I am. Your friend, Zabelle. From camp. The girl who wrote you so many letters. I cared about you long ago, and then I was so mad at you, so hurt. But now that doesn't matter. All that matters is that you live. Please, try very hard to live. Do it for God or for your soldiers or for your mother and father—your dear father who was just here. Who loves you so much. And . . . and do it for me, Peter. Live for your Zabelle. I promise I will leave you alone. I won't write or visit. We have our own lives. But live."

The tears wouldn't stop as she watched the silent man and concentrated hard to hear him breathing, soft, difficult breaths.

Slowly she reached out and placed her hand over the sheet covering his hand. Softly she touched it. Then she stroked his scratchy beard all the while humming a silly song they sang at camp, one she hadn't thought of in years. When she finished the tune, she whispered again, "Please live."

She touched his face again, and Peter opened his eyes.

Green! Like the clover that grew behind the Citadel, brighter than the Durance River on a summer day.

"Hey," he whispered.

That was all, but she saw the way his lips curved upward, and she saw a movement in his hand.

"Stay," he whispered.

Isabelle nodded.

He looked fragile, in pain, desperate.

His eyes closed again, his breathing remained shallow. She felt a tug of fear, then heard him take a deep breath.

She sat back in the chair, fingering the Bible, and remembering her promise to Monsieur Christensen. *"I will watch over Peter for you . . . I'll stay here until he gets better."*

47

PETER

He could barely keep his eyes open; his lids were so heavy.

Stay awake!

But they closed regardless.

Later—how much later, he did not know—he looked up and saw a mirage: a young woman sitting beside the cot, arms folded across her chest, head bent, eyes closed.

"Hello," he whispered, and she startled, shook herself awake, and met his eyes.

"Bonjour," she said, and her cheeks flushed.

> A beautiful shade of pink
> Or maybe coral
> Or maybe the color of the sun
> Setting at just the moment after the ball
> Seemed to sizzle into the ocean.

That was her description of a blush, written in French in one of her poems long ago.

"I'm Isabelle," she said in French.

"Oui . . . *fille*."

"Yes. The girl. I'm the girl you saved . . . I came to say merci."

Peter nodded slowly, felt the dizziness return, then whispered, "Water, please."

She held up the glass of water and placed the straw between his lips. He sucked on it, tasted the cool refreshment, sucked again and felt his head clearing. "Thank you."

She set the glass on the bedside table, and as she did, they spoke in English at the same time, "I know who you are . . ."

They both looked down, then back up at each other, the question mirrored on their faces.

"Zabelle?" Peter mumbled. "*Pas possible*. How can it be?"

"Yes, impossible, and yet here we are." She leaned in close, speaking in French, "Peter, I came because you asked for me." Those crystal blue eyes—oh, how he remembered them—staring deep into his own. "And because I wanted to. I needed to. To thank you in person for saving my life." She reached for his hand under the sheet and squeezed it gently. "It was very brave of you, Peter."

He forced his eyes to remain open and pronounced with great difficulty, "Stay. Please stay."

Her lips turned up, her hand touching his cheek, his forehead. "I'm not leaving. I promised your father I would stay. Rest now. And don't worry, I'll stay."

The next time he awoke, he felt his stomach grumbling. The girl, Isabelle—Zabelle—was still in the chair. "Hungry," he said in English, and then he felt a smile crease his lips. "Thirsty too."

"*Mais alors!* Aren't you bossy?" she replied in French. "I'll get you some food."

The first time he tried to sit up, he was overcome with dizziness. Then she helped him, pushing the pillows behind him as he leaned his head against the wall.

For long, silent minutes she fed him little spoonfuls of soup that slid down his parched throat and into his stomach. This wasn't a dream or a nightmare. Zabelle sat beside him, beautiful Zabelle.

When Céline came by, she clapped her hands together. "Ooh là là! You're awake, sitting up, and eating! You've got color in your face. You've turned the corner." She winked. "Isabelle is good medicine for you."

When they were alone again, finally Peter met her eyes. "I'm sorry, Zabelle." He wanted to explain, had so much to say to her, but perhaps these few words would be enough to start the conversation. "So sorry," he repeated.

She met his gaze, her eyes that startling blue—deep and expressive, tired and angry and sad. The same eyes that had communicated such emotion when she was just a young teen. The same eyes that didn't flinch, that stared back, almost daring him to look away.

He didn't.

"Sorry for the way I hurt you long ago. I was wrong."

Did her eyes soften the slightest bit?

He tried again. "I'm sorry I stopped writing, that I never explained." He looked at her, felt another wave of fatigue and hoped she understood what he meant. "I was wrong, and I regret it deeply . . . Zabelle. And I'm grateful for the chance to tell you this."

48

RENÉ

At daybreak, René headed out in the German truck, hoping to cover the one hundred fifty kilometers between Sisteron and Montélimar in half a day. Instead, the truck ran out of gas somewhere between the towns of La Rochette and Saint-Auban, and René knew there was no more petrol available in the whole of southern France. He continued on foot for hours, his canteen, knapsack, and his father's watch with the compass his only companions, along with the wildflowers blooming beside the road. As he walked, he thought of his last conversation with Delphine, how she had held on to him as if she might never see him again.

"You must be careful. It's going to be a horrible battle. I don't know how I know this, but I do. Many people will die. You cannot die, René. You must come back to me. You are my family, remember? But if you come back to the camp, and I'm not here, I'll be in Lyon. I will go back to Papa's chocolate shop, Levy's of Lyon, and to our apartment. As soon as Lyon is freed, I'll go there and wait for my parents. Don't look sad. I believe they are still alive. They are strong, stubborn people."

He had forced some sort of neutral expression on his face, even while his gut told him her parents would never return.

She was still talking. "When the war is over, please come find me again. Let me know that you're okay. Then we can walk to the Penitents together and climb to the top and wave to La Baume and St. Michel and The Camp Between the Hills. And later we'll visit Mme Nicolas, and she'll serve us blackberry jam. Promise me we can do this."

"Of course," he had said with a forced levity in his voice and a tug on one of her pigtails. "I promise."

But for all the times Delphine had spoken about the future with assurance, this time they both had known it was just a hopeful dream.

The sun had set behind the hills when René entered the town of Dieulefit. He barely had the strength to acknowledge the name of the village, but under his breath, he said, "Dieulefit. The name of this stinking town is 'God did it.' What did you do, God? Tell me! What in the world have You ever done for me, for any of us?"

Of course, there was no answer, just verdant countryside with wild lavender and honeysuckle. No army vehicles, no jeeps or tanks, and not a German in sight. In fact, no soldiers at all, no bombed-out buildings, no Jewish children, no orphans. Just silence with darkness descending.

Soon that would change.

René took out the crushed buds of lavender from his pocket, held them to his nose, and drew deep, calming breaths. He thought of his rage and his anger at the Almighty and everyone else. "Show me something You've done, just show me," he whispered, maybe as a prayer or an accusation or a dare.

Delphine is safe, the children are safe, Isabelle is safe.

Yes, true.

"Thank you," he murmured and felt something settle in his gut. Hope.

Just in case God was up to something, René added, "Give me

one other thing, God. You know I've not only wanted to win the war, but I've wanted revenge. Yet revenge feels like anger and hatred and bitterness. I don't want to feel that way anymore. So please take away that desire for revenge and let me simply do my part. Let me protect my friends. That's all, God."

He filled his canteen at the fountain in the town square, checked his compass, and saw the sign: *Montélimar—30 km.*

Antoine had warned the next part could be tricky.

Ten kilometers farther toward Montélimar, René climbed a rugged hill, removed the binoculars from his knapsack, and groaned as he peered through them. The next section of road between Dieulefit and Montélimar swarmed with Germans fleeing to the north. German tanks and artillery littered the countryside.

Antoine's instructions were clear. *"Stay to the south of the main road and come to the* lavoir *in La Touche. We're hiding out in village homes, but we meet at the old washhouse each evening at 20H00."*

René had visited the ancient village that was south of Montélimar many times before, had strolled through it on a guided tour with his parents long ago, had heard the history and stood under the open-roofed lavoir, where women in past centuries washed their laundry in the spring water that flowed into the huge cement basins.

At last, he walked into the village square, guided by flickers of light from cigarettes. Sure enough, huddled around the basins by the fountain that sprayed water from iron spouts, there stood the Durance Maquis, all of them. Didier, Etienne, Samuel, Bastien, Gabriel, and, of course, Antoine.

His brother's face lit up when he caught sight of René, and he hurried over with an outstretched hand. "Welcome back, little brother." Grasping René's hand, Antoine's dark eyes shone with both relief and fatigue. "You made it just in time for our next adventure."

René held his hands under the spraying water, gulping it in handfuls, then splashing his face with the chilly liquid. Afterward, he greeted each of the maquisards, shaking their hands. This time,

Gabriel offered his too. He even handed René a cigarette and lit it for him.

"Whole lot of Germans heading straight into Montélimar," René began.

Antoine nodded. "Hopefully into a trap. But it's been slow on the Allied side. In the afternoon on Monday, the front-runners in Task Force Butler made it to the forest on the high ground north of Montélimar. They brought in armored vehicles, tank destroyers, and Stuart light tanks, unpacked all their artillery, and started fighting."

"We could hear the gunfire even from here. It echoed across the river for hours." This came from Etienne.

"The Boches who were heading north along the eastern shore of the Rhône got mighty scared when the Allies started firing their shells—looked like geysers of dirt and mud shooting into the sky," Bastien said.

"Monday night there was so much shooting going on around Montélimar that nobody noticed when we blew up a road bridge on the Drôme tributary. Yours truly helped with it," Antoine said. "We needed you, René, but I managed okay. And while we were taking out the bridge, the Allies pelted a whole convoy of Wehrmacht trucks. At least fifty of them exploded—you could see them burning all through the night."

René absorbed this news his comrades shared, one after the other. "So we're beating them back? Capturing them?"

Gabriel shrugged, then produced a hand-drawn map. "Little by little, the Allied troops have rallied, but the Germans are stubborn. Might be retreating, but they're still showing plenty of defiance. Monday was bad, but yesterday was worse—heavy fighting between the Boches and the Allies. Not just with tanks either. The German Cavalry is there too."

"And us? What's our next adventure?" René asked.

"Bridges again. The Maquis have been tasked with destroying all the bridges on the Rhône and Drôme Rivers for fifty kilometers." He patted his brother on the back. "Most of them are down, but don't worry, we've left a few for you to blow up." Another pat on the back.

Gabriel flicked his cigarette to the ground. "But we've got to keep moving fast. The goal is for the American divisions to encircle the German troops. Here and here." He pointed to the map. "With all the bridges gone, they'll be blocked by the Rhône to the east and the Drôme to the north. We hope. Word is that the Allies are afraid many of the Boches are going to escape."

"Not if I can help it," René said with a smirk.

"I know you feel that way," Antoine said, "so I brought you a little gift." He handed René a pistol.

"Where'd you get this?"

"Where do you think? Off the body of a German."

Gabriel perched on the side of one of the basins. "Listen to this, just in: 'Early this morning, Algerian infantrymen accompanied by Sherman tanks entered the streets of Marseille. They were cheered on by the citizens, who were still in their nightclothes.' Our French troops have done it. Marseille will be liberated by the Allies in the next few days."

Back slapping followed as the Maquis absorbed the hopeful news from the ports of Marseille and Toulon. "Looks like the Allies will have their port on the Mediterranean soon," Etienne said.

Gabriel continued, "We've still got plenty to do here in Montélimar. The Allied divisions are finally showing up with fuel and vehicles and men, though the Germans aren't running scared yet." He motioned to them all, then focused on the map. "We'll split up into two groups. Antoine, Etienne, and René will take these two bridges. Bastien, Samuel, and Didier, these two. Let's get going. We've got four bridges to destroy before dawn."

Throughout the night, René again found himself clambering under bridges like a monkey, hanging explosives, twisting wires together, then crawling back out and watching the ensuing explosions light up the night as if it were Bastille Day as iron beams and huge chunks of cement tumbled into the dark river below. Pride and terror competed in René's gut each time enemy fire reverberated from across the river. But the bridges came down without enemy reprisals up close. Adrenaline pumped in René's veins as the threesome made their way north and joined the other trio of men at dawn.

"Gabriel's been meeting with two other Maquis and someone from the Allies' Task Force," Didier said. "We're supposed to join up with him ten kilometers north of Montélimar by late afternoon. For now, he wants us to stay here, lay low, and sleep for a few hours."

No one complained about those instructions. They slept in a field outside La Touche with the sounds of battle in the distance a faint yet constant droning like an off-key lullaby. When they awoke, they found a basket filled with cheese and sausage and bread.

"Villagers came with food a little while ago." Bastien began distributing it, and again no one complained.

They reached the arranged meeting place at four p.m. and waited there for Gabriel.

Five o'clock came . . . six o'clock. Nothing.

When Gabriel finally arrived, he bent over, hands on his knees, trying to catch his breath. "Just got orders to head fifteen kilometers farther north toward Loriol. We're to help block the route up to Lyon—the way the Germans are heading. Bridges are down, men, but now we must create a roadblock and then get the heck out."

He didn't need to explain further. They knew the Germans were all around them. One false step and enemy fire would come raining down on this ragtag group of saboteurs.

"I'm up for all of that," replied René, "except for the part about leaving."

"I know you want revenge," Antoine said to his brother. "We all do. But at the end of this war—and it *will* end—I want to have a brother still. This is no time to be pigheaded. We've got to be careful, methodical."

René took a slow breath, remembering his prayer at Dieulefit, and nodded.

"Exactly," Gabriel agreed. "I've talked to a few men in the Task

Force. Come nightfall, one of them will meet us here with a truck that we can load with bricks and cement and fallen trees. Whatever we can find to block the road to Lyon."

⟡

The soldier was young, boyish-looking, covered in grime and ash, but René recognized him before he introduced himself to the maquisards. "I'm Lieutenant Frank Jamison."

When his eyes met René's, they registered surprise, but he said nothing to indicate to the others that they had met. "I'm afraid we're gonna have to start over with the roadblock. A battalion from the 141st Infantry successfully cut Highway 7 before dawn, but by early this afternoon the Germans had broken through both borders. We gotta find a way to stop them. We'll take the truck up toward Loriol. Townspeople and other resistants will join you there to create the roadblock. General Butler intends to send some troops up your way tonight. Hopefully."

They crammed into the truck and drove with the young soldier to a field, where they dismounted and joined with more soldiers and maquisards, all of them hurriedly loading trucks with debris. Villagers traipsed toward them through the fields, dragging carts and plows and machinery.

An older man was leading a mule attached to a cart filled with rocks and bricks. "He's a tough one," the man said, slapping the mule on the rump.

René kept watching the young soldier, the one called Frank. With an armful of rocks, René went over to him. "I saw you in the infirmary over at Castel-Bevons. You were talking with my cousin. I'm René."

The soldier nodded, but obviously didn't understand his French.

"Cousine. Isabelle. Aumonier." What had Isabelle called the soldier who saved her? "Chaplain."

Frank frowned, tilted his head, then grinned. "The girl at the hospital. Yeah. You were there with her. You weren't very excited to meet me." He ruffled his forehead, concentrating, and said, *"En colère. Toi."*

310

René blushed. The soldier knew a little French. "Oui. I was mad."

"It's okay. I'm mad a lot too."

"Aumonier saved Cousine Isabelle."

He grinned, then nodded. "The chaplain, good ol' Ginger. Your cousin is the girl Ginger saved! Exactly. And I'm his assistant."

"*Assistant?*" René said in French. Then in English, "Same word?"

"That's right, same word. I help the chaplain."

"Chaplain okay?"

The soldier frowned. "No, he's not okay. Our chaplain sustained multiple injuries. Hurt. Bad."

"*Blessé,*" René said, pointing to the bandage he still wore around his arm.

"Yes. Hurt. Blessé."

"He will come here?"

"I doubt that. Not here." He stuck out his hand. "But we're glad you're here. Merci." He shook René's hand and added, "See you after the battle." As he walked away, he said something in English to Antoine.

His brother translated, "He told us to be careful. The whole region is littered with Germans, and they aren't giving up. He said they lost four men from the Task Force just this afternoon."

Throughout the evening, Didier, Etienne, Samuel, Bastien, Antoine, René, and Gabriel rode together in trucks alongside the American soldiers, then dismounted, gathered debris, walked beside the trucks, and unloaded the debris across a long stretch of land. Other resistants and Maquis joined with villagers in dragging felled trees across the road and field. Several burnt-out vehicles were added, as well as large pipes and concrete cubes.

Back and forth they drove from field to village to the chosen area as the nerve-racking race to build the blockade continued through the night. René thought back to Isabelle's stories from camp, how it had been built back from the ruins. And here they were, piling up discarded machinery and parts of nature. The hope was that their ruins would stop the enemy.

At dawn, René stood with his binoculars, staring across the field at what looked to be hundreds of Germans hunkered down, their arms at the ready. And they had tanks.

Antoine cursed. "Those Panther tanks are so close you can feel the heat from their motors."

"We need to get out of here before the sun is up," Bastien whispered.

Gabriel motioned them forward. "This way. Quickly."

They had walked no more than a kilometer from the blockade when Gabriel stopped, held up his hand, then motioned for them all to lie flat on the ground. As they did, René saw the terrified look on Antoine's face.

No more than ten meters to their left, leaning against a rock wall, guns by their sides, sat a dozen Germans, sleeping.

Somewhere, a branch cracked, and one soldier stirred. The maquisards remained still. For a minute. Then two. Then five. The wait felt interminable. René expected at any moment the Germans to wake and tear them apart with their machine guns. Instead, one by one, waiting in between for five long minutes, the Maquis slithered away on their bellies like lazy snakes, René bringing up the rear.

Only when the Germans were out of sight did the Maquis shift to a squatting position, becoming now like ducks, waddling away, until finally Gabriel stood, and the rest followed at a trot.

René fingered his pistol. He could use it. He *would* use it if necessary. And yet, when he had been close enough to see the sleeping enemy, his resolve had faltered. They were just boys like him, perhaps only fifteen or sixteen, wearing dirty uniforms, their faces grimy. Young men knowing they were facing defeat but not allowed to leave.

As the sun rose, the sound of fighting in the distance shattered the countryside as well as René's nerves.

Then came a shout. One of the German boys was pointing their way. Others were turning toward them.

René stopped and backed up without making a sound and scurried behind a truck, taking out the binoculars. Gabriel and Antoine and Bastien were already in the field, and calling to them would only alert the enemy. What to do?

René looked through the binoculars, focusing on a German officer, older, who was pulling on his boots, running his hands through his hair, and replacing his hat. When he straightened, he towered over the boys.

René shivered.

One of the soldiers holding the gun on René walked closer. He was taller than the other men by a hand, his hair whitish-blond. And his pale blue eyes were cruel, proud, mocking. He lifted his pistol, held it inches from René's head . . .

The soldier who had almost killed him after the raid at the farmhouse, the one Isabelle called Tomas. That same soldier now stood across the field from René, shouting at his men to get up as he raised his pistol toward where the three maquisards were crouching. The soldiers turned, all of them, close enough for René to see blue eyes, the snout of the pistol, to hear the command in German.

Then a shot rang out, and more Germans were turning.

"Get back, *les gars!*" Gabriel yelled, his eyes frantic as he shooed the maquisard behind him.

Another shot, and Gabriel fell to his knees.

René stepped from behind the truck, aimed his pistol, saw a glint of silver across the way and fury in the eyes of Isabelle's German. They fired at the same time, and René went down, pain exploding in his side.

More gunfire, bullets flying all around. Shouting in French, shrieking, the Maquis calling out to one another, "Get back! Watch out!"

More shouting in both German and English.

From where he lay, René saw a blur of American soldiers, kneeling, firing, yelling at the Maquis to fall back, the Germans a breath away.

This is the end, he told himself. *I'm sorry, Delphine.*

Across the hill from where he lay, two Panther tanks were burning, then one exploded. Closer still lay bodies in German uniforms, perhaps the same young German boys he had watched only minutes earlier. Then René was being dragged away by his legs, his arms and body trailing behind. As he watched the grass turn red around him, he saw it. A helmet on the ground and a soldier with white-blond hair and cruel blue eyes staring lifelessly in a puddle of blood.

49

ISABELLE

D-DAY+9
AUGUST 24, 1944

Peter Christensen's apology had worn him out. He slept for hours. Deeply. But he had spoken. He was better. And she was sitting beside the bed of the only boy she ever really allowed herself to feel something akin to love for. She had felt plenty of other emotions too, of course: anger, betrayal, even hatred. She'd heard it said that there was a fine line between love and hate, and she'd straddled that line and crossed back and forth to both sides all those years ago as a desperate young girl trying to figure out faith amid tragedy, unraveling matters of the heart amid the distressing truth of her life. And she'd let Peter's silence complicate everything.

Well, perhaps now his spoken regret, his "I'm sorry" could untangle the threads in her mind.

While he slept, she repeated over and over his recent words, words he'd pronounced with difficulty, with purpose, with hope, with a deep sincerity that stung her heart: *"I'm sorry, Zabelle. . . . Sorry for the way I hurt you long ago. I was wrong, and I regret it deeply. . . ."*

315

Then she heard Ginette chiding her: *"Forget what happened all those years ago. You can at least try to forgive him, Zabelle."*

She thought about the kind of healing that happened inside a person, in one's soul. The kind the Bible spoke of. She knew what Céline and so many others in this place were trying to do—heal the injured of their physical wounds.

But inside?

Yet with those few words from Peter, she knew. Of course she would forgive him. In fact, she realized that she already had forgiven him. The blessed calm that forgiveness produced had slipped into her heart somewhere between Ginette's reprimand and Monsieur Christensen's kindness and Peter's heartfelt *"Stay."*

The next time he woke up, she'd tell him.

He was ravenous for food and for real conversation. Isabelle was happy to comply, feeding him little spoonfuls of soup while she gave him equally small portions of the happenings in her life. As he gained strength, Peter Christensen returned to the boy she remembered: playful, teasing yet capable of genuine concern. They volleyed between English and French with such ease as he asked question after question. But the latest question made her gut flutter with pain.

"How are things in the city? Have the water lines been restored yet?"

"No. It's all a disaster." She realized that she was twirling a strand of hair around her finger. This question was too painful. "My friends in the Resistance, they say it will be months, years even, before we recover. You saw it. I imagine that's what a battlefield looks like once the fight is over. I can't believe that the Citadel, our stronghold, is in ruins! First the Germans took it over, and then the Allies destroyed it. Now the Citadel and the city and the citizens are all battered, Peter."

He gave a slight nod. "Yes. I'm so sorry." Then, tentatively, he added, "But you're free."

"What good does it do to be free if we are broken beyond repair!" she barked.

316

"I'm sorry. I didn't mean to sound trite."

They sat in silence as she continued to twirl the strand tighter and tighter around her finger.

He tried again. "I don't believe you're broken beyond repair, Zabelle. Not you. Not the people of Sisteron. You've fought hard during the occupation. You'll keep fighting. To rebuild the city, to rebuild your lives." Peter looked into her eyes. "Do you remember what my father used to say? That verse he cited?"

She rolled her eyes. "You mean when we were sweating in the insufferable heat and lifting those huge rocks, breaking our backs? Yeah, he'd be in the trench with us, lifting much heavier loads and quoting from the Bible. I made myself forget that verse."

But even as she said it, she turned to Peter, and in unison they quoted in English the passage from the book of Isaiah: "'And they shall build the old wastes. . . .'"

When Peter dared a glance at Isabelle, she had the beginnings of a grin on her lips.

"I guess I do remember it pretty well," she said.

"You weren't great at breaking codes, but you memorized Scripture faster than anyone I'd ever known."

"Faster than you did, that's for sure." She stuck out her tongue.

"Silly girl!" Peter winked.

"We were all silly girls. We all had crushes on you. You were Monsieur Christensen's teenaged son." She laughed. "We watched you every day. Did I ever tell you that? We spied on you."

Peter chuckled. "Spied on me, huh? Little did you know that I was spying on you too."

She felt as if she were fourteen again, flirting and laughing, a laughter that made her ribs hurt, and she was grateful for the pain. She was grinning, and he was laughing, those eager green eyes lit up and with that same teasing smile like long ago when she thought he could see into her heart.

"I liked watching you help your father, your obnoxious red hair curling all over the place. You've lost the curls but not that fire-red color. I'd never seen anybody with red hair like yours." She quieted, and she imagined her face was red like his hair.

"And I'd never seen anyone with eyes as brilliantly blue and as beautiful as yours."

As a deep blush crept across her cheeks, she shrugged. "We were kids. Silly adolescents."

"True, and we're not kids anymore, yet your eyes are just as blue today as they were then."

The sun was setting, and still she sat by his bed, offering water and soup and other food that Céline brought to them. The nurse winked with pleasure as she observed their banter.

It was as if Peter was coming back to life. And perhaps so was she.

They were talking so easily that she dared ask, "Did you hear my rants the other night? My confessions? I'm so embarrassed that I shared them, so I'm hoping you didn't hear."

A smile spread wide across his face. "As it happens, I did hear them. Somewhere in my foggy mind I mixed them up with another girl who smoked cigarettes and gossiped and talked about Protestant penance." He chuckled, low like his father. "And she walked a long way to ask forgiveness."

Isabelle made a face. "I'd just as soon you forget about that past incident as well as my present rants."

Then Peter's face lost its levity, and his eyes softened. "I didn't register all the 'rants,' as you call them, but I remember you were very mad at God, at life, at how unfair it seemed, at all the pain and suffering your family had endured. I remember that."

"Yes, unfair."

"It was unfair, and 'I'm sorry' seems like another trite answer, Zabelle, but I *am* sorry for all of it."

He was staring out the window, his brow furrowed under the bandages. "In my job, I stay behind with the wounded. I listen, I carry them to stretchers, I close the eyes of the dying. I write letters to their families. And sometimes I grow angry. At the evil, yes. At the injustice too. But also at all the euphemisms of war. At the words I must use."

When Peter spoke, he seemed to have wandered off in his mind to another place and time. Perhaps a battlefield or a grave.

"They're calling the first days of our military operation a 'huge success.' That's what the world will hear. Everyone will camouflage the truth with euphemisms such as 'light casualties' and 'few troops lost,' assuring those back home that the Allies fared much better than the Germans. We'll say just about anything to paint a hopeful picture. That's how it must be in war." He turned his head, and his eyes, only moments ago a dancing bright green, had dulled. "But I know the individuals. I'm beside them in the trenches, and it's hard to rejoice when death is all around."

"But you do it. You still have your sense of humor. You tease, you smile, you . . . care. How do you do this, Peter Christensen? How?" Before he could respond, she continued, "Deep down, or maybe right on the surface, I'm so mad! I hate this war! I hate it!"

"Of course you do—"

"Don't say 'Everybody hates the war'!" Her anger felt palpable again. "Don't tell me that everyone feels that way!"

"No, I won't. Keep going, please."

"What do you mean by 'keep going'?"

"Tell me your story."

"You know my story—that Maman died giving birth to my baby brother who was stillborn."

"Then tell me the parts I don't know."

She twirled another strand of hair as she spoke very softly. "I thought Papa would die of heartbreak, but we survived. And then my father, my beloved papa who forged papers, who saved countless children, was captured by the Germans and locked up in the Citadel. He leaked innocuous information so they would take him and spare the Martin Network. To protect the children. To protect me."

Should she tell him the next part?

"They locked him up, but we—we call ourselves the Silo Resistants—we had a plan to rescue him, to rescue all the prisoners." Eyes down, hands twisted together. "We each had our jobs. Mine was to distract a German officer . . ."

319

No more details!

"We rescued them all. It was a daring plan, but it worked. But five days later, all the rescued prisoners were massacred as they were going to a safe house. Papa was murdered . . ." A sniff. "And then my aunt was killed at her farmhouse. She and some maquisards, murdered. And only my young cousin, René, and the Jewish girl they were hiding survived. And we knew someone had betrayed us—had given the Germans information about the freed prisoners and the Jewish children we were hiding. That meant that the children were in danger. We needed to find another place to hide the children, so we took them to the camp, *your* camp, Peter. And then the Allies bombed our city, and Tito died, and . . ."

And then you sacrificed yourself for me and saved me from getting killed. But she didn't dare say that. Instead, she repeated, "I hate this war. I am so angry at it all!"

For the longest time, Peter did not reply, and Isabelle wondered if he had fallen asleep. But she glanced his way and saw a strange look of conviction on his face. "Your anger is important, Zabelle. No one has time to grieve right now. That's the horror of war. But we must grieve at some point, in some way, and then let grief teach us its lessons."

She looked up with a frown. "What can grief teach me?"

Now his eyes were closed, and he looked completely worn out. She wanted to tell him that it was okay, she didn't have to know the answer, that he needed to rest now.

But without opening his eyes, he said, "Grief has taught me many things. How to help others, how to love them well when they are grieving. And if we let it, grief can teach us how to grab back on to God, even if we're blaming Him."

She pondered that. "I had to blame someone, so I blamed Him."

"That's fine. If God is God, He can take it."

She found his answers irritating and confusing.

He didn't notice but continued, "What is the book of Psalms but one long, groaning, grief-filled complaint. One after another, one long lament. Of course, there are praise psalms too. Thank the Lord, often the lament and praise are in the same psalm. But it doesn't take away from the psalmist's anger, his cursing." Peter opened his eyes and looked up. "Sometimes in my darkest moments, I just grab an imprecatory psalm and pray for all it's worth that God will wreck the enemy, that He will bash their brains out!"

Isabelle gave a tiny smile and cocked her head. "That's such an odd thing to say."

"Odd perhaps, but honest. And it's in the Bible."

"You remind me of your father," she said, picturing Monsieur Christensen only a few days ago in the hospital. She let her mind travel back to her days as a Scout at the camp, with the cobalt blue sky and the Baume and St. Michel rock formations providing a magnificent backdrop as Monsieur Christensen taught the entranced kids. "Your father would lift his hands high into the air, and he'd say the strangest things, just like what you just said, Peter. Things like, 'If you're mad at God, just tell Him! It's all right there in the Psalms. One long lament!'" She looked off to the mountains, then turned back to Peter. "Do you remember him saying that?"

"Of course I remember."

"I guess I never really learned to view the Psalms that way. When I met you at camp, it seemed like for once something might go right. I know I was just a gangly teenager, but meeting you, knowing you, hearing from you, your letters, it all gave me hope. Yes, hope that life still held good things.

"But then you disappeared from my life. Like Maman and my baby brother, only I knew where they had gone. With you, the wound remained open." She glanced up at him. "I would wait and pray and wonder. I'd pray that a letter would arrive from Algeria. I ran home from school every day, and every day I opened the little mailbox with my key and there was never a letter from you. I prayed and nothing changed, and it hurt, Peter. It hurt so badly. So I stopped praying, and then I became mad at God."

Feeling ashamed, she stopped speaking, mortified by her admission, by the anger and hurt that had finally escaped her lips. Suddenly she had a strong urge to get up and leave the room. Instead, she whispered, "And when I first realized who you were, that the boy who had sliced my heart in two a decade ago had saved me,

From the Valley We Rise

I-I was furious. At God and at you. I wanted to hurt you, Peter Christensen. I wanted to hurt you as bad as you hurt me."

He reached out and touched her arm, and she felt a sizzling pain, the pain of a long-ago love, the pain of her broken ribs and her broken heart melded together.

"But I don't want to hurt you anymore," she whispered.

By the sixth day after the bombing in Castel-Bevons, Isabelle knew that Peter had indeed turned a corner. She no longer needed to sit by his bed through the night, afraid he might take his last breath. She slept on her own cot in a room down the hall.

The next morning, after she had fed him a small breakfast, Peter asked, "Could you please find my sketch pad and pencils in my knapsack? I'd like to sketch for a while."

She regarded him and raised an eyebrow. "I remember that you liked to sketch."

His face darkened with embarrassment. "Of course you do."

"I loved your letters."

He grinned. "And I loved writing them and designing those envelopes, thinking up those comics to put on the front. And . . . and you sent me your poetry."

She blushed. "You were very kind to read my poems. They weren't very good."

"I enjoyed them. Do you still write poetry?"

"No. I have tried, but the only things that came out were dark and angry." She shrugged. "I guess I lost my inspiration."

"I'm sorry."

"It's okay."

"No, I mean it. I was immature. I was a coward. I-I had other plans, and you were the most wonderful distraction."

"Peter . . . don't exaggerate."

"I'm not. Believe me, I've had time to think about it all. I was a coward, a big fat coward."

"We were kids. It's okay."

"Zabelle, I can see in your face that it was not okay. You taught us all about asking for forgiveness. You taught us that at the Penitent cliffs, and then I just strung you out to dry. Sure, I was a teenager, but I knew better."

It was time to say it. Still, she struggled. "You're right. You hurt me, but I forgive you." She looked up and found his eyes. "I mean it. I hadn't forgiven you. I'd stuffed it way down inside me. But in these last days, seeing you, hearing your confession"—she managed a smile—"well, you've said you're sorry, and I've forgiven you. So let that be enough. Okay?"

"Okay."

The look he gave her felt more than okay.

Something slid way down inside and settled softly in her gut.

Hope.

Peter's presence gave her hope in something beyond the destruction and the loss of war, hope in the goodness of life, hope that her life was important, that the God she had encountered at the Scout camp all those years ago was still the same God now.

And she felt something else in her heart. Grateful. Grateful for life, yes. So grateful. Grateful Peter had turned a corner. Yes, of course.

And grateful that she had promised Monsieur Christensen that she would stay with Peter. She had an excuse. She didn't need to leave his side quite yet.

50

PETER

D-Day+10
August 25, 1944

A week had passed since the bombing of Castel-Bevons. Hour by hour, Peter grew stronger in his mind. Hour by hour, he felt torn between staying here with Isabelle and joining the soldiers.

His body remained extremely weak, however. His injuries, all of them, were healing, but slowly. Céline insisted he was in no shape to return to the battlefield, that he might never be ready. But Peter wanted, needed, to leave. Occasionally, when Isabelle was talking, he would not really be paying attention as he wondered what was happening on the battlefield with the men. What was happening in Montélimar?

Though she didn't say so, Peter could tell Isabelle had noticed his internal struggle. "You're getting better, aren't you?"

He nodded. "As Céline said, you've been good medicine."

"I don't know about that, but I'm very thankful you're on the mend now."

"I'm hoping to head out soon—as soon as there's a vehicle

with enough fuel to get me to Montélimar. It doesn't sound like it's going very well."

"Yes, you want to be there with the Allies. Only . . ." She gestured toward his head and arm and leg.

"Sure, I've got serious injuries." Earlier that morning he had gotten to his feet and had limped to the toilet. His left arm was in a cast, his head and right thigh still wrapped in bandages. "But I won't be on the battlefield. I don't carry a physical weapon, but I hold the weapon of prayer. I can listen to the men; I can hold their hands and pray away their fears and comfort the injured. I don't have to be in perfect physical shape to do any of that. And you have other things to do too."

She looked out the window, then said, "You're right. The children are safe at the camp, but I need to get back there."

Yes, the children in this region were safe, but what about the other children? And his parents? He thought of his father's visit. *"Your mom is back in Algeria . . . to hide the Jews . . . baking cookies . . . many other children hidden farther north . . . I'm heading that way."*

He knew for sure that his parents weren't concerned about safety for themselves.

"Thank you for staying here with me and for letting Frank head out with the Task Force. He sends a big merci."

I need to go. I want to go. And yet . . . I don't. I want to stay right here with you, Zabelle.

"I was thankful to be able to stay here . . . so that he could go."

"You being here, well, it changed everything. You really are good medicine."

Tell her, Peter! Tell her how you're feeling. Tell her you want to see her again.

But her kindness was a duty, an obligation to Frank because I had saved her, and a promise to my father so he could leave me. She certainly doesn't want or need me in her life again.

But the coincidence—finding her like this. It feels so strange. Like something precious and holy and important. Perhaps it was just so I could apologize.

"Peter?"

How long had he been talking to himself in his mind?

"Yes, I was saying that you've been such good medicine. Much better than Frank . . ." He paused, waited until she met his eyes, and took a deep breath. "What I really want to say is that I need to leave, but I hope I can see you again, can write to you. I would like that very much."

She looked at him, surprise and maybe fear in her eyes. "No. I can't have you write to me." She was shaking her head, staring at her shoes. "No, Peter. I've enjoyed these days. And I'll miss you like the last time. But now that I'm grown . . . this was just a coincidence, right? A happy coincidence, so that you could save my life and then tell me you were sorry for long ago, and I could hear it and forgive you and laugh again." Those crystal blue eyes filled with tears. "I'm terrified that you'll get up and walk away again like you did all those years ago."

Peter lowered his eyes and grimaced as he struggled to sit up in bed. He nodded and said, "I know you're afraid. I'm afraid too. I don't know why we are here like this. It seems cruel and wonderful and terrifying all at once."

It was time to tell her what had happened in the past decade of his life. "I don't know the 'why' of right now, but may I tell you my story?"

She gave the slightest shrug.

He took a deep breath and began. "I stopped writing to you because I liked you too much, and I wasn't ready for love. I was young, you were younger, and I realized that if I continued writing to you, I wouldn't go back to America to attend college and seminary. I'd move to France after finishing high school in Algeria so I could be near you . . ." He paused, silently praying for the right words. "And I couldn't do that, Zabelle. I'd felt called to the ministry ever since I was a teenager. If I didn't go, I thought I'd be disappointing my parents, myself, and more importantly, God."

He reached for his Bible and took out the envelope. "I've kept this letter with me all these years because in it, you encouraged me to be a pastor. I kept it to prove to myself I was making the right choice. That I had made the right choice." He stared down at the envelope, then up at her. "I did it wrong and poorly and then I did so many other things wrong. When I got to America, I was miserable at first. But gradually I started understanding America and liking the courses I was taking, and then I met Helen.

"And I liked her a lot. But sometimes when I was with her, I thought of you and the way we shared with each other. It wasn't like that with Helen." He felt his face turn beet red. "And then I made myself not think of you. It hurt to remember talking like we're talking right now. I made myself not think of our walks by the stream at camp, of the way we spoke in French and English, of our letters, of how much I longed to see you again. After some time of making myself forget, I let myself love Helen. And you will be glad to know that she hurt me, perhaps like I hurt you. She broke my heart. She didn't understand me, didn't know how to help when the hardest thing happened."

He paused again, worn out by his words.

"Go on," she whispered. "I'm listening. I want to know about the hardest thing."

"It was my biggest mistake. Worse than a mistake. A tragedy. I had finished seminary, and I was the pastor of this lovely country church in the state of Kentucky, where everyone was poor, and many children went barefoot to school and their parents worked hard and lived simply. My first pastorate, fresh out of seminary. I loved that little church, and I loved those people. I hoped to be at this church for many years.

"There was a little girl, Libby; she was six or seven. A beautiful child with curly, blond hair, a radiant smile and a kind heart. She loved church and Jesus. And she liked me and would visit me after school. She called me Uncle Pete. One day she came to me, looking—" he struggled with the image that flashed in his mind— "looking destroyed, like the life had gone out of her. She showed me bruises on her arms, big black bruises that she covered with her long-sleeved blouse even though it was hot for a fall day. Bruises that came from her father . . ."

Isabelle gasped.

"And worse." Peter swallowed, tried to clear his throat. "When she told me what he did to her, I was young and fervent and angry and horrified. I knew her father. He was a deacon in our church, respected." Peter tried to calm his heart so he could continue. But it was thumping, the pulse drumming in his temples. "I was new to the church. I didn't know this man had a strong liking for liquor and that he had a terrible temper when he was inebriated."

Isabelle had reached over and was holding his hand, tightly, as if she knew he would need her strength to keep telling the story.

"Libby was afraid to tell me what he'd done to her. She said he made her promise not to tell, that it was . . . a 'special secret' between them and that if she told anyone, people would be jealous of her father's special love, and bad people would make him go away."

Peter took a deep breath. The telling was agony. "I didn't know what to do. But when she came to see me again, only a few weeks later, when I saw that all the brightness in her eyes was gone, well, it tore me up. So I went to see her father. I tried to talk to him. It was the wrong way to go about it, but I didn't know. In seminary, I had not learned what to do when a child was molested by her father. I didn't know about incest in real life. I went about it all wrong." He cleared his throat and continued, "Not a week later, that poor girl, little Libby, was dead by her father's hand."

"Non!" Isabelle sucked in her breath.

Peter's grip tightened on Isabelle's hand. "I-I reported to the county sheriff what Libby had told me about her father—what I'd seen on her arms, in her eyes. I had never felt such deep sorrow and such fury at the same time. I thought I was doing the right thing. But I was so wrong. Libby's father was a cruel drunk. He coerced his poor, battered wife to give him an alibi. Oh, and he was also the wealthiest man in town. His lumber mill supplied jobs for half the men, and he 'owned' the sheriff."

Peter took a deep breath, watched how his hands shook.

"Libby's father turned the murder against me. Everyone in the church knew that Libby liked me, that she called me Uncle Pete. That she came to see me. He accused me . . ." Peter struggled to give voice to the next words. Head in his hands, he remembered the horror of Libby's death, combined with the terror and pain of his accusation. "He accused me of molesting and murdering his daughter."

He stared at the way Isabelle's hands were interlaced with his, tried to let that peaceful image replace the one of a child's bruised and bloodied arms.

"The sheriff threw me in jail. Everyone knew the father had done it. I saw it on the faces of the whole church. But they were afraid. That man wielded so much power in the town. He had done other things, evil things, before . . ." Slowly, Peter pulled his hand from Isabelle's grasp and buried his face in his palms. The movement brought a sharp physical pain. "Two days later, the sheriff told me that some of the church people came to him in secret with proof that I was innocent. He declared me not guilty of any crime and then begged me to leave town immediately and never come back. He was concerned that Libby's father would kill me too. So I fled. It was wrong what I did, but there was no way we would get justice for that little girl."

Silence. When he dared to glance at Isabelle, he realized she was crying.

"*Je suis desolée.* I am sorry for such pain, Peter." This she pronounced slowly in English. "But you have forgiven yourself? It was a mistake, yes? It was not your fault."

"*What is so terrible in your past that you cannot forgive yourself, Ginger? You preach forgiveness to the men, you vibrate with love for God, but deep inside there's a wound, and you use a knife to continue to cut yourself and remove the scab.*"

"Sometimes it still feels raw," he admitted, "and I'm afraid I'll make another terrible mistake."

"And you will not be forgiven?"

"God will forgive me. It's much easier for me to accept God's forgiveness than to forgive myself. Sometimes . . . sometimes I just try to ignore and forget it."

"I do that too." She gave a timid smile. "I have a hard time forgiving myself also."

"Grace."

"What?"

"You know. Grace. Like my father always preached. God's forgiveness is free. And enough. He said it a thousand times. 'There's good and bad in all of us, Pete. Always remember that. Ain't one of us off the hook. All of us need God's grace.'"

"Yes. Grace. For ourselves. For others."

Let it go, Peter. Give up the guilt. Let God have that too.

"After the debacle in Kentucky, my father told me about the chaplains. He thought that my being a chaplain could work for me. I knew I would never work in a church in America again. Who would want me? I'd been accused of murder, even if later I was released as innocent. But the Army needed me. You see, the day Libby was killed was the day Japan bombed Pearl Harbor.

"My greatest failure," he whispered, "and yet I found God's mercy. The Lord led me to the front lines of a different war where I could offer help and hope again to others in need."

Peter glanced over at Isabelle's hand, thought of reaching for it again but did not. Instead, he went on with his story. "The missionaries were told to leave Algeria when the war began. My parents and sisters came to America, living in Georgia when I was in Kentucky. But shortly after I joined the Army, my father disappeared. I'd heard rumors about a group of missionaries spying on the Nazis. And I suspected he was part of that group. I hadn't heard from him after I joined the army, other than seeing him once in Algeria in 1942. But then a few weeks ago, I received a strange letter from my mother, talking about my dad rescuing children and being betrayed and these children needing to be taken to the camp. There were lists of kids I was asked to put into the camp code."

Her head jerked up. "You wrote the lists in the camp code?"

He nodded.

"I'm the one who broke that code. You wrote that code for me!"

He reached over and took her hand again. "Well, I'm not surprised. You had a good teacher way back when." He gave her hand a gentle squeeze. "And then I stumbled upon you, literally. The strangest coincidence of my life. And now we're here together."

Deep breath. "I hope I can leave soon, though. I need to be with the men."

Say it.

"But when this war is over, Zabelle, I want to be with you."

It took a moment for his comment to register with Isabelle, but when it did, she let go of his hand and scooted back in the chair, her eyes wide. "No, no, Peter. Don't say that."

He waited a moment. Took a breath. "Zabelle, surely you remember how the camp was in ruins when my father purchased it. You saw the photos. And you remember how we built it back, stone upon stone, year after year, until it became what it is now—a safe place where children can be hidden and saved. The camp has become a spiritual stronghold for good, and God has a strong hold on it and on us, Zabelle. And I believe that Sisteron can be built back again, just as the camp was. I know it will happen." This he said with conviction, but then with much less conviction, he added, "I believe that perhaps we, too, can build back our relationship—"

"Peter, please don't promise to come back. Don't write me letters either. You did that before. Even if you mean it this time, you may end up dead tomorrow, right next to the men you pray for. Please, let's pretend this, our meeting again, never happened."

"I'm not very good at pretending, Zabelle."

"Do it for me. If you truly care about me, pretend it didn't happen. Or forget that it did."

He raised his eyes toward the bandage around his head and touched the raw scar on his forearm. "That'll be difficult."

"Stop it!" Her fists were balled, but he took them in his hands and pulled her into his chest, holding her tight, her head nestled into his shoulder, the one that was throbbing with pain.

"I just want 'easy' now, Peter."

"The girl I knew didn't do anything the easy way."

"It's different now. Life has beaten me down."

"Life has brought us back together."

She backed out of his arms. "Don't twist the words—it's not a puzzle to be solved. It's hearts to heal or break. You used to understand these things."

"I still do, Zabelle. I do."

"Then you know why I'm afraid. It hurts too bad."

"I don't want to hurt you again. I promise I don't."

"Then go away, and please don't look back."

He shook his head. "I can't do that. But I can promise you this. If I'm still alive when the war's over, I'll find you, wherever you are. And if you'll join me, we'll walk together to the Penitents and climb up and stand among them and look out over the valley. And then we'll help build back Sisteron."

Lee Johnson drove the jeep, glancing often to where Peter was stretched out in the back seat. "Battle's been going on for six long days. The Task Force has finally received fuel, tanks, artillery, vehicles. And the 36th Division showed up to help. But we've lost a lot of men, Ginger." He gave a shrug. "The Germans have lost more."

Peter noticed the stench first, of rotting animals, rotting flesh. Then he saw it, the road from Montélimar strewn with many German corpses. The world thought of them as evil monsters, but here where they lay, dead and mutilated, Peter saw men doing their duty for their country.

He'd told Isabelle that in war it was clear who the enemy was—who were the good guys and who the bad guys—but in reality, was it not just a matter of perspective?

No! In some cases, it really was clear. Libby's evil father, for example. But then what did Peter know of the man? What was his background, what of his wounds, scars, habits, the inner workings of his soul?

"There's good and bad in all of us, Pete. Always remember that. Ain't one of us off the hook. All of us need God's grace."

His father's familiar words haunted him as the jeep bumped past the carnage and the sounds of battle pierced his ears. Lee pulled the jeep onto the side of the road and said, "This is as close as we can get for right now, Ginger. The battle is fierce."

Was it shell shock he saw on Lee's face?

"We'll take you to your tent."

Three other soldiers soon joined Lee and lifted Peter out of the jeep and onto a cot. His head swam, and he was thankful when the soldiers set him down and helped him into a field chair, placing a cane beside him. Perhaps this was a mistake. He flinched at the blinding pain in his head, then took long sips of water from his canteen as he settled in with his wounded leg stretched out in front of him.

Lord, give me Your grace to stay with these soldiers, to offer whatever they need.

They needed him. The relief on their faces when the soldiers saw Peter caught him off guard. They came to him, one after another, saying, "So glad you're okay, Ginger," which was followed by tears and the shaking of heads. And finally, "It's been hellish. Worst fighting we've seen. German cavalry came in on both sides, and the whole route is strewn with dead horses and dead men."

He listened and nodded and prayed with them. Leaning heavily on his cane, he stood beside the bodies of two boys, one from Arkansas and the other from Iowa, who had played cards with him on the *Nevada.*

"*I hate this war!*" Isabelle had said.

Yes. He understood what she'd meant by that.

Later, back in his tent, he called to a private, "Could you find Lieutenant Jamison for me?"

"Yes, sir." The soldier removed his helmet and wiped the sweat from his face using his shirtsleeve.

When Frank arrived, his expression was one of torment. "Thankful you're here, Ginger. Hate to bring this news, but it's Andy. Could you come with me?" He shook his head. "Don't look good at all."

Not Andy, not the prankster, the one who had prayed and been so afraid and then had been so brave. Not the boy who loved Judy.

Two other soldiers helped Frank get Peter into a jeep, and the four men bumped across the fields until finally they came to a first-aid tent, now an infirmary. They carried Peter inside past row upon row of wounded men, who lay moaning on their pallets. They set Peter down next to Andy's bed.

"Hey, buddy. Ginger's here," Frank whispered.

Peter reached for Andy's hand, not looking at the soldier's torn body but into his eyes.

"Gin . . . ger," the boy murmured.

"Yes, Andy, it's me. I'm right here." He squeezed Andy's hand. "Judy . . ."

"I'm gonna pray for you now. I'll pray for Judy too." Peter removed his hat and said a prayer for his dying friend. Later, he wept.

All through the day, Peter sat beside the injured, listening, praying, comforting them. Andy was "lost." So many were lost. His head swam, his body felt as if on fire. He was so tired . . .

Peter was dozing, his head resting on his chest, when Frank returned to the infirmary late in the afternoon.

"Ginger, you awake?"

Peter opened his eyes. "Hey, Frank."

He took a seat beside Peter and removed his helmet. "I'm thankful we were able to get you here." He looked around and grimaced. "It means a lot to us." A pause, then he choked out, "I know it meant a lot to Andy."

Peter nodded. "And I'm thankful to have been there for Andy . . . to be here for all the men."

Frank pointed to Peter's bandages, the cast on his arm. "You're barely out of the woods yourself, and if you don't mind my saying so, you don't look so good. How about we find a medic to check your injuries, maybe change those bandages? And then you keep on resting for a while."

Peter fidgeted on the cot, every wound screaming out. Sleep would not come. He sat up, awkwardly removed his sketch pad and set of colored pencils from his knapsack, and using a flashlight, he studied the drawing he'd made of Isabelle as she was sitting beside his bed some days prior. He'd caught a hint of the fire in her eyes and a trace of a smile.

It had taken a long time, so many words, for her eyes to take on that gleam he remembered from long ago. Hours to sit and talk and share and remember and forgive. Of course she was terrified. So was he. He held the sketch pad, his finger caressing her cheek, and prayed, "Lord, give Zabelle hope. And, Lord, I want to see her again."

Tell her.

He fumbled again in the satchel, took out a crinkled envelope, and began to draw.

⁘

At dawn, Frank found him dozing again, the sketchbook open on his lap.

"Hey, Ginger." He handed Peter a tin cup of steaming-hot coffee. "You been sketching in the night for us?"

Peter took a sip of the coffee and tried to smile, but it came out as a grimace. "Something I drew when in the hospital."

Frank glanced at the sketch. "I recognize her! Pretty good likeness. Did you ever get to talk to that French gal? Isabelle, right?"

"I did." Another sip, and he felt his head clearing. "And you won't believe it."

"Tell me."

"I know her."

"Good, you got to know her."

"No, I knew her from our camp, years ago. I wrote her letters, decorated the envelopes." He pointed to the envelope he had covered in different colors during the night. "And then I broke her heart. And if that ain't the strangest thing, then I saved her life."

"You knew the girl whose life you saved?"

"Yeah."

"That is . . . hard to believe."

"But it's true."

Frank tilted his head, sipped his coffee, and said, "Well, here's another thing that's hard to believe. Her cousin is here somewhere—he's with the Maquis. A skinny kid, but brave. Shot a German right in the head a few days ago. Saved his leader's life and helped the Maquis get away while we took up the fight with the Boches."

"Are you talking about René? Isabelle told me about him."

"That's him. He came to see her in Sisteron. I met him there, and he was madder than that girl. He recognized me here. Was asking about you, wanted to know if the chaplain was okay. I told him you were hurt bad and didn't think you'd be joining us. No idea where he is now, but I bet he'd like to meet you."

Isabelle's cousin. The only one who survived a massacre. Here? Just a bizarre coincidence. Nothing more.

"We never have believed in coincidences, have we, Pete?"

His whole life, it seemed, had been a series of strange coincidences, one after another, with the God of the universe bending down from His footstool in heaven, picking Peter up, and giving him another chance.

51

<hr/>

RENÉ

D-Day+11
August 26–28, 1944

"Hey, kid."

René tried to open his eyes. They felt glued together. When he finally managed to pry them apart, it took a moment to focus. Then he saw an angelic face looking down at him. He squinted, focused again, and cursed in his mind.

Gabriel.

If he's here, then I've woken up in hell.

With his eyes closed, he heard Gabriel yelling, "Antoine! *Il s'est reveillé!* He's awake. Come, come!"

Then his brother was kneeling beside him, patting him, crying. "You stubborn kid. What were you doing, saving good-for-nothing Gabriel? I told you to be careful."

René felt his lips twitch. "You gave . . . me the pistol. Force of habit . . . to shoot."

Antoine brushed his little brother's hair off his face and swiped at his own tears. "You're mighty brave, little brother."

René gasped at the stabbing pain in his side.

"You took a bullet, but don't worry. You're still all in one piece."

"Where are we?"

Antoine sat back on his haunches and chuckled. "Where are we? We're at a four-star hotel! It's so fancy they took down the walls and the roof. Nature all around."

"Sounds nice," he managed to say.

"Oh, yeah, it's nice."

"Battle?"

"We're still near Montélimar." He cursed under his breath. "This battle's been going on for a while. Pretty mean."

"Did we win?"

Antoine grimaced, then said, "Not quite. We're all here, though, the Task Force—6th Army of Americans, the F.F.I. from all over. Everybody's fighting. Lots of broken-down chariots, dead horses, dead soldiers. But those Germans don't seem to want to give up Montélimar." Then a smile. "But you killed a German, René. Saved Gabriel's life and killed a German SS officer."

The German. Tomas. He pictured the helmet beside the fallen soldier, the way the blood stained his white hair. The German who haunted his dreams and Isabelle's was dead.

"You protected us all."

Please forgive me, take away the desire for revenge, and let me simply do my part. Let me protect my friends. That's all, God.

He looked up at Antoine, shook his head, and whispered, "Not me, Antoine. Dieulefit."

The next time he opened his eyes, another angelic, boyish face was staring into his and speaking in English.

"Hey, kid. Remember me? Lieutenant Frank Jamison. Truck . . . roadblock . . . sorry you're blessé."

Then an Army medic was talking to Antoine in broken French. ". . . brother . . . lost a lot of blood . . ."

René knew those words. Everything was so blurry, so quiet—too quiet. Was he sleeping? Or dying?

The next time he woke, he saw Gabriel again. The Maquis leader's face looked pained. "Come on, René. We need you to pull through. You're a good man. A big man with guts." He cleared his throat. "Stay with us. You hear me? We need you." A rough hand patted his hand. "I'm not gonna tell you thank you for saving my life. Not till you're sitting up and looking me in the eye, you hear? Come on, kid. You can do it."

Antoine was there again, wiping his head with a cool rag and holding a canteen to his lips. "Take a sip, brother, please. And I've got food too. When Lieutenant Frank told the other American soldiers what you'd done, they started bringing me some of their rations. They'd like to keep you alive. So would we."

Keep me alive for Delphine.

Later, Antoine was speaking again, his voice hoarse with emotion. "We're all here, René. All the Durance guys. It's August twenty-eighth. Gabriel's got good news from the coast."

He heard Gabriel's voice as a far-off echo. "I've been getting reports from our buddies in the south. Listen up." He began reading something, something important.

Concentrate.

"'Toulon and Marseille have been liberated! The Allies have taken the port of Marseille . . . a tricolor has risen over Fort St.-Nicolas in Marseille . . . a month ahead of what was predicted in Operation Dragoon. The German commander has surrendered . . . French soldiers found him at dawn in an underground burrow with two telephones and a plate of Gruyère cheese . . . church bells have been ringing in jubilation for an hour . . . thirty-seven thousand prisoners have been taken in the two port cities. . . .'"

Such good news.

As René heard his comrades laughing, congratulating each other, as he heard the clinking of wineglasses and smelled the smoke of their cigarettes, he felt himself slowly drifting away.

"René."

He struggled to open his eyes. An American soldier was leaning over him and speaking in French, "René. My name is Peter. I'd like to pray for you."

Concentrate.

Too hard. He was drifting off again.

"René." The soldier was shaking him gently. "Hang in there, buddy. Come on . . ."

A cool rag was placed on his forehead, and a hand came under his head, lifting him gently. "Take a sip of water. That's right. Another . . ."

The soldier laid René back down on the coarse blanket. He could feel the hard earth beneath him. A bird was chirping somewhere.

A bird. Maybe the battle is over.

"Lavender," he whispered.

The soldier leaned closer. "What'd ya say, René?"

"Lavender. Pocket."

The soldier called out, "Hey, I think he's asking for lavender. Anybody know what he's talking about?"

Antoine came beside René again. "Isabelle told him that lavender has healing properties. He keeps a wad of it in his pocket."

His brother started feeling in his pocket, then laughed. "*Punaise!* They're still here." Antoine held the lavender buds under René's nose. "Can you smell it, frangin? Can you? That's right. Let it heal you."

Then the American soldier was speaking again, still in French. "Thank you for helping my father—Monsieur Christensen, Monsieur Martin—with the kids . . ."

René's eyes had closed again, but the man kept talking.

"Your cousin Isabelle, I know her too. Somebody will let her know you're okay. Don't you worry."

Am I okay? Tell Delphine.

But he couldn't pronounce the words.

When the soldier bent lower, René saw he was covered in bandages.

"You're the . . . aumon . . ."

"That's right. I'm the aumonier."

340

The chaplain who saved Isabelle's life. The chaplain whose father had shoved him into a cave at The Camp Between the Hills, whose father was Monsieur Martin. The chaplain who had helped dig the cave where Delphine and fifty other kids were hidden.

Delphine.

He thought of her last words to him, how the battle would be harsh. He had no idea how she knew such things, only that she'd been right. It seemed this battle would never end.

"Many people will die. You cannot die, René. You must come back to me. You are my family, remember?"

René turned his eyes to the chaplain and squeezed out the words, "Pray . . . that I will not . . . die."

Throughout the long night, with the sound of artillery shells exploding in the distance, the chaplain sat beside René as he struggled in and out of consciousness. Each time he awoke, the chaplain was still whispering prayers into the night. "Let him live, Lord. For the Maquis, for his brother, for Isabelle, let him live."

And René would add in his mind, *For Delphine.*

PART IV

52

ISABELLE

SISTERON AND LYON, FRANCE
SEPTEMBER 1, 1944

Isabelle felt the stones in her gut, their heaviness weighing her down. But this wasn't a time to grieve. It was a time to celebrate. She watched as the last child left the camp, little Anne Rocher, walking between her foster parents, Yannick and Laurette.

A week ago, Monsieur Martin had contacted Isabelle, Ginette, and Mme Nicolas and given the okay to release the children hidden at the camp. "The Germans are gone. The Milice are being punished. It's safe now." He'd sounded so calm, so absolutely sure.

Isabelle wondered at the timing, but she trusted Monsieur Martin. Monsieur Christensen. Peter's father.

Peter.

No. Don't think about him.

She'd received no word from Peter.

You begged him not to write to you.

But there had been word from Antoine. Three days ago now.

"René's been shot. Not looking good. Don't tell Delphine."
So her silence sat like heavy rocks in the pit of her stomach.
Think about now. About this.

For the past five days, as the French and American soldiers and the Maquis continued to liberate the towns in the Rhône Valley, men and women came at all times of the night and day to The Camp Between the Hills to reclaim the children hidden there.

Isabelle, Ginette, and Mme Nicolas had watched as one by one or two by two the children embraced their foster families. The smiles of the children, the tears of relief of the adults. Such brave children, such brave men and women. Thank God the children had not lost these caregivers. Every one of them had rejoiced to take back their charges.

Relatives of the children orphaned by the bombing of Sisteron also made their way to the camp. And these were heartrending, bittersweet reunions. But those children would also be cared for.

Thank You, God. Thank You for holding us fast.

That was a phrase Peter had taught her, the words to one of his favorite hymns.

At the last moment, little Anne turned around and ran to Isabelle, kissing her cheeks again. Yannick and Laurette had assured Isabelle earlier, "We're beginning to put the apartment back together, just as the city is beginning to put itself back together. We want to have Anne back with us."

"I was so afraid the Germans had found you and taken you. The apartment was in such a state. I found excrement . . ."

Laurette said, "Ginette saved us all. She came in the middle of the night. I'll never forget the fear in her eyes as she whispered that the Germans were coming. Begged us to give her little Anne. It was terrifying. But she was right. And we're all okay. And now we will take Anne back home with us."

Fifty-one children. Reunited.

Fifty children, Isabelle reminded herself. Delphine had nowhere to go. No family would be coming for her. Rumors had circulated for days of terrible casualties in Montélimar, of a never-ending battle. And Isabelle had that note from Antoine . . .

Please, God, keep René alive. Antoine needs him. I need him. Delphine needs him. He's our family. Please, God . . .

She prayed like she'd prayed for Peter throughout those long nights in Castel-Bevons.

Please.

Yesterday, Jean-Yves had convoked the Silo members in secret. "We're needed in Lyon. Their resistance has been compromised by someone within our ranks who has given the Germans information about the Allies' tactics. The Germans are bent on destroying everything and everyone before they leave. Word is they are retreating but blowing up the bridges."

It would never be over.

"You'll stay with me," Mme Nicolas said, her arm around Delphine as they waved good-bye to the Rochers.

Isabelle turned her focus to Delphine. "You'll be sure to take good care of Mme Nicolas for us, right?"

Delphine chewed on her lower lip, big eyes filling with tears. Then Delphine was pleading, "I can't stay here." She was still holding on to Mme Nicolas. "I want to, but I need to go to Lyon. To see Papa's store. Please take me to Lyon, Izzie. Please! The Allies will liberate the town soon, and Mama and Papa will come home. I must be there to welcome them."

Isabelle knelt beside the girl. "Delphine, you know the war is not over. It may be months, years before we know if . . ."

"If they survived? They're strong. Of course they will survive. And I'll be there to welcome them. I'll find our home by the river and wait for them there. And René knows to come find me in Lyon. Please take me with you."

René may not be coming. Ever.

"Delphine, the Germans are still in Lyon."

"They're retreating. The Army is chasing them. The Maquis too. You said so, Isabelle."

"Yes, but it's still dangerous. Where will you stay?"

"I'll stay with you, of course. I must be there."

Something about this girl. She said such strange things, had such strange convictions.

Delphine whispered, "God told me to be there."

Mme Nicolas held out her hand to Isabelle. "Let her go with you, dear." Then, looking down at Delphine, she added, "You will always have a home here if you are in need."

The Germans were retreating, but they did not leave quietly. In Lyon, throughout the night of September 2, reverberations from explosions and bridges being blown up echoed all across the Rhône Valley. Awakened by the noise, Isabelle watched from the window of the apartment overlooking the Saône River as first one bridge, then the next erupted in fire. Why had she allowed Delphine to accompany her here? At least the girl still slept.

The vision from this window brought back the nightmare of her view from her apartment in Sisteron on August 15. Was that just over two weeks ago?

They had traveled to Lyon together, the whole Durance Maquis, arriving the night before, crowded into the apartment of Muriel, a fellow resistant in Lyon. Jean-Yves, Amandine, Ginette, and Maurice were combing the city in the night, following the leads they had been given. What did it matter now to find the traitor if the Germans were gone, if the threat was over and the children safe?

Revenge?

She was too tired for revenge.

All she wanted was to go back home with Ginette and bring Delphine to live with them there. René and Antoine as well. Little by little, her cousins could restore the farmhouse. Little by little, she and Ginette and Delphine would help clean up the city. She would return to the library, Papa's library that was hers too, and begin her work there.

And wait for Peter.

Foolish girl. She'd asked him to leave her alone.

Another explosion. She shuddered.

Let it be over soon, God.

By the next morning, September 3, the words were whispered and shouted and written across the city and by Lyon's two rivers. "They're coming! The Allies! Our troops are coming. Today! Now!"

People were pouring into the streets below the apartment.

Delphine had awakened early and was planted by the window. "Please, let's go down, Izzie. The Allied soldiers are coming now. I want to celebrate. Can't we please take a moment to celebrate?"

And so they left the apartment and joined the masses on Rue de la République.

Every balcony along the wide boulevard was filled with cheering people, waving French flags and clapping. Crowds huddled on either side of the road, making a long pathway with human borders for the soldiers to pass through. The noise, such joy, made Isabelle break into a smile. At last, something to celebrate. Delphine was right to insist they participate. There had been no celebration following Sisteron's liberation.

Isabelle sheltered Delphine, holding her close as they moved forward with thousands of others to the Place des Terreaux in the heart of the city. The magnificent Bartholdi Fountain in the square showed Neptune's hands raised while below four galloping stallions literally sprang from the granite. The mood in the square felt every bit as intoxicating as the beautiful fountain with its splashing water.

Men and women and children dressed in their best clothes, the men and boys in suits and ties, the women and girls with brightly colored dresses, waved their tricolors and screamed with a frenzied joy. Isabelle and Delphine joined thousands of other French citizens, cheering the French and American troops who rode through town.

Half a dozen young women had climbed onto an American tank and were waving flags as the huge vehicle lumbered across the open square, now packed with pedestrians. Other girls ran out to the jeeps as they passed by and kissed the French soldiers full on the mouth. And everywhere the crowd roared.

Suddenly, Delphine let loose of Isabelle's hand, squealing, "This is why I'm here! This is why I needed to come to Lyon."

Isabelle grabbed her by the arm. "Delphine, you can't go running into the mob. Arrête!"

Her face lit up. "But of course I can, Izzie. Can't you see him? It's René."

Surely not.

Delphine pushed through the crowd, screaming, "René! René!"

René is alive? René is here? Thank you, God!

Isabelle hurried to catch up with Delphine when her cousin turned his head and his mischievous blue eyes widened. He stood in the jeep, clutching his side with one hand and waving with the other.

Isabelle burst into happy tears and watched as Delphine climbed onto the jeep with several other teenagers. She glanced back at her with a look Isabelle would never forget. Supreme joy.

53

RENÉ

SEPTEMBER 3, 1944

Surely he was dreaming, hallucinating. But at least he had awoken in heaven this time. Paradise. With Delphine by his side.

After all the nightmares, the sleepless nights, the chaplain beside him praying, Antoine begging, even Gabriel pleading, René had come back to life. While the Maquis and the French and American soldiers chased the retreating Germans up the Rhône Valley, he had lain in that field outside the demolished city of Montélimar, smelled the lavender, and let Antoine tend to him. The chaplain's prayers had worked. His own prayers had worked. He had protected his friends, he'd stayed alive, and now he was in paradise with Delphine.

Only it was real. *She* was real.

Gabriel was driving the jeep with the rest of the Maquis crowded inside: Didier, Etienne, Samuel, Bastien, and Antoine. Hands reached out to shake theirs, girls tossed flowers to them, music played, people clapped. And Delphine sat scrunched beside him.

The crowds cheered, for the whole of southern France was now liberated.

Delphine chattered excitedly, almost oblivious to the celebration around them. ". . . For two days we didn't have bread or anything but soup. But then it was over, and the families were coming back to the camp. Ginette and Isabelle were welcoming them while the children were finding their families and crying happy tears. I didn't have a family come get me, so Mme Nicolas said I could stay with her, but then Isabelle was coming here to Lyon and I just knew I had to come too. God told me to come. I thought it was for Mama and Papa, but now I know it was for you—"

"Shhh, Delphine. Slow down. It's hard to hear you over the cheering around us. Later you can explain it all. For right now, I'm just glad you're here." René's whole body ached, and she was pressed so tight against him. Another irony. Delightful pain.

Antoine reached over and tweaked Delphine's nose. "It's good to finally meet you, sis," he said.

I'm alive. Delphine is safe.

Dieulefit. Dieulefit.

René closed his eyes, leaned against Antoine's shoulder, and fell asleep while thousands of French citizens shouted their joy, and one young girl held tightly to his arm.

54

PETER

SEPTEMBER 3, 1944

Peter savored the joy, the exuberance that surrounded him as the citizens celebrated the liberation of their beloved Lyon. The war wasn't over, but on this day, as the Task Force drove through the city, they let the people's joy seep into their souls.

And their gratitude. He saw it on every face, bright eyes shining with tears of gratefulness and hope.

The tragedies in Sisteron, the excruciating long battle of Montélimar, the drive up the Rhône, had culminated in a party. A citywide, impromptu festival where champagne corks popped into the air, and the bubbly liquid sprinkled the heads of soldiers as they slowly wound through the sea of civilians.

Peter felt such pride for the soldiers, though today they were fresh-faced, bright-eyed boys. Today he would not let himself dwell on the ones who were "missing." He would embrace the euphemisms that they were "lost" and "in a better place." For today that was enough.

Today was for honoring the exemplary courage of the Task

Force and the 6th Army of the French, the maquisards and resistants. He watched as they all soaked in the gratitude being
expressed, their necks adorned with wreaths of flowers, cheeks
splotched with the bright red marks of women's lips.

And the music!

Bands of old men stood in their World War I uniforms, proudly
playing their trumpets, trombones, clarinets, oboes, flutes, and
drums as if they had been practicing for months. Perhaps they had.
The group of ragtag musicians played "La Marseillaise" in front
of the Bartholdi Fountain. The crowd joined in, singing, "Allons
enfants de la patrie . . ."

Somewhere up ahead, another vehicle filled with brave maquisards inched between the cheering horde, a young boy among
them. He thought of the night he'd spent beside René, praying,
wondering if he would perish like Andy.

But Isabelle's cousin had lived.

Zabelle.

Was she still at the camp with the children? Had his father contacted her again? Surely the children could now leave the camp. Antoine had told him of the German soldier René had killed, and later,
René had explained that this was the man who had terrified Isabelle.

It was all so strange, amid the war, the coincidences that seemed
somehow like divine appointments. Like destiny.

Like God's grace.

Not your fault. Forgive yourself yourself . . .

Libby's bright, happy eyes flashed in his mind while children
all around him sang and cheered.

Grace.

In that moment, in the joyful cacophony of liberation, Peter
felt a lightness, a freedom from that tenacious guilt.

The music played louder as they drew nearer to the fountain,
the throngs pressing closer. A head turned, bright eyes, a face.
Peter's heart stopped, then accelerated. He squinted. Surely not . . .

She turned at the same time, and her eyes widened. She gasped,
reached out as if to touch him, reaching and then pushing through
the crowd, calling, "Peter! Peter!"

55

ISABELLE

SEPTEMBER 3, 1944

Isabelle had jogged alongside the jeep, calling to Delphine, "Be back at the fountain at two," and Delphine had nodded.

Now Isabelle was jogging beside another jeep, and Peter was reaching out, laughing, pulling her up as she held on to the door.

Then she was seated in the jeep, on his lap, out of breath.

"I didn't mean it," she said, touching his cheek, staring straight into his eyes while Frank and two other soldiers whistled and patted Peter playfully on the shoulders.

"What didn't you mean?" he asked, but his eyes were teasing.

"Oh, don't be impossible! Do what you promised, Peter. Please. Write to me. Come back to me."

He smiled, and his freckled and scarred face lit up with pleasure. "I will." Then Peter leaned over and pressed his lips against hers. For just a moment.

Soon she was back on the street. Strangers were laughing and shaking her hand, and everywhere there were smiles.

She touched her lips. What had just happened? A dream?

354

A hallucination? She had not even asked him where they were headed or if she could see him again in Lyon.

For now, it was enough. Much more than enough. That kiss, that smile, that promise would last until the next time.

While the crowds had thinned, hundreds of people were still milling about Place des Terreaux. It was three in the afternoon, and as each minute ticked by, Isabelle worried. Delphine was an hour late. Had she lost her way among the mass of people? Would René bring her to the fountain? Surely the Germans were gone, and the men with René would keep Delphine safe. Why had she let her loose in this mob?

Fifteen minutes later, Delphine arrived out of breath, red-faced, with a wild look in her eyes that caused Isabelle's stomach to wrench.

"What is it?"

Gulping, Delphine choked out, "The crowd, Ginette . . ."

Delphine grabbed Isabelle's hand, yanking her across the immense cobblestone *place* and weaving through the narrower streets, between the crowds of joyful townspeople who filled every corner of the city.

"Hurry, hurry!"

They entered a smaller square, packed with men and women. Yet the shouts and jeers she heard coming from the crowd shocked her. "*Collabo! Collaboration horizontale!* Whores! Traitors!"

A dozen women stood encircled by the crowd, their heads shaved, their clothes torn, their eyes turned down. One of them was Ginette.

A low moan escaped Isabelle as she bent over, doubled in pain, one hand pressed against her belly, another at her throat to keep the bile at bay. When she managed to straighten again, she hurried to where Delphine had scrambled onto the wall. They held each other, shaking, and then Ginette's eyes caught those of Isabelle. Only for a second. But she read the terror, the soul-wrenching truth.

Ginette was the traitor!

Isabelle's astonished eyes met Ginette's briefly.

Impossible! Ginette?

The fury of the crowd sent chills running through Isabelle.

"They're so angry," Delphine cried. "They're going to hurt them—hurt Ginette!"

Did you betray me? Is my father dead because of you, Ginette?

The women's screams grew louder, high-pitched, hysterical. "Au secours! Help! I'm sorry! I'm sorry!"

And the furious crowd responded, "You slept with the enemy!"

Two women fell to the ground, then another.

"We've got to stop them! They're going to hurt her, Izzie!" Delphine's eyes, so knowing, accusing. "If we let them hurt these women, we're no better than the Nazis."

Ginette screamed as a middle-aged man slapped her across the face. With a punch to her stomach, she fell to the ground.

Delphine jumped off the wall and began to push her way through the crowd with Isabelle following. Together they squeezed through the bodies, felt the fists on their heads until out in the open, where Delphine shouted, "I'm a Jew! I watched my parents beaten and carted off to work camps by the Nazis. My host family was gunned down by them. Are you no better?"

Isabelle fell to her knees, sheltering Ginette with her body as the mob continued to spew insults. Isabelle heard a shot, and then Delphine screamed. Then another shot. Maurice, pistol in the air, fired one more time. "Arrête! Enough!"

Finally the crowd began to disperse, and as Isabelle raised herself to a sitting position, her arms around an unconscious Ginette, she saw the blood on Delphine's dress and the dark, gentle eyes of Maurice as he held the child in his arms.

Isabelle paced back and forth in the narrow hallway of Muriel's apartment as Amandine tended to both Delphine and Ginette. Jean-Yves lit his fourth cigarette and tugged on his skinny mustache. Maurice had his face buried in his hands.

At last, Amandine came out. "The girl will be okay. I thought the blood was from a bullet wound, but it's from two badly scraped hands and knees. Courageous kid."

"Thank God," Isabelle whispered. "And Ginette?"

"Yes, how is Ginette?" Maurice's expression showed more than concern for a friend. "How is she?"

"Sleeping. Bruised. I don't think anything's broken, but they carved . . ." Amandine broke down in tears.

"A swastika in her forehead. I saw it." Jean-Yves's anger spilled forth. "She deserved it. They all did!"

"Jean-Yves!"

"We knew there was a traitor among us."

Isabelle's stomach cramped. "We don't know that for sure."

"You're just protecting your friend," Jean-Yves shot back.

Maurice walked up to Jean-Yves, his face only inches away. "Who turned her in? No one knows her here in Lyon. Did you do it, Jean-Yves? If so, *why*?"

Jean-Yves shook his head. "They're accusing her of sleeping with Germans. Collaboration horizontale."

"That's impossible! Who is saying this?" Isabelle asked.

"One of Muriel's friends, Philippe, here in Lyon. Their top explosive guy. I've met him. He came to Sisteron the week before the bombing." Jean-Yves shrugged. "We needed his expertise. Ginette hadn't shown up to help." He scuffed his shoes on the floor.

"She was helping me with the kids, and that's all," Isabelle said.

"Maybe. But it's not what he said. He recognized her when we were all out last night. He was positive too, and furious. He said when he was in Sisteron, he'd seen her with that German. 'She was completely entangled with a German officer,' he said. 'Eerie, handsome chap with white hair. You don't forget that.'"

Isabelle swallowed and squeaked out, "With Tomas?"

"Sounds like it."

Isabelle slid to the floor and buried her head in her hands.

Alone in a bedroom with Ginette, Isabelle stared at her best friend, with her shaved head, a bloody swastika carved in her forehead.

"You were the traitor, Ginette? It was you?"

No, no! It couldn't be. Not Ginette.

"My father is dead because of you? My father, Ginette!"

Ginette was hunched over, her face black and blue, her lips swollen. Her eyes too, almost swollen shut. Slowly she shook her head back and forth. "No, Zabelle. I won't let you believe that. I helped them escape. All the prisoners. We took your father, took all of them to a safe place."

"And then what? You told Tomas and the others where they were hidden?"

"No one told them where the prisoners were hiding. They figured it out."

"How do you know that?"

"Because Tomas bragged about it to me."

"Then it is true? You were sleeping with Tomas?"

"Yes."

The force with which she slapped Ginette's face left Isabelle's hand stinging.

Ginette's hand on Isabelle's arm was just as forceful. "Stop!" she yelled. "You can believe what you want, Zabelle. But first you must hear me out. Don't I deserve that much after all of this?" She motioned to her hair, her head, to the scars on her wrist. "If I'm guilty, then you can turn me over to them again. You can have me killed. But *please*," she pleaded and sank to her knees, "hear me out."

Isabelle tried to make her face blank, tried to calm the pulsing in her ears, the way her heart was ramming against her ribs. But she remained standing, arms crossed tightly over her chest.

Ginette's usual confident smile was nothing but a trembling mess. "The night after the attack on the Amblard farm, Tomas found me. I was giving information to Jacques at the café when they came in. Four or five Germans. Tomas was bragging about killing the Maquis and laughing about a boy who had survived. He was drunk with whiskey and pride."

Ginette's hands were shaking, her whole body shaking.

"I left the café, going out the back door, but Tomas came after me. He didn't know I had any part in the prisoners' escape, but he had seen me with you in town one day, Zabelle."

Ginette had folded into herself, shivering. She began to speak in a harsh voice. "He grabbed me and said, 'You are friends with Geraldine, n'est-ce pas? I've seen you together. Are you working for the Resistance too?' He asked me this, Zabelle."

She looked up, her eyes glassy.

"'What do you mean, sir?' I asked him.

"'Geraldine was a decoy, non? To distract me. All of you were trying to distract us.'

"'Geraldine, a decoy? Believe what you want. I don't think she's smart enough to work underground. But she is my friend. This is true.' He slapped me when I said that. I tried to act mad and said, 'How dare you!'" Ginette gave a harsh grunt. "Foolish me. He cut me then with his knife. He sliced through my wrist right there on the street behind the café."

Isabelle gasped and sank to the floor beside Ginette.

The lost look of a child came over Ginette, and she whispered, "Blood everywhere, but he only laughed and said, 'I dare because I can. And you *will* tell me about your friend.'"

Ginette's hand went to the ugly scar on her wrist, the one she had kept bandaged for weeks, the one she claimed she'd cut while planting explosives.

"I fainted, and when I came to, he had bandaged the wrist and carried me into a room. I kept saying you were innocent, that you weren't the type to spy. 'You've been with her. She is nervous, a little simple, but she likes men.'" Ginette closed her eyes as Isabelle's arm came around her. "Oh, Zabelle, what could I say? Tomas was so drunk. He bragged about the massacre of the prisoners—how they found them, how they drew the Maquis out that morning with rifle fire. How they . . . killed them. And then he bragged about the ambush at the Amblard farm, saying, 'We attacked the farm because we thought there were many Maquis in the region. But there were only four and a boy and his mother.'"

"They didn't search the cave the first time when Delphine was hidden there. When they killed Dominique . . ." Ginette stifled a sob. "But later that night, Tomas went back to the farmhouse. He suspected something. He said, 'We found evidence of someone hidden there. It smelled like a Jew.' He slapped me then and shouted, 'So I don't believe your friend is innocent or stupid.'

"Knowing he was going to torture me to get the information, I decided another way. I-I offered to spy on you, on the others. But it was to protect you, Zabelle, and to save myself, at least for a little while. 'What do you want me to do?' I asked him.

"'I want you to find the Jewish swine hidden in the region. We have received word from an ally in Nice: Jewish children are hidden here. And now we know they were keeping a Jew at that farmhouse. You find the other Jews—tell us where they are. And you and your dear, innocent friend may live.'

"I pleaded with him to give me a few days to find out about the Jewish children. He was so mad, so livid, so determined to have the information. I needed to distract Tomas, to buy us time. I asked him, 'Why haven't you taken Geraldine to bed? She is too good for you perhaps? Am I too good for you?'

"I used all the tricks I taught you, Zabelle. I seduced him, like I had told you to do. Better that than to be raped and killed, I thought. I-I didn't know what else to do. He knew. All along he suspected you were a resistant, that I was a resistant."

Ginette was holding Isabelle's wrist so tightly that her fingers had turned white. She averted her eyes as if she could still feel the knife's blade, see the blood.

"After Tomas let me go, I wrote to Monsieur Martin and begged him to get the word out that the Silo Network had been compromised. Someone in Nice had found out about it." She was taking shallow breaths. "But I was also afraid. If they tortured me again, I would . . . betray the Silo. Betray the children. So I lied to you. Sometimes I wasn't planting explosives. I was with Tomas." She looked up, her left eye now swollen completely shut. "As soon as Monsieur Martin got the word to hide the children, I lied to Tomas. I gave him wrong information. Think of it. They didn't know about the Silo; they didn't find the children."

And I did the same. I lied to Tomas, made up a story on the spur of the moment to save myself, to save the Network from being discovered.

Ginette continued, "You were right to suspect a traitor. You were right to hide Delphine at the camp. The crowd today was right too. I had slept with the enemy. But each time it was to protect you and our friends and the children. And yes, to save myself. Better a ruined woman than a dead one. I kept telling myself that." She coughed, then whispered, "Perhaps, though, I was wrong. Perhaps I would be better off dead—like Dominique, like Tito . . ."

Her friend's immense suffering melted any rage, any doubt Isabelle still clung to.

Ginette was still talking. ". . . I told Tomas about hiding the messages in our mailbox. But I put the wrong information there. They didn't know about the Silo, about the camp, about Monsieur Christensen. About you. I tried to protect you all." She paused and gave a deep sigh. "It was not easy to keep ahead of them, to lie to you, to warn the families. I took the Alain children first. The family left so that the Germans would find the house empty. They destroyed it. We were all saving the children, and I hurried, and you hurried. I had to give Tomas a few addresses. Twice I put the right addresses of families in the mailbox, but not until I had warned the family ahead of time, not until they had left, the children gone. Of course, Tomas would have killed me if he found me again, because the information I supplied was wrong. But I never saw him again after the children were safely hidden. I too hid at the camp."

"Are you saying there was no traitor?"

"In Nice, yes. But here, only me. Yet I was worse than a traitor. I lied to *everyone*. I thought . . . I thought it would save some . . ."

"But they found the Rocher apartment. Destroyed it!"

"Because I told them the child was there. But the family escaped first. They escaped. And the child was hidden. You saw that. All the children were hidden and safe. All taken to the camp."

What had Laurette Rocher said? *"Ginette saved us all. She came in the middle of the night. I'll never forget the fear in her eyes as she whispered that the Germans were coming. She begged us to give her little Anne."*

"What could I do? I told Tomas, but the families knew first. I had to tell him something. He would have killed me. And you. He was so evil." Ginette's shoulders were bare from where the townspeople had ripped her favorite pale blue dress, the one that had brought out the color in her eyes.

"And the only thing that saved me, Zabelle, was the bombing of Sisteron. It's a horrible thing to say, but Tomas would have found me again. He knew I'd been lying. Ironic, n'est-ce pas? The bombing of the town saved me. Everything is twisted around."

Ginette leaned back against the bed and stared at the ceiling. "It doesn't matter if you believe me, if anyone believes me. I know what I did. What we all did to survive, to save others. We lied, we killed, we stole. Were we evil like the enemy? We did the same thing. For our cause, for freedom."

"But we did it to save innocent lives."

"Perhaps. Then 'the ends justify the means,' n'est-ce pas?"

Confused, Isabelle's head was pounding now. "I don't know."

"I know. And I would do it again and again. The same things, because it was right, because it was all we could do. Because I wanted to protect the people I love. To protect myself. I wanted to *live.*"

Ginette rested her head on Isabelle's shoulder and whispered, "None of us wants a badge of honor. We did what we had to do. Now we want to forget. And the ones who want revenge, let them have it. I know what I did, and I would do it again." She wrapped her hand around Isabelle's. "For you."

Maurice sat beside the bed as Ginette slept. Amandine and Jean-Yves had joined other resistants as the city continued to celebrate and spy. Delphine lay on the leather couch in the salon, talking excitedly. "I thought I needed to be in Lyon for my parents, Izzie. I hoped, I dreamed. Then I thought it was for René. But I was wrong. It was for Ginette. Will she be okay?"

"I think so." Isabelle brushed the hair off Delphine's sweaty forehead. "Dear child, you are so brave. And you listen, don't you? To God."

"*Shema*. It is Hebrew for listen. But it means more than simply 'to listen.' It means that whatever you hear, whatever God asks you to do, you obey."

"That's beautiful."

"You do shema too, Isabelle. You have listened and obeyed and worked so hard, and now it will be okay."

"I hope so. I think you're right. For now. Tomorrow we'll go home. You'll stay with me. With us."

"And I know René will come back sometime. I can't believe I found him. He told me how he almost died, but then your chaplain prayed for him."

This was the third time Delphine had repeated that story, along with the information that René had shot and killed Tomas. The girl was still chattering, but her eyelids were growing heavy.

"Shush now, Delphine. Rest. Just rest."

"Okay. But remember, once we get home, we'll visit the families with the children, we'll help clean the city, and you'll open the library again."

"Shhh."

Delphine's chocolate eyes slowly closed, and she grinned. "And we'll wait for Peter and René to come home."

Isabelle drove Ginette to her parents' farmhouse ten kilometers from Sisteron. There, Ginette could hide away until her hair grew back and her wounds healed. While Delphine waited in the car, she walked her friend to the simple farmhouse.

"Do you want me to stay and talk with your parents?" She had known the Duprés since she was a child, had often spent the night at their home. Ginette's parents were good people.

"No. I'll be okay. They know not to ask too many questions." She hesitated. "It was quite amazing to hear what René did. You're sure? He really shot Tomas?"

"Yes. And when he explained it to Delphine, he said the strangest thing. That God had answered his prayers to protect his friends. That he felt sorrow for Tomas and the young boys they had killed."

Ginette shrugged. "Yes, there's so much we will do to protect those we love. Even kill. So confusing. So much doesn't make sense."

"But some things do," Isabelle whispered. "Courage. Friendship. Love."

"Yes, those. And Delphine will stay with you, with us?"

"Eventually. I'm taking her to the camp tonight. She wants to check on Mme Nicolas, to help her for a few weeks. But then she'll come live with both of us." Isabelle placed a kiss on her friend's cheeks, then touched her forehead to Ginette's scarred one. "Rest. Heal. Then please, come back."

She nodded. "I will." Tears slid down her face. "And have you heard from Monsieur Christensen?"

"No. But I didn't expect to."

"Neither did I. And what about your chaplain?"

Isabelle gave a faint smile. "Only time will tell."

"I'm sorry for it all."

She embraced Ginette and kissed her swollen cheeks again. "I'm sorry too. That I ever doubted you. For this, for all of it. Merci. Merci for everything."

Once again, Delphine talked nonstop as Isabelle drove from the Duprés' farmhouse to The Camp Between the Hills. As soon as they bumped onto the rocky driveway, Delphine cried out, "Stop! I want to surprise her myself."

Isabelle watched as the young girl flew out of the car and down the hill, slipping on a few rocks and standing at the doorway, knocking. When Mme Nicolas opened the door, the child melted into her arms, and Isabelle imagined that even Mme Nicolas could not hold back the tears. Delphine pointed up to where Isabelle stood beside the car, and the elderly woman and the young girl both waved to her.

⊰⊱

Isabelle turned toward her apartment building, watching as the villagers continued to pick through the ruins and slowly build back her city. She didn't know what was next for her. Would she stay and help, or did the Silo resistants need her again?

She opened the heavy door and walked into the dark corridor of her apartment building, past the row of wooden mailboxes where the instructions had been hidden. The children were safe, all placed again with families. Delphine was at the camp, René traveling with the Maquis. And Peter? He was most likely praying with the soldiers as they continued to chase the Germans.

She turned back to her mailbox, inserted the key, and opened it out of force of habit. One brightly covered envelope lay inside, an envelope that looked like the ones she had received so long ago. She held it, almost reverently, brushing her fingers across a comic-strip drawing of a girl with bright blue eyes and black hair, sitting beside the bed of a green-eyed, freckled-faced soldier with a bandage around his head and red hair curling over it. He was talking, and the bubble coming from his mouth held her address.

She felt a smile cross her lips. Turning the envelope over, she saw strange symbols scrawled across the back. The camp code. Even she could break the few words it represented.

See you soon, Zabelle.

EPILOGUE

DELPHINE

SISTERON AND THE CAMP BETWEEN THE HILLS
AUGUST 15, 1954

The cemetery sits on an incline below the massive Citadel. Today, many of us are gathered as the mayor lifts the wreath and nods to the other town officials. A children's choir is singing "La Marseillaise." Then the mayor reads a communique about the war, about the bombing, including the names of all who were lost on this day ten years ago.

I hold Izzie to my breast. She is so young, so innocent. She won't remember this ceremony or the one tomorrow, but she'll grow up hearing the stories. Nothing will be forgotten.

In May, when the letter arrived, that brightly colored envelope with the equally bright invitation inside, I turned to where Izzie slept in the crib and whispered to my daughter, "I'll be back soon."

In truth, I only walked five steps into the kitchen and picked up the receiver, held it to my ear, and dialed the number on the invitation.

"*Allô?*" When I heard that voice, deep, booming and familiar, my throat constricted.

"Bonjour, Monsieur Martin. This is Sarah. Sarah Levy. I'm calling about the invitation we received." Then I whispered, as if the walls of my home were listening, "I-I was one of the children." The flood of tears surprised me.

"Sarah!" His voice sounded pleased.

I could not make my mouth pronounce the next words.

"Sarah, are you there?"

"Yes," but the emotion was too great.

"Sarah Levy," he whispered reverently.

"Do you remember me?"

"Of course. Delphine. You were Delphine Amblard. How are you?"

"I'm still Delphine Amblard," I said finally, and my lips turned up despite my tears.

"Ah." He chuckled. "I thought I had heard a rumor."

"We have a daughter. Isabelle. I call her Izzie."

Now his voice was quiet, and there was a catch in it. "It's a beautiful name."

René called out, "Delphine, who are you talking to?"

I caught his eyes, and he saw the tears and came close, raising his eyebrows, worried. He's protective in that way. I shook my head, covered the mouthpiece of the phone, and mouthed, "It's okay." Then I said to the man on the other end, "We'll be there."

Philip Christensen is stooped, but his eyes are bright, and he still towers over the rest of us. Peter is holding his father's arm, standing in between his parents, his other hand intertwined with his petite mother's. As his parents take a seat in two Adirondack chairs, watching their grandchildren play pétanque in the sandpit behind the house, I catch her voice.

"Dell! Dell, what in the world are you doing? Put that down right now. Quit teasing your brothers!"

She's speaking in English, hands on hips, with her back to me. The little girl, Dell, twirls around, and I laugh. Her hair is a tangle of bright red curls. She sees me and starts running toward me.

"Auntie Sarah! Uncle René! We've found blackberries."

The child too is speaking in English, but I know what she is saying because of the dark stain around her mouth.

Peter calls out, "French, Dell! *Il faut parler en français avec Tonton et Tatie.* You know you speak in French with your aunt and uncle."

She frowns at her father and switches languages. And then Isabelle turns around and sees us. She starts crying, of course. Her hair is swept back from her face in a long French braid. She is heavy with child. Their fourth.

She embraces me with a kiss on each cheek and whispers, "Thanks for coming. He was hoping you would be here."

"We wouldn't miss it for the world!"

Peter takes out a bottle of champagne, the one he procured from the cave where all of us lived for those weeks. The one Mme Nicolas had told me was going to be used for a very special occasion.

She was still alive when Isabelle and Peter got married in the village chapel with Monsieur Christensen performing the vows. The meal afterward in this garden lasted until the wee hours of the morning. There was lots of champagne on that night eight years ago. I remember, I was there.

But this bottle is for a different type of celebration.

The village looks beautiful on this late August afternoon. The golden stones on every building fairly sparkle as the setting sun casts its spell on them. Ivy grows up the archway between the front two buildings, giving it a welcoming feel. Lavender is planted in the Anduze pottery beside the doorway to the Christensens' home.

I think of how that bat flew out and scared me to death all those years ago. I can almost feel the slick rain that cooled us off, can almost hear Isabelle joining me as we whispered the Psalms of Ascent. René and I sing them sometimes. In memory of Mama and Papa.

They never returned, but I learned they were brave until the very end, as I knew they would be.

368

And last year we took over the chocolaterie, Levy's of Lyon.

The camp is completely renovated. Monsieur Christensen says, "It only took us thirty years," and he laughs and pats his wife's hand. He joined Dotty in Algeria after the war was over. They finally retired this past spring after forty-five years in Algeria and France. They are here at the camp for one more visit before they move to the States permanently.

For one more celebration.

The camp is used year-round now—for missionary families, for Scout camps, and for church events. Peter and Isabelle live here permanently. Peter is the chaplain and pastor, while Isabelle does just about everything else.

René and I attend a little Protestant church in the town where we live to the north of Lyon. We each embraced the gospel, the Master, at some point during the five summers we worked at the camp, from 1946 to 1950, first as campers, and then as counselors. It was the only time we were able to see each other. Otherwise we wrote letters.

René and Antoine lived at the farmhouse with their father, who came back from the prison camp. I lived with Isabelle and Ginette for the first year after the war, and then with Isabelle and Peter after they married in 1947. Isabelle wouldn't even let René take me on a date until I turned sixteen.

But at camp, René and I corralled the kids and created new camp codes and lifted stones and listened to Peter preach. We still listen. Peter's voice isn't quite as intimidating as Monsieur Christensen's, at least that's what Isabelle says, but he raises his hands and talks about grace and forgiveness, with La Baume and St. Michel keeping watch behind him and dozens of campers' eyes fixed on his bright red curls.

And then he tells the story of the camp, of building it back, of building back Sisteron, and of a God who will help us build back our lives, no matter what we've been through. He'll hold us fast.

Finally, after spending all those summers helping at The Camp Between the Hills, René took me down to the stream and asked me to marry him. I had just turned eighteen.

"When are the others supposed to arrive?" I ask.

"Anne is coming tonight with Laurette and Yannick," Isabelle says. "Peter's picking them up at the train station."

"Ginette is driving from Montpellier with Maurice and the kids tomorrow morning. And then the whole crew from Sisteron and the surrounding villages will arrive tomorrow night. Every bed will be filled."

It's a mini reunion of the Martin Network for the kids and foster families from the Basses-Alpes. The first ever. Ginette had the idea when she learned that Monsieur Christensen was retiring. She and Isabelle spent six months contacting the foster families, finding addresses for the children. No one has spoken of the Network in all these years, certainly not Monsieur Christensen. But when Peter asked him to come, he said his dad's eyes got awfully misty.

The cicadas are chirping, and the air is fresh. The children are all asleep, and the last of the wine is finished. Peter holds out his hand to Isabelle.

"Walk with me," he says with a smile.

They're going to the stream, their nightly routine. He walks with a limp, the only visible remains from his injuries.

She laughs and turns to us. "See you bright and early tomorrow, right?"

"We'll be there."

In the cool of the morning tomorrow, before the evening festivities with the other families, we'll drive beside the Durance River to Les Mées and walk up the path to where the Penitents look over the valley. Peter and Isabelle with their kids, Dell, Ginger, and Andy, and René and I with little Izzie strapped to René's back.

Peter's arm is tight around Isabelle's protruding stomach. "Zabelle has promised she is up for it." He grins, pats his leg, and says, "She still walks faster than I do, even with that belly of hers."

René shakes his head. "That's my cousin for you."

"Look who's talking," she shoots back. "You walked from the Penitents to Sisteron when you were half dead."

I wink at my husband. I remember that walk in the middle of the night when I was begging God to keep him alive.

René pulls on my arm and whispers, "Oh, yeah. That's when I promised to tell you."

"Tell me what?"

"That you're pretty, Sarah Levy." He tweaks my nose as if we're teenagers, then says, "And I love you."

AUTHOR'S NOTE

This story was inspired in part by events that happened in 1983, when my teammates and I, all young North Americans, first arrived in France for ministry service. We took a group of college-aged Americans to a ruined medieval alpine village near Sisteron called Entrepierres, which literally means "between the stones." We spent two weeks hauling rocks and digging ditches to help build back the dilapidated village.

Heading up the work project was Dudley Ward, a visionary British missionary, who challenged us in our thoughts about faith, work, and love. He created a retreat center for full-time French pastors and missionaries. God has mightily used Entrepierres, the inspiration for The Camp Between the Hills, to bless families, including my own, and bring healing and health to hundreds of people throughout the years. Entrepierres is a living metaphor for Isaiah 61:4, the verse referenced several times in this book.

Although I've lived in France for over thirty-five years, I had heard very little about Operation Dragoon and the Allied invasion of Provence. A few years ago, I ventured to Entrepierres for a week. While there, I visited nearby Sisteron and learned not only about the bombing of the city on August 15, 1944, due to the Allies' miscalculation, but also of the rescue of the prisoners from the Citadel in July 1944 and their subsequent massacre five days later.

When I returned to the city, I wandered through the andrones and up to the Citadel to attend the memorial service held at the cemetery every August 15 for those who perished during the bombing.

Afterwards, I spent weeks trying to understand the huge implications of Operation Dragoon—watching documentaries, reading essays, studying maps, and basically wearing out my civilian brain. I was also inspired by the stories of World War II chaplains and enjoyed learning about missionaries who became spies during the war.

And the nearby Penitent Cliffs in Les Mées haunted and enthralled me. Paul and I explored their grottos and climbed the snaking path to the top of the cliffs for a breathtaking 360-degree view of the region below those old, petrified monks. The themes of penance, confession, forgiveness, and forgiving oneself slid into the story line.

Years ago, I was challenged and inspired by Lilias Trotter, who left a promising career as an artist to become one of the first British missionaries to Algeria. You can find out more about her amazing life, her writings, and artwork at LiliasTrotter.com.

While I knew little about Operation Dragoon, I've been fascinated by the courage of those in the French Resistance for many years. When my family moved to Lyon in 2003, I dove deep into research about the Resistance for my novel *Searching for Eternity*. For this novel, as I learned about the Resistance and the Maquis in and around Sisteron, I came across the story of René Amblard, the lone survivor of an attack by hundreds of Germans on a farmhouse in July 1944.

In the weeks and months following D-Day in Normandy, the *épuration sauvage,* or "wild purge," of those believed to have been traitors was spontaneous, unofficial, and brutal. Women accused of "horizontal collaboration," or sleeping with the enemy, were targeted by vigilantes and publicly humiliated. Their heads were shaved, they were stripped half-naked, smeared with tar, paraded through towns, and taunted, stoned, kicked, beaten, spat upon, and sometimes even killed.

There is a wealth of information available in books, online, and in documentaries about civilians risking their lives to hide Jewish children, but my first interest came from hearing about how a pastor and many of the residents of the French village of Le Chambon-sur-Lignon helped shield Jewish children and other vulnerable people from the Germans. That operation saved the lives of thousands of refugees, including about 5,000 Jews.

To my knowledge, no Jewish children were hidden in the cave at Entrepierres, but the cave itself does exist, and I have stepped inside it!

The Martin Network in my story is loosely based on several real networks in France that rescued Jewish children. The 2024 movie *One Life*, starring Anthony Hopkins, is another accurate portrayal of such a network. According to my research, those who headed up the rescues did not speak about their service or work for many decades.

For the plot and timeline in the novel, I brought the children, families, and rescuers together in the epilogue after ten years. It never gets old, telling stories of ordinary citizens who display extraordinary courage in the face of danger and tragedy and who desire no credit for their acts of heroism.

ACKNOWLEDGMENTS

I am indebted to:

Dudley and Jill Ward for their sacrificial service at Entrepierres (PierreVivantes.org). In 1968, Dudley and Jill began acquiring and rebuilding Entrepierres as a place of rest and refreshment for Christian workers serving in Europe. Dudley, also an author, has many true and miraculous stories of God's provision there.

Jonathan and Rachel Ward, who now manage Entrepierres and offer counsel and hospitality, along with their dedicated staff. I loved how Jonathan's face lit up when I explained the plot of *From the Valley We Rise* and how the fictional village would house Jewish orphans. He immediately took me to the huge cave he and Dudley dug many years ago. It looks a lot like the one in my story.

My dear friend Rob Suggs (RobSuggs.com), a renowned author and cartoonist, whose brightly colored comic-strip drawings on envelopes blessed me as a teen and inspired Peter's creations.

The wonderful, gifted team at Bethany House Publishers. A huge *merci* to Rochelle Gloege, Luke Hinrichs, Genevieve Smith, and Kate Jameson for the way you have embraced this story and made it so much better, expertly catching all my snafus. Also to Joyce

Perez, Raela Schoenherr, Lindsay Schubert, Rachael Betz, Emily Vest, Bria Conway and many others at BHP, *merci* for all you do behind the scenes. Your expertise is invaluable and reassuring.

Jori Hanna, my delightful, savvy marketing assistant. You're a joy to work with as you keep me sane and laughing, all while managing a mountain of information. It's a privilege to watch you develop your own business in the publishing world. You will go far.

Chip MacGregor, my long-time agent and friend, who retired without my permission and much to my dismay. *Merci pour toutes les années ensemble.*

All my cheerleaders in the Goldsmith and Musser families. Thank you for your support throughout our years on the mission field and my years in writing.

So many friends on both sides of the Atlantic who pray for the work of my hands. I can't begin to name you all, but please be reminded that your prayers have been answered each time I birth a book.

My Transformational Fiction prayer partners: Lynn Austin, Sharon Garlough Brown, Robin Grant, Susan Meissner, and Deb Raney. We have prayed each other through so many joys and sorrows on this journey as writers and sisters in Christ. Thank you.

My family at One Collective. Thank you for receiving what Paul and I have to offer with grace and for allowing me to pen my stories.

Andrew and Lacy, Chris and Ashlee—my sons and daughters-in-law. Paul and I feel deep joy as we watch you navigate your lives in ways which honor the Lord, your families, and so many others around the world.

Jesse, Naj, Quinn, Lena, and Cori. I still can't believe I am blessed not only to have grandchildren, but to enjoy so much time with you all. Your love of life inspires me. Can you find where I winked at you in this story?

Paul. Always to you, my better half, my partner in love and life, and the hidden hero in every one of my love stories. You care for and support my every endeavor and then take it all to the Lord. Thank you for loving me so well as our journey together twists and turns. You remain my favorite soccer player. I love how you make life lighter with so much laughter, while giving godly wisdom from your great big, kind, and humble heart. *Je t'aime tant.*

My dear readers. You make my day repeatedly with your comments and photos on social media and your heartfelt emails. And what a joy to get to meet some of you in person!

And finally, to Jesus, my Savior and Lord. Thank You for calling me to Yourself and for rebuilding my life one stone at a time. Day by day, You reveal more of Your mystery, holiness, and extravagant love and grace to me. I owe everything to You—my life, my love, my all.

READING GROUP
DISCUSSION GUIDE

1. Throughout the Bible, there is a beautiful metaphor of building back ruins, as in Isaiah 61:4. This metaphor also runs throughout the novel. Discuss the transformation that happens at The Camp Between the Hills, as well as in the lives of Peter, Isabelle, and René. How does grace factor into their arcs?

2. What do you think of the imagery of the Penitent Cliffs and the idea of Protestant Penance? *This would be a Protestant penance. . . . She'd share her heart with this soldier who looked as frozen and still as the monks, who could not answer, but would hear. And . . . if this brave chaplain took her rage and anger and heartache to the grave, perhaps that would somehow heal her soul.*

3. Isabelle, Peter, René, and Ginette all struggle with grief. Near the end of the novel, Peter says to Isabelle: *"No one has time to grieve right now. That's the horror of war. But we must grieve at some point, in some way, and then let grief teach us its lessons . . . How to help others, how*

to love them well when they are grieving . . . how to grab
back on to God, even if we're blaming Him." How have
you dealt with grief in your life? Discuss what grief has
taught you.

4. When Isabelle admits she is mad at God, Peter's response
surprises her. "What is the book of Psalms but one long,
groaning, grief-filled complaint? One after another, one
long lament." Have you ever admitted to being mad at
God? What happened? Are you familiar with the spiritual
discipline of lament? If so, how has this been helpful in
your life?

5. Both Isabelle and Peter reflect on the difficulty at times of
spotting the enemy—in the Resistance, in war, and inside
the walls of the church. Have you ever been blindsided by
an attack from someone or some group to whom you felt
loyal? How did you respond?

6. Tito points out that the enemy would like nothing more
than to have the resistants fighting each other. How have
you found this true in life, spiritually as well as physically?

7. Both Peter and René experience the benevolence of the
enemy. Have you ever experienced a situation where you
found unexpected moments of kindness or understanding
among those you considered an enemy?

8. Discuss René's trajectory about revenge. What helps him
change perspective? Have you ever been motivated by
revenge? What happened?

9. Isabelle's father tells her: "Remember that courage is not a
lack of fear, my darling child. Courage is fear that has entrusted the outcome to God. We pray and we do what God
Almighty asks of us." Do you agree or disagree? Why?

10. Isabelle is afraid of the Nazis and the evil around her, but she is also *"afraid to open her heart, to let in any more love . . . She would not let herself love anyone else."* She feels that it *"costs too much."* Have you ever felt that way? Why or why not?

11. Despite knowing God will forgive him, Peter has trouble forgiving himself after the tragedy in Kentucky even though he knows it was a *"terrible mistake."* The Allied bombing of Sisteron was another terrible mistake that many characters wrestle with. Discuss making mistakes, not being able to forgive oneself, and living with guilt. Do you find it hard to forgive yourself for mistakes?

12. What do you think of this quote? *"Remember what Saint Augustine said: 'Hope has two beautiful daughters. Their names are anger and courage; anger at the way things are, and courage to see that they do not remain the way they are.'"* Have you ever needed to face a situation with both anger and courage? What did that look like for you?

13. Before reading *From the Valley We Rise*, were you familiar with Operation Dragoon and the Allied invasion of Provence? Had you ever heard of the important role the French resistants and Maquis played in World War II? Discuss the acts of courage on display in the novel.

14. Peter, Isabelle, and René each have thoughts about the use of euphemisms in war. How do you view euphemisms? When are they necessary and helpful, and when are they harmful?

For more from Elizabeth Musser,
read on for an excerpt from

By Way of the Moonlight.

Allie Massey's dream to use her grandparents' estate for equine therapy is crushed when she discovers the property has been sold to a contractor. With weeks until demolition, Allie unearths some of Nana Dale's best-kept secrets—including her champion filly, a handsome man, and one fateful night during WWII—and perhaps a clue to keep her own dream alive.

Available now
wherever books are sold.

1

ALLIE

Atlanta, Georgia
Thursday, March 5, 2020

Dinosaur Bones Found in Buckhead Backyard

It was the silliest of presuppositions, only the alliteration worthy of notice, and I loved alliteration. And yet . . . dinosaur bones.

When I read it online in the *Atlanta Journal-Constitution*, I normally would have laughed out loud. Instead, I burst into tears because I knew exactly whose backyard it was and exactly who those bones belonged to. And it wasn't a dinosaur.

It felt like death to me. I wanted to scream that some crazy backhoe was unearthing my whole life—my history and my future—and would it please, please stop?

My cell beeping a familiar tone pulled me out of my morbid mood.

"Hey, sis. I guess you saw the article in the *AJC*."

"Yep."

"I blinked about a thousand times when I read it. Those were almost your exact words from twenty years ago! Remember? 'Someday someone's going to dig up the ring and think they've found dinosaur bones in Nana Dale's backyard!'"

"Of course I remember! It was funny back then. A joke. Now reality is crashing in, and I hate it!"

"Hey, don't go down that road of self-incrimination. This is *not* your fault. You put up a fight worthy of a T. rex."

"Ha. Thanks, bro." But my words sounded flat. I knew that Wick was staring at the article from his computer screen somewhere in France. I thought of my months' long fight and of his frustration at being far away.

Wick had loved genealogy since he learned he was named after our maternal great-grandfather, Jeremiah Wickliffe Butler. He had recently gotten his master's in historic preservation and combined the two skills in many unusual ways, the most recent being a twelve-month contracted job at the Louvre in France. He had already come back to the States for Nana Dale's funeral and the reading of the will back in December. He couldn't leave again.

Nevertheless, I said, "I wish you were here. You could help me straighten out this huge mess."

"It was all straightened out in January. This is not your problem anymore."

"But that's just it! Not being my problem *is* my problem. It was my dream, my life's ambition. Everything." I let out a muffled sob because I did not want to cry on the phone with my brother. "More important, it was *her* dream too. She commissioned me to keep it."

"Hey, I'm sorry. Yeah, I know it stinks, but there's nothing you can do about it. Have you finished cleaning out the house?"

So much for sympathy.

"Almost," I lied. I had yet to pack the first box.

But Wick knew me too well. He gave an exaggerated sigh. "Sis, if you don't go through and pick out what we want, everything will get sold or given away. Please."

"I will. I promise."

"And let the estate-sale agency help you, for heaven's sake."

"I don't trust them."

"It's not their fault. Or our lawyer's. You know that."

Silence on my part.

"C'mon. Let someone help you."

I was thankful he didn't bring up Austin.

"I'm going to see the bones!" I snapped, desperate to change the subject.

"What?"

"The dinosaur bones." I gave a dry chuckle. "I'll bet they haven't found half of them yet."

"For crying out loud, just leave it all alone. You've got enough living things to worry about without . . ." He hesitated, suppressing his deep chortle. "Without helping the *AJC* reporter solve the mystery of the dinosaur bones."

I shut out the thought of childhood games and the muggy summer days when our parents dropped us off at our grandparents' estate while they gallivanted around the world. "Gotta go," I said.

"You behave yourself, sis. Promise me that?"

I didn't answer, and I knew Wick wasn't surprised.

I set down my cell phone and stood up abruptly, dislodging my cat, Maggie, from my lap. She glared at me, green eyes intense, fluffy white fur leaving its residue on my black leggings. On purpose.

I grabbed the keys to my Hyundai, left my eleventh-floor studio apartment in Buckhead that overlooked Peachtree and East Paces Ferry roads, and drove ten minutes down West Paces Ferry to Nancy Creek Road and the neighborhood that housed so many memories and so many dreams.

The people who used to live in my grandmother's Buckhead neighborhood had built their homes with their bare hands when Atlanta was still recovering from the Civil War and the roads were made of dirt. They'd worked hard, scraped by, and loved their neighbors. But now it was a mishmash of old wealth and new wealth and weasel-eyed contractors destroying perfectly beautiful homes so they could plant cluster mansions on land that used to boast of columned manors and horse stables.

I slowed down in front of my grandparents' house, the one that was supposed to become *my* house. It sat far back from the road, tall hickories blocking the view so that one had to peek through an abundance of new spring leaves to see the redbrick-faced beauty just over a small hill of manicured fescue. I passed the rock driveway and the house on my right and turned into a second rock driveway.

My little Hyundai bumped down a steep descent that eventually headed back up the hill, old hickories and dogwoods and oaks lining the road. *These woods are lovely, dark, and deep.* I quoted Robert Frost in my mind as a squirrel dashed across and up a tree, fat gray tail swishing as it climbed frantically to a waiting limb. My stomach lurched. How I loved these woods and the wildlife that happily inhabited the property.

"For heaven's sake, don't let them cut down the healthy trees!" my grandmother had ordered—so the story went—when an ice storm had knocked down a dozen of them, along with power lines all over the city, in 1973, long before I was born.

"They're gonna level it all now, Nana Dale," I whispered as I parked the car in the clearing. I shook away the anger, choosing instead to get out and take the path on the left, back up the hill, an acre or two farther behind the house, instead of veering to the right on the flat rocky path that led to the barn.

I arrived in the riding ring, where a backhoe stood, its steel-cage mouth gaping empty beside a mound of Georgia red clay. I stared at the flattened expanse where the wooden fence and the jumps and the paddocks and the trees used to stand.

Dinosaur bones, indeed.

The driver of the backhoe paid me no attention. Dressed in mud-caked overalls, his back to me, he was stamping out a cigarette in the clay. And as his smoke swirled lackadaisically in the air, I heard Nana Dale's umpteenth warning: *"Never ever carry a match near the barn!"*

"How dare you smoke here!" I shouted. "When the whole thing could go up in flames!"

He turned slowly, looked over at me with a smirk, lifted his bushy gray eyebrows, and motioned all around him to the red clay that went on for yards and yards around us. "Ain't much chance of that, Miss Allie."

I caught my breath. "Barnell!"

I walked over and threw my arms around his hunched shoulders.

"Miss Allie," he repeated, a smile spreading across his face, the wrinkles interspersed with a thick gray beard. "You ain't s'posed to be traipsing around here, you know."

"I know, and I don't care. How'd you get to be the one to dig everything up? Do you know the contractor?"

Barnell made a nasty face. "Everyone knows that contractor and his reputation." He shrugged. "I was real sorry to hear your grandmother sold it to that scoundrel, Miss Allie. Figured the least I could do was be the one to dig it up."

"Thank you for being here. What a nice surprise on such an awful day. Came out of retirement to do it, didn't you?"

He gave me a sympathetic nod. "I'm real sorry about all of this," he repeated.

"Have they taken the bones away?" The question came out harshly, but when I turned to look at Barnell, he was laughing, his beard moving up and down with the rhythm of his chuckle.

"Dinosaur bones! Of all the inane things to say."

I shrugged back tears. Funny how I felt like giggling and bawling at the same time.

"How many of them did you bury back here, Barnell? Three?"

"Yes, ma'am. And my papa buried two others. And I ain't dug up but the one."

We grinned at each other.

"Can I see the bones?"

"C'mon," he said, motioning with his head as he swiped his tanned face with a ratty bandanna, then wiped the back of his neck, bright red from the sun.

We walked to the center of what used to be a riding ring, with an outside track that was one-quarter of a mile around. I closed my eyes and saw myself as a teen cantering around the periphery on my mare, then cutting diagonally across, where she and I jumped effortlessly over the brick wall—made of plywood and painted red and white—and then took five strides before going up and over the white coop. Then we'd weave between several tall pines and canter around a thick oak before heading back across the ring in another diagonal, leaping over a row of green and white poles, all the jumps that had made up my childhood and teenaged years.

Now the whole thing was a flattened bed of red clay, except for where it looked like a crater had fallen from the sky, creating a mammoth indention in the ground.

Barnell and I walked over to the gaping hole. "Had three reporters over here yesterday morning," he said with a chuckle.

I glanced up at him. "How'd they find out about the bones?"

He shrugged, then threw his head back in his robust laughter.

"You called it in, didn't you?"

"I couldn't help it, Miss Allie. I remember all them times when I was over here repairing a fence or fixing the waterline or something else and you and your big brother would be tearing around this ring playing that you were the Flintstones and chanting about burying dinosaur bones. Thought it was worth a good story."

"And they actually believed you?"

Forensic experts will be examining the bones in the next days to determine their age, the article in the *AJC* had stated.

I took a seat in the clay, beside the hole.

"Any idea which one this is?"

"It's No-No Nicotine," he said, reaching for another cigarette, which I found delightfully ironic.

"Sweet Nicky," I whispered. "She was the last one to be buried here, wasn't she?"

"Yep, she was."

"Who was the first?"

"It was your Nana Dale's pony. . . . Can't remember his name, but he was buried up here before I was born. And then there was a mare called Krystal, I believe. My papa buried her up here when I was about ten or eleven. And of course, there was that beautiful dappled gray mare, the one she called Essie. I helped my daddy bury her. Like near ripped all our hearts out, that one."

Essie. Oh yeah. Of course. I'd heard plenty of larger-than-life stories about my grandmother and her prized thoroughbred. In the house were numerous black-and-white photos of my grandmother on that mare, soaring over jumps, or standing together,

Nana with her fresh-faced smile wide, holding a silver trophy. My grandmother used to serve homemade biscuits or a hock of ham on silver platters engraved with things like *Chastain Park Shriners Hunter Show, Champion, 1947.*

Nana Dale had told me stories about her beloved mare from the time I was small. *"Most striking markings I'd ever seen on a horse,"* she'd say. *"Steel gray with dapples as white as snow, a flaxen mane and tail, and white legs, every one but her right back leg, which was pitch-black up to the hock."*

I hadn't known what *flaxen* meant, but when I looked it up, I was disappointed to find it basically meant "off-white." I'd imagined a much more exotic color.

Barnell peered down in the hole, then knelt and retrieved a bone bigger than any human specimen. "Yep. Still can picture your grandma out here, yelling at me to get that hole dug for Nicky faster, 'before the police come around and arrest us for burying horses in the Atlanta city limits.'"

I remembered it too. I was no more than six or seven when I had sat, much like I was sitting at the moment, in a pile of red clay that Barnell's backhoe had dumped to the side of the hole. I'd walked over and peered in before he could grab me by my ponytail. The body of a bay mare lay in the hole.

"Why's Nicky sleeping like that?" I'd asked, even though my mother had explained to me the night before that my grandmother's ancient mare was dead.

Now I reached into that same hole and let my hands wrap around a thick bone. "It's been over twenty years, hasn't it?"

"Yep. 'Bout nearly killed your grandmom, burying that one, almost as bad as when she buried Essie."

Every horse my grandmother buried had cost her dearly. Nana Dale had been one of the feistiest, most stubborn women on the planet. Hard like steel. Except about her horses.

And now the legacy she had wanted me to prolong, the property that had been part of the family since right after the Civil War, was sold, and the back acres were being cleared so that the rocky road from the street could be paved and three new houses planted in the riding ring, where so many of my memories were made.

"Thought ya might want to keep this, though."

Barnell handed me a metal box, and as I opened it, my eyes clouded over.

When my grandmother buried her beloved horses, she sent each into the ground with a small metal box. Nicky's body had long since decayed, but the metal box, covered in clay, was intact.

I opened it and saw four rusted horseshoes. For reasons that made no sense to anyone but Nana Dale, she would have a blacksmith remove the horseshoes before burying each horse. *"Wouldn't want them to be uncomfortable up there in eternity"* was her odd explanation.

I stared at the horseshoes. "We never did figure out why she buried these separate from the horses, did we?"

Barnell tilted his head and almost looked embarrassed. "Truth is, Miss Allie, long time ago, your grandmom told me, 'Barnell, if I ever lose Hickory Hills, promise me you'll dig up the bones.'

"Thought your grandmom had suddenly lost more of her marbles till she explained it." Here Barnell's eyes softened again as he pointed to the tin box. "She said she wanted you to have the horseshoes. Said you would put 'em to good use, Miss Allie, like she used to. Said it would be her gift to you. She was mighty insistent. Made me swear on Essie's grave that I'd do it." His grin was bittersweet.

I swallowed twice, cleared my throat, and took a deep breath as the memories cascaded around me. One summer when I was about twelve, I had watched as Nana Dale nailed old horseshoes to wooden plaques so that each shoe stuck out at a right angle, allowing us to hang a bridle or a lead shank or a halter from it. Before the nailing, she'd allowed me to stain the wood and burn each horse's name onto a plaque with the woodburning kit she'd given me for Christmas that year.

After that, whenever a new horse came to board at the barn, we'd repeat the same ritual. Nana Dale kept a stash of old horseshoes in the tack room just for that purpose. Then the plaques would be attached to the wall beside each horse's stall.

"Jeff Jeffrey was the first one to give me the idea when I was a girl not much older than you," Nana Dale had explained. "I think it's mighty appropriate that we continue what was started so long ago."

I stared down at the four horseshoes and the yellowed piece of monogrammed stationery where Nana Dale had written in her lovely cursive script *No-No Nicotine (1962–1995)*.

"Horseshoes are for good luck, Allie," she'd often remind me as we worked. "In this life, we need all the luck we can get." The first time she'd said it, she'd stared out the window in the tack room where we were working and said, "I don't like to call it luck, though. I call it faith."

I'd never thought of my grandmother as especially religious. She attended church, as did most people her age. But Nana Dale was filled with secrets and surprises, not the least of which was barnyard wisdom that often included phrases that sounded a lot like they came from the Good Book.

I lifted the horseshoes out of the box and cradled them in my hands. How many times had I stood outside the barn area down below watching as the blacksmith shod one of the horses or ponies?

"Thanks," I said, trying to push past the knot that had lodged itself in my throat. "Thanks for convincing the contractor to let you be the one to dig them up." Then, staring straight at him, I asked, "You'll call me when you unearth the other ones, won't you?"

He met my gaze with his dark brown eyes still twinkling. "Don't you narrow those perty turquoise eyes at me, young lady. I knew you'd read it in the paper, Miss Allie. I was just waiting for you to show up." Then he shrugged again. "But yeah, I'll call you when I bring up them other bones." He fished in his overalls and brought out an ancient cell phone. "I got your number in here somewhere." He let his eyes roam the whole expanse. "Might take me a while to do all the diggin'."

"Taking your time, aren't you?"

"They hired me as the expert to dig up them trees, which I done.

Now I can take all the time I need. I hinted that we might find a passel of other bones. Keeps me busy and keeps that weasel away from the barn."

"He's gonna tear it down in a blink."

"I know."

"When will they implode the house? Has he mentioned a date?"

Barnell fiddled with another cigarette. "Believe they've set the date for March twenty-eighth."

His eyes bore into me.

Three weeks away. Three weeks, and there'd be no going back. Three weeks, and my family could let out a sigh of relief. *"Thank goodness she's finally got to give up! It's about killed her, trying to save it. Nothing worth saving now."*

Barnell interrupted my thoughts. "Where's that fiancé of yours gone off to, Miss Allie?"

"He's not around anymore." *Couldn't save that either*, I reprimanded myself silently.

"Sorry to hear that. What, don't he have no sense in his head?"

"I think he has way too much sense," I mumbled. *"Allie, sweetie, sometimes it feels like you love the land more than you love me."* "He got real tired of me spending all my time trying to save the house and the property."

"Know how much this place means to you. To all of you."

"Yeah."

I'd wanted to argue with Austin when he said it, but then I admitted that perhaps he was right.

And now I'd lost the land and the house and the guy I loved. All of it was gone.

I drove away, the rusted horseshoes sitting on the seat beside me, taunting me with thoughts of good luck when I knew all my luck had run out right when Barnell's backhoe opened its mouth and started to chew.

Elizabeth Musser writes "entertainment with a soul" from her writing chalet—toolshed—outside Lyon, France. Elizabeth's award-winning, bestselling novel *The Swan House* was named one of Amazon's Top Christian Books of the Year, one of Georgia's Top Ten Novels of the Past 100 Years, and was awarded the Gold Illumination Book Award 2021 for Enduring Light Fiction. All of Elizabeth's novels have been translated into multiple languages and been international bestsellers. *Two Destinies*, the final novel in THE SECRETS OF THE CROSS trilogy, was a finalist for the 2013 Christy Award. *The Long Highway Home* was a finalist for the 2018 Carol Award. Her novel *The Promised Land* won the 2021 Carol Award for Contemporary Fiction and was awarded second place in Literary Fiction at the 2021 Georgia Author of the Year Awards. *By Way of the Moonlight* is a *Publisher's Weekly* Top Ten Pick in Religion and Spirituality and a Christy Award finalist.

For over thirty-five years, Elizabeth and her husband, Paul, have been involved in missions work in Europe with One Collective, formerly International Teams. The Mussers have two sons, two daughters-in-law, and five grandchildren. Learn more about the author and her novels at ElizabethMusser.com.

- @ElizabethMusserAuthor
- @elizabeth.musser
- @EMusserAuthor

Sign Up for Elizabeth's Newsletter

Keep up to date with Elizabeth's latest news on book releases and events by signing up for her email list at the website below.

ElizabethMusser.com

FOLLOW ELIZABETH ON SOCIAL MEDIA

Elizabeth Musser   @Elizabeth.Musser   @EMusserAuthor